Tessa Had Known Many Men— But Never Before A King

Tessa knew well the reputation of King Charles II of England. Even his most humble and loyal subjects told bawdy stories of his insatiable appetite for women. As Tessa lay in his bed, she thought about all of the beauties from every station in life, with every erotic skill and every exotic appetite, who had preceded her to this legendary place of pleasure and pleasuring.

Tessa already had journeyed far on an odyssey that had taken her from a paradise of ecstasy to a hell of unspeakable degradation. Yet now her most dangerous challenge and golden opportunity still lay ahead—as she saw the royal shadow cutting off the lamplight, and felt his touch upon her flesh. . . .

The Stewarts of Stormhaven is available
from Popular Library:

Have you read these other books by Marilyn Ross,
available in Popular Library editions?

PLEASURE'S DAUGHTER

MARILYN ROSS

POPULAR LIBRARY • NEW YORK

PLEASURE'S DAUGHTER

Published by Popular Library, a unit of CBS Publications,
the Consumer Publishing Division of CBS Inc.

ISBN: 0-445-04316-4

Printed in the United States of America

10 9 8 7 6 5 4 3 2 1

To my good friends
Sir John Mills and
Lady Mary Hayley Bell Mills

BOOK ONE

London, 1663

Chapter One

The foppish Sir Julian Dorley smirked and touched the end of his thin mustache with a bony forefinger as he said, "I vow, madam, this Tessa whom you claim as daughter wears little more in public than most young ladies do when bedded!"

Elegant Lady Pleasure Farr glared at her companion. "This is not a time for your dubious jests, friend Julian. The moment of the reunion of a mother and daughter must be one of tender sentimentality!"

Tessa, sitting opposite the two well-dressed people in the private parlor of the Maybury Inn, felt embarrassed and unhappy. When they had arrived in the village in their elaborately decorated French carriage a short while ago she had been busy doing her pony-riding act. She had been vaguely aware of their presence but had been too busy concentrating on her fancy riding tricks to pay much attention to them.

Now she sat before the two, her pert oval face drained of color. She was sixteen and had long black hair which she wore draped about her shoulders and which streamed behind her in graceful fashion when she rode around the circus ring on her pony. Her circus costume was cut low, and her skirt was only of knee length, to make her riding easier. Already her body was filled out with a feminine appeal, and her foster parents, Tom and Ina Shaw, considered her the star of the small traveling circus.

Tessa said defensively, "My dress is short for my act. I wear a proper dress when I'm not working."

Lady Pleasure Farr gave her a cool smile. "I'm sure you do, my dear. You must not mind Sir Julian, and you must accept the fact that you are my daughter."

Tessa felt trapped and filled with astonishment. She told the older woman, "I have always regarded Tom Shaw and his wife as my father and mother!"

The middle-aged woman in her stylish brown-velvet dress and broad-brimmed hat with a feather showed a resigned look on her attractive face. In her cultivated way, she explained, "I gave you to the Shaws for adoption years ago. They promised to look after you and bring you up, in exchange for a yearly payment from me. You are the child of my first marriage and I feared my second husband, Lord David Farr, would resent you. So I parted with you, even though it near broke my heart!"

The foppish fellow in purple coat and breeches rose and spread his hands in an exasperated gesture. He told Lady Pleasure Farr, "Fie on you, madam! Be honest with the girl! Let her know she was born to you between your marriages and you did not wish to present His Lordship with a bastard!"

Lady Pleasure crimsoned and rebuked the thin dandy with his powdered wig. "How crude you can be, Sir Julian!"

"Let us call a spade a spade," he shrugged. "Otherwise you will leave this poor girl more confused than she is already!"

Lady Pleasure's arrogant, lovely face took on a patient smile as she explained to Tessa, "What Sir Julian said is true. I hoped to spare you. But since it has been revealed, I will tell you. You were born to me of a romance with a fine man killed in a duel before I could wed him."

Sir Julian smirked again. "I fear there have been many such fine men in your life, dear lady. How fortunate that Lord Farr is so tolerant!"

"Julian!" Lady Pleasure snapped at the fop, who was leaning on his walking stick and thoroughly enjoying himself.

Tessa felt impelled to speak up again, "I have been trained to work in the circus. I plan to marry Bob Wills, our acrobat. I'm happy here and have all I want of life."

The older woman smiled in that overbearing fashion once again. She asked, "What do you know of life or what you want of it? Life, my dear, is a great deal more than a squalid little circus traveling from village to village. Lord Farr has agreed to adopt you as his daughter. You will be able to take your rightful place in society."

10

"Why not let me remain here, since I'm happy?" Tessa asked forlornly.

"Your mother has told you," the foppish Sir Julian said. "She wishes to make a great lady of you!"

"But I do not want to be a great lady!" the girl protested.

"You are sixteen, a mere child!" Lady Pleasure said. "Stirring things are happening in England in this year 1663. Charles the Second is on the throne, and one day you may be presented to him at court! Think of it!"

Tessa stared at the two rebelliously. "This is my home and my life. If you take me from these familiar things, I have a mind to run away!"

"Never!" Lady Pleasure replied. "You could not be so ungrateful to me! I have humbled myself to appeal to Lord Farr and get you this opportunity. When we leave the inn tomorrow morning, you will come with us. I have already settled it with the Shaws!"

"I shall die of unhappiness," Tessa said tremulously.

"I hardly think so," the foppish Sir Julian said with a mocking smile on his thin face. "Let Lord Farr introduce you at court in a revealing gown, and the king will be at your feet! His taste inclines to seeing a lot of woman rather than a lot of style!"

The fop laughed in a high-pitched tone at his own joke while Lady Pleasure regarded him with annoyance again. Tessa felt humiliated and ill at ease with the two and could not believe that this fading beauty of a woman was truly her mother.

The scene between the three in the dusty little parlor of the inn was interrupted by a knocking on the door. Sir Julian went over and opened the wooden door to reveal the circus owner, Tom Shaw, standing there respectfully.

The stout Tom Shaw, his hat in hand, came nervously into the room and in an apologetic voice said, "If Your Ladyship will forgive me, the crowd are asking to see Tessa ride again! Since it will be her last day with us, I would be greatly obliged if you would allow it."

Lady Pleasure frowned slightly and then acquiesced. "I suppose it will do no harm. But mind that the girl is ready

11

to travel with me in the morning and explain to her again that all I have told her is true. I do not wish her to mope after I've removed her from the circus."

The stout Tom bobbed his gray head. "You can count on me, Your Ladyship." And to Tessa he added, "Come along, lass. Let me see you do your act once again. I swear there's not a pony-rider your equal in all of England!"

Tessa followed the stout circus owner out of the room, and as the door closed behind them, she heard Sir Julian make some mocking comment to her mother and then burst into his high-pitched laughter once more. Instead of feeling excited and happy at being claimed as the daughter of a rich and titled lady, Tessa felt humiliated and crestfallen.

She halted in the doorway of the inn and appealed to the man she had known all her life as her father: "You cannot let me go this way!"

He touched a fat hand to her arm and with a sympathetic look on his round face, he said, "You are her daughter, lass! I kept it from you because she asked it. But now that you have this great chance to make something of yourself, you cannot turn your back on it!"

"I'd rather stay with the circus."

"Forget the circus! It's a bloody awful life if the truth is to be told—all right for the likes of us, but not for a lady born like you!"

Tessa's hazel eyes were pleading and her pretty oval face was sad. "I've been trained to be a circus star. I've given my promise to wed Bob Wills!"

"Wed an acrobat!" Tom Shaw said and shook his head. "Never, my girl. He's not for you, nor you for him. You must both marry your own kind!"

"You and your wife encouraged us!"

He looked guilty. "That was before I knew of Lady Pleasure's plans. I've talked to Bob just now and explained to him. He agrees you should go to a fine home and riches. He'll not keep you to your promise!"

"But we love each other!" she said, near tears.

"Come, girl! Time to do your act! The crowd is wait-

12

ing!" The stout man grasped her by the arm and hurried her outside to the warm September afternoon sunshine. The circus had set up its ring behind the inn, and the field was crowded with spectators ringed around the entertainment center. At the moment Bob Wills, a stalwart, blond young man, was doing a series of handstands, somersaults and the like and getting rounds of applause.

A baker shouted his wares on the outer edge of the crowd as Tom Shaw shoved Tessa forward. Bob Wills took his final bows and came out of the ring just as she prepared to enter it.

The good-looking young man smelled of sweat from his exertions as he leaned close to her and said, "We'll do a bit of talking after the show!"

"We must!" she agreed. And then the circus owner's plain wife came forward in the spangled costume she wore for her juggling act, leading a trim, white pony by its red halter. She passed the reins of the pony to Tessa with a kindly look on her thin, worn face.

At once Tessa became the professional that long training had made her. She smiled for the applauding circle of village folk, then, sending the pony off to circle the ring at a quick pace, she gracefully sprang up onto its back and performed a number of skillful balancing feats on the bare back of the obedient animal.

Tessa was a favorite with the country folk who had come to attend the traveling fair. She had been taught to ride by Tom Shaw himself, and many of her fancy tricks were the result of acrobatic training by flaxen-haired Bob Wills. This sturdy young acrobat stood on the edge of the circle now, watching and encouraging her.

She tried desperately to concentrate on what she was doing, but her mind was too filled with confusion to allow her to be at her best in the ring. Somehow she managed to get through the act and to bow to the applauding crowd. Then she quickly ran from the ring, and Ina Shaw led away the white pony.

Tessa went straight to Bob, and taking him by the arm, she led him around behind the inn where they could not be observed by the patrons of the fair. A Punch and Judy, show was now under way in the middle of the ring, causing loud bursts of merriment from the crowd, mixed with the raunchy voices of the Punch and Judy.

Tessa's lovely green eyes were sad as she gazed up into the youthful face of the acrobat. "You know what's happened, Bob? This woman who claims to be my mother wants me to go away with her tomorrow morning. She says she wants to make me a great lady!"

"And so she does!" Bob said soberly. "Tom Shaw has told me about your good fortune!"

"The best fortune I can ask is to remain here and marry you!"

"Nay, lass," Bob said, "I cannot stand in your way. I'm only a poor fool capable of entertaining country bumpkins! And even if I should reach the top as an acrobat, I'd be nothing compared to a fine lady!"

"I do not like this Lady Pleasure!" Tessa said unhappily. "She is hard, I can tell! And from what that fop with her says, she is loose of character! If that is a lady, I do not wish to be one!"

"Hard and loose she may be," Bob said, "but she is your mother. And she has a great name, money, and position. You would be a fool not to take advantage of her offer."

"But why does she wish to do this for me?"

"Perhaps she feels some shame for deserting you," he said. "Tom claims she paid him regularly for your keep. Now she wants to do more for you."

Tessa sighed. "I am a bastard, you know. She claims my father was a titled man whom she loved dearly and who died in a duel before I was born."

"It could well be the truth."

She reached out and took the stolid young man by the arms. "Bob, my darling, I love you so much. How can I be parted from you?"

"It is best," he assured her. "And perhaps one day we'll meet again, when you're a great lady."

"Never!" she mourned. "If I lose you now, it will be the end." Her eyes met his shyly. "And I have given myself to you. Have you thought of that? Because we were to wed, I have let you make wanton love to me!"

The first sign of emotion showed on his round face. His smile was almost tender. "Aye, lass, we have truly loved! But that will remain a precious thing, for us both to cherish in memory."

Her cheeks flushed at the thoughts of their hours spent together in close embrace. In a soft voice, she told him, "I shall miss you so. What shall I do without you?"

"You will find someone else. Someone more suited to you," he said.

"Never!"

Now he took her in his arms and spoke softly in her ear, "I shall come to you tonight, my Tessa. We'll have a last good time to remember."

"You promise?" She hoped that if he came to her in the night, he might be won over to her plan for them both to run off together.

"Aye, lass," Bob said. "Now I must get back to the ring!" And as the Punch and Judy house was swiftly removed by Tom and Ina Shaw—who had played the roles of the two comic characters—Bob hurried away to take up the entertainment of the country folk.

Tessa stood alone in the fading sunshine of the September day and tried to straighten it all in her mind. She would be content to remain with the circus and wed Bob. But everyone else, including her husband-to-be, considered her daft not to take advantage of her mother's offer of open adoption. She had never dreamed of riches or social position. Though she'd been vaguely aware of another world out there, it had seemed too far distant from her own vagabond existence to consider. Now this different way of life was being offered to her!

After a moment she had an idea. She'd consult old Madame Normand, the fortune-teller with the fair. Madame Normand looked like a monstrous toad. She had one wall eye, but the other was keen. She wore a fur cap on her head in all seasons, which duly impressed the country folk, and her dark tent was filled with grim souvenirs—such as a huge bat, stuffed and hanging from a string, a yellow human skull, and a murky crystal ball. When Tessa reached the small tent, an old country woman was just leaving with a folded paper, doubtless containing a powder of some sort, clutched in her hand.

Tessa waited until the country woman was out of the way before entering the shadowed tent. Old Madame Normand sat with the crystal before her on a small wooden stand with the yellow skull beside it. At the moment she was counting the coins the country woman had given her. On hearing Tessa enter she looked up with a frightened air; then, recognizing the girl, she used a clawlike hand to wave her to sit down on the stool reserved for visitors.

Madame Normand hid the coins somewhere under the bench and then gave her attention to Tessa. The one keen eye riveted her. "What is it, girl?"

"I have come for advice," Tessa said in a nervous voice.

The old woman in the fur hat let a smile crease her brown, emaciated face. "You think I don't know? You're asking about whether to go with your mother?"

"Yes. Did Tom Shaw talk to you about it?"

Madame Normand leered at Tessa. "I have my own ways of finding things out. Your precious mother was here to consult me earlier."

"Lady Pleasure came to question you?"

"Why not?" the old woman snapped. "I have predicted the futures of great ladies and gentlemen before. I have been called on for advice by some of the top gentry!"

Tessa leaned forward in the shadows. "What did you tell my mother?"

"I predicted great happiness if she adopted you properly," the old woman said smugly. "It made a deep impression on her. She has plans of gaining favors at the king's court by using you."

"How dare she?" Tessa said angrily.

The old woman lifted her clawlike hand to silence her. "It is but the game of life, lass. You might find the experience most pleasant. Riches and a fine marriage would be true blessings! You'll never find them here among us."

16

"I'm not sure I want them," Tessa said.

Madame Normand stared at her with her one good eye. "Would it make a difference if I told you I was once young, and like you, with the man I loved, I did acrobatics in a traveling fair like this. But the bairns came, and we grew older. One day he was run down by a wagon. No one wanted a middle-aged female acrobat with a bad eye. So I became a fortune-teller. And when I grow too old for this, I'll be abandoned and die in a ditch somewhere! This might well be the story of your life if you stay here with us!"

Tessa felt a cold chill run down her spine at the bleak picture the old woman painted. It was true—one did not stay forever young! What about that day? If she were unfortunate enough to lose both Bob and her looks, who in the circus would want her?

She shivered. "It surely wouldn't turn out that badly!"

"It could!" the fortune-teller rasped. "Better listen to Tom Shaw. He wants the best for you."

"Is that all you have to tell me?"

"There is one other thing," Madame Normand said with a crafty smile, revealing sunken, toothless gums. "You may know it for a farthing!"

Impatiently Tessa searched in her dress pocket and produced the coin. She tossed it over beside the crystal ball. "There's your pay!"

The old woman's claw of a hand snatched up the coin greedily. Then she bent over the crystal and in a low voice whispered, "I told Lady Pleasure that taking you home with her would bring much happiness. But I didn't tell her all. The happiness will be yours; for her part she will experience nothing but frustration! Go with her, girl! It is a favorable move for you!"

Tessa left the old woman's tent with these words still echoing in her ears. The visit to the fortune-teller had made her see that there were hazards in remaining with the circus troop and marrying the stalwart Bob. But she still found it difficult to imagine any other sort of life.

Dusk came and the fair ended. The country folk went on their way and the circus people began to pack up. As

17

darkness came, the troop gathered in a back kitchen of the inn around a huge plank table. The innkeeper had prepared roast pig hocks and other delicacies for them, and they would remain there overnight. The more humble workers would sleep in the open with the wagons while the owners, Tom and Ina Shaw, and the stars, like Tessa and Bob, had small attic rooms in the old inn.

Tessa was already at the table—seated between the fat man, who weighed nearly four hundred pounds, and Madame Normand—when the foppish Sir Julian Dorley appeared in the candlelit room. The loud conversation at the table ended as he showed himself.

The white-wigged dandy came to where Tessa sat with mincing step, and in his high voice he said, "Dear girl, your mother asks that you join us in the front parlor for dinner."

"Thank you," she said, looking up at the thin face with its long beaklike nose over the mustache. "But since it is to be my last night with my friends, I prefer to remain here."

Sir Julian raised his eyebrows. "Very well. I shall deliver your message and trust Lady Pleasure will understand your sentimentality." He moved on but halted by where Bob Wills was sitting and touched the young man's biceps. "Dear me, what a strong fellow you are!"

Bob raised a belligerent face towards him and asked, "What's it to you?"

Sir Julian smiled nervously and withdrew his offending hand. "Nothing, dear boy! I only hasten to say that a magnificent physique like yours would be appreciated by some of my friends in London. Have you ever thought of going there?"

"No!" Bob said. "Gents of that sort don't appeal to me!"

"More's the pity!" Sir Julian commented coolly with a shrug, and he went on out.

The clamor of conversation about the table resumed. Fliglen, the fat man, paused with a pork hock in his hand to say to Tessa, "That the fellow you're going off to marry?"

18

"Hardly!"

The fat man's face was all grease. He laughed. "Thought not. But you're a lucky one. Not many of us can rise above this. Not even with that grim Cromwell gone and Charles on the throne!"

The party went on in a raucous manner. Tom Shaw began to be a little drunken, and with slurred speech he proposed a toast to Tessa. With his wife's help he struggled to his feet and held aloft his mug of strong beer.

"To Tessa," he said, "who will one day be a lady and do us all justice!"

There was applause and laughter, and everyone joined in the toast, even Bob Wills. But the young acrobat gave Tessa a look of meaning afterwards, and her eyes blurred with tears.

"Speech!" Tom Shaw called out.

"Yes, a speech!" Madame Normand chuckled and pounded an emaciated hand on the plank of the table.

"Come along, Tessa!" the fat man urged, forcing her to her feet by placing a hamlike hand at her back and literally propelling her upward.

Her tears came more freely and ran down her cheeks. She sobbed out, "I'd rather remain here with all of you than ever be a fine lady, whatever that may mean!" And she turned and ran from the kitchen out the back door to the yard of the inn.

A moment afterwards the skinny Ina Shaw, wife of the circus owner, came out. She placed a thin arm around Tessa and said, "You mustn't feel like this, child. You should be happy. Tom and me are happy for you, even though we hate to lose a talent of your sort. We never had a better acrobat or pony rider. You'll never be properly replaced."

Tessa sobbed out her sorrow with her face pressed against the woman's painfully bony shoulder. When the worst of her sorrow was over, she dried her eyes and said, "I must say I'm disappointed. No one seems to expect I should want to stay with the circus. And no one has begged me to stay!"

Ina Shaw said, "That is because we care for you, child. We want you to do what is best for you."

"I love Bob," Tessa said in a choked voice. "I shall miss him!"

"I know," Ina consoled her. "But he is an average sort. Not nearly good enough for you."

"We were to wed!"

"You will wed someone else in proper time," the older woman assured her as they stood together in the darkness. "You have a warm, loving nature and you will find a good man!"

"Will I grow up to be like my mother," Tessa wondered, "a hard, arrogant beauty who gives herself to anyone when the mood is on her?"

"Child!" the older woman said in reproval.

"That is what that Sir Julian said in front of her, and she didn't deny it. I have the same hungry need for love. I am her daughter. How can I deny it?"

"Don't think about such things," was Ina Shaw's halting reply. "Now it is late—time for you to be up to bed. You must have a good night's rest for your long journey tomorrow."

"I have such a confusion in my mind, I doubt that I shall sleep at all," Tessa complained.

"You're young and healthy. You'll sleep," Ina Shaw told her. "In the morning I'll help pack your things in the cloth bag we gave you. It's not fancy, but it will hold them."

When Tessa returned inside, she avoided entering the rear kitchen, where the circus folk were still carousing. She made her way up dark and narrow back stairs to the tiny attic room that had been assigned to her. Its slanting roof did not allow her to stand up at the outer wall of it, but there was a tiny window, a small pallet of a bed, and a chair of the most plain type.

A tiny amount of moonlight filtered into the room through the pane of the murky window. By the moonlight she undressed and folded her clothes on the chair. When she at last stood naked and waiting in the shadowed room, she began to tremble slightly. She had known such moments before when she waited for Bob.

From the time months ago when they had first frantically made love on a deserted hillside long after the others were asleep by the wagons, she had come to realize her hunger for carnal love and her great capacity for it. Ever since she'd first been aroused, this nagging need had remained with her.

At times it shut out all other thoughts, as it did tonight. Even her fear and grief at leaving her friends for a new life was forgotten in her anticipation of Bob's coming to her. She caressed her firm, small breasts and lithe body, and her hands came to linger at her thighs. A fresh shudder ran through her, and she stretched out on the bed and waited.

Soon she heard voices and footsteps outside as the others made their way drunkenly to their rooms. Her heart sank as she worried that Bob might not come to her. But after a time she heard a creak of a floorboard outside; then the door opened slowly and Bob came in.

He closed the door and stood staring at her. Then he came to kneel by her naked form on the bed. As he lifted her head tenderly to kiss her, he whispered, "You are a beauty!"

After they kissed, she spoke thickly, "Hurry!"

Bob was not slow to remove his clothes. And in a moment she felt the comfort of his embrace, his lean, muscled body on her and his awakened manhood firmly penetrating her. Their bodies molded together to become one, and she was lost in the ecstasy of this overwhelming passion. Their bodies combined in a rhythm of burning beauty that she wished would last forever, shutting out all else but this glorious, consuming desire! As his vigorous probing mounted in intensity, she reached a peak with a tiny, awed cry—and they lay back, close together, exhausted.

She did not speak for a long while. Then she whispered, "Must we lose all this?"

He turned to her solemnly. "I love you, Tessa. I will not deny it."

"I have never doubted it."

"But you are of different clay. You can tell that just to look at us. I'm common, born in a workhouse. You are of the gentry!"

"I don't care!"

"I do. If I robbed you of this chance to take your rightful place in life, I would always be ashamed of myself. And in time you would come to hate me!"

"No!"

"I dare not keep you," he said soberly. "You must have this chance. If it turns out ill, you can return to me!"

"You will marry someone else. You'll never wait!"

"Do not fear about that!"

Her eyes were wide as she kissed him on the mouth, the neck, the shoulder. In a small voice she said, "What is worse, I cannot trust myself! I have a hunger and need for love. I'm too much like her, Lord forgive me! You taught me the joy of passion. How can I manage without it?"

"You should not," Bob said, "nor will you."

"You see me becoming a wanton creature like Lady Pleasure—with lovers so numerous I will not be able to remember their names?"

"No," he said. "I expect you will meet some fine man and fall in love."

"How will I know?"

"You will know," Bob told her. "What we have is a kind of love. But it is not the sort that a girl like you should have."

"I do not understand you," she said unhappily. And seizing him again, she hungrily pressed her lips to his.

He laughed softly and stared up at her. "I think it fitting we make love again, since this may be our last chance for many a day!"

She submitted silently, and once again they were locked in a rapture which excluded any outside thoughts. After this second, longer interlude of love ended, they were too weary to say much more. She dropped off to sleep. And when she wakened to the morning light, Bob was gone and the blanket was tucked tenderly about her.

She lay there for a little, lost in rapturous thoughts about the night enjoyed, but fearful of what this morning might bring. She was soon roused into activity when Ina Shaw arrived to help her dress and pack.

She and Ina breakfasted alone in the big kitchen of the inn. "The others have gone on ahead," Ina explained. "I have the small carriage and will catch up to them later in Dulford."

Tessa eyed her sadly. "I'm sure you made them go early so the parting wouldn't be too hard for me."

The older woman smiled. "Well, maybe it was Tom who thought of that. Anyway it was done. And now you've only me to bid good-bye."

"I shall miss you," the girl said, impulsively reaching out and taking the older woman's hand.

"Aye, lass, and I shall miss you. You were like a daughter to Tom and me."

"Someday I'll be back."

"Sure you will," the older woman encouraged her. "You will come back and find us all waiting to welcome you."

Tears came to Tessa's eyes. "And Bob?"

"Bob is happy because he thinks you are doing the proper thing," the older woman said.

"We are so much in love!"

"You'll always have your memories," the circus owner's wife consoled her. "And you may well find others you love. If not, you and Bob will surely seek each other out again. In either case, you see, it should end well."

It was a rather childish simplification, but in her distress, Tessa was willing to accept it. She lingered at breakfast with the older woman until the innkeeper brought her a message that her mother demanded her presence—they were ready to leave. She tearfully kissed Ina Shaw good-bye and went to join her mother in the front parlor.

Sir Julian Dorley, clad in a purple velvet suit, sat at ease in a comfortable chair, his silver-headed walking stick languidly in hand. On sighting Tessa in her proper long brown dress and bonnet, he exclaimed, " 'Pon my word, girl, you look as bedraggled as a pigeon caught in a hailstorm!"

Lady Pleasure Farr, standing by him, gave him a reproving glance. "We need none of your court humor, Julian. The girl's clothing is plain, but it will do until our return to Wilton, when my dressmaker will fit her out with a new wardrobe."

The fop laughed and told Tessa, "I much preferred you in your abbreviated circus outfit, when I could enjoy so much more of you!"

Lady Pleasure came between the thin man and Tessa and gazed sternly at the pack her daughter was carrying. Ina Shaw had bundled Tessa's clothes in a sheet and tied it around the top to make a pouch. "Is that all you have to carry your posessions in?"

"I'm afraid so," the girl said in a small voice. "We travel light with the circus."

"So it would seem," her mother said with disdain. "No matter. Give it to the driver, and he will place it with the other things at the rear of the carriage."

"Yes, ma'am," Tessa said in a low voice and started on out.

"Don't say that!" Lady Pleasure snapped irritably. "I am your mother. When you address me, use my name in that way. Call me 'mother!' "

"Very well, mother."

"What maternal instincts you have, Lady Pleasure!" Sir Julian observed, rising. "And I sense a compatability between you. You both have a secret dislike of each other!" He chuckled at his joke.

Outside, the ornate carriage was waiting as the driver and his assistant bustled about, piling and tying the luggage—including Tessa's poor handmade pouch—at the rear of the vehicle. Then they all stepped up into the carriage, which smelled of horses and straw, and sat back on the rather hard seats. The innkeeper and his wife were out front to see them on their way.

The driver flipped the reins and shouted to the horses, and they were off. The inn and the yard where the fair had been located were now racing away from them. Tessa

24

leaned forward to glance out the window and see the grounds where she had performed her circus act for the last time. Then she settled back in her place beside Lady Pleasure with a sigh.

Her perfumed and elaborately clad mother gave her an austere glance. "We have had enough of your sighing," she informed her daughter.

Tessa looked down at her hands, folded in her lap. She managed to reply, "Yes, mother."

The carriage rocked with every rut and turn of the long, winding road. Along the way they passed through many small villages like Maybury, with their inns and often large churches. They went by farmhouses and farmers in the field. Then they came to a more deserted area of the road, where trees and bushes grew fairly high on either side of the dirt road and there were no signs of farms or habitations of any sort.

Sir Julian peered out one of the side windows with a bleak look on his thin face. "Damn me, this is the back road! It is not nearly as well-settled as the other."

"Control your uneasiness," Lady Pleasure begged him. "You will only serve to upset my daughter!"

Sir Julian shot her a glance and settled back in the hard seat again. "Ods-bobs!" he said, "I suppose you'd call me a pessimist, always building dungeons in the air!"

Tessa could not help bursting out with laughter at his wry quip. And then at once she became silent and looked at her mother in a shamefaced manner. But her parent did not reprove her.

Instead, Lady Pleasure herself laughed. "I'm glad you can do more than sigh and show tears, my girl! Julian is a strange fellow! You do well to enjoy him!"

Sir Julian leaned on his walking stick and told her, "I'm not nearly so stupid and odd as most people think. I prefer to be myself!"

"And you are surely different," Lady Pleasure told him. To Tessa she confided, "Sir Julian is our nearest neighbor at Wilton. And since your stepfather couldn't make this journey because of other pressing matters—"

"A pressing dairy wench from his farm, I've been told!" Sir Julian chuckled as he interrupted.

Lady Pleasure's once lovely face showed annoyance. "Don't be such a fool with your continual interrupting, Julian. You will try me once too often."

"Forgive me, Your Ladyship," he murmured with mock respect.

Lady Pleasure turned to her daughter again and finished her earlier thought, saying, "My husband sent Sir Julian along as company for us. But he is no relative; you may be thankful for that."

Tessa asked respectfully, "How far is Wilton from London?"

"Not far," Lady Pleasure answered. "Your stepfather and I often attend the court in Whitehall."

"That is true!" Sir Julian agreed as the carriage rolled on. "Your mother is no stranger to the king!"

"Julian!" Lady Pleasure reproved him. "What ideas you are apt to give the child!"

"I simply tell the truth," the elegant fop said. "Charles the Second has an eye for true beauty. He encourages lovely ladies to grace his court."

Lady Pleasure showed a thin smile. "In that case, I accept your compliment, Sir Julian." And to Tessa she added, "In time, when you have learned the manners and speech of a lady, you may be presented at court."

"Do you have any other sons or daughters?" Tessa wanted to know.

"I have two stepsons and a stepdaughter, all children of Lord David's first marriage. We have not been blessed with any offspring of our own. However, I'm happy to play the role of mother to Harry, who is a lover of the outdoors like his father, as well as to my younger stepson, Horatio, who is frail of health and a scholar. My stepchild Mary is a pretty, quiet girl of your own age. You and she will share the same governess."

Sir Julian spoke up. "Let me make it more plain for you, my little filly! Harry is a handsome womanizer like his father, Horatio a mean fellow with a bad liver which ruins his temperament, and Mary a plain, nice girl too de-

26

mure to present at court. You will be a prize for your stepfather and his son Harry. You'll bring new life into the castle!"

Lady Pleasure bridled. "Must you always be so coarse, Julian?"

"But I merely speak honestly," the dandy complained. "I say you need the youth and charm this child offers. Your own fading beauty, though still fascinating, is no longer enough. This Tessa, molded in your same loveliness, will be a continual reminder to all of your unequaled splendor!"

Lady Pleasure weighed these words for a moment. "I swear you wish but to confuse me," she accused him. "You speak from one side of your mouth and then the other! You praise me in one sentence and mock me in the next, so I do not know how to respond!"

The thin fop extended a bony hand to touch one of hers and said, "I shall for all time be your most ardent and admiring servant!"

"Pretty words!" she said with some dryness. "I think it is past time for us to halt and refresh ourselves. I had the innkeeper pack us a good lunch."

"By all means," Sir Julian agreed. "Especially as we seem to be still in the middle of this damned woods, with no other tavern in sight. I could do well with some good ale or wine!"

"You will find drink in the lunch basket," Lady Pleasure assured him.

"You have wisdom above rubies," the pleased Sir Julian returned.

Lady Pleasure lifted the flap at the front of the carriage and informed the driver that they wished to stop and have their lunch. Tessa took it all in, still stunned to near silence by this new world into which she'd been plunged.

The driver halted the horses at the first clearing they came to, and they all left the carriage. Then the driver and his assistant fetched the basket filled with food, and laying a white cloth, they began setting out the good things the innkeeper had packed. They were all standing, about to enjoy the feast, when suddenly there was a sound from the bushes behind them. Tessa turned with the others to see what the sound might indicate. It indicated nothing pleasant!

Standing smiling evilly at them were two masked ruffians. One held a pistol directed at them, and the other stood ready to do his bidding. "I bid you stand and deliver!" the ruffian with the pistol said sternly.

Chapter Two

The whole thing had happened so suddenly they were all taken by surprise, the driver and his assistant as well as Tessa, her mother, and Sir Julian. The ruffian with the pistol had a black bandana covering half his face; the other was a younger man with a short red beard showing below his mask, and thin slits of eyes. The driver, who apparently was armed, made a move to reach under his coat.

"None of that!" the black bandana said, fixing the pistol directly on him.

"Drop your weapons!" the red beard ordered them harshly. "Then we'll take your gold and silver and any precious things!"

"Don't try to hold none back!" Black Mask warned them. "Your only chance to live is to obey us and do it without delay!"

Lady Pleasure Farr quavered, "We are but poor folk on our way home. We have little of value!"

Black Mask laughed harshly. "I can see that by your rings and your expensive carriage!"

Red Beard went to pick up the pistol the driver had dropped. With it in hand he advanced to Sir Julian. "Empty your pockets," the ruffian rasped.

Sir Julian gave him a vindictive look. "Honesty pays, dear chap. But evidently not enough for you."

"None of that!" Red Beard growled. "Let's have your money and your rings. And that gold watch!"

"My father's, kind sir," Sir Julian said, hesitating with the watch in his hand. "Of great sentimental value. May I not bargain with you for it?"

"Listen to him!" Black Mask guffawed and added, "You've got nothing to bargain with, mister! Get his watch!"

"Aye!" Red Beard agreed and snatched the watch from the fop's thin hand. Then he took the money he'd received from him and stuffed it in his pockets.

"Don't miss the rings!" Black Mask ordered his partner.

"Right!" And Red Beard quickly pulled the rings from Sir Julian's thin fingers.

"Must you be so rough?" Sir Julian cried unhappily.

"I don't plan to hold hands with you, Squire," Red Beard said with an evil grin.

"Not so much talk and on to the others," Black Mask ordered him.

"You shall hang for this," Lady Pleasure said as she gave up her pocketbook and necklace. "I shall remove my rings myself!" And she did so imperiously and gave them to Red Beard.

"Now the girl!" Black Mask said, coming towards Tessa.

"I have nothing!" she protested.

He grinned at her evilly. "You are far too modest, miss. You have a neat body and a pretty face. If you are short on valuables, maybe Red and me will be satisfied with what you have to offer!"

Red Beard came up by the man with the pistol and said, "I think that right smart. Mix a bit of pleasure with business, eh, my buck?"

Lady Pleasure cried, "I beg you to let the girl be. She's a virgin!"

"The same couldn't be said for you, old hag!" Red Beard jeered.

Red Beard smacked his lips. "Let me test her first!"

"No, you hold the pistol on them, and I'll be first to taste her sweetness," Black Mask told him.

Tessa had been watching and waiting tensely. Now that the two were facing each other on the point of argument, she made the swift move she'd been planning. Using all the precision of her teaching, she quickly somersaulted, upturning her bare thighs to the startled bandits and kicking Black Mask in the face—to send him spinning backward, taking his partner down with him!

Before either of them could recover, she retrieved the gun Black Mask had been holding and with the expert skill of a marksman shot a bullet through the right shoulder of

Red Beard. He screamed with pain. Letting go of the pistol he'd taken from the driver, he rolled on the ground in agony. A pool of his blood spread out beside the still stunned Black Mask.

"Move quickly!" Sir Julian ordered the driver and his assistant.

The driver sprang forward and picked up the pistol that had fallen from Red Beard's hand. Directing it at the recovering Black Mask, the driver shot him directly in the face as he attempted to get up off the ground. The face was covered with blood as Black Mask fell back dead. Meanwhile Red Beard had staggered back into the woods, bellowing with pain.

The driver turned to Sir Julian, "Shall I go after him, sir?"

"No," Sir Julian said. "He'll likely die from loss of blood anyway. Let us quickly get out of here!"

"You are wrong, Julian," Lady Pleasure Farr spoke up. "Go after the villian, both of you! He has our money and valuables! Don't let him get away!"

"Yes, Your Ladyship," the driver nodded, and preparing the pistol, he rushed on into the woods with his assistant following.

Sir Julian came over and took the other pistol from Tessa's hand. He said, "That was remarkably quick thinking, my girl. You saved the situation. I daresay the sight of your lovely bare thighs stupefied those two as much as the strong kick that followed!"

She blushed. "It seemed I should do something. And I have studied pistol shooting. We did a sharpshooting bit in the circus."

Her mother came over to her. "We have to be grateful to you; however, you gave a most immodest display of yourself."

"Fie on you, Pleasure," Sir Julian replied. "Better to see those lovely bare buttocks than be at the mercy of those robbers."

Lady Pleasure delicately waved a hankie before her. "I declare, I may faint. Can you not remove the body of that ...creature?"

Sir Julian eyed the dead man with distaste. "Nothing more than mutton, my lady. Turn your back on it!"

Tessa accompanied her mother back to the carriage. They were both standing by it when they heard a shot in the woods. And a few minutes later the driver and his assistant returned with triumphant looks on their coarse faces.

"Got him!" the driver announced happily. "And I've got the goods as well." He then began a distribution of the money, rings and other precious items among them.

None of them had any appetite for food, but fortified with wine they began their journey again. Tessa could not believe that they'd had such an exciting adventure. She was pleased to be accepted as the heroine of the occasion, even if her mother had been shocked at her wanton display of herself. Sir Julian showed a keen appreciation of her exposure as well as of her excellent marksmanship.

It was late evening when they arrived at the huge gray stone building that was Farr Castle. They were all dusty and weary from their journey. Servants came hurrying out to greet them, and Lady Pleasure gave Tessa into the care of a gaunt older woman by name of Mrs. Hess.

"Mrs. Hess will take you to your room and give you hot water to freshen up," her mother told her. "And when you have washed and changed, you may come down and meet the rest of the family."

"Thank you, mother," Tessa replied dutifully.

Mrs. Hess guided her up a winding stairway. Her room, on the third floor of the old castle, was larger than any she'd known before, with a four-poster bed and canopy, rich drapes at the window, dressers, and a commode—on which the older woman had placed a pitcher of warm water.

Tessa began her ablutions alone after declining the help of a maid. She was still in a dazed mood from the sudden change in her life-style. She could not believe she was to be part of this great house and this noble family. She worried that her mother might have done her a bad service. Surely she would have been better off to have remained with the circus and married Bob.

She found herself still debating this and feeling sad for her friends of the circus as she changed from the dusty brown dress to her best, a pale green silk with lace at the low-cut neck and sleeves. Lady Pleasure had promised to provide a new wardrobe, but Tessa couldn't picture any dress being more suited to her than this green one.

She'd barely put it on when there was a soft knock at her door. She went over and opened it to discover a girl a few inches shorter than herself standing in the hallway.

The girl was dark-haired like herself, with a fine-featured face, a spread of small freckles over her milk-white skin, and gray eyes that were bright with friendliness. She smiled and said, "I am Mary Farr, your stepsister. May I come in?"

"Please do," Tessa said, pleased at the attractive appearance of the girl and her friendliness.

Mary, who wore a white gown, asked excitedly, "Did you really shoot one of the bandits and save the lives of all the party?"

"Hardly," Tessa said. "I did manage to take the two by surprise. And I put a bullet through the arm of one of them. The driver and his assistant did the rest."

Mary smiled. "You are too modest."

Tessa laughed. "Mother thinks I wasn't modest enough, since I did a somersault as part of my surprise attack."

"I know," Mary said. "Sir Julian told me. He's ecstatic about it."

Tessa blushed. "I wish I could have done otherwise. Too late to worry now."

"And no need of it," Mary assured her. "You should be looked upon as a heroine. You saved them."

"Mother made it plain she would have preferred I had not acted so rashly."

"Fie on her," Mary said petulantly. And she leaned close to Tessa. "Let me say *she* is not so terribly modest where men are concerned. It is well known she turned my father's head with her wiles, and now she openly cuckolds him!"

Tessa's eyes widened. "With Sir Julian?"

Mary laughed merrily. "Never! All of us are safe with

Julian! He enjoys women only as companions. When he lusts, he looks for different company."

"Ah, I suspected that," Tessa said. "We had such men in the circus from time to time!"

"You must tell me about the circus! What a life you must have had!"

"I left it reluctantly," Tessa sighed.

Mary's eyes twinkled. "Your mother intends to make a fine lady of you!"

"So she says! From what you tell me, she is not exactly a lady herself!"

"Oh, she's a lady, all right. By birth as well as by title. But she has a loose nature, which makes her see every man she meets as her natural prey. My father has been patient, but I can see that he is weary of her behavior. I think she tries him too much."

"It sounds so," Tessa said. "He must be a man of good nature to endure it."

"He is a kind man," Mary agreed, "though one of strong sexual passions. I was so disgusted once I wanted to go to France and enter a nunnery there. My father heard about it and was so shocked he dismissed my French governess. Now we have a stiff English widow who is good in heart but cold in manner."

"And she shall be my governess as well," Tessa said.

"That is the plan."

"And your brothers?"

"Are the privileged characters here," Mary said with some annoyance. "They go about doing as they like. Harry plays the lute and drinks a lot between hunting and fishing expeditions. He will inherit the title. And Horatio is a lean, aloof scholar who seems to hate the world and love only his books."

"I hope they will approve of me," Tessa worried.

"My father and Harry will," Mary said. "And watch out for them. They have an eye for a pretty girl. Horatio will be sure to disapprove of you. He despises youth and beauty, and he also hates your mother. He has never accepted her as stepmother, and he has boasted to me that since you are a bastard, he will never be civil to you!"

34

Tessa was shocked. "He said that!"

"He often talks that way," Mary said. "Pay no attention to him. I think him a little mad. In fact I distrust all men. What about you?"

Tessa hesitated. "I can't say that I do."

"You were in a traveling circus," Mary said, staring at Tessa. "I should have realized. You are bound to have had a lover, or even lovers."

Tessa shook her head. "I am not my mother's daughter in that way. I think sex indulged in without love is a sad thing. I want no part of it!"

"I'm happy to hear you utter such sentiments," the dark girl said. "But I warn you that popularity at the court of Charles the Second is impossible if you stay with such ideals."

"I care little for the attitude of the court. I hope I shall never have to appear before the king."

Mary smiled. "You may change your mind. He can be charming when it suits him. Now I must take you downstairs. They are waiting dinner for us. No doubt Sir Julian has regaled them with his wild version of your exploit!"

And Mary was right. Sir Julian had given the family a lurid account of the adventure in which Tessa was the rather brazen heroine. She sat blushing beside Mary at the large table. Her mother sat at one end, regal in dark satin, while her stepfather, Sir David Farr, sat at the other. Sir David was a good-looking man with a square, determined face bronzed by much outdoor life—very much the genial country squire.

Across from Tessa sat a smiling Harry Farr, who would one day inherit his father's title. He looked much like his parent, handsome in a coarse, outdoor fashion, with a quick smile and ready wit. At his side in drab and rusty black sat Horatio, the scholar. His face was long and thin, and he had bad yellow teeth that made him even more unpleasant to look at. His manner was cold and he said little at the table. Most of the time he glared at his plate or offered Tessa an occasional glance of hatred. Sir Julian sat on the other side of the cold Horatio and did his best to keep the conversation going well.

During one lull, he said, "They say at court the king's latest mistress has a passion for clothes, none of which return her affection!"

"I know her well," Lady Pleasure commented. "She is Barbara, Countess of Castlemaine. And she has a horrid, nasty disposition."

"But a trim ankle that pleases the king," young Harry Farr said with his eyes twinkling. He included Tessa in his glance, and she looked down and blushed.

Sir David Farr said, "Barbara Palmer's title is a masquerade to cover up her harlotry, of course. Yet for all the looseness of the court, we live in better times than when we were ruled by Cromwell."

"God save the king!" Sir Julian said piously and rose to drink the sovereign's health. All the men at the table rose, and the ladies joined them. Tessa followed suit and solemnly drank the toast.

When they were seated again, Sir David Farr smiled at Tessa down the table. "We all wish you happiness here, my dear. Your mother has great plans for you. We shall all join with her to try to make them come true."

"Thank you," she said quietly. "You are too kind."

"And you are a young woman of talent and experience, if what we have heard about your defeating the robbers is true," young Harry Farr said.

Tessa smiled wryly. "I think my actions have been exaggerated a good deal."

"Not at all," Sir Julian said with an airy wave of a thin hand. "I drink to Tessa, the heroine of the day!"

All drank except Tessa—and Horatio, who sat sullenly and paid no attention to the proceedings. When the others took their seats again, he gave Tessa a cold look and in a low voice said, "Wickedness is weakness! You are no Farr!" And he rose abruptly and strode out of the great dining room with its richly tapestried walls.

There was a shocked silence following his dramatic exit. Then Sir Julian poured more wine into his own glass and declared, "Fie upon the young gentleman! He has maggots in his liver, and they upset his temperament!"

"Let us speak of more pleasant things," Sir David suggested. "There is to be a hunt ball this Saturday. We must have Tessa make her first appearance in public on the occasion."

Tessa listened in a state of confusion. Mary had warned her that Horatio would be unpleasant, but she had not imagined his being so cruel and blunt. He was surely not going to try to make her advent at the castle a happy experience.

When they left the candlelit dinner table, young Harry singled her out and took her to the gardens for a stroll under the stars. As they walked together, he showed every consideration for her.

"You must forgive Horatio," he said. "I often think he is not right in the head."

"He hates me without reason," Tessa said. "It is my mother's wish that I am here, not mine."

"We all know that," Harry agreed. "We shall try to make you happy. I shall talk to my brother privately and warn him to mind his manners. Father will also lecture him."

"You mustn't do it for me," she told him. "I do not want to be the cause of any ill will between brothers."

Harry smiled at her as they paused at the end of the grave garden walk. He said, "You have all the beauty of your mother and some extra quality as well."

"You are too kind."

"I mean it," he said. "A man would not find it difficult to fall in love with you."

Tessa said, "Love is a thing apart from the lust that seems so prevalent these days, both at the court and away from it."

Harry laughed. "I did not expect such puritanism from one accustomed to the circus life."

"We have our morals in that world just as people do anywhere else," she said stoutly.

"I'm sure you do," he apologized. "But this new kind of living we call loose morals is surely only an expression of rebellion against the strict standards of the Roundheads, under whom we suffered so many years."

"So now there is an excess of debauchery?"

"If you would call it that," Harry said.

"What else can I call it?"

They had begun to stroll back and were walking arm in arm. He said, "They did it better in the days before Cromwell. Life was lived to the fullest, but there was not the excesses of license which we know now."

"Perhaps things will return to that normalcy one day."

"I think so."

"What do you do for activity?" she asked.

"I play the country squire, so that when I inherit the title I shall not be ignorant of what is expected of me. It takes study and experience to be a proper member of the gentry."

"I thought you were all born to the purple," she teased him.

"Hardly," he said. "It takes a certain fine flair to be a nobleman. Our new king led the way when he returned here from exile. He gave all first offenders in prison a pardon on his first day on English soil. You would have to have visited some of our foul prisons, like Newgate, to know what a lease on life that was for many."

"I have seen the country prisons. They are filthy places not fit for human beings. Only prisoners with money can buy themselves decent food or comfort."

"And that is a scandal in itself," Harry said. "Making one law for the rich and another for the poor. The man with money can live on the right side of Newgate prison and not suffer too much, while the poor wretch on the paupers' side must sleep in slimy filth and eat crusts the rats might refuse!"

Tessa listened with excitement, for she knew something of these things. She told him, "We had a girl join the circus once. When she took off her dress, we saw the deep welts from the whip on her back. She told us she was whipped at Newgate and was raped by more than one of the guards there! She thought it a miracle that she had escaped alive."

"Many don't," Harry said grimly. "If my brother Horatio were truly inclined to do good deeds, it would seem he

38

could make a career of looking after the welfare of those in prisons. There must be some reform."

"It seems he is a theorist when it comes to good deeds," she suggested. "He is not ready to put his beliefs into action."

"That is true," Harry said with surprise as they arrived at the entrance of the castle. "You have a fine head on your shoulders. And you speak very well! How does this happen in a circus girl?"

She smiled. "The traveling show draws every sort of person, especially at the low levels. All kinds of human discards came our way. We had one such fellow whom we called the professor. He drank a good deal, and so he became a clown. Until the day of his untimely death he schooled me."

"And did an excellent job," Harry said. "Your mother ought to be pleased that she will have so little to do to make you a fine lady."

"I cannot tell about her," Tessa mused. "I think she is both drawn to me and repelled by me."

The young man frowned. "Yet she went to much trouble to see you were taken care of. And now she has sought you out and brought you here."

"I know," Tessa admitted. "Yet I still have a strange feeling about her. An old fortune-teller told me I was to bring her unhappiness."

"I do not believe in fairy tales," Harry admonished her. "We are all delighted to have you here, except for Horatio. You will brighten our mundane lives."

In the weeks that followed, it seemed that Harry's prediction was to be proven right. Tessa and Mary became the best of friends. And under the tutelage of their stern governess they acquired both knowledge and etiquette. Tessa's mother remained politely aloof, and now that she was at home again, she began carrying on in the old manner with her several lovers.

The handsome Sir David Farr spent much time in London and seemed to want to remain ignorant about his wife's affairs. It was impossible not to sympathize with him. Horatio crept about the house, always with some heavy book in his hand. His silent, venomous progress about the place made Tessa think of a loathsome lizard. His drab, dark garb increased the effect.

Harry went about the business of the estate and also did a good deal of hunting with other members of the local gentry. He remained Tessa's good friend and often took time to have long chats with her.

When she and Mary had gone for a stroll in the fields one cool October afternoon, she had asked her stepsister about Harry's romantic interests.

Mary gave her a knowing look, "You have met Lady Eve Murray?"

"Yes, I went to the home of her family on the night of the Hunt Ball. My first appearance in society here."

"She and Harry are betrothed," Mary said.

"But she is such a plain girl," Tessa recalled. "And she has a stutter."

"True," Mary agreed. "But it is best for our two families if the match is made. Lady Eve will have a good dowry, and it will mean a joining of the two estates."

Tessa asked, "What about true love?"

"I think Eve loves Harry, but he cannot truly be attracted to her. It is a pity. Yet he will marry her and seek his love somewhere else."

Tessa was shocked. "You consider that a good solution?"

"Many accept it," her stepsister said.

The days went by pleasantly, and Tessa was beginning to settle into the contentment of her new life. But the humdrum surface was only part of the picture, as she was soon to learn. She went to a guest room one evening in search of a book that had been lost somewhere and that she badly wanted to read. When she opened the door and entered the room, she came upon her mother and a strange man naked on the bed in a frantic lovers' embrace!

Had Tessa not been so shocked, she might have escaped without their seeing her. But so strong was her reaction that she stood for a moment in the doorway, a frozen creature. Then her mother's head rose, and Tessa could see those maternal features twisted in anger by the light of the candle at the bedside.

"Get out of here!" Her mother's screech was that of a fishwife in anger.

The order brought Tessa to life. Shamed, she stumbled back and groped her way out of the almost dark room. She stood in the hallway a moment, pale and nauseated. Then she went to the stairs to go up to her own room. She met Mary on the landing.

Her stepsister took one look at her, and realizing there was something badly wrong, she touched Tessa's arm and asked, "What has happened?"

Tessa looked down. "Ugly!" she said.

"Tell me!" Mary said urgently as they stood together on the shadowed landing.

"My mother!"

"And a man?"

"Yes. I came upon them. Back there!" She waved a hand to indicate the room.

"Sir Rupert Hazen," Mary said angrily. "He never calls when Father is at home!"

"He came a while ago. Then they both vanished."

"An old trick of Lady Pleasure's," Mary said grimly. "Later on they'll show up all smiles and innocence, and she'll talk about a stroll in the garden. A stroll in the garden, indeed!"

"How can she?"

"Do this to my father?" Mary asked. "I don't know. And I can't think why he stands for it. He is well liked, and he has been true to her since they were married."

Tessa said with disgust, "He should throw her out like something rotten!"

"You're beginning to sound like Horatio," Mary warned.

"I can't help it. She screamed at me to leave them!"

Mary looked worried. "I hope it doesn't mean trouble."

"I don't care," Tessa said bitterly. "I'd rather go back to the circus. Life was clean there, in comparison."

"You mustn't leave because of this—I should miss you dreadfully," Mary said.

Tessa was on the verge of tears. "I was happy in the circus. I was in love, and we were to be married. I gave it all up for this! They thought it would be such a fine opportunity for me. They didn't know!"

Mary put an arm around her. "You mustn't think too much about this. Regard your mother's behavior as a strange illness. That is how I have forced myself to think. It is the best way. She is aging and soon she will no longer be attractive to men. Maybe my father will know peace in his last years."

"A slim hope," Tessa said with a deep sigh.

The sequel to this came the following day when Lady Pleasure summoned Tessa to her room and then shut the door so no one would overhear what was being said. Her mother's face was noticeably painted though it was early in the day. It seemed she could not bear to study the ravages of time on her face in the bright daylight.

The older woman paced back and forth—she was wearing a silk robe with much lace trim—as Tessa sat primly in a plain chair waiting to hear what she would say.

Her mother began, "About yesterday—"

"I would rather we didn't discuss it," the girl said in a low voice.

Lady Pleasure showed anger. "That is always the way with you. And it is the cause of most of the trouble. You are ignorant of important facts and refuse to understand."

"I don't want to understand."

"Listen to me," her mother said, grim-faced. "Lord Rupert is a dear friend of mine."

"That was obvious," Tessa said, sounding sarcastic without wanting to.

"Be careful what you say!" her mother warned. "I knew him long before I married Lord David. Poor Rupert has an invalid wife. He must seek love outside the marriage bed."

"So he finds it with you?"

"Is that so evil?" her mother asked, the crimson on her cheeks deepening beneath her heavy makeup. "I consider

42

it charity on my part. An attempt to help an old friend in trouble."

"You seemed to be enjoying the charity you dispensed so willingly," Tessa observed.

"You have an acid tongue, girl!"

"I'm sorry. May I go now?"

"Not until you understand!"

"I understand."

"You are a willful, silly girl," Lady Pleasure stormed. "And all the fine training I have squandered on you appears to have been wasted."

Tessa looked at her mother with imploring eyes. "Then perhaps you will let me go back to the circus."

"Never," her mother said harshly. "You want to return to your lover. I can see through you. Don't tell me you've never been in bed with a man. I can see the guilt written all over you!"

"I would never soil my marriage bed as you have!" the girl shot back.

"You'll pay for that!" her mother hissed and slapped her hard across the face. "How dare you speak to me in such a way? You'll never escape. Do you hear me? You can run away as much as you like—I'll pay and pay well to bring you back!"

"Simply to make me suffer?"

"To make you show proper respect for your mother," Lady Pleasure declared, recovering her arrogant dignity. "Now you may go. But think well about what I have said. Keep a civil tongue and pray for forgiveness!"

"Why should I pray for forgiveness?" the girl demanded.

"Because you have been cruel to your mother!" the older woman said righteously. "Cruel to me, who has only shown love for you! Go!"

Tessa needed no urging to leave the room. She rushed into the hall, only to find herself confronted by the twisted Horatio. He stood there, book in hand, a scowl on his pale face. There seemed every likelihood that he had been listening to their conversation.

He looked at her in his mad fashion and in a low, intense voice said, "A whore calling on a whore!"

"Hold your tongue!" she retorted angrily.

Horatio moved on a step, then turned and said, "You have brought another shadow of wickedness to this house. Why don't you leave?"

"Why do you hate me so?"

"Because you exist," he said in his low voice. "Go away, or that existence may be short." And he moved slowly on along the bleak corridor like a great black beetle.

Tessa stood where she was for a little. She did not know what to do. She had no idea where the circus might be by now. It traveled in all directions, wherever the performers could find some work. She would have to make lengthy inquiries and in all probability would have difficulty locating it.

Never had she needed friendship more. But her mother had warned that if she tried to join her former cronies, she would be brought back in disgrace, and no doubt Lady Pleasure would be as vindictive as she dared towards the circus people. Tessa did not wish to bring trouble on the Shaws or on Bob. And she knew how little it would take for a moneyed member of the gentry to cause trouble for a humble circus owner. Lady Pleasure would simply have to say the word, and it might be Newgate or an equally grim prison for the Shaws and Bob. Tessa did not dare risk her mother's vengeance on them. But could she remain in this house with what was going on?

She went downstairs with her dilemma unsolved. Mary had gone to spend the afternoon with Harry's fiancé, Lady Eve Murray. She had asked Tessa to come along, but Tessa found Lady Eve so dull she had begged to be excused. She could not imagine the lively, good-humored Harry marrying such a girl.

Fortunately, Sir Julian Dorley arrived shortly after she went down to the living room. He was wearing a new red velvet coat and fawn breeches, and his ruffled shirt was also of a new style. He eyed Tessa with his quizzing glass, a smile on his thin face.

"Where is Lady Mary?" he asked.

"Gone to visit Lady Eve. I declined."

"You find Lady Eve dull?" he asked with a light in his pale blue eyes.

"Yes," she admitted, "if I must be honest. And her stammer bothers me."

The fop nodded. "I understand. She has the same effect on me. She cannot be blamed, poor girl. She was the child of a father badly eaten with the pox! 'Tis said she has inherited the dread disease, though as to that, I can neither confirm nor deny the rumor."

Tessa was shocked. "I have heard that some such children do suffer, though they seldom live to be adults."

"So perhaps Lady Eve is not infected but only marred by her father's disease," Sir Julian suggested.

"Either way, it is an ugly business. Why does Harry intend to marry her?"

"To get her land," Sir Julian said bluntly. "The Farr estate is badly in need of fresh farmlands."

Tessa was shocked. "I cannot think that Harry would be part of such a mercenary arrangement."

"That is how we gentry survive," Sir Julian said, with a wink. "I am perhaps the single exception. If I marry, it will surely be for love!"

"You will never marry," she told him.

"That is probably quite true," the fop agreed. "But there is a ring of nobility in my declaration of intention."

She smiled at him despite her upset state. "You are the utter cynic," she told him.

"I should be disappointed to learn I have any peers," he admitted.

So the week went on with Tessa growing more unhappy all the time. She had nearly made up her mind to risk going back to the circus, regardless of the harm it might bring those she loved. Then, one pleasant autumn night, she found herself alone in Harry's company under strange conditions.

She was standing in the living room when the handsome young man entered with a weary look on his face.

"I've had a bad night," he told her, sinking heavily into a wing-backed chair. "My favorite mare has hurt her leg. If it doesn't get better, she may have to be shot."

"Oh, no!" Tessa protested. She was fond of the brindle mare.

"I've just come from her now," Harry said wearily. "I don't think there is anything else we can do. The coachman made a bandaged support for her leg."

"I wonder how he bandaged it," Tessa said. "It makes a difference. We had several horses and a pony in the circus. I've had some experience in the treatment of such troubles."

Harry's face brightened. "I'd forgotten all about that. Of course, you're bound to know the best methods."

Tessa said modestly, "The owner of the circus was said to be a true expert. He gave me instruction."

"You must come out and see if Nell's leg bandages are right," Harry pleaded. "It might mean the saving of her life."

Tessa didn't hesitate. Her love for animals was paramount in her emotions. She said, "Take me to her."

Harry led her out to the stables and lighted a lantern for her to see the mare in her stall. Tessa went to the uneasy animal quietly, speaking to her in soft tones. The mare whinnied nervously and moved about a little.

"Calm, Nell," Harry said, doing his best to help with the tense animal.

Kneeling by the bandaged leg, Tessa saw that the bandage was not tied correctly, nor was it as tight as it should be. She began to unwind it. After she'd done this, she began to bind the leg again, this time making the bandage much more taut.

"Excellent," Harry said with admiration as he watched her work.

"This will be better," she promised, rising. "Look at it again in the morning. I'll check it if you like."

"We can come here together," he suggested. "You're a remarkable girl, Tessa."

She managed a smile. "You learn many things in a circus." And she started out of the barn.

She had walked only a little way when Harry came to stand in front of her. Next to him was a stall that was empty except for straw on the floor. He was staring at her in a strange fashion. In a husky voice, he said, "Tessa, I love you!"

"No!" she said, frightened. "Please let me go!"

"I can't," he said thickly. "I won't! I'm madly in love with you, Tessa!"

"What about Lady Eve?"

"I despise her," he said, taking her in his arms. "It is you I love, you I want!"

She felt the warmth of his embrace, his frantic lips on hers. And she was aware of a new feeling within herself. The hunger which she had kept in check so well was asserting itself. Her legs became numb and she was unable to fight him off as she wished.

"Harry, please!" she moaned. "I like you. Let's not spoil it! Wait until we can talk about this!"

"No!" he said, hoarsely, already tearing at her clothes.

"You mustn't!" she said weakly. But she knew it was too late. Harry was physically overpowering her, and her own inner weakness had come to undermine her as well. She was herself filled with a burning desire that made no sense!

Now she was naked and on the straw and Harry was upon her. His rough penetration of her was more cruel and at the same time more satisfying than anything she had experienced with Bob. They played their macabre game of love stretched out in the straw. Harry was relentless in his probings, and Tessa was filled with a blinding passion that for the moment shut out shame and fear.

Then she was aware of others coming up to stare at them, and she heard the cruel voice of Horatio saying triumphantly, "I told you where you'd find them!"

Chapter Three

"Slut!" There was no mistaking her mother's angry voice ringing out loud and clear!

Harry uttered a low curse and lifted himself up, at the same time hastily arranging his clothing. Then he turned and fled blindly from the stall, leaving Tessa naked and trembling on the straw as her mother and a gloating Horatio, with a lantern held high, hovered above her.

"You whore!" her mother screamed, her dark hair in disarray around her shoulders. "You would criticize me!"

"Seductress!" Horatio said, his sallow face more ugly in its hatred.

Tessa gazed up at them in the glow of the lantern; as her confusion faded away, she made a futile attempt to cover her nakedness. She realized she had been disgraced before the family and servants. No need to try to explain that it was Harry who had led her to the barn and then had so wantonly attacked her! No point in explaining she'd been cruelly raped, no reason to hope for understanding! Her mother had caught her and was ready to make the most of her daughter's discomfiture—to cover her own falls from grace!

"Stay with her," Lady Pleasure said harshly. "I know how to make her understand!" And she turned away to the darkness of the barn.

Horatio remained on guard over Tessa as she reached out for her torn clothes and began to cover her nakedness. She was on her feet when her mother came striding back. Then she saw the long whip in her mother's hand.

"No!" she cried out plaintively and stumbled back.

"You have a lesson to learn!" her mother said grimly. She raised the whip as Horatio looked on with approval.

Tessa saw the whip descend, and retreated as far into the stall as she could. It wasn't far enough. The curling whip lashed down, striking her naked breasts and raising a livid scar below her nipples. The pain was searing, unbearable!

48

"Please!" she screamed for pity, turning her back to her mother.

This seemed to goad her parent on to crueler heights. Lady Pleasure had a look of maniacal delight on her face as she brought the whip down on Tessa's back again and again. And each time its thin, snaky coils struck, large red welts were raised across Tessa's lovely back. Blood coursed down to her bare buttocks, and still the abuse went on.

"Mother!" she mumbled repeatedly through her torment. Finally she slipped down on her knees, too weak and hurt to stand any longer.

"Scum!" Lady Pleasure cried and raised the whip once again to strike her daughter across the shoulders.

This was the last blow Tessa remembered. At this point in her mother's cruel game of torture, she lost consciousness. A kindly velvet blackness descended over her. She was content, even anxious for this escape. A deep sigh came from her lips as she sprawled out on the straw.

When she opened her eyes again she was in her bed, and Mary was bending anxiously over her. Her stepsister's face was pale with horror. And Tessa was suddenly aware of a scorching fire which enveloped all her back.

Her throat was parched and her mouth dry from the pain. In a low voice, she told Mary, "It wasn't my doing!"

"Please! You mustn't worry about it," Mary said, placing a cool hand on her forehead. "You have such a fever! I had you brought up here to your room and Mrs. Hess has covered your back with a soothing salve which she says will surely heal it."

Tessa stared up at the girl. "My mother?"

"Is a madwoman," Mary said with disgust. "I shall marry as soon as possible and get away from this unhappy house."

"I'm sorry," Tessa said.

"You have no need to be," Mary told her. "I know Harry's nature, his wildness where women are concerned. He has gone away from the house. I know it was he who must have been to blame."

"Neither Horatio nor my mother were willing to believe he raped me," Tessa said.

"Because it pleased them not to think so," Mary said grimly. "You are not the first young woman Harry has attacked . . . though before you, they were only servants on the estate and it was hushed up. Now they plan to protect him by blaming you."

Tessa said, "I fought him at first. Then I was carried away by a passion of my own."

"Do not try to understand or discuss it," Mary said.

"I cannot remain here," Tessa said. "I shall leave as soon as I'm able."

"My father will be home soon," Mary told her. "I will talk to him and be sure he knows the truth. He will be on your side."

Tessa stirred, and pain rose like flames, causing her to moan. She closed her eyes, "I should never have come here."

"I'm glad you did," Mary said. "You've given me the courage to escape this house. Lady Eve Murray has a cousin, Charles, who is anxious to marry me. I intend to accept him."

"My mother hates me," Tessa said in despair. "She hates me because I found her out in her wrongdoing."

"Sir Rupert is only one of a host of men who have been in her bed," Mary said with disgust. "The shame of it has made my father avoid going to court. Everyone in Whitehall knows about Mother's looseness."

"He should leave her or drive her from the house," Tessa said.

"The pity is that in a way he still loves her. He sees something in her beyond her insatiable desire for sexual fulfillment. His thought seems to be to try to save her. But her wickedness towards you will do much to make him see her as she really is."

"She will lie to him."

"I shall speak with him first, and he will listen to me," Mary said quietly. "Now you must rest."

And Tessa did rest. In the morning when Mrs. Hess came to place the healing salve on her back again, she was able to take a small amount of broth, and the pain was bearable if she did not move about too much.

Mary came to her in mid-morning and said, "I have talked with my father. He is enraged with Harry—and with Horatio and your mother."

"Has Harry returned?"

"No, he's gone to London to wait until the trouble blows over. It's an old trick with him."

"To think I trusted him," Tessa sighed.

"I should have warned you," Mary said. "For all his charm, Harry is without character. Neither of my brothers are men to admire."

"I should be able to leave by tomorrow," Tessa said. "In the meantime, will you let it be known I do not wish to see my mother."

"I doubt that she will have the face to visit you," Mary said. "But my father plans to come talk with you, and I urge you to see him."

"I shall," Tessa said, giving Mary a look of gratitude. "You are a true sister to me!"

"I hope I may always be," Mary said as she bent and kissed her gently on the cheek.

Tessa lapsed into an exhausted sleep for a while. When she awoke, the sun of the autumn afternoon was setting. She found herself feeling a little better. She was able to move about in bed without being tormented by pain.

Again Mrs. Hess came and applied the healing salve to her wounds. And she tried some food. After she finished her lunch Sir David Farr appeared, and Mrs. Hess discreetly retired from the room.

The handsome nobleman wore a blue jacket and gray breeches. His curled wig gave him an imposing air, its stark white contrasting with his bronzed, manly face. There was a strength in his features that was not apparent in Harry's face, though the son did resemble the father in many ways.

Sir David came to Tessa's bedside and gazed down at her soberly. "You have been sorely mistreated, my girl."

She looked up into his kindly face. "I wish to cause

you no more trouble. It is my intention to leave this house and return to the circus."

He studied her soberly. "You no longer wish to be with your mother?"

"I cannot think of her as my mother. I'm sorry."

"No need to apologize," the middle-aged man said. "I understand your feelings."

"Thank you," she said in a low voice.

I frowned. "I know my wife better than most people think. In the end she will destroy herself. And I know my sons. Harry is greedy to possess all that he sees, and Horatio is a cold fish of a scholar. I have only my daughter, Mary, to be proud of."

"Mary has been very kind to me," Tessa said.

"I agree you should leave here," Lord David said. "And I'm going to make you a rather shocking proposition."

"What?"

"I want you to leave here in my company."

She stared at him. "In your company?"

"Yes. I have rented a town house in London, not far from the court. I planned to use it as a base when Lady Pleasure and I returned to court circles. Because of her actions I'm delaying that, and instead, I wish you to journey to London and live with me in the house. In due time I shall present you to His Majesty, Charles the Second, as was planned when my wife and I brought you to live with us."

Tessa was staggered by the offer. "You are suggesting I go with you to London and live with you there as your mistress?"

The older man responded with a weary smile. "Does the idea repulse you?"

She considered for a moment and decided to answer him as honestly as possible. "No," she said. "If I were to sell my body to anyone, I would weigh your offer very seriously. I'm sure you are a kindly and considerate man, and not without wit and intelligence."

"Thank you."

"You would doubtless treat me better than many a younger man making the same offer."

"You may rely on that."

She looked up at him sadly. "But I do not want to give or sell my body to the first interested bidder. I would prefer to return to the circus and marry the man to whom I was betrothed."

Sir David sighed. "I fear you may not find it so easy to go back to that world after sampling this one."

"I shall try," she said.

"Let me make you a more interesting offer, one which you have earned," the nobleman said. "Come to London and live with me as my attractive companion. Let my wife and all the world think you are my mistress, but be secure in my assurance that I shall not lay a hand on you."

"I cannot agree to such a one-sided bargain," she protested.

"It would be quite fair," Sir David insisted. "You would be doing me a service by making my wife madly jealous. It is my only hope of bringing her into line."

Tessa listened with a new interest. "You really think it could help?"

"Being unfaithful to her is a course of action I have forbidden myself," Sir David said. "In this instance I have a chance to try its effects without demeaning myself. And perhaps the arrangement may be of value to you as well."

Her eyes met his knowingly. "My mother will hate me doubly."

"I cannot see that it matters any longer."

"Nor I," she agreed. "But how am I to believe you— that you will not try to rape me as your son did in so disgraceful a manner?"

The older man spread his hands. "I can only give you my word as a gentleman. Is that enough?"

"I believe it is."

"Thank you," he said. "I will not deny that I am attracted to you. You are certain to develop into a beauty who will turn men's heads. You are more lovely than your mother now. You should have a fine future, and you must not throw yourself away on circus life."

"I found my circus life honest and good."

"Not good enough," Sir David said. "I shall introduce you to the court and to the king. At the same time, Lady Pleasure shall be banned from the court until I give permission for her to attend. The king is my friend, and he will grant me this privilege."

Tessa said soberly, "That may work out well. But I have been told that both the court and the king are dissolute. Even under your protection, would I not be easy prey for the debauched there?"

"Under my protection you might be in danger," Sir David admitted. "But under the king's protection you would be completely safe. Charles will do me the favor of giving you his protection."

Tessa managed a wan smile. "So my mother's promises will be fulfilled. I shall see the court and king after all."

"If you choose to go to London with me," her stepfather said.

She hesitated, frowning again. "Lady Mary will believe I've given myself to you. I wish that could be otherwise. I have come to care for her."

"My daughter will be informed of the truth," Sir David said. "As for Harry and Horatio, let them gnash their teeth in frustration, along with Lady Pleasure. I shall take great delight in allowing them to think so young and charming a creature as yourself has agreed to be my mistress."

"I will do it," Tessa said, knowing she was taking a great chance but willing to gamble on the older man's word of honor.

He smiled. "Well done, Tessa. You are a girl after my own heart. Will you be well enough to leave in the early morning when the rest of the house is still asleep?"

"I shall manage," she promised.

"When we reach London in mid-morning, we shall proceed straight to the house I have rented," he said. "And the first thing I shall do is have a physician come and treat you."

"The salve Mrs. Hess has given me is working well enough. I shall ask for a supply from her to bring along."

54

"As you like," Sir David said. "Be prepared to leave at four in the morning. I shall come here for you."

So the strange bargain was made. It gave Tessa something to hope for. All during the rest of the day and evening she lay in bed, excitement growing in her. She knew there were dark aspects to the agreement, knew she would be marked all her life as the mistress of the old nobleman. No matter how many explanations were offered, there would always be those who would insist that she had sold her body to him.

But she did not care. It was a way to pay back both her mother and Harry. All of the county, and London as well, would laugh at the young nobleman who had ravished a lovely girl, only to have her jilt him for his father! Yes, over their tankards of ale the men would laugh heartily at such a story. Still, if Tessa met some man she truly loved, he would believe her version of it all, for did not complete trust come hand in hand with love?

She would risk her reputation to survive and to avenge herself on those who had been so cruel to her. Mary came to the room later and let her know that her father had confided his plan to her as he'd promised Tessa he would.

Mary warned her, "Your reputation will suffer, though I know my father will keep his word and not touch you."

"That is all I ask."

"In the meantime, the arrangement will serve Lady Pleasure and Harry right, not to mention my loathsome brother, Horatio. He is so pious it disgusts me, especially since it is false piety."

"Please don't hate me for what I am going to do," Tessa begged of her.

Mary smiled. "I love you for it. I'm sure it will help my father settle his score with Lady Pleasure. That is enough for me!"

Tessa was pleased at her stepsister's reaction. Now everything depended on her ability to travel in the morning. Thus, with Mary's aid, she got out of bed and made a few feeble circlings of the big room. Her head was dizzy and she leaned on the smaller girl's arm for support, but she tried to put her weakness out of mind. Then they together packed her small hoard of belongings in a case Mary gave her. The wardrobe her mother had promised had never materialized.

Before leaving her, Mary gave her a warning: "If Sir Julian Dorley visits you and Father in town, you must not let him suspect it is all a charade. He'd be sure to come mincing back to Lady Pleasure and tell her. There is nothing he likes better than gossip."

"To him I shall be your father's mistress," Tessa agreed.

"He is one of the ones who must be deceived," Mary emphasized. "Lady Pleasure is bound to send him spying on you."

"I shall remember," Tessa said.

That evening Mrs. Hess came and treated her back for the last time, after which she gave the girl a container with a good measure of the soothing salve. "I shall be here to help you dress shortly after three," the gaunt woman promised. "And may the good Lord look after you!"

"You have been so good!" Tessa told her gratefully.

"No more than my Christian duty," said Mrs. Hess.

Tessa slept little that night. Between the soreness of her back and her mounting excitement, she found it impossible to rest for more than a few minutes at a time. She worried as to whether she had made the wrong decision and wondered if she should have returned to the circus. At least she understood the rules there, where life was so much simpler. But her spirit of adventure urged her to sample what London offered.

There was no moon. It was the darkest of nights. Her bedchamber was wreathed in shadows until Mrs. Hess gently opened the door and came in, bearing a candle in her hand. There were furtive whisperings between Tessa and the older woman. Tessa dressed as quickly as possible and then, assisted by the good woman, went down the stairs.

Sir David, waiting in the reception hall for her, was wearing a heavy dark cloak. He said, "Everything is

56

packed. We have only to get into the carriage and be driven away."

"I'm ready," she said.

"Good." Sir David smiled at her. Then, after thanking Mrs. Hess, he and Tessa made their way out to the carriage in the darkness and got in. She gazed out the window of the carriage, wondering if she would ever see the great stone castle again. But almost instantly the carriage was under way, and the great adventure of London lay ahead.

Sir David turned to her in the darkness of the carriage and said, "I have blankets here. Make yourself comfortable and sleep if you can. We have a long and weary journey before us."

Thanking him, she fixed the blankets around her. When she finished, he gently folded a blanket at her back so as to protect it from the jarring of the carriage over the rough roads. When she was completely wrapped in blankets she relaxed, and to her surprise she actually managed to fall asleep. By the time she came awake, it was daylight and they were entering London!

Her stepfather gave her a warm smile. "You amazed me. You slept all through the journey!"

"I'm sorry I was such a dull traveling companion," she apologized.

"Think nothing of it. I had more than forty winks myself."

She turned to the window. "Are we really in London?"

"You are, indeed," the middle-aged man said heartily. "It is ranked among the wonders of the world, but in many ways it may disappoint you!"

As Tessa looked out into the narrow street, all seemed to be confusion. There were rows of ancient plaster and timber houses, leaning sloppily against each other and threatening to topple into the cobblestone street with its sewer running down the middle of it—a loathsome, open gutter into which human and animal offal was dumped, to be flushed into the Thames when it rained—the mighty Thames River, at once a highroad and a sewer.

57

Tessa said, "It is not what I expected. Where are the stately houses?"

Her companion laughed. "You will see them. But more of the city is like what you are seeing now. It is not a collection of fine palaces."

She studied the shops and warehouses lining the narrow cobblestone streets and heard the roaring confusion of hackneys and drays as they fought for a right of way. Then there were the cries of the apprentices standing before various shops and intoning, "What do you lack?" Everywhere there were pedestrians, and from all sides hawkers bawled their wares—fruits and vegetables, milk, custards, herring, oysters, old clothing and Newcastle coal.

"So many people!" she marveled.

"They claim we have a half million if all could be counted," Sir David Farr said with some pride.

"So many!" she said in awe.

"When King Charles returned to London from exile and paraded through the streets, I declare the whole lot of them turned out," Sir David said warmly. "As you know, the king declared a free Parliament and pardoned all first offenders in the prisons. In every street that night rumps of beef were roasted at open fires to celebrate the end of the Rump Parliament. The king paraded down the Strand to Whitehall with a glorious company, and the city exploded with joy!"

"They were glad to have a Stuart on the throne again."

"They were," Sir David agreed. "The streets were strewn with flowers, the church bells clanged, the fountains ran with wine, and the city companies appeared in livery with banners and gold chains. The windows and balconies along the Strand were crowded with ladies and gentlemen in velvet, gold, and silver. There were blaring trumpets and thundering drums to issue in the brave new world."

Tessa smiled at him. "And is it as brave and new as was hoped?"

"I fancy not," he said lightly. "But it is better than before. Charles's weakness for the ladies has led him into

58

exchanging titles for harlots' favors on occasion. Nonetheless, among the weeds grow lovely flowers. I vow you shall be one of them."

"I give you my trust," she said and turned to stare out the window again.

Now the streets were wider, and there were houses of brick and stone—a more stately city, the London she had imagined. This was a mile westward from the city of Westminster. Here was the fine old palace of Whitehall, where Charles the Second lived when he was in London, and the imposing Westminster Abbey, the Parliament Buildings, with piles of brick and stone set along the river bank. Behind them, away from the river, were St. James's Park, St. James's Palace, and the new exclusive neighborhoods of Pall Mall and St. James's Square.

As they were driven along, Sir David pointed these things out to her and explained that midway between these western suburbs and the limits of the city was the Covent Garden district, bounded by Drury Lane, Longacre Street, St. Martin's Lane and the Strand.

The house Sir David had rented stood in the fine area of St. James's Square. It was a solid-looking brick edifice, rather narrow but three stories tall. The carriage halted outside it, and they descended to the street as the driver began gathering their baggage to take inside.

The door was opened by a snobbish-looking young man whom Sir David addressed as Hobbs and whom (he told Tessa) was the butler of the establishment. Tessa received the impression that this pale, bewigged Hobbs ran the house. He offered her a condescending smile of welcome.

Sir David showed her about the elegantly paneled and richly furnished living room. He indicated the paintings and tapestries on the wall, saying, "They have been chosen with good taste. A patron of the arts owns the house."

"It is wonderful," she said.

"It will do," he agreed. "Not so large as the castle but still a good size for London. Now I will take you to your room."

They went up a broad stairway to the second floor, and her room was at the top of the stairs immediately adjoining his. The nobleman offered her a knowing smile, "There is a connecting door. You shall have the key."

"We must preserve appearances or lose our evil reputation," she replied.

"You have a sense of humor," Sir David said approvingly. "And to be able to exhibit it in your condition is courageous, in truth!"

Her bedroom was a good size and furnished much as her room at the castle had been. A maid had already brought up her things and was installing them in a long dresser. After helping the girl, she freshened herself with the warm water that had been sent up. Then she went downstairs to lunch with Sir David.

She was well aware of the sly looks given her when the servants thought she wasn't aware of them. She had no doubt that the servants' quarters were alive with gossip about the nobleman and his young mistress. And she demurely played the role as planned. She wanted the adventure to turn out well.

She and Sir David sat down to luncheon in a fine dining room with a long table and several large paintings on its walls. Over their lunch he told her, "I have already sent for a Dr. Hyslop, who has been well recommended to me."

"It could have waited," Tessa said, though her back was still dreadfully sore.

"Not a minute longer than necessary," the nobleman said. "Such injuries can be dangerous. I have known several to die from after-effects of the lash."

The enormity of her mother's evil could not be denied. Tessa enjoyed the idea that her present enterprise must have already caused the bad-tempered Lady Pleasure a good deal of annoyance.

Sir David said, "After the doctor has seen you, we will make some other plans."

Dr. Hyslop arrived late in the afternoon and found Tessa resting in her room. Sir David brought the old man in and introduced him. The doctor was thin and watery-eyed, but his wrinkled face had a kindly look—which turned to distress when she removed her clothing to allow him to examine the welts on her back.

The old man made a clucking noise. "What a cruel business! I have seldom seen such brutality with a whip outside the prisons."

Sir David, who had remained for the examination, said dryly, "Her mother was responsible."

"I would find it hard to forgive her," Dr. Hyslop said. "The welts are healing nicely—thanks to the salve, whatever it may be. But clear scars will remain."

Sir David frowned. "The scarring will be permanent?"

"I fear so," the old man said sadly. "It is fortunate the wounds have healed as well as they have. Had pus set in, this girl's life might have been in danger."

Tessa replaced her blouse and buttoned it up. "I owe my recovery to Mrs. Hess."

Dr. Hyslop nodded. "I would agree with that. You must take things quietly for a week or two. No violent exercise and not too much moving about."

Sir David assured the old man, "I promise good care will be taken of her."

Dr. Hyslop closed his medical bag and bowed to Tessa. "If I can be of further service, let me know."

"I shall," she promised.

After the doctor and Sir David left the room, Tessa sat down and tears came to her eyes. She had been proud of her lovely body, and now her back would always bear ugly scars. She would never be able to wear a dress styled low in the back without showing deep red welts.

After a moment the door opened to admit Sir David again. Seeing her weeping, he came over to place a hand gently on her shoulder. "I'm sorry," he said. "I can never really forgive Harry or your mother. Between them they caused you this harm."

"It was not in any way your fault," she said, wiping away her tears with a tiny hankie.

"I swear always to think of you as my daughter," the handsome older man vowed. "And you shall be included in my will along with my blood children."

"There is no need," she protested.

"I think differently," he said. "In any case, our immediate concern is to restore your health. You must remain in the house and rest for a little until I am able to introduce you to the rest of London."

So began Tessa's convalescence. Sir David, who attended various functions in London, reported that it was a staple of the court gossip that he had taken a young mistress, the daughter of his second wife, Lady Pleasure. This news had been bandied about with glee by those who had reason to dislike the arrogant lady he had married.

One afternoon about two weeks later, when Tessa's back was almost completely healed, she had a visit from Sir Julian Dorley. It happened that Sir David was out when the fop arrived, and so she had to entertain him on her own. This was not too upsetting. She had expected Sir Julian sooner or later, so she resigned herself, ordered tea and cakes brought to the living room and went down to meet her caller.

The dandy, who was wearing a yellow waistcoat and white breeches, drew a lace-edged hankie from his sleeve to tend to his nose.

"Law, what a stir you have caused!" Sir Julian said.

"Truly?" Tessa murmured with feigned innocence.

" 'Tis whispered the doctor had to come and give your mother some sort of physique to make her sleep. She was like a wild woman in her rage."

"Yes," Tessa said quietly. "I know something of her bad temper."

The thin fop chuckled. "The thought that you and Sir David are living happily here together while the court talks about it has her feverish with rage!" He produced a snuff box of gold, pinched a squeeze in his long, thin nose, and immediately was seized with racking coughs.

Tessa asked worriedly, "Can I fetch you anything?"

He shook his head but continued to cough until his eyes watered. When at last he calmed down, he waved for her to be seated again. "It is naught but the snuff," he gasped.

"It must be too strong," she suggested.

"No, I happened to breathe wrongly when I was taking it," he said. He eyed her with admiration. "What a true hussy you have turned out to be!"

She smiled thinly. "Let us say I was whipped into it!"

He burst into a giggle. "Good! Excellent! Lady Pleasure did not know what she was doing when she whipped you after your little turn with Harry! They say he ran from the barn pulling up his pants! I should have liked to have been there."

"Would you?" she asked quietly.

"Fie! I did not mean that," Sir Julian blustered. "I wish I could have arrived to warn you in time. Tell me, who beds you better, the father or the son?"

She pretended shock and hurt. "How dare you put such a question to me?"

He wagged a bony finger. "I venture more has been put to you than that. Tell me, which of them is the best womanizer? Lady Pleasure says the old man is all but impotent!"

Tessa chose to look superior. "Perhaps he was with such a loose woman. But you can pass the word that he pleasures me delightfully and compares my charms with hers to my advantage!"

Sir Julian fairly bounced on his chair with delight. "I shall tell her! 'Pon my word I shall repeat your words exactly, and she will burn with jealousy."

"You may also tell her," Tessa said archly, "that I hope soon to appear at court. They tell me the king is a true sovereign when it comes to lovers! I shall be delighted to offer her my report later!"

"Shameless, brazen hussy!" Sir Julian chuckled and pointed his forefinger at her again. "I shall tell Lady Pleasure. And she will writhe with the misery you'll be giving her!"

"I did my writhing earlier, under her whip," Tessa said with scorn. "But it was well worth it. I have her London house, her husband, and a welcome at court—which, I understand, is denied her at the moment."

"You have more than evened the score," Sir Julian agreed. "I had a suspicion that you and Sir David were merely playing a game on Lady Pleasure—that you were living here as friends and making a show of being lovers!" He eyed her with his quizzing glass.

"Must I have him pleasure me in your presence to set your doubts at rest?" she asked.

Sir Julian crimsoned. "Law, no! Your new manner and language proclaim that you have taken on a different role. You talk like a true bawd!"

"I have become one, thanks to Harry and my mother," Tessa said with a cold smile. "And I mean to make it pay as well as the best bawds do."

Sir Julian nodded. "You are right," he said. "Do you know the latest? Nell Gwyn has taken the king's fancy, and Barbara of Castlemaine is beside herself . . . not to mention the poor queen, who has yet another rival for her royal mate's affections."

"Nell Gwyn?"

"Have you not heard of her?" Sir Julian wondered.

"I think not."

"You shall. She is going to be the toast of London, I promise you. Lovely girl—with golden, curly hair and a pretty face. Better than that, she has a rollicking manner and warm disposition. The king is supposed to be charmed with her. He regularly attends her performances in the King's Theater."

"She is an actress, then?"

"One of the new lot who have taken over now that it is no longer fashionable for men to play the feminine parts—though I must say I preferred the men," Sir Julian added with a toss of his head.

"I'm sure you would," Tessa said dryly. "Is this Nell Gwyn a good actress?"

"Dryden is fond of her and sees she has a part in all his new plays. She was merely an orange girl earlier, going about the pit selling oranges and the like to the patrons. Now she is the king's darling!"

"Does she have a good background?"

"Law! She has no background at all! Her sister Rose is known to have sold her favors in the streets; her mother is a gin-soaked old ruin; and Nell, naturally, is a bastard!"

"So many of us are," Tessa purred with a smile.

"Lovely!" Sir Julian said with delight. "I swear you are more witty and entertaining now that you have become a bawd!"

"I suggest you be on your way before David returns," she said.

"So it is 'David' now!" Sir Julian remarked with awe.

Tessa smiled knowingly. "Titles are more clumsy than night shirts when two are abed!"

"You will kill me!" Sir Julian said, chortling with high-pitched laughter. He rose to go, his walking stick in hand.

She rose to see him on his way and said, "Please tell Lady Pleasure that while she prefers to remain an amateur, I'm finding that there are advantages to being a professional."

"I shall," Sir Julian promised. "I shall tell her you've entered the role of bawd with joy rather than shame! And it is the only way! I vow it!"

She saw him out. Then she went back to the living room to indulge in a good laugh. She enjoyed more laughter when she recounted the gist of the conversation to Sir David. The handsome older man smiled; at the same time, he seemed embarrassed.

Standing by the fireplace facing her, he said, "I'm sorry you had to demean yourself in this way to convince him."

Tessa shrugged. "I enjoyed it. It was like being in the circus again. Sometimes I played roles in short dramas."

"Nonetheless, Sir Julian Dorley will blacken your character in every corner of the city and the county," Sir David warned. "He is the worst of gossips."

"All the better," she said firmly. She paused; then, "What do you know of Nell Gywn?"

Sir David looked surprised. "I have met her. How did you hear about her?"

"From Sir Julian."

"I might have known," Sir David said with a wry smile. "She is an actress and a good one. She is also a pleasant girl. And at the moment she has won the heart of the king."

"So I've heard," Tessa said. "I would like to see her. I'm much better now. Would you take me to the play one evening?"

Sir David smiled. "Of course, staying in this grim house must be trying for you. I shall take you to the King's Theater tomorrow afternoon if you like. Nell is playing, and there is a rumor the king will also be there."

Tessa clapped her hands with delight. "You are so kind to me! I can wear one of the new gowns you've had made for me."

"You must look as beautiful as possible," the nobleman agreed with a smile. "All London has been talking about us. Now they shall see us."

The next afternoon they arrived at the King's Theater a little before three and settled themselves in their box seats. But just before the play was to begin there was a rustle of excitement in the crowded playhouse, and Tessa watched with interest as the box opposite them was occupied by King Charles and his party. There was a roar of approval from the pit where the ordinary folk stood, and those in the boxes rose to express their respect for the monarch.

King Charles II, his sardonic face shadowed by a heavy black periwig, bowed in recognition as his party sat down. This afternoon he was giving a good deal of attention to his petite queen, the Portuguese Catherine. Catherine smiled at the crowd nervously, showing her crooked teeth.

On Charles's other side sat Barbara, Countess of Castlemaine, in an adjoining box. Still mistress to the king, she was dressed in gorgeous colors, in diametric contrast to the drab dress of the queen. Still, she looked sullen in her dress of red satin, her husband at her left.

Sir David whispered to Tessa, "You will note fair Barbara's sour countenance. She would not come to see her rival Nell act unless His Royal Highness had insisted upon it. So she is in a bad mood."

"That appears obvious," Tessa agreed, adding, "I see a great many eyes focused on us."

"I know," the old nobleman said. "The wagging

tongues have made us well known. It's not every man runs off with his wife's daughter!"

"Fie on you for making it sound so villainous," she teased him. "I have never been so happy since I left the circus!"

"We shall come to the play often," Sir David promised.

As Tessa glanced across towards the king's box once again, Charles looked directly at her. His keen eyes met hers, and there was no mistaking the admiration in his glance. The look made her blush and cast her eyes down. So the king had also heard about her and her stepfather lover!

Chapter Four

Tessa whispered to Sir David, "Is it true that Nell Gwyn was once an orange girl in this very theater?"

The nobleman nodded. "The King's Company granted Mrs. Mary Meggs, a widow, the right to sell oranges, lemons, fruits and sweetmeats of all sorts. Nell was one of the three girls engaged to help her."

"And now Nell is a star in the same theater."

"And a favorite of the king," Sir David added.

As they waited for the play to begin, Tessa avoided looking in the direction of the king again, fearing that he might make some other sign of noticing her. She watched the orange girls parading about with their baskets of eatables. They stood in the pit by turns, with their backs to the stage, crying out their wares. The girls were all attractive, impudent types, all of them dressed in coarse gowns that were topped by handkerchiefs around the neck.

For this performance the theater was full. The King's House was a large, barnlike wooden structure about a hundred feet long by sixty feet wide. It had a glazed cupola that let in some measure of light—Sir David joked that it also let in enough rain at times to send the audience running from the pit. The place was draughty, its only heat the animal warmth of the patrons, added to the flames of candles along the walls and over the stage. The young bloods of the town stood in the pit, joked with the orange girls, made bold advances to the drabs wearing vizards and pretending to be ladies of quality, laughed, quarreled, and paid scant attention to plays or players.

The dignitaries and the beauties of the court sat in the side boxes where the king was always seated and across from which Tessa and Sir David sat this afternoon. These boxes were raised high enough above the pit so that amorous exchanges took place on two levels. More quiet folk sat in the middle gallery, and the poor found places in the upper tier, where footmen and coachmen were admitted free to see the last parts of the play.

The musicians under the stage were offering sweet music as a background to the orange girls' cries and the loud talk of the audience. Footmen arrived early to hold seats for their masters and retired when the late-arriving dignitaries came to take their places.

But at last the play began, and Tessa found herself lost in the wonderful spell of the stage. It was the first true stage acting she had ever seen. The play was Fletcher's *Humorous Lieutenant,* and she was caught up in the bawdy comic web about the efforts of a king to seduce his son's lowborn sweetheart, played by Nell Gwyn. When Nell appeared on the stage, merry-faced and lovely with her chestnut hair tumbling over her shoulders, there was a great round of applause.

Nell's part was rich in opportunities for displaying her comic style. She insulted the bawds who brought her to court and dressed her in rich gowns; she overcame the lecherous king in a fencing scene; she ridiculed her high-minded lover, Prince Demetrius.

At the interval Tessa turned to Sir David and said, "She is a fine actress!"

"None can question that," he said, pleased that Tessa was enjoying the play. "I'll take you back to meet her after the performance."

"Would you really?" Tessa's eyes were wide with anticipation.

Sir David was looking across at the royal box; he told Tessa in an aside, "The king is taking a great interest in us. I fear you have caught his fancy."

"Do you think so?"

"Yes," Sir David said. "He has an eye for beauty. I do not think you are ready to deal with him yet, but you may have to summon your resources. He is a powerful man and greedy when it comes to having his way with women."

"I have you to protect me," she said, glancing at him.

Sir David sighed. "I shall do my best. But even my efforts must be feeble where the king is concerned."

At that moment a stout man with protruding eyes, dressed in somber gray, came into the box where they were sitting. Bowing to Sir David, the stranger offered him a pudgy hand.

"I am Samuel Pepys, Clerk of the Admiralty," the little man said by way of introduction. "We spent an evening together at the Mermaid Inn some months ago. But perhaps you have forgotten me."

Sir David was on his feet. "Not at all. I remember you well. You are a cousin of Montagu."

"Only a poor cousin, I fear," Samuel Pepys said. "But I am doing well at the Admiralty, I'm happy to say."

"You should have your hands full if war comes, as it seems it must," Sir David said.

"That is so," Pepys agreed. He smiled at Tessa. "And this is the pretty young lady of whom all London is talking."

Sir David responded with a dry smile. "Is our liaison that scandalous?"

The little man with the protruding eyes chuckled. "It is a subject of many conversations, sir. You are envied by the men and hated by their wives. Indeed, my own good wife has spoken of you as a satanic person. I write a diary nightly, and I must confess I have made mention of you in it."

"Thank you," Sir David said. "I would not wish posterity to miss the account of how a titled man ran off with his stepdaughter."

"I have set it all down, my lord," Samuel Pepys said happily. "I promise you that." He bowed. "May I ask if you are enjoying the play, Miss Tessa?"

"I'm completely taken by it," she said, "and by Nell Gwyn."

"Nell Gwyn," he repeated approvingly. "She is the best of all the new crop of actresses here in London. And with the king's backing, she is certain to be a great star."

'She is one now," Sir David said.

"True," the stout man acquiesced. Then he bowed again. "Excuse me, I must be on my way. The play is about to resume and I do not wish to miss anything."

He bobbed out the back and left them alone again. When she was sure he was out of earshot, Tessa laughed.

"What a strange little man! Do you suppose he really put anything down in his diary about us?"

"They swear he makes entries assiduously every night," Sir David said. "And are we not as good a subject for his writings as the other scoundrels and lechers of the town?"

She shook her head in awe. "I had no idea our charade would bring us so much notoriety."

The play resumed with Prince Demetrius convinced of his beloved's iniquity. Nell played her role to the hilt and Tessa again was lost in admiration of the actress, at the same recalling how much she herself had enjoyed being the pony riding star of the circus. She loved this business of amusing people. It was in her blood.

If only she could find someone to teach her the fine arts of acting, perhaps she might be able to go on the stage and be a star equal to Nell! She could think of nothing she would like more. But would Sir David approve? Would he allow her to go on the stage, when the theater was known to be a hotbed of licentiousness? She had to be submissive to his wishes since he had saved her from her mother's cruelty and brought her to London.

Their pretense of being lovers had made them famous. Even the king was casting sly glances of her and Mr. Pepys was certain of their evil passion. What a shock it would be if the gossips were to learn the truth! But they would never know. She and Sir David could not afford to let their charade be revealed for what it was.

The play ended when Demetrius, after a long agony, learned that Celia had been chased and not caught and that she was truly a virtuous princess in disguise. Joyfully the prince took her to his bosom.

"I like a happy ending," Sir David approved, joining with the others in applauding.

Tessa was ecstatic. "I've never had so much enjoyment," she told him.

"Now I shall take you backstage," the nobleman promised.

And he did. They made their way onto the dark backstage area to a corner where Nell was holding court for some friends and admirers. When she saw Sir David approaching, she left the little circle and came forward to greet him.

"David Farr!" she exclaimed with delight as, still in her stage costume and makeup, she threw her arms around him. Sir David kissed her on the mouth and they hugged each other once again. Then he introduced her to Tessa.

Tessa kissed Nell on the cheek and said shyly, "You are the best actress I have ever seen."

The chestnut-haired beauty laughed pleasantly and said, "But then perhaps you have not seen many."

Sir David told the actress, "Tessa was once an entertainer herself."

"You were?" Nell was all interest.

"Yes," Tessa said demurely, and explained briefly that she had for some years been with a circus.

"So you have also entertained audiences," Nell said.

"Yes. I would like to be an actress."

"Are you sincere in that?"

"More than in anything else," Tessa said. "I should like to study and play on the stage."

Nell gave Sir David a questioning look as she said, "We all know that this young lady is the special prize of your old age. Would you allow her to study for the stage?"

Sir David showed a little surprise, but after considering for a moment, he said, "I would not mind—if she is serious about it."

"I am," Tessa told him, plaintiveness in her tone.

"Very well," he said. "If you can find a proper teacher, I will not object."

"Charles Hart is your man," Nell said at once. "You saw him play the king tonight. He is a fine actor and good director. He played female parts in the days when all such roles were done by men, and he can make an actress of you in a short while. We are looking for more actresses of talent."

Tessa thought she would burst with happiness. She said, "I'd love to meet him."

Nell laughed. "That is easy!" And turning back to the circle, she cried out, "Charles Hart! Come here! Some folk wish to speak with you!"

A thin, handsome, dark man disengaged himself from the group and came towards them. The moment Tessa saw his sensitive face and recalled his fine performance on stage, her mind was made up. She agreed with Nell: Charles Hart must be her teacher.

He bowed to them. "You saw the play?"

"We did, and you were excellent," Sir David said. "My young lady friend would like to study for the theater, and Nell has suggested you."

The dark man looked at Tessa in a friendly manner. "You really want to be an actress?"

"I desire it most truly. And I would put my future in your hands."

Charles Hart rubbed his thin chin and eyed her thoughtfully. "You speak prettily enough; you have the looks, and you carry your body with grace."

"And she knows audiences," Nell put in. "She worked in a circus as a pony rider."

"Excellent!" Charles Hart said. He gave Sir David a questioning look as he told him, "All London envies your conquest, Sir David. Are you willing to trust this frail beauty to my hands?"

"I have full confidence in you as a gentleman and an actor," Sir David replied heartily.

" 'Zounds! I like that! I shall make an actress of this lovely wench, and perhaps even a great star."

"You're making no mistake, Charles," Nell Gwyn encouraged him, winking at Tessa slyly so as not to be caught.

Charles Hart said, "You will have to come to the theater every morning at nine. I shall coach you in private for an hour, after which you will work with the company for two or three hours each day. It will be time-consuming and arduous."

"I do not mind," Tessa said.

Sir David smiled. "And I shall not complain, as long as I have her evenings—and provided that one day I shall see her here in a starring role."

"I'm sure that will come about," the handsome Charles Hart said. And to Tessa he added, "I shall expect you

73

here on this stage tomorrow morning at nine." With a bow, he walked off to return to the group at the other end of the stage.

Nell came to Tessa and gave her a quick kiss. "You see? It is all settled! Now I must run! The king is waiting!" And she hurried away, to vanish in the backstage shadows.

Sir David turned to Tessa and said, "I didn't know what you had in mind when I brought you back here."

She looked up into his bronzed face. "Are you upset with me?"

"No," he said. "I want you to do whatever makes you happy. But you must be able to keep up the charade that we are lovers. I do not want anyone to suspect otherwise for a time."

"You may depend on it."

"I hope so."

"It will be to my benefit," she pointed out. "As long as I'm known to be under your protection as your mistress, I have an excuse for putting off amorous advances from others."

"Very sharp of you, Tessa," the older man said with warm approval. "I vow I shall be proud of you one day when you are a star like Nell."

"I shall never be her equal," she predicted. "But I believe I can be as good as many of them. I'll surely try."

Sir David smiled. "We shall celebrate by going to the Cock and Pye Tavern for dinner and something to warm our gullets. This is a night we should remember."

It was dark when he escorted her to the cobblestone street, nonetheless, he had to push aside the mob of people still gathered about the theater. He found a hackney cab with a lantern, and they boarded it to be taken to the tavern. After a short drive through narrow streets, with their huddle of houses, they descended from the vehicle to enter the cheery interior of the noisy tavern.

The ruddy-faced tavern owner, quick to notice gentry entering, came to greet them. Wiping his hands on his apron, he suggested they take a table down at the other end of the crowded place. They followed him, heading

74

toward the wide fireplace, which had a great hunk of beef on a spit over the blazing coals.

Their progress across the busy room was noticed by many, and some shouted jeering remarks. Coarse jokes were made on the spot about the old man and his lovely young lady. The tavern owner found the empty table and pulled out Tessa's chair for her to be seated.

He said, "You must not mind those coarse fellows. They know no better."

Sir David sat down and nodded. "Just so long as we have some good beef and plenty of your best wine."

"On the way, my lord," the tavern keeper said with an exaggerated bow.

A melancholy-looking old man immediately presented himself by their table and played a sweet tune on a flute with great sadness of expression. The air was haunting, and it cut off some of the noise of the other revelers in the tavern. When he finished, Tessa clapped her hands and smiled, and Sir David gave him some silver. The old fellow bowed several times, expressing his gratitude; then he went off with his flute in one hand and the coins in the other.

"It is noisy but a popular place," Sir David told her.

"I like it," Tessa said. "Does the king ever come here?"

Her escort eyed her with good humor. "I can see His Highness made an impression on you."

Her cheeks crimsoned. "Not really!"

"No need to protest," the nobleman said. "He is a comely fellow and has a way with the ladies."

"That is surely true."

"But remember, he has his choice of mistresses. And at this moment, Nell Gwyn heads the list of his favorites. If you wish her aid in the theater, remember not to cross her with the king."

"I wouldn't dream of such a thing!" Tessa protested.

Sir David looked wise. "You think not. But fate plays odd tricks. You could find yourself in an unforeseen dilemma. That is why I warn you in advance."

"I will remember," she promised.

The wine and food were set out on the table for them.

Sir David ate heartily, and Tessa had more than usual, too. The long afternoon had whetted her appetite. They finished the meal and were lingering over goblets of wine when suddenly a young man came up to the table and bowed.

Sir David rose at once, and recognizing the young man, offered him his hand. He said, "Tom Montagu! Delighted to see you again. I had heard you were away on naval duty."

The young man laughed in a pleasant manner. "I was, but I'm now returned between wars. I have not seen your son Harry of late."

"Neither have I," Sir David said dryly. "May I introduce you to my close friend, Miss Tessa Shaw!"

The handsome, flaxen-haired man turned his keen blue eyes to meet Tessa's glance and said, "My great pleasure! All London speaks of your beauty."

Because she was at once taken by the tall young man she observed with a sly smile, "And of my usurping my mother in Sir David's favors?"

The young man actually blushed. Awkwardly, he said, "I believe there have been stories. I pay little heed to gossip."

"Good for you, Sir Thomas Montagu," Sir David said. And he explained to Tessa, "Thomas is the son of one of my oldest friends. His father was a friend of my youth. And I look upon Thomas almost as my own son!"

Sir Thomas smiled warmly in response. Then he turned to Tessa again. "I saw you at the play. You seemed to get true enjoyment from it."

"It was a great treat for me."

Sir David said, "Tessa plans to study with Charles Hart. Perhaps one day she will rival Nell."

The flaxen-haired young man showed interest. "You wish to be an actress, Miss Shaw?"

"I do. I shall work hard at it," she said.

Sir David smiled with wry humor and said, "She is not content merely to be an old man's darling."

"That is to her credit, sir," Thomas Montagu said quietly. "I wish you well in your career, Miss Shaw."

"Thank you."

Sir David told him, "We are living in the town house I've rented in St. James's Square."

"I think I know the place," the young man responded.

"Are you returning to sea in the near future?" Sir David asked.

"That depends on the Dutch. I do not know which way this war will go."

"England must finally prevail over the Dutch," Sir David said sternly.

"Not before we have a damn' difficult time subduing them," the young man responded. Then he quickly apologized, "Forgive my coarse language, dear lady."

Tessa smiled. "I understand the concern that made you utter those words so grimly."

The young man in his blue jacket and breeches sighed. "I wish the fools at the Admiralty were as aware of the dangers."

"We met a clerk of the Admiralty at the theater," Sir David put in. "A stout fellow, Samuel Pepys."

"Popping eyes?"

"Yes. They were most noticeable," Tessa agreed.

"I know him," Thomas Montagu said with wry amusement. "He is a gossip, and they say he has a book in which he writes everything down. If it be so, that diary will no doubt be his ruin one day. Folk do not like all their doings recorded."

"Very true," Sir David agreed.

"But then he is not often in the company of the gentry or the court. He writes of middle-class folk like himself, and so the dangers are minimized. I have it on good authority that he is a distant cousin of the Montagu family, but I swear I see no sign of it in his common face or dumpy body."

Sir David laughed. "I spent a night drinking in his company. He has pretensions beyond his position."

"That is well known," Thomas Montagu agreed.

Sir David said, "I invite you to come by and visit us. We have little company and Tessa often becomes lonely.

We would welcome you." He turned to her. "Is that not so?"

She was surprised by his invitation but tried not to show it. Could he have sensed that she had been taken at once with this young man? It seemed he was rather pointedly creating an opportunity for her to know Thomas Montagu better. She said, "It would be pleasant if you called."

"Then I shall," Thomas Montagu said, looking straight at her. "I trust you will not be away at the theater when I pay my visit."

She said, "I will be working mostly in the mornings at the start of my training. You would surely find us at home in the evenings."

"I will keep that in mind," the young man said. Then he bowed, and saying good night, he went on his way.

Sir David sat down and gave Tessa a teasing look. "You like him," he said. It was not a question.

Her cheeks burned. "Was it so obvious?"

"I know you well enough to tell," the nobleman said. "It was a most modest display, nothing you should be ashamed about."

"I'm glad of that," she said quietly. "Thomas Montagu is nice. Too nice to be a friend of Harry's."

"He and Harry were only casual acquaintances," Sir David told her. "Never close friends. Thomas's father is a stern man, one not to be opposed. My only worry in your having a friendship with Thomas is that his father might not approve."

"Still, you invited him to the house," she said.

"I know you are starved for company."

She said, "I shall have the theater now and its people."

The older man shook his head. "Not the same. You should have some company from your own class."

Tessa was forced to smile. "Come! I'm not truly of the gentry!"

"You are more a lady than your mother," he declared.

"You think so?"

"In every way."

"You are too kind."

78

"I merely state the truth," he said with a sigh. "When I think of Sir Edward Montagu and what his opinion might be of you because of the deception I've practiced, it worries me. I fear I may have done you a terrible wrong."

Tessa said, "Let them think what they will. When I find the right man, he will love me despite gossip and marry me without questioning my past. You need have no fears."

He stared at her in wonder. "Dear child, who knows so little of the world. You make all seem so simple and direct, but most real-life situations are complicated and devious."

She smiled at him. "Thus far, what we have done has brought me only happiness."

And she truly believed this as they made their way home that night along the narrow cobblestone streets, dotted with their occasional lanterns. Along the way they passed the night patrol man walking his shift and crying out, "Nine o'clock and all is well!"

The following day Tessa began at the theater. And although it was a new experience, this training recalled her days with the circus. It made her remember the fat lady, her foster parents Tom and Ina Shaw, and most of all Bob Wills. She had been ready to marry the young acrobat, but he had turned her down and insisted on her having her chance to be a lady. What irony there was in life! Now the lady was ready to become an entertainer again.

The dark-haired Charles Hart was waiting for her when she arrived at the playhouse. Not one to waste a moment, he immediately directed her to the stage and gave her a part to read while he cued her by playing the other parts. She felt desperately awkward when she began to read, but after a little she gained more confidence.

When they finished the scene, the thin actor stood studying her a moment. "Not bad," he said. "You need a lot of work, but you have the basic instincts for a theatrical career."

She said, "I'm willing to work hard."

His smile was thin. "When anyone studies under me, that is taken for granted."

And he was a hard taskmaster. Tessa worked an arduous hour with him every day and then spent another two hours playing small roles with the company. She filled in for whoever was absent through illness, because of travel away from the city, or through having a big head after a night of too much drinking. She read and acted male and female roles.

Nell laughed heartily at her when she played the role of a knight-in-armor, saying, "I swear you are better at it than the fop who plays it in the afternoons."

Tessa's friendship with Nell grew along with her acting experience. Gradually she realized that soon she would be asked to appear with the King's Theater company in regular performances. She often wanted to query Nell about her friendship with the king, but she always stopped short of posing the leading question.

Sir David Farr was patient with Tessa's attention to her theater work. He encouraged her with it and often read the cues for her part when she had to memorize a long and difficult role. Life went on so pleasantly at the house in St. James's Square that she almost forgot the scars on her back from the beating given her by her tyrant of a mother. And the terrifying rape she'd suffered at Harry's hands seemed now like a vague, distant dream.

Some of these memories were brought back to her, however, when Sir David took her into the living room for a quiet talk one evening. When she was seated, he began, "I have had a letter from home."

"Oh?" she responded, immediately nervous.

He stood by the fireplace and with a sigh clasped his hands behind his back in a familiar attitude. He said, "You may have guessed I heard from Lady Pleasure."

"She was certain to contact you sooner or later," Tessa murmured, trying to hide the fear this news aroused in her.

Sir David continued calmly, "This is not the first time she's sent me a message. I have kept the others from you."

"Why?"

"I did not wish to worry you needlessly."

80

"And now?" The cold fear was closing in on her.

"Now certain events have taken place which I feel I must report to you."

"Please go on," she begged, though she was sure she would rather not hear what he might be going to reveal.

His manner was quiet. He said, "First, Harry has married Lady Eve Murray. You knew they were betrothed?"

"Yes," she said bitterly. "He made fun of the poor plain creature. How can he be so cruel as to make her his wife when he cares nothing for her?"

Sir David looked grave. "I fear my son Harry cares for no one besides himself. He proved that in his treatment of you. Now he is proving it again. We can only pray he will try to reform and be a different sort of person."

"That would be a miracle."

"An unlikely miracle," Harry's father agreed. "In any event, he and Lady Eve have come to live at the castle. Harry is managing the estate in my absence."

"I wish them happiness," Tessa said in a taut voice.

"That is generous of you," the nobleman said dryly. "There is also Mary."

"What about Mary?"

"She has left the castle."

"She said she would."

"She is living with the family of the man who is to be her husband. They plan a marriage in the spring. I trust I shall be able to attend it."

"And I," Tessa asserted. "Mary is a fine girl. I think of her as a sister."

"Touching!" he said with sincerity. "Now to mention one whom I'm sure does not meet with the same approval from you—my son Horatio!"

Tessa gave the older man a level look. "I fear he does you no honor."

"I have the same fear," Sir David said. "Suffice it to say that he had a violent quarrel with your mother and left the castle with the stated intention of entering a monastery."

"He has not the quality of character for a holy life," Tessa said.

"That is true," Sir David said. "No doubt he will wander about the countryside aimlessly and return in due time to play the saint and scholar in his feeble fashion. He is sure to cause me concern all his life."

"I'm sorry."

He shrugged this away. "Now we come to the most important news," the nobleman said.

"That is?"

"A message from Lady Pleasure, your mother. She asks forgiveness for what she did to you. And she begs that I speak to the king about her being allowed to show herself at court again."

"Will you do it?"

"Not yet," Sir David said sternly. "My wife still has much to pay for. And if my information is true, she is even now taking secret lovers to her room at nights. She continues to defile our marriage bed."

"In a sense she is mad."

"Likely," Sir David said. "But in her letter she prays for my return, offers forgiveness and even sends her mother's love to you."

"I find her hypocrisy revolting."

His glance was tolerant. "I do not blame you for not wishing to forgive her."

"Do you intend to forgive her?"

He shrugged. "I cannot truly say. I'm surely not ready to forgive her as yet."

"But you will one day."

"Probably," he said. "Though I swear we shall not live as man and wife again. She can have her men friends and I will live my own life."

"That would be wise."

"I'm willing to do neither yet." He paused for a moment, appearing to search his mind. Then he added, "Nothing will change our arrangement here until we have you securely launched on the stage."

"Charles Hart is working hard at that."

"And so are you," Sir David said. "I give you full credit."

The discussion ended, but the subject continued to disturb her. She knew that her mother would contact Sir David once again, that, in fact, she would be likely to bother him until he gave in and forgave her. Tessa could not bear to think of this happening.

She knew her mother for what she was. Lady Pleasure was a self-centered, disagreeable woman with a mad need for sexual gratification. Sir David would never know happiness living under the same roof with her. But Tessa could not stand in his way if he decided on a reconciliation. And if this were to come about, what would become of her? She did not know. She would somehow have to make her way on the stage; but without the protection of Sir David, this would be more difficult. Because he was still thought of as her lover, she was treated with deference by all the actors.

She was unhappy because Thomas Montagu had not paid the promised visit to the house in St. James's Square. She did not dare mention this to Sir David; nonetheless, she wondered and worried about it. Was it because Lord Montagu disapproved of her studying for the stage? Was he revolted by the supposed fact that she was Sir David's mistress? Or did he simply fear that his father would be angry at any interest he showed in her?

When she returned home from rehearsal one afternoon, she found Sir David already in an easy chair in his study. He invited her in with him for a moment to say, "I had an audience with King Charles this morning."

"Oh?" She sat across his desk staring at him, wondering what he was about to reveal.

"He wishes me to undertake some duties of state for him. It will mean my being away from here for a few days at a time."

"I assume it is an honor to be asked to take over these duties," she offered.

Sir David smiled wearily. "Most men would think so. I fear I'm not impressed. I have never been of a political turn of mind."

"Still, you should accept the undertakings," she opined.

"They have to do with the estate of the Duke of Buckingham," Sir David explained. "The king wishes certain information that only a trusted friend can secure."

"I wish you well."

"Thank you," Sir David returned. "You know, you have grown even more lovely since I first brought you to London.

"It is because I have been happy."

He smiled. "The London gossips will say my love has made you bloom."

"I wish they would."

"I'm not so sure," Sir David said with a slight hesitation in his words. "You see, the king is showing an interest in you. Nell has been silly enough to praise you loudly for your looks and acting ability. And the king sets store on what she says."

Tessa frowned. "Nell should have known better."

"She meant you well," he pointed out. "She is all heart. The king is most fond of her. But now he wants to meet you."

"Oh, no!"

"I'm afraid it is true. I tried to put him off, but he would not hear of it. He has asked that I arrange a meeting with you, and soon."

Tessa was shocked. "What can we do?"

"I don't know," Sir David sighed. "I honestly don't know. That you are my supposed mistress makes little difference to him. He plucks men's wives from them as if they were flowers grown for transplantation to his garden."

"So?"

"I have put him off for a few days. I asked that he wait until I returned from his first mission. To that he agreed."

"But then?"

He shrugged. "I will try to think of something."

She said, "You might say that I am betrothed to Thomas Montagu."

Sir David laughed bleakly. "That would not save you. The supposition would only whet Charles's appetite."

"Thomas Montagu has never made his promised call," she said unhappily.

84

"At least I can bring you good word on that score. I have heard that Montagu was suddenly called away from London on navy business. I had it from no less an authority than Samuel Pepys, Clerk of Admiralty!"

Tessa laughed. "That old gossip!"

"Ah, but Mr. Pepys thinks himself a man of importance," Sir David said with amusement. "In this spring of 1664 there is no man in London whose prospects Pepys favors more than his own!"

"I doubt it not," Tessa assented. "Did he stare at you with those bulging eyes?"

"Searched my very soul," the nobleman agreed with relish. "He wanted to know if you had stayed with me through the winter and if you were still living under my roof. I told him we were still together and were more contented than ever."

"I vow that must have upset him," she said.

Sir David smiled. "He seemed disappointed. And then he went on to talk of the navy, and so I heard the news of young Montagu, which I regarded as fortunate."

"But he has returned now?"

"Yes.".

"Then perhaps we may see him," she said, feeling better at the prospect. And for the moment the dilemma of the king's interest faded from her mind.

The following day Sir David left London on his errand for the king. When Tessa returned from her exertions at the theater late in the afternoon, she was weary. She also felt strange about being in the great house without Sir David. Tonight her only company would be the elderly female servant who acted as both cook and housekeeper since Tessa's and Sir David's needs were small.

Tessa had a sleep, but when she awakened she felt more on edge. Somewhat surprised by her new feeling of fear, she prayed that Sir David might soon return. The prospect of spending several nights alone in the house with the single servant did not please her. She considered asking one of the actresses to come and stay with her, but Nellie was the only one she would want, and Nellie was too busy with acting and the king. Besides, Nell now had her own fine home in Pall Mall through His Majesty's generosity.

Tessa changed into one of her lovely, low-cut gowns, thinking that being dressed up might make her feel more at ease. Then she went downstairs to dine alone. But dinner at the long table by herself was not a pleasant experience. She felt ridiculously overdressed in her elegant gown and thought she read disapproval in the old servant's glance. When dinner was over at last, the woman vanished and Tessa breathed a sigh of relief as she went to sit by the blazing fire in the living room fireplace for a little before going to bed.

She realized, however, that her uneasiness still had not left her. She was staring into the fire when she heard a knock on the front door. A twinge of fear tightened her muscles. It was early in the evening, but she was not expecting visitors. She got to her feet and waited to see if the housekeeper would answer the door, but the deaf old woman did not appear. The silence lengthened. At last Tessa nervously made her way to the reception hall, where she stood for a moment in shadow as the knocking was repeated.

Fighting her fear, she went to the door and slowly opened it. To her horror she saw a familiar figure standing there. He quickly stepped inside. It was the repulsive Horatio, dressed in his usual drab black, his long, humorless face washed with a jaundiced pallor, and his eyes bright in a way that hinted dementia!

Chapter Five

"You!" Tessa gasped as she closed the door on the foggy night.

The bedraggled Horatio stared at her oddly. Then he asked in his croaking voice, "May I speak with my father?"

"He is not here," she answered, wary of the strange, young man whom she knew despised her.

"I have journeyed far." His tone was plaintive. "May I not stand by the fireplace and warm myself before I leave?"

"If you wish." She wished him gone, but Sir David might be upset if she turned his son away.

She led the way into the living room, and Horatio followed slowly, taking in the details of the house. Finally he went to stand facing the fireplace, warming his hands.

After a moment, he turned to say, "You have a fine house here."

"Your father picked it out." He did not seem to hear her. After an interval she said abruptly, "What are you doing in London?"

The mad, too-bright eyes fixed on her. "I came to join a holy order, but they would not have me."

"I see," she said. She had heard this.

"I will continue my search," the odd young man went on. "I shall eventually find some order that will accept me."

"Are you sure you wish to retreat from the world?"

His long face twisted into a grim expression. "It is an ugly world of evil. I shall not regret losing it."

"Many things in the world are not ugly," she said with unexpected feeling. "Surely not young people nor young animals."

He glared. "You ruined our home, made us all the laughing stock of London. I do not care to philosophize with your sort."

Tessa edged a little away, still watching him closely. She said, "Then, do please leave me!"

As she was held by the mad eyes, which never wavered from her, she began to realize she had made a dreadful mistake in opening the front door. In spite of the warmth of the blazing fire, she felt chilled and terrified.

In his grating voice, Horatio said, "Do you know that Mary has left us? She ran off and was married because of you!"

"She planned to marry. She told me so."

"Harry has brought his wife into the house," Horatio went on, "but she feels disgraced because of what is going on here between my father and you!"

"Please be on your way!" Tessa pleaded. "You are warm now. Your father is not here!"

"I knew that before I came," Horatio said with a leer. "I have been waiting for this opportunity!"

She took a step backward and stood with a chair between them, certain now that her visitor intended nothing but trouble. "You had better go, or I shall have the butler come to put you out."

Horatio shook his head. "There is no butler. I know more than you guess, harlot!"

"You're mad!" Tessa gasped.

"And you are a whore straight from hell!" Without warning, he swooped down on her and caught her in his strong hands.

"Let me go!" Tessa cried, struggling to free herself.

He gloated at her fear and struggling. She could smell the fetid odor of his breath as his smile revealed his yellow fangs of teeth. "I have come to pay you for what you've done, harlot!"

"Your father will settle with you!" she protested as she struggled in vain to get away from his insane grip.

Little by little he dragged her toward the fireplace. When he was close enough, he snatched the poker from its stand and thrust it into the fire. Then, still managing to hold her despite her battling, he used his free hand to tear away the bodice of her dress so that her lovely breasts were bared.

"Let me go!" she sobbed, clawing at his face and drawing blood as her nails dug into his cheek.

Horatio seemed oblivious. "I shall brand you for what you are, harlot!" he hissed. "Spell the letters out on your breast!"

"No!" Tessa screamed, struggling anew without freeing herself.

Snatching the poker from the blazing fireplace, with mad delight Horatio waved its red-hot tip before her fear-distorted face. Then he brought the torture weapon to her breast. She screamed in agony. The pain from the poker's touch was beyond belief. As in a nightmare, she saw a vertical line being seared into her bosom. Frantic with pain, she thought, This must be the end. The mad Horatio would torture her to death before he let her go.

Suddenly she was aware of a stirring in the background and a man's loud angry voice. The odor of her own poor burning flesh nauseated her, and between this and the pain she was on the verge of collapsing. But as faintness overcame her, Horatio suddenly let her fall to the hardwood floor and darted back. And sprawled out before the fireplace, sobbing, eventually she realized what was happening—the dark clad, bug-like Horatio was being put to rout! A young gentleman in a red cape and jacket and a plumed yellow hat had attacked the madman with his sword, and Horatio was making a hasty retreat to the front door.

Tessa looked down at her bosom. The rounded inner side of her right breast bore a burn mark about two inches long. *Harlot,* Horatio had called her. No doubt he had tried to brand her with the letter *H*. The seared flesh hurt terribly, and all the front of her dress had been torn away to reveal her nakedness in a most shameful fashion.

For a long time, it seemed, she heard the voices of the two men from the reception hall. Then the man in the red cloak returned. His sword still drawn, he anxiously knelt by her. "Did the scoundrel harm you greatly?" he demanded. And she saw that it was young Thomas Montagu who had been her rescuer.

Tessa raised a hand to cover the mark. "He was trying to brand me!"

"Let me help you into a chair," Thomas Montagu said with grave concern. "Is there a woman here to look after your care?"

"Yes," Tessa whispered as he helped her into the nearest chair. She pulled the torn section of her dress up to preserve some vestige of modesty.

"The maid is old and deaf," Tessa said, biting her lip from the pain and trying hard not to faint. "She'll likely be in the kitchen."

"I'll get her," Thomas said. And he vanished, leaving Tessa in a state bordering on unconsciousness. She had forgotten to ask what had happened to the mad Horatio, but in fact she no longer cared. It was enough that he was no longer there to threaten her.

Thomas Montagu returned with the frightened old woman, whom he ordered, "Get your mistress some brandy at once!" And of Tessa, he asked, "Who is your doctor?"

"Dr. Hyslop," she murmured. "He is old. I don't know if he can be reached tonight. He lives somewhere down the street."

"I'll find him," the young man said, preparing to go.

She looked up at him in terror. "What about Horatio? What if he returns?"

Thomas Montagu looked grim. "I doubt that he will. I put my sword tip through his arm, and he is a craven fellow! The last I saw of him, he was running into the darkness."

"I shall have no ease until you return," she pleaded.

"I will not be long, and the woman will be here to keep you company," he replied, giving her a concerned look before hurrying off in search of the old doctor.

The brandy helped revive Tessa, and its soothing effect quieted some of the pain from her breast. She felt herself relax a little as she sat back in the chair with the old woman hovering over her, waiting for the young man to return. How ironic, she thought, that Thomas Montagu's visit, so long delayed, had come at a moment when she needed him desperately!

Within twenty minutes he was back, dragging a startled Dr. Hyslop along with him. When he saw Tessa, however, the old doctor at once recovered his professional aplomb, inspected her mutilated breast and attended to it.

Afterward he gave her a troubled look. "You seem to have an unhappy tendency to being a victim of violence," he observed. As her eyes filled with tears, he went on, "This is a foul piece of work. The man responsible should be in Newgate."

"I agree," Thomas Montagu said emphatically.

"Once again, you have a scar you will carry for life," the old doctor told her. "The potion I have given you should be applied to the wound at regular intervals. And take the powders I have left when you wish to sleep."

"Sir David Farr will be told of your kindness in coming to me," she said.

Dr. Hyslop glanced at Thomas. "Give the credit to this young man. He dragged me from my bed. I shall look in on you tomorrow, my girl."

Thomas Montagu saw him to the door and then returned to stand by Tessa's chair. He said, "I will not remain long. I know after such an ordeal you need to rest."

"Pray remain for a little," she begged him. "I'm still fearful of being alone. Horatio is mad and wily. He could return when he thinks I have no one to protect me."

"In that case I shall remain here for the night. And the devil take him and his evil plans."

"Had you not come when you did, he would have killed me."

"Do not think about it," the young man said stoutly, drawing himself up to his full height in his colorful crimson and yellow justancorps. "I've been serving in the King's Navy against the cursed Dutch. Otherwise I would have been here before."

"Mr. Pepys told Sir David about your being called to duty," she said.

"So you knew why I had not shown myself here."

"Yes."

He sighed. "I do not know how long it will be before I'm called on again. Probably not long. You see, I'm captain of my own ship, and there are only a few of my age with a solid knowledge of navigation and fighting at sea."

"I'm sure that must be so," she said.

"The Dutch are strong, and one can never be sure when they will attack again," he went on. Then, changing the subject: "Who was that fellow?"

"Sir David's son by an early marriage." She paused before adding, "He hates me."

"Because you are living here with his father?"

She lowered her eyes, pained by the knowledge that she could not divulge all the facts to him. In a low voice, she said, "Yes."

The handsome young captain of the king's navy stood there rather unhappily. "It was a family quarrel, then. Nevertheless, he must be insane to have carried it to such lengths."

"He is mad," she said, her voice flat.

"I'm still slightly incredulous," he remarked. "His father is so different—a fine man. Indeed, I cannot help realizing why a young woman like you might be drawn to such an older man, however unfortunate the liaison may be."

"Sir David has shown me only kindness."

"I believe that. Gossip has it that you and he fled his castle in the middle of the night. And that your mother has placed a curse on you for stealing her beloved husband."

"There was no true love between them," Tessa declared with scorn. "My mother is a cruel wanton of a woman who betrayed her husband so often that he came to hate her. That is why he came here with me."

Thomas Montagu listened with serious interest. He said, "Dr. Hyslop mentioned something about your being badly whipped before you arrived here. I inferred that he had treated you then and that you would always bear the scars. Was that why Sir David fled with you? Because you had been beaten so badly?"

She nodded. "By my mother."

"I'm sorry," he said. "I would not have come here, had not Sir David given me a warm invitation."

"We wished you to visit us."

"I do not wish to intrude," he told her soberly, "but I would like to be your friend."

"You have shown yourself to be that tonight," she replied.

His eyes were grave with concern. "I have no right to be keeping you here talking this way. Let me carry you up to bed."

"I can manage on my own," she insisted. But when she struggled to her feet, the room whirled about her, and she almost fell.

Thomas quickly swooped her up into his arms. "You are not as well as you would believe," he admonished her. And following the elderly woman servant, he carried Tessa up to her bedroom, where he deposited her gently on the bed and said good night.

When he had gone downstairs, the old woman helped prepare Tessa for bed. "See that Captain Montagu has a bed," Tessa told her. "He plans to remain here to guard us through the night."

"I shall look after it," the housekeeper promised, but she would not leave the room until Tessa was safely in bed.

Alone at last, Tessa tried to sleep. She had taken one of the powders left by the doctor and hoped it would soon work. She was relaxed and grateful that Thomas was remaining in the house for the night. She could tell he was unhappy in believing her to be Sir David's mistress, and she wished she could tell them of their arrangement, but she could not think of that unless Sir David would acquiesce.

Where had the mad Horatio gone? Had the wound in his arm been of any consequence? His father would surely be much upset when he returned. These thoughts circulated in her mind as the powder began to work and she sank into a deep sleep.

In the morning she felt better. Her breast pained only when she moved about. The old woman came early with some gruel and tea for her, and later Dr. Hyslop showed himself and dressed the burned area once more.

"No sign of complications of pus as yet," he assured her. "You healed well before. I think your sturdy health will stand you in good stead this time."

She looked up at him wanly from her pillow. "Am I always to be the object of mutilation, Doctor?"

"I should hope not," he said. "The burn made by that madman is bound to leave a red scar. But if you have your dresses cut carefully, you will be able to cover it, and there are cosmetics to make it appear less ugly."

"But I will always know it is there."

"I know," the old man sighed. "I hope the scoundrel pays for what he did."

At the doctor's request she remained in bed. But Thomas came up and had lunch with her. He sat on her bedside and told her about his adventures in fighting the Dutch and about his home and family. Tessa learned that his father, Sir Edward Montagu, was one of those who regretted the end of Cromwell's reign. Sir Edward, a Puritan, even opposed Thomas serving the new king in the navy.

"But it is my own life," Thomas said with a smile, "and I intend to do as I wish."

Propped up against several pillows, Tessa smiled gently at him. "I'm sure you do."

"You think I'm right?"

"Yes."

The young man gazed at her earnestly. "I cannot help begrudging Sir David such a jewel as you."

Tessa blushed. "I'm not so extraordinary."

"I disagree," he said. "And if you or he should decide that your affair is over, I would like to know."

Her lovely eyes fixed on his handsome face. Softly, she asked, "Would you?"

He bent forward and gently kissed her on the lips. Then he kissed her again. "Do you believe me?"

Her face was a delicate crimson. "Sir, you make it hard for me to deny your good intentions."

94

The young man gave a deep sigh. "And good intentions they are."

"I'm certain of that," she said, reaching out her hand to touch his cheek.

He took the hand in his two and held it for a moment. Then he burst out, "Why pretend? I have fallen in love with you, Tessa. I know I have no right. But I cannot help it."

"Thank you for telling me," she said.

"You're not angry with me?"

"Surely your love is a compliment."

He looked troubled. "I come into this house where you are the kept woman of an older friend of mine, and I declare my love for you. Is that playing fair?"

"I do not wish to judge you," she said, her voice trembling. "You cannot deny your feelings."

"I cannot," he agreed. "What about you? What feelings do you have for me?"

It was a question she had hoped he wouldn't ask, but since he had spoken his heart so clearly, she felt she owed him the same sort of truthful answer.

In a hushed voice, she said, "From the moment of our first meeting I have had a special affection for you—different from any I've felt for any other man!"

He leaned close. "My dearest!" Then he frowned. "I am a man of honor. What am I to do?"

She managed a smile for him. "Be patient, my Thomas! When Sir David returns, I shall talk with him and plainly reveal my feelings for you."

"I can ask no more. I deserve not as much," the young man said, immediately happier.

By mutual agreement, they spoke no more on this subject, but Thomas came to pay her a visit each day while Sir David was absent. She sent word to the theater that she was ill but gave no explanation. Her breast was healing quickly, like her earlier wounds, and soon she was able to come downstairs and move freely about the house.

Thomas came on Wednesday afternoon with a gift of white violets, which she put them in water before coming to sit beside him. They were talking pleasantly when they had an unexpected visitor. It was the irrepressible Sir Julian Dorley, wearing a new outfit of pale green that was set off by a white plumed hat. The housekeeper had let him in without consulting Tessa, and so he came bursting into the living room to surprise them.

"Law!" The fop exclaimed with a roguish gleam in his eyes. "I have come at an awkward moment!"

Thomas jumped to his feet and said, "We are most pleased to see you. Tessa and I were but talking."

Sir Julian chuckled and waved his hand as if to dismiss it. "You need not worry," he assured them. "I shall keep this all in confidence."

Tessa reproved him. "You must not make wrong of this. Thomas is a good friend of Sir David. He is like a son to him."

Sir Julian pursed his lips. "Perhaps even more than that," he said with malicious delight. "I take it Sir David is still away on the king's business."

Thomas eyed the fop angrily. "No insinuations, sir. He invited me here before he left."

"That is so," Tessa agreed.

Sir Julian rolled his eyes. "My dear, it makes not the slightest difference to me. I have come merely to give you some news. Grave news, I fear!"

"What news?" she asked, afraid it might be word that Sir David had suffered some mishap.

"News of your stepbrother, Horatio," the fop said. "Two nights ago he attacked a bawd in a public house and very nearly strangled her. It took a half dozen men to pull him away from her."

Tessa gasped. "I do not doubt it. He has become a madman!"

"Exactly!" Sir Julian said. "I'm glad you've realized. The authorities have the same opinion, and your stepbrother is now locked up in Bedlam!"

"He was taken into custody?"

"Yes, they found him too mad for a mere prison like Newgate, so they detained him with the lunatics. In my opinion, the poor chap will not last long there. Few do."

She was silent for a time before murmuring, "Sir David will be distressed when he hears."

"I came here to let you know, so that you might break it to him," Sir Julian said.

"Thank you," she said in a troubled voice.

Sir Julian leered at her and the young man. "I'm going to Wilton, where I shall visit your mother and Harry at the castle and break the news to them. Your mother has been fearful about Horatio. She claims it was your bedding with his father unhinged him."

"He was mad before that!" Tessa said sharply. "I do not care to hear more of this."

Thomas Montagu moved towards the fop in a threatening manner, his hand on his sword hasp. He said, "You have heard the lady! She wishes you to leave!"

Sir Julian moved back nervously and said, "Fie on you both!" in his high-pitched voice. "It would seem the daughter is as wanton as her mother! Be forewarned, I shall let all London know about you two!" And with that he made a hasty exit, fairly bounding out the front door and slamming it after him.

Thomas growled, "The evil fool! I should have put my sword through him! London would be a better place for it!"

Tessa put a restraining hand on his arm as he glared after the vanished Sir Julian. She said, "No need of that. He is not half as clever as he thinks."

Thomas looked at her unhappily. "Pray, what does that mean?"

It was then she broke her word to Sir David and explained her situation to Thomas. She felt she was justified. She had tried the young man's love for her to the breaking point. She told him the whole story from the start, explaining how Sir David had planned to punish his unruly wife, who happened to be her mother, and emphasizing that she was not Sir David's mistress but his ward—under his protection because his son had wickedly raped her and his wife had cruelly beaten her afterwards.

Thomas was overcome by her revelation. He took her in his arms and with great gentleness said, "I should have guessed the slanders against you were wrong. I love you so, Tessa."

"And I love you, my Thomas," she whispered. And as she leaned close to him, the fires of her passion stirred mightily again.

"You shall be my wife," Thomas promised. "We shall be wed before I return to war against the Dutch."

"I'm sure we will have Sir David's blessing," she said. "He cares deeply for me, and he approves of you."

Thomas said, "I will speak to my father, make him aware that you are pure. There can be no doubt that he will agree to our marriage once he knows you are not a party to the court scandals and not the mistress of Sir David."

"May I continue my career at the King's Theater?" she worried. "I'm soon to be a regular member of the company."

The young man smiled. "For a time, at least, if it pleases you, though perhaps you will have to retire from such activity when we are wed. My father is a hard-headed Puritan where the theater is concerned."

Tessa listened without worrying about it very much. The important thing was that she had told Thomas the truth and he had believed her. Nothing the gossips, like Sir Julian, could do would come between them. Thomas would arrange it all, and she would be forever happy in his love!

It was not surprising that Thomas remained all night. And that they shared her bed. His lovemaking was gentle as he eased her on the bed. His lips caressed her naked-ness, and he was most careful where her breast still re-mained sore. She was delighted with his superb body. He was all she had expected and more. His firm maleness en-tered her and stirred her own passion. She met him with a great, surging desire of her own. Their bodies pulsated in a unison of delight. Great waves of fulfillment broke over them as they were lost to all but each other.

Their passions climaxed and they lay back gasping. Tessa had never experienced such lovemaking. She was more than ever certain this was the one man in the world she wished to marry. She lay contented in his arms as he murmured words of his love to her. And she remained there after she had drifted off to sleep. It was a night of ecstasy. She and Thomas would repeat it many times, but never would it have the meaning of that first night.

Thomas left her reluctantly the following morning. And she went to the theater for rehearsal for the first time since Horatio had branded her. Charles Hart was pleased to see her and announced that she was scheduled to appear at a regular afternoon performance in the new piece by John Dryden.

Nell took her aside and with a sly smile said, "You are radiant today, little Tessa. Could it be you were abed with more than mere sickness?"

Tessa blushed. "You should not think such things."

"There is something," the pretty mistress of the king insisted. "I can tell."

"You are right," Tessa confided in a whisper. "I have fallen in love as never before."

"What about Sir David?" Nell Gwyn wanted to know.

"He will understand."

Nell's eyes widened. "I can promise the king would not have such understanding," she said. "I hope you are more fortunate with Sir David."

"I'm sure it will be all right," Tessa maintained. And then they were both called to go on stage, and the discussion ended.

In a way Nell had been right. The task of informing Sir David was more difficult than Tessa had imagined. When the nobleman returned from his errand for the king, he was weary and looked older. They dined alone, keeping the conversation light. But afterwards as she sat with him in the living room, she felt she must broach the graver subjects. She said, "I have some things to tell you."

"Indeed?" the dignified old nobleman said.

"First, there is evil news about Horatio."

Sir David leaned forward in his chair with a frown. "Tell me at once."

She did, ending with her rescue by Thomas. She said,

"If he had not appeared, I know Horatio would have murdered me."

"The villain!" Sir David fumed. "I shall make him pay for this! Is your breast healing properly?"

"Yes, it is fine," she said. "And I fear Horatio has already paid for his madness. He attacked a prostitute in a public house and the authorities took him. He tried to kill the girl. They decided he was insane and locked him up in Bedlam. That is where he is now."

In a shocked voice Sir David said, "My son in a lunatic asylum!"

"Perhaps you may be able to secure his release."

"Not unless he is improved or I can find another private asylum in which to place him," the older man said bitterly. "I cannot let him roam about the country mad, a menace to all who come in his path and especially dangerous to you!"

She added, "Lady Pleasure circulates the story that our behavior unhinged him."

"Lies! He was mad long before we came to live here!"

"I know," she sighed.

The gray-haired man sat back in his chair. "Perhaps the time has come to end the charade, to let those who are important to us know the truth."

"I leave that to you."

He gave her a worried look. "I do not wish to do you irreparable harm."

"You have always been most kind to me," she said gently.

Sir David's smile was weary. "My only regret is that fate made it impossible for us to be lovers."

Tessa hesitated, thinking that in a way she loved this man, too. "You have been a father to me," she said at length. "I had never had a true one. Tom Shaw was good enough when I was in the circus. But he could never show the kindness to me you have. I feel I'm truly your daughter."

"Then I am happy," Sir David vowed.

"There is something else I must tell you." At his nod, she continued, "Thomas Montagu and I are in love."

100

"I'm not surprised. I could almost see it in both of you. You think he is sincere?"

"He has asked me to be his wife."

"Capital!" Sir David exclaimed. Then, his manner changing abruptly, he looked directly at her. "Have you two lain together?"

She lowered her eyes and in a shy voice said, "We made love for the first time the other night after I had told him the truth about us. Before that, when he believed I was your mistress, he would not even speak of it."

Sir David sighed. "I cannot blame you for your love. But I do worry a little."

"About what?"

"About his father, Sir Edward Montagu."

"Thomas has promised to talk to him," she responded quickly.

"He may find himself in a difficult discussion. Sir Edward will have heard the slander about our living together. To make matters worse, he hates the king and all the members of the court, including myself, and so he is not apt to accept the story of your purity as quickly as his son did."

Tessa's eyes widened with apprehension. "You think he may be against the marriage?"

"I fear it greatly."

"Thomas will win him over!"

Sir David frowned. "I don't know about that. Only time will tell. Sir Edward is a hard man, capable of turning his back coldly on anyone of whom he doesn't approve."

"Thomas is so different."

"There is no question of that—as Harry and Horatio are different from me. You cannot judge the father by the son."

"Thomas did make some mention of his father's difficult disposition," she admitted.

"I'll warrant he did," Sir David said gravely. "And then there is the business of your studying at the theater. Sir Edward considers the theater licentious."

Tessa drew herself up. "It is not like that at all.

101

Charles Hart and his company are dedicated craftsmen. Even Nell thinks more about her acting than she does about the king, I'll be bound."

"But she is the king's mistress as well as an actress. Many of the actresses are kept by noblemen. To all outward appearances, you have been one of the same group."

Tessa stood up and began to pace restlessly. "I can't give up the theater. I want to act."

"You also want to wed Thomas. You may have to make a choice."

"He said I could appear with the company until I married him."

Sir David shrugged. "Perhaps his father will show a side of his nature new to me and give you his blessing. But I rather doubt it."

She turned to face her stepfather, concern clouding her pretty face. "What am I to do?"

"Be patient," he said. "We will soon know Sir Edward's reaction."

"Sir Julian was here. He saw me with Thomas and made much smirking of it."

"I have no doubt," Sir David said, grimacing. "I'll seek him out and silence him. He is much in debt to me because of his gambling. He cannot afford to ignore what I say."

She gave the old man a worried smile. "I fear you are paying more heavily for your kindness to me than you should."

"Not at all," he said with an answering smile as he rose to place a good night kiss on her cheek. She gave him a grateful look. For a moment they stood close to each other, saying nothing, and when Tessa left him to go upstairs, it was with a sense of sadness that their pleasant interlude together was ending. She knew she would miss the quiet happiness of that time.

The very next morning Sir David went to Bedlam—and discovered that he was too late. Horatio had hung himself the first night he'd been taken there. The nobleman was able to rescue his son's body from a pauper's grave, but it was small consolation. Although he had been sorely tried by the erratic young man, Sir David felt the loss of his son the more deeply because his grief was mingled with guilt.

Tessa felt an immediate change in the dignified man. His shoulders slumped in a way they never had before. He was always in a more solemn mood, and now he began talking of deserting London and returning to Wilton. He had no intention of allowing Lady Pleasure to be present at court again, but he was ready to live with her in the country.

Meanwhile Thomas and Tessa continued to see each other regularly, with Sir David's approval. And when it was rumored at the theater that the king had found still another new mistress, Tessa was glad, since that would mean he would no longer have time to show interest in her.

The time for her debut at the King's Theater drew near. Sir David had promised to be on hand and so had Thomas Montagu. Several evenings before the announced performance, Thomas came to see her at the house in St. James's Square. He greeted her as usual, but when she saw his drawn features, she was at once conscious that he was upset, and she urged him to tell her what was bothering him.

The handsome young navy captain sat down beside her and said heavily, "I had a long session with my father today."

"And?"

He sighed. "He was more unreasonable than I have ever known him to be."

Tessa looked her lover directly in the eye. "About me?"

"Yes," he said unhappily. "He refuses to believe you have been living here as a ward of Sir David rather than as his mistress."

"He would rather believe the gossips than his son?"

"So it would seem."

"I could ask Sir David to speak to him directly."

Thomas shook his head. "I'd have no faith in that. My

father would more than likely snub him and refuse to believe him."

She was shocked. "Sir David is a gentleman. No one would distrust him if he gave his word of honor."

"I fear my father would," Thomas said bitterly. "When I told him I was determined to marry you, he forbade it."

Tessa looked down. "Perhaps you had better obey him."

"Certainly not!"

"You are the one who will inherit his title. Your wife must be beyond reproach."

"You are beyond reproach!"

"You may believe that," she said with a sigh. "But the London gossips tell a different story."

Thomas went on fervidly, "Not content with throwing up the business of your living here with Sir David, my father also brought up the matter of your making your debut on the stage."

She felt a twinge of despair. "Sir David warned me that might cause trouble."

"He uses it against you," Thomas said with disgust. "But he would use anything. He does not want me to marry you."

"How did your discussion end?"

"With my walking out in a rage." He made a helpless gesture with his hands. "I'm sure my brother overheard us. Claude is a sly one, always playing up to my father and trying to win his approval. Nothing would please him more than to have the Dutch kill me in battle so he might inherit the title and the fortune that goes with it!"

"That must be an exaggeration!" Tessa exclaimed surprised.

"It is the unadorned truth," the young man replied. "Claude and I have always disliked each other. Besides, being a second son in a titled family is frustrating. Claude is greedy to take my place."

"He does not sound as if he could," Tessa said. And after a moment she added seriously, "Thomas, I do not wish to rob you of your inheritance. I will give you up, no matter how painful it may be, so that you will get the title."

Thomas said, "There is no question of that. We simply must wait until I get father's approval. It may take a while, which means delaying our marriage."

"I can wait," she said.

"I knew you'd feel that way." He managed a wry smile.

She suggested, "Perhaps if I could meet your father, I might be better able to let him see the kind of person I am."

Thomas nodded. "Perhaps we can arrange that. I'll wait for the right moment."

Later she told Sir David about this, ending with, "It would appear you were correct in your opinion of Sir Edward. He is dead set against the marriage."

"I feared that," Sir David said.

"So it seems I shall have to wait to be a bride. I do not mind."

Sir David frowned. "I would like to see you settled before I return to the country. I plan to remain in London for your opening night, but then I must leave."

"I shall miss you," she said.

"And I shall be bereft without you," the older man returned with a sad smile, touching her chin with his hand. "The time here living with you has been one of the best periods in my life."

"So it has been for me," she said. "When you go, I shall try to find other quarters."

"There will be no need. I have taken a continued lease on this house. You may live here until you marry Thomas—or as long as you wish. The rent will be paid from my estate."

Tears brimmed in her eyes. "As usual, you are far too kind to me!"

"It is the least I can do," he said. "But you will be alone except for the housekeeper. Perhaps you should ask a suitable girl from the theater to come here and live with you."

"I'll try," she promised, "but if I don't find anyone, I will manage on my own."

He nodded. "You have no real enemies, now that Horatio is gone."

"None that I can think of," Tessa agreed. Later on she was to realize that taking this for granted was a major error on her part. Even as she expressed the sentiment, a serious threat was hanging over her head. But she was still happily unaware of this; besides, she was too excited about her debut at the King's Theater to worry about anything.

She could not have known then that the afternoon of her opening would also bring a major disappointment. She was seated in a small dressing room with Nell Gwyn, ready to don her costume, when a page arrived with a message.

Tessa took the message and read it. Nell must have known from the expression that came over her face that something was wrong.

"Bad news?" the actress asked sympathetically.

Tessa nodded. "Thomas isn't going to attend the play this afternoon."

Nell stood up. "Not attend your first performance! Why not?"

Tessa showed the other girl the note. "It is not his fault. He has been called back to his ship for active duty—the Dutch are threatening us again!"

Chapter Six

"Blast the Dutch!" the good-hearted Nell exploded with annoyance.

Tessa managed a rueful smile. "I expect that is what Thomas plans to do."

Nell came and put an arm around her. "Poor little duck!" she said. "Never you mind. It will be a good day for you. You are fine in the part. The king will be here and so will your Sir David."

"Yes," Tessa said, feeling better. "Sir David has been looking forward to seeing my stage debut."

"And it will be well worth his interest," Nell said. "Come, my dear, time for us to get into our costumes."

The theater was crowded, both pit and boxes. The orange girls called out their wares as loudly as usual, and the gossips laughed and talked and were an attraction in themselves. Sir David Farr sat in a box with none other than the colorful Sir Julian Dorley at his side. While Sir David looked stern and scarcely seemed aware of the crowd of playgoers around him, Sir Julian, in contrast, was thoroughly enjoying his prominence in the box. He picked out friends in various parts of the theater by squinting through his quizzing glass; and from time to time he smiled, called out, and waved to various other London types whom he knew.

Just before the play began, King Charles arrived, looking somewhat gloomy. With him was his wife, who always seemed to have an air of uneasiness in public. And into the box next to them came Barbara, Countess of Castlemaine and her husband. All eyes were upon this group for a short while. Then the play began.

It was Beaumont and Fletcher's old melodrama *Philaster*, with Charles Hart in the leading male role and Nell playing Bellario, the love-sick girl who followed the hero disguised as a page boy and who, for her pains, was most unjustly accused of seducing the heroine. Tessa had the less rewarding role of the heroine. The Bellario role had first been written to be played by a boy actor, and as written it was not a humorous character.

But Nell's talents in a breeches part like this gave scope for much bawdy humor. She and Hart were excellent, and the audience responded. Tessa gave her part full values, speaking out clearly, being properly demure and appealing. The patrons were generous at the end and gave her an especially loud burst of applause.

Charles Hart embraced her backstage and told her, "You have the makings of a star. Your time and mine has not been wasted."

"I owe so much of it to you and Nell," she said, breathless with happiness.

Nell left a group of admirers to kiss and hug Tessa and say, "From now on I must look to my laurels. You are destined to be a favorite."

But it was Sir David Farr's tribute that Tessa appreciated most. The old man came and kissed her and said, "One day you will be a star. London and all the world will know your name."

Perhaps it was too high-blown a compliment, Tessa reminded herself. Of course it was premature on the basis of one performance. On the other hand, she knew it was sincere, a statement of faith, based on the older man's true love for her. Once again she was aware that she would never have a better friend.

Sir David had arranged a special dinner party in her honor, to which all the members of the company were invited, as well as a number of other people. The affair was to be held at the Bell and Star Tavern. And although this was only a few short blocks from the theater, Sir David, intending that Tessa should remember the occasion, had arranged to have her transported by means of a sedan-chair through the smelly streets with their open ditches.

When she left the theater, the sedan-chair was waiting for her. It glittered with gold leaf and was glassed in to protect its occupants from the weather. Two sturdy chairmen were ready to carry the dainty conveyance; in addition, a lad carrying a flaming torch led the way, and a footman, armed with a crab-tree cudgel, followed behind the chair.

Nell arrived at the Bell and Star still wearing the page-boy costume and was the center of attention. She put her arm around Tessa, confiding, "Ods-bobs! It's almost as if the party was for me!"

Tessa did not mind. As long as everyone had a good time, she was happy enough. Still, it was not a true celebration for her, since Thomas could not be with her. He had missed her performance and he was now missing the party. She did not allow herself to show her sadness, however, but worked hard at being merry for Sir David's benefit.

Sir Julian Dorley, proposing the toast to her, waxed poetic about her purity and ability. It was evident that Sir David had warned him to make good the harm his gossiping had done. Whatever the motivation, the speech was a splendid one; afterward, when all drank Tessa's continued success, Nell whispered to her, "Is it you he meant or was he talking about one of the saints?"

There were endless toasts, along with much drinking and eating, and the evening went on endlessly. Near midnight, when the merriment was at its height, someone overturned Sir Julian's chair and he fell to the hard boards sputtering annoyance. He had to be helped up to a sitting position, and only after he was plied with a huge glass of brandy did he recover his good humor.

Even later Samuel Pepys staggered around to where Tessa and Nell were seated and made an exaggerated bow, which nearly overturned his stout body. His protruding eyes were glazed with drink and he was a picture of happiness.

"I enjoy a party such as this," he declared.

"And don't we all?" Nell agreed.

He eyed her owlishly. "It is a pity the king cannot be here," he observed.

Nell gave him an annoyed glance. "The king may choose his own company, little man. Tonight's group is not all to his liking."

"God bless the king," Samuel Pepys said righteously. "And to hell with the Dutch and the Papists!"

"Well spoken," Nell approved. "When next I see Charles, I shall inform him of your stout friendship."

Samuel Pepys looked delighted. He beamed at the actress. "I shall put you down in my diary tonight, Nell." He turned to Tessa. "And our guest of honor as well. Pepys records it all!" And with this, he swayed and stumbled back to his seat.

"What an odd little man," Tessa exclaimed.

"I have been told he does good work at the Admiralty; some say they have not yet promoted him in accord with his talents," Nell said. "The king finds him amusing, though he only sees him occasionally."

Tessa was not sorry when the party finally ended. It had been a noisy, wearing evening, and it seemed to her that all the men were down with drink except Charles Hart and Sir David. Bidding Nell good night, she went to speak with Charles Hart before he left.

His message was, "You've had your fun tonight, but tomorrow morning you report for rehearsal."

Sir David had a hackney cab waiting for them. They had to leave the sleeping and limp Sir Julian off at his lodging place. The fop was snoring drunkenly as the driver lifted him out of the cab and carried him to the doorway of his London house.

When they were on their way again, Sir David smiled in the semi-darkness of the cab's interior. He said, "Sir Julian did himself proud tonight. He verbally placed a halo around your head."

Tessa allowed a small laugh. "I noticed that and decided you had frightened him into lauding me so."

"I had a small part in it," the nobleman agreed dryly.

"You've been too generous. I didn't deserve such a party."

"Indeed you did. As did most of us. It has been a long, troublesome year, and no doubt we haven't seen the end of problems yet."

"Things must be tense, or Thomas wouldn't have been called to duty just when I so wished him to be here."

Sir David showed sympathy. "True," he said. "Well, at least a few were here to join in your triumph!"

"Half of London, thanks to you, dear Sir David," she said, hugging him.

A few days after the joyous party Sir David Farr left to return to Wilton and his castle. When all his luggage had been piled on the rear of the coach, he returned to the front door of the house to say good-bye to Tessa.

Tessa felt he had never looked more distinguished—or more sad. He took her hand and kissed the back of it. "It is hard to bid good-bye to a great lady," the gray-haired man told her.

"You must come to the city occasionally and visit me," she insisted tearfully.

He smiled. "Perhaps. I shall have your mother to deal with. If I dare come to London without taking her to court, there will surely be trouble. Lady Pleasure is a proper shrew, so let us have her bury her talents in tiny Wilton."

Tessa laughed through her tears. "Be sure to let her know I am a great success at the theater and don't neglect to mention that I will be marrying a title."

"Do not fear, I shall turn the knife in the wound," he promised. "And Harry, that lumpkin, shall hear about your good fortune as well—as will Mary, who loves you, when I write her."

He kissed her again and was on his way. Tessa saw the coach vanish down the square and felt a great sadness come over her at the thought that she was going to be in this great house by herself.

She at once applied herself to her acting and spent the evenings quietly. Once in a long while she had a few friends from the company, including Charles Hart, join her for an evening meal at the big house; but most of the time she kept to herself, with only her memories of Sir David to fill the melancholy rooms and corridors of the big house.

She received an occasional letter from Sir David and, more rarely, a hurriedly written note from Thomas. Her lover was occupied with the operation of his ship on a

111

wartime basis. Things were not going extremely well for the English. Thomas always stressed his loneliness and his continued love for her. He promised to return as soon as possible but could not set a day.

So Tessa waited with impatience. Meanwhile, she continued to gain a following at the theater. John Dryden himself spoke to her about writing a new comedy with starring parts for both herself and Nell. The playwright enjoyed writing his plays around stars and claimed his synthesis went a long way to the success of both play and stars.

Sir David's communications were full of country life, highlighted by the tantrums of Lady Pleasure, who was still trying to coax him to allow her to return to London and the court before her looks were irrevocably gone. As always, he turned a deaf ear to her pleas; and in return—to make him pay for his decision—she continued to have other men in her bed whenever she had the opportunity. Sir David confessed he no longer cared; he was sure, he wrote, that this spoiled some of Lady Pleasure's fun, though her whoring went on unabated.

As to other news, Sir David reported that Harry, who was doing a poor job with the estate, had sired two sons by the plain Lady Eve. Nonetheless, Harry spent most of the time in an adjoining village in the company of a wench who was married to a magistrate there. The magistrate was elderly and near blind; he considered the young nobleman's attentions to his wife a compliment. " 'Tis much like one of Dryden's plays," was Sir David's observation.

There was also news of Mary, who had married the young man of her heart and gone to make a quiet life in the north. She had two children as well, both girls, and she sent Tessa her love through her father. The letters were warming, and Tessa often read them over and over again.

One dark winter evening in early 1665, Tessa sat writing a letter to Thomas. She knew the war was under way with the Dutch. Some said the vessels of the Dutchmen had so far made their way up the Thames that the sound

112

of their guns in battle could often be heard in London. She was asking him about this and other matters when there was a knocking at the front door of the house.

A new housekeeper had replaced the old one, and since this woman was much more alert and responsible than the old servant, Tessa went on with her writing and let the woman answer the door. A few minutes later the housekeeper came into the small parlor where Tessa was seated and told her she had a visitor.

Tessa looked up from her half-finished letter with an expression of surprise on her lovely face. "A visitor at this time of night! Who?"

"A fine gentleman," the woman said. "A Sir Edward Montagu."

"Sir Edward!" Tessa cried with pleasure. "Of course I will see him." She put aside her writing to go welcome the old gentleman, feeling delighted that he had apparently come around at last.

He stood waiting for her in the living room, ramrod stiff of back, wearing a white wig, a dark coat and matching breeches. His dress was severe, with none of the ruffles that were so fashionable among the gentry. He turned to Tessa as she came into the room, and she slowed her pace as she took in his cold slab of a face, the high cheekbones, the thin-lipped mouth, the steely eyes.

She extended her hand. "My dear Sir Edward, I'm heartily pleased by your call. Thomas has spoken so much of you."

He bowed coldly and pointedly did not take her hand. He said, "I would have a few words with you."

"Do be seated," she said, ignoring his coolness and the insult of his not accepting her hand. She was so eager to please him, she was ready to put it down to embarrassment on his part.

"Thank you, I shall stand," he said in the same clipped manner. "But I beg you to seat yourself."

"Very well," she said, still anxious to make a good impression on him. "I was only now writing to your son."

"Were you?"

"Yes. We exchange letters as frequently as possible.

113

We are much in love, as you know. And when he has time from his war duties we hope to marry—with your approval, of course."

His gaze was icy. His eyebrows raised slightly. "With my approval?"

"Of course. I would not wish to marry him without that," she said.

"That is most commendable of you," he said dourly. "This is the house in which you lived with Sir David Farr?"

She felt her cheeks burn at his insinuation. "Yes. He is my stepfather."

Sir Edward's thin lip curled. "All London knows about your relationship."

Hurt, she said, "I was under the impression that Thomas had set you right about that. Sir David and I were not lovers."

"I see," Sir Edward said. "You prefer to be thought of as his mistress!"

She rose. "No!"

He waved a gloved hand. "Pray do not call on your training as an actress to exhibit hurt feelings for me."

"You have pained me, sir, and most unjustly condemned me!"

Sir Edward regarded her as if she were some unnamable but repulsive sort of insect. He said, "I have come here to tell you I will never consent to a marriage between you and my son."

Angered, she said, "In that case, we shall marry without your consent!"

"My, you change your tune quickly!"

"You force me to, sir!" she shot back.

Sir Edward stared at her, then said, "I am a powerful man and a wealthy one. While I may not be in favor with the king and his court, I have a great influence in London."

"Pray, what has that to do with the matter?"

"I will explain," the elegant Sir Edward said. "If you persist in trying to marry my son, I will have you murdered."

114

She was stunned. "You will what?"

"You heard me. I have agents at my disposal who will do away with you and hide your body. You will vanish without explanation—another mystery for this ancient city."

"You cannot be serious!" she gasped.

"I am deadly serious," he said, emphasizing the word *deadly*.

"You would not dare!"

Sir Edward sneered at her. "I would not soil my hands on the likes of you. But there are certain . . . ah . . . persons of low esteem who will gladly do my bidding."

Tessa felt nauseated by his cold hatred, but she said, "You have only made me more determined."

"That is too bad," he replied in the same icy manner. "A harlot like you surely has a few good years left. If you use your talents where they'll be most appreciated, I'm sure you can go on living in wealth like your sister of the stage, Nell Gwyn."

"You're not fit to clean Nell's shoes!" she spat out.

There was a brief flash of anger in his eyes, but he said only, "We have had our talk. I trust you will mull it over in your mind."

"I will see a justice and tell him of your threat," she warned him.

"He wouldn't believe you."

"I will have my servant's word for proof."

"No one would take the word of you and your servant if I made a statement to the contrary," Sir Edward assured her calmly. "I'm known as a man of principles in this city. I'm respected for my religious views and for the purity of my conduct."

She stared at him. "Purity of conduct! You have just threatened me with murder!"

"Since the majority of harlots meet a violent end one day, I would be merely pushing your fate ahead a little. But at the same time I would be saving my son from a most disastrous marriage!"

"How well you have settled it with your conscience," she said in disgust.

He nodded. "I look upon you as an ugly threat. Once I have you removed, I will not think of you at all. You are as nothing in my mind."

She raised her chin in challenge. "God be thanked, your son doesn't feel that way! Thomas shall hear of your threats! I will write him this very night!"

Sir Edward shook his head. "Save your time, woman. He would not believe you either. He has grown up with great respect for me and my sense of fairness."

"You are a villain!" she gasped.

"I do what is necessary when I must," he said. He bowed again. "Good night to you. I trust you will heed my warning and save your skin."

He left her standing there aghast and went on out, closing the door after him. She heard his coach clattering away over the cobblestones, and then all was silence. She began to tremble and thought she might faint. Slowly she made her way back to the parlor and her unfinished letter. She sank into the chair and stared at the letter. Great tears flooded her eyes. Laying her arm over the letter, she bent her head forward on her arm and sobbed loudly.

When she recovered from the worst of the shock and tears, she was faced with the question of what to do. It was like a dilemma in a nightmare. She wanted to let Thomas know what his father had said to her, but she was certain Sir Edward was only too accurate about how his son would respond. If she wrote bluntly that Sir Edward had threatened to have her murdered, she would only confuse her lover. Thomas would not believe her; he would probably think she was writing wildly to upset him.

Instead, she decided to write him that she was afraid in the great house, where she was alone except for a single servant. In the letter she would also hint that the streets of London were becoming more dangerous for a woman on her own. She would further hint that she felt Thomas's father would never consent to their marriage and that they had better adjust to this and make plans to marry anyway. She would beg Thomas not to write Sir Edward about their marriage plans. "First let us get our plans in

116

order and carry them through. We can inform your father later," was how she would end the letter.

She finished writing it that night and sent it off to Thomas in the morning. During the days that followed, as she waited for his reply, she was bound to be uneasy. She counted on the likelihood that Sir Edward would take no action against her until he was sure she was ignoring his threat. So she kept silent and waited, hoping that Thomas would arrive any day, longing for the day when they would be married. Then she would tell him what his father had so coldly said to her.

The one bright spot in this dark picture was her success at the theater. She played in a revival of *The Wanderer* and won the acclaim of all who witnessed her in the rather dull piece.

Nell, high in the king's favor again, was absent from the theater a good deal, since the erratic Charles demanded that she spend more time in his company. This meant that Tessa was soon playing many of Nell's parts. And although she never quite caught the hearts of the people as Nell did, she steadily gained in popularity.

One early afternoon in March she played in *The Lady of Pleasure*. She was in a blue mood: She had not had a letter from Thomas since she wrote him insisting they be married without his father's consent. After the performance, Samuel Pepys came around to invite her and Charles Hart to have a bite with him at the Gull.

"I would most surely appreciate your both joining me," declared the plump little man with the bulging eyes.

Tessa knew him to be a friendly soul despite his oddness. She acquiesced, "If Charles will come, so will I."

That was how it came about. Charles Hart was in a mood for conversation, food, and some good ale. The three of them wound up at the Gull. And it was there that Samuel Pepys gave them a most disheartening account of the way the war was going.

"Our losses are heavy in naval battle," the little clerk of the Admiralty reported worriedly. "I cannot give you the exact information, of course. That is a state secret, and they would have my neck for it!"

"I have not heard from Thomas, and he always writes when he can," Tessa said.

The little man sighed. "The reason is clear enough to me. He has not had the opportunity to write; in fact, it is even doubtful whether your letter reached him."

Until now, this possibility had never crossed her mind. "You think it may have gone astray?"

"It could well have," Samuel Pepys said earnestly. "If I were you, I would write him another letter exactly like it."

"I will," she promised. "Thank you for telling me."

Charles Hart held up his empty ale tankard for the tavern keeper to refill and said, "I thought we were supposed to be more than a match for those Dutchies!"

Samuel Pepys said, "I'm certain we shall win ultimately. Victory shall be ours. There can be no question that they are extending their line of battle too far. But it may be months before our successful emergence from the war is assured."

"I pray it be soon," Tessa said fervently.

"I agree, my girl," Pepys said. "At least there is no concern nor sadness in this place." He was right. The tavern was alive with boisterous laughter, singing and loud talk. Like most of the other taverns in the center of the city, it was always well filled.

Charles Hart took a deep drink from his newly filled tankard and said, "Fie on you and your war, Mr. Pepys. I'm more interested in John Dryden's new play. He tells me he has a fine comedy in hand, and it will surely be a success with Tessa in the leading role!"

Samuel Pepys broke into a wide smile and lifted his own tankard. "To a great playwright and a fine actress! I shall put the good news down in my diary before I go to bed this night!"

"In your diary!" Charles Hart said, roaring with laughter. "What a quaint fellow you are, Pepys! But a damn fine host, none the less!"

It was Samuel Pepys who escorted Tessa home in a fine hackney cab that night. The little man, feeling the spirits he'd inbibed so freely, was talking a good deal as the cab made its way through the dark, rough streets. He complained of the way things were being done at the Admiralty and the way frightened civilians were being ruthlessly picked up by press-gangs in the streets and shipped away to serve their King.

He bobbed beside her in the dark of the cab as it rumbled over the cobblestones and told her, "I watch these unhappy men shipped off, and I see the distress of their women! Lord, how some poor women do cry! And in my life I've never seen such a natural expression of passion as I see here now that so many of these women come searching, bewailing themselves and running to every parcel of men that are brought, one after another, to look for their husbands. They weep over every vessel that sails away, thinking their men might be on it. I have seen these poor women looking after ships as far as ever they could see by moonlight, and I grieve in my heart at the sight!"

Tessa said unhappily, "We women of the officers are not much better off, even though our men go by their own wish. War is a sorry business."

"I know it," Pepys said. "Every naval contract placed by the government is an invitation to profiteers. I have been forced to remark that it is impossible for the king to have things done as cheaply as other men do."

"Can you not reform the office?"

"Small chance of that. I have worked into the night trying to cope with the shortage in money. Meanwhile, seamen's wages are in arrears, and ropes rot on the masts of ships for want of replacements."

Feeling a sudden need to confide in someone, she told the stout man beside her, "Not only am I worried by lack of word from Thomas, but I am living in perpetual terror. My life has been threatened by someone I dare not name."

"Dear lady!" Samuel Pepys was horrified.

"It is true. I only feel safe when I am at the theater. This madman who has threatened me may decide to strike at any time."

"Surely you can ask the authorities for protection," Pepys suggested.

"No," she sighed. "I cannot do that. So I must bear the burden of fear alone. At nights I'm unable to sleep. And I have only one servant, a woman."

Samuel Pepys said at once, "You must have a bodyguard—someone to stay in the house with the single duty of protecting you."

He was right, she realized. "I would feel much safer for it."

"May I take the responsibility for finding you such a fellow?" Samuel Pepys offered.

"If you would, I would be most grateful."

"Consider it done, dear lady. And if I get any word about Thomas Montagu or his ship, I will let you know at once."

"I would appreciate that also," she said, "since the Admiralty always has first word of the movement of naval vessels."

The little man escorted her to her door and saw her safely inside before he left. His promise that he would find her a suitable servant to act as a bodyguard gave her a feeling of relaxation she had not experienced since Sir Edward Montagu's cold threat. With two servants in the house, she ought to be relatively safe, she thought, pleased also that Pepys had promised to give her early word by messenger when Thomas's vessel was due back.

The next morning a burly fellow who gave his name as Tim Burke presented himself, saying he had come at the direction of Samuel Pepys. Burke had a history of service in the navy and was a big, brutal-looking fellow who seemed likely to be a match for anyone who tackled him. When Tessa offered him what seemed a fair salary, he at once accepted the position as general handyman and guard.

Tessa was grateful to Samuel Pepys for his prompt help in this regard. With the lifting of some of her burden of worry, she was now able to give her best to the theater, and she regained much of her light-heartedness. All that remained was to wonder when she would have a message from Thomas. But although she kept writing, months passed, and still she received no reply.

120

Then, gradually, the shadows began closing in again. She was playing in a revival of Beaumont and Fletcher's *The Knight of the Burning Pestle,* an amusing play—but the theater crowds had fallen off some and there was much talk of war in the air. Nell Gwyn knew Tessa's concern for Thomas and tried to cheer her up, but Tessa had the black feeling that something was wrong, a premonition that Thomas had come to harm and word had not reached her. She realized that even if his family had been informed, they would not let her know. Sir Edward would enjoy the idea of her waiting and suffering without hearing anything!

Then one late afternoon, as Tessa was leaving the theater, she was approached by an elderly man, who bowed to her and said, "Are you not Miss Tessa Shaw?"

"I am."

The man reached into a pouch of leather that he carried with a strap over his shoulder and produced an envelope sealed with wax. He said, "A personal message from Samuel Pepys at the Admiralty."

"Thank you," she said, taking the envelope in hands that trembled slightly. She knew the message within might bring her great joy or devastating sadness, yet she could not resist the desire to open it immediately.

She stepped into the hackney cab that regularly waited to take her home after the performance. She had hired the driver by the month, and he had proven most reliable. As soon as she was seated in the cab and on the way home, she ripped open the envelope and strained to read the message sent by Samuel Pepys.

It read, "My Dear Tessa: I am saddened to have to inform you that Captain Thomas Montagu's ship, *The Unicorn,* was sunk by the Dutch, with a loss of almost all hands. There has been no word that Thomas survived. I fear you must accept the worst. Your good friend, Samuel Pepys, Esq."

Tessa sank back in the cab's seat and stared up into the shadows. She feared she might collapse. She was shivering, and a chill gripped her spine. She crumpled the message in her hand. Then sorrow and grief wracked her, and she began to sob loudly.

The driver was startled by her condition as he helped her from the carriage. He took her by the arm and led her to her door. "What is wrong, my lady?" he asked.

She made an effort to stifle her sobbing. "A personal tragedy. I am sorry."

The old man eyed her with sympathy. "Then you will not likely be at the theater tomorrow?"

"No," she said. "I will not be there. You may inquire later about my return."

"I hope you may recover from the blow soon, milady," the old man said respectfully.

She thanked him and went inside, where she had to face the scrutiny of the manservant, Tim, and the housekeeper. Tessa told them that a dear friend had been killed in a naval battle. And she sent Tim to the king's theater with a message for Charles Hart informing him she had learned of the death of Thomas Montagu and would be retiring from playacting for a while.

So, knowing she should not, she nevertheless became a kind of recluse in the great house in St. James's Square. When she tried to write Sir David and tell him the bad news, she could not put the grim facts on paper. Most of the time she spent in bed, crying. Sometimes in the evening, she would go down and sit by the fireplace for a little.

She could not help wondering if Sir Edward Montagu had heard the news. She assumed that he had. She did not know what his reaction would be, and she could not find pity in her heart for one who had declared himself such a merciless foe. It was ironic that he would not need to carry through his threat to have her murdered because Thomas had himself been killed. She no longer had the burden of the threat, yet she no longer cared.

As a result she discharged the burly Tim, whom Pepys had found for her. The guard was loath to go, but she explained to him she was no longer in danger and since she was not working, she could not afford to pay an extra servant. So she was back to being alone in the house with the housekeeper, who also did the daily marketing and brought back whatever news she heard in the shops.

One evening Charles Hart came to visit her with the intention of coaxing her to appear in a new play by John Dryden. The dark, handsome man said, "My dear Tessa, it is a magnificent opportunity. Nell is spending almost all her time entertaining the king. We need you at the playhouse."

She sighed. "I would be no use to you. I'm not in the mood to play a comedy."

In desperation the director said, "Then I'll put the comedy aside and find you a tragedy. We can do a revival."

Tessa offered him a gentle smile. "You are kind, Charles. And I would like to oblige. But quite simply, my heart is broken. I loved Thomas more than any other man I've ever known. Without him I am at a loss. I have no purpose in living!"

The volatile Hart knelt before her and took her hands in his. "You cannot allow your own life to end because of the death of another. I know how dear Thomas was to you. But there are other men."

"I am not interested," she said.

"There was a time not long ago when the king himself showed an interest in you," the director said. "Perhaps it might be revived. You could reign over the court."

She shook her head. "No. Let poor Nell be the king's mistress. It is an uneasy role she fills. I want no part of it."

The handsome Charles sighed. "I would woo you myself, but you know it would be a charade. Long ago, when I played female parts, I formed a pattern of affection for men. It has stayed with me, though I now direct the company and play the most manly of heroes."

She was touched by his confession and leaned forward to kiss him. "Dear Charles, you are my friend—my best friend. I would not ask you to try to play the role of lover and husband. I'm content to have your love and loyalty as things are."

He stood up in a mood of desperation, running his

hand through his long black hair. "I cannot bear to see this air of resignation in you, to have you hiding here in this great house. You are playing the role of one whose life is over."

"That is how I feel."

"You should not give way to your sorrow in this fashion," he protested. "Many have griefs and continue on with courage. You have a talent, and you owe it to yourself to use it. If you refuse, you may one day curse the very fact you were born."

She looked up at his troubled face. "I'm sorry, Charles. Of course I know these things, but arguments cannot change emotions. If I have a change of heart, you shall be the first to know."

"You must soon come out of this melancholy state," he insisted.

"I hope I may," she said. "Just now I feel as dead as my poor Thomas."

Charles left with her promise that she would at least attend a rehearsal the following week as a first step in trying to revive her interest in living. Making the promise, she felt certain that nothing could accomplish that. But the very next night something took place which changed her life and attitude more than she would ever have believed.

She had retired early and was awakened from her sleep by the frightening feeling that someone had intruded in her bedroom, that she was not alone. She rose on an elbow and called out the housekeeper's name. On receiving no reply, she added in a taut voice, "If you are there, don't be afraid to speak! Answer me!"

There was no answer. But a board creaked on the floor close by her bed, and as she stared into the dark shadows she was gradually able to make out a figure standing over her—the figure of a gigantic male!

"I see you!" she gasped. "Who are you? Why are you here?" Her voice rose in her terorr.

No reply! And into her mind came the threat Sir Edward had uttered. Had he decided to go through with it anyway? Had he made up his evil mind to take vengeance on her even though his son was dead? She had not

124

thought of this possibility. But now it seemed natural enough that a man so dark of nature might enjoy snuffing out her life even when she was no longer an annoyance to him.

In a taut voice she asked, "Are you from Sir Edward?"

Still no answer, but now the figure moved and in the next moment pounced upon her. She drew back in the bed and tried to escape the huge body, but her struggle was in vain. She was seized roughly and her mouth was bound. Then her hands and ankles were tied. She vaguely realized there were two intruders, one of whom was giving the other orders about robbing the valuables in the house.

Suddenly she was lifted up and carried sack-like over her attacker's shoulder. Renewing her struggle, she fought to break the bonds at her hands and ankles, but she could scarcely breathe with the suffocating gag around her mouth. She felt herself being taken down the stairs just before she lost consciousness.

Later she came to, experiencing a cruel cold. As her senses gradually returned, she realized she was in the back of a rough wagon of some sort, which was rolling through the streets at a good speed. She was being bumped about incredibly. In the wagon around her were things stolen from the house, including several rugs which had been roughly rolled up.

The rugs helped cushion her from some of the bumps. There was a tarpaulin tied over the top of the wagon so she could not see out, but she was aware it was still dark. The ties at her hands and ankles were cutting into her fearfully now, no doubt because her flesh had swollen. At least the air was fresh in the wagon; so it was easier to breathe in spite of the rough gag which still hampered normal breathing.

She was a prisoner—no question about that! And it seemed to her that the fact of the kidnapping precluded the possibility of her being the victim of ordinary robbers. The men who had come to her house must be the minions of the villainous Sir Edward. She had let her guard go, considering herself safe, and then he had struck in a most dastardly way!

To what avail? Thomas was dead. There was no longer any possibility that Tessa Shaw might darken the Montagu name. Nothing but sheer hatred on the part of her lover's father could have motivated this.

Ironies seared her mind. She had wished herself dead, had been existing as if her life were over, and now she was going to be murdered! Charles Hart had been right in condemning her attitude. She had been a fool not to see the folly of her resignation!

Chapter Seven

The wagon halted with a fearful lurch. Briefly, the low, rough voices of two men consulted with each other; then the canvas that had been tied over the top of the wagon was pulled back, and hands groped in to drag Tessa out of the vehicle. Once again she was slung over someone's shoulder like a sack.

She tried to get some idea of where she might be. It seemed a narrow street lined with hovels, but before she could form a clear impression, the man carrying her descended a flight of stone steps and went around to the back of the building. There was a moment's hesitation as he opened a door and then bent down so that he might get her inside without striking the top frame of the door.

Now she found herself in a shadowed room. Here she was set down roughly on what seemed to be a pile of dirty blankets. She lay there, her body crouched, her eyes fearfully trying to seek out her captor. After a moment a candle was lighted and set on a wooden table at the end of the room.

It was then she had her first glimpse of the man who had taken her prisoner. He was a huge fellow, tall and broad of build. His hair, black and oily-looking, fell around his ears and on his forehead. He had a patch over one eye, a black patch, but the other eye was sharp and strangely pale blue. His face was rawboned and his skin almost as brown as that of a gypsy. His clothing was nondescript and ragged, but he carried himself with a regal air. She could not help thinking this youngish man with his strong features was no ordinary criminal.

He was standing there outlined in the candle's light and smiling at her grimly. She fought against her bonds and tried to speak, but all that she could manage was an absurd gurgling sound. She appealed to him with her eyes and moved her thinly-clad body slightly in her efforts to free herself.

The man's deep, rough voice growled at her, "You might as well be still! Struggling won't help you!"

She was too weak to fight anymore. She closed her eyes and prayed for help. It seemed to her this was a punishment inflicted on her for turning her back on life. She had insisted she didn't want to live; now she knew she was not at all ready to die. And she was especially anxious not to be the victim of the evil Sir Edward Montagu!

She heard the door open. Now another man came in, carrying a rug and a valuable vase, both taken from her house. This second man was small and wiry, in contrast to his partner, and he had a face with foxlike features and furtive eyes. His thatch of hair was brown and in disarray, and his clothing was as old and drab as the big man's.

The little man threw the rug into a corner and set the vase down carefully on the table. He nodded at it. "That will be worth a good penny!"

"What about the rest of the stuff?" the big man asked.

"Mad Reevy ain't your servant," the foxlike man said harshly. "What's to stop you bringing in some of it yourself?"

"I've looked after the girl. We're being paid more for her than all the rest will fetch!"

"And she's more nuisance!" The one called Mad Reevy spat on the floor in disgust.

The big man said, "I think you'd better take that rug and vase and put them back in the wagon."

The little man looked thunderstruck. "Why?"

"I don't want them here. We had better keep the loot at your place until we get rid of it!"

Mad Reevy looked annoyed. "And have me take all the risk?"

His partner gave him a look of disgust. "Who put you onto this job?"

"You did," the shifty-eyed man admitted reluctantly.

"So I did. And we'll make a fair, good thing of the night's work. But if they trace that stuff and link me with the girl's death, it's Dick Henry's neck will be stretched!"

The smaller man nodded. "I see what you mean, Dick!"

128

"That's new," the big man said with sarcasm. "Now get these things and yourself out of here. I have work what's to be done before the dawn."

"What will you do with her body?"

"Mother Thames," Dick Henry said. "That's where all the useless baggage what takes their own lives ends up!"

"She ain't taking her life. You are."

"Just you and me are to know that," Dick Henry retorted roughly. "Now get on with you!"

"Making me drag things back and forth to no account," Mad Reevy grumbled. Nonetheless, picking up the rug and the vase, he went on out.

The big man came back and stood over Tessa with a hard look on his brownish face with its stubble of beard. "You!" he said.

She tried to respond with a look in her eyes, but she feared she was not reaching him. She feared more that in a moment Dick Henry would take her out and drop her in the muddy waters of the Thames. In a few days her bloated body would float to the surface among the sewage and other debris. She had often seen great dead rats drifting along in the current.

Dick Henry was studying her intently with his one eye. He said, "I don't like this sort of job. Only hard times has brought me to it!"

She shut her eyes and fought against being ill. If she became nauseated, she would surely choke with the filthy rag still bound tightly over her mouth.

The big man came close and said, "You ain't too comfortable. If I take off that gag, will you make no fuss?"

She nodded, meaning that she wouldn't and hoping he would understand.

He apparently did. Kneeling by her, he said, "Calling out won't do you no good! We're in the cellar of a deserted house on the riverbank. Being near the river makes it easier for me." He went about taking off the gag.

When he threw it to one side, she gave a deep gasp of relief. "Thank you," she said in a hoarse whisper.

Dick Henry continued to contemplate. "You're a pretty

one! And you can act! I seen you from the gallery many a time!"

Tessa stared up at him. "You know who I am?"

"Most people in London do," the big man said with a wry grin. "And there are those who don't want you around."

She stared at him. "Sir Edward hired you to murder me."

"Makes no difference who wanted it done."

"I know who it was."

"Then you know," the big man said, still kneeling by her. "I was the one who won the bid."

Her eyes widened in horror. "You mean he actually had bids out on me?"

"For doing away with you," Dick Henry said calmly. "A lot bid for the job. I was the lowest, so I won out."

"How could anyone be so wicked!"

He smiled bleakly. "You're lucky I won the bid. I'll be as gentle as I can. I'm not a murderer by trade like some of them. I don't enjoy hurting people."

"You're satisfied to rob and kill them!" she accused him.

He continued to smile, and she noticed, unwillingly, that his was a strangely attractive face. Was it the black eye patch that gave him the jaunty air of a pirate? she wondered.

He said, "I've done my share of thieving. And I've killed some men in fair fights. You're the first female to find death at my hands."

"You have sunk to being a murderer of women!" she said with disgust.

"If I let you go this minute, you'll be killed anyway," Dick Henry told her. "The man who wants you dead has more power than most realize. The whole of the London underworld knows you're worth a penny dead. If I don't finish you, others will step in to do the job!"

"This information has been given out?"

"Yes," Dick Henry said. "So best be content with me. I'll make as comfortable an end for you as I can."

"You're a brute!" she said. "Without feeling!"
130

He stood up and gave her an annoyed look. "You are
~~rong!~~ I have my good points. There's been many a lass
~~st~~ their hearts to me—a good many even since I lost my
~~ye."~~

"Your missing eye is not what makes you repulsive,"
~~he~~ said. "It is your cruel soul!"

Dick Henry smiled bleakly. "I'm not one for fancy
~~ords~~ or thoughts, though I did like you well enough
~~hen~~ you acted with Nell."

Tessa groaned. "My wrists and ankles are paining.
~~lease~~ free them."

He hesitated. "You won't try to run off?"

"Does it seem likely?"

"Wouldn't do you any good. There's only this one door
~~o~~ outside. You'd never get past me."

"Then why make me suffer needlessly?"

"I'll take them off," he conceded. And he knelt by her
~~gain~~ and cut away the cords which bound her. She at
~~nce~~ began to move her arms and legs. It was a while be-
~~ore~~ feeling returned, and even then the pain continued.

"Better?" he asked.

"Yes," she said in a strained voice. Suddenly she was
~~ware~~ that her thin nightgown was her only covering. He
~~ould~~ surely see through it.

Dick Henry smiled. "I have a greed for women what
~~lmost~~ matches Old Rowley's. But you're the first quality
~~emale~~ ever to be in my room!"

She knew Old Rowley was what the people called King
~~Charles~~ behind his back. It was the name of one of his fa-
~~ous~~ stallions. She was acutely conscious that Dick
~~Henry~~ was becoming more aware of her body each mo-
~~ent.~~ She said, "If you let me go, I'll leave London. No
~~ne~~ need ever know you didn't kill me."

He shook his head. "No good. You'd never get out of
~~he~~ city without someone knowing and telling him. And
~~e~~ would have you followed and see you were done in."

She was seated on the pile of blankets now, her legs
~~urled~~ under her. "I see," she said. "So my plight is
~~opeless."~~

"That's a grand way of saying you are to die."

"So be it," she said.

The big man looked uneasy. "You are a beautiful creature. Do you know that?"

"I will be less beautiful when my bloated carcass float in the Thames," she said bitterly.

He waved a big hand. "We don't need to dwell o that."

"I must contemplate my future," she told him.

Dick Henry was silent for a moment, just staring at he with his one eye. Then he said, "It's too bad. You're to young and lovely to die. What did you do that got you i this?"

"I loved the wrong man too much."

He chuckled. "A lot of women do well by loving th right ones."

She said, "You're talking about lust! You have no ide of the sort of love I mean."

"Do I not?" he asked. "Am I some sort of brute then?"

"You will soon be a murderer of women," she replie in a quiet voice. "Can you sink lower than that?"

"A lass died for me!" he said belligerently. "A swee wench, killed when we was robbin' a merchant in th Strand. She saw the blood from the musket woun spreading over her blouse, and she came running to m arms. I got her away and she died in my arms, here i this same room!"

"How noble of you to put her in such danger!"

"She was my woman! She wanted to rob with me!"

"I do not understand," Tessa said. She turned her fac away.

Dick Henry was pacing back and forth now, obvious upset. He turned to tell her, "There's little about peopl of my sort you know! We have to live as we can! W don't choose to be thieves nor our women to be whores We are forced to it if we want to survive! I was thre when my father, an honest rat-catcher, was run over by nobleman's wagon, and there he was, his life snuffed ou of him like one of the rats! My mother sold her body o

132

he streets to get a few pence to keep me and my three brothers alive."

He finished his speech in a state of frustration that made her almost pity him. He was not sly enough to make up such a story, as his partner, Mad Reevy, might be. It was clear that this statement was an anguished searching of his heart. And Tessa knew what he said was true. At the bottom layer of London life the all-important consideration was to survive.

"I'm sorry," she told him. "I know something of the truth in what you say. I have been out in the world with only myself to depend on."

He gave her a sarcastic look. "You know nothing of that sort of misery! Are we mongrels of the gutter, to sink into the mire without a struggle so the king and his court may play their games of license and thievery? There is more theft in high places than in low!"

Tessa knew this was true, too. The account Samuel Pepys had given her of the goings-on at the Admiralty had emphasized that graft extended all through the system. She said, "I'm not against you."

"I believed that when I saw you on the stage from the pits in the King's Theater. I thought you were speaking as much to me as to those wealthy swine in their fancy boxes!"

"I was," she agreed. "Actors are sincere in their work."

"But off the stage you wish to play the lady," he accused her.

"I try to be my own person," she defended herself. "A person of honor. And I know it was one of the nobles who put a price on my head."

"But you still favor them?"

"I would dearly love to wreak vengeance on the man who condemned me and hired you as my official killer!"

"Now you're speaking from your heart," the big man approved. "Would you like some find brandy before you say goody-bye to the world? It must be done before dawn. But I vow I could do with some of the warming brew."

"Thank you," she said. "I'm still suffering pain from my ankles and wrists. The brandy might help."

133

The man with the black patch over his eye gave her a knowing smile. "I have the best. Straight from the cellars of one of London's most reliable vintners!"

"I do not doubt that. If one is going to steal, it is sensible to steal the best!"

"Damn it if the wench hasn't wit!" Dick Henry said as he removed a dusty bottle from a cupboard. He pulled the cork from it, put the bottle to his mouth and drank freely. When he at last put the bottle down, he wiped his lips with his other hand and declared, "Makes your veins run with fire, it does!"

Tessa took the bottle from him and followed his example of drinking straight from it. She had no idea how much of the burning liquid she downed. Had she not been overtaken by a fit of coughing because of its strength, she might have drunk more.

Dick Henry laughed as he took the bottle from her and drank again. Then he said, " 'Tis a good way to go! No member of the gentry could do better than meet his end afloat in the best of brandy."

Her courage having returned—partly because of the brandy—she said acidly, "It seems *you* are to enjoy the fine liquor without having to pay for it with your life."

"The difference between you and me!" he said.

"I'm well aware of it," she retorted.

He was staring at her again, and there was a gleam of lust in his single eye. He said, "I've been told that all the women at the King's Theater are whores to the king. Were you one?"

"Had I been one of the king's favorites, no one would have dared to put a bounty on my head to all the underworld of London."

"True," Dick Henry admitted. "But how could he come to miss someone of your grace?"

"Perhaps because it was known I loved another."

"Some fine lord, I'll be bound!"

"A captain in the King's Navy, who gave his life for the England you speak of with such disgust!"

"A pox on that! I'll tell you what I think of England—if the time came, I would fight for her along with
134

the other gutter rats of London. Even we have a love for British soil!"

"You have small reason for such a love."

"But it is there, a part of us," the big man said.

"You continually surprise me."

"Stand up," he ordered her. And she did, her cheeks burning. She knew he was appraising her as some men evaluated fine horses. He said rather thickly, "It pains me to destroy such a beauty—and one who has such power with words!"

"All gone in a twinkling," she said. "I shall be a cold and lifeless lump of flesh."

"No!" Clearly, the idea disturbed him. He took another huge swig of the brandy and then offered the bottle to her. "You need it?"

"Not as much as you," she said calmly. "You are the one about to stain your hands and your character."

"Damn me, I'll not take that!" he said, in a rage again. "You taunt me when I am helpless to change my course."

She managed a wan smile. "I suppose I shouldn't blame you. The one to blame is the one who wishes me dead. I'm doomed in any case."

He slowly put the brandy bottle on the table. In a low voice, he ordered her, "Drop your nightgown!"

Tessa stared at him. "What would you have me do?"

"Strip naked! Naked as when you were a babe!"

"Why?"

"So I may see you fully. Appreciate your beauty before I have to destroy it!"

She shook her head. "I don't understand you!"

"Hurry, lass! Dawn will come all too soon!" he said, and his voice was filled with urgency.

Tessa knew well what she might expect—a cruel rape before she had her throat slit and was thrown in the river. Yet there was something about this man that made her suspect he might not want the obvious. She had found him strangely different, just when she'd tagged him as a beast. Beneath his cloak of the ruffian there was something better. True, this side of his nature had not developed as it would have in other conditions, but there was a sensitivity in him that was unexpected in a hired killer.

Having made a decision, with a swift movement she let her nightgown fall. He came close to her and she saw the look of awe on his brown face. Strangest of all, he was trembling! Actually trembling! He moved around her and she heard him gasp.

"Your back!" he said. "And your breast? Who abused you so?"

Her own voice had a quaver in it. She said, "I told you I have experienced some of the cruelties of this world."

"And you did not lie to me," he said tensely. "What villains would mar so lovely a body?" And in the next moment he had her in his arms, and his lips caressed her mouth and then her breast where it had been burned, and then he let his lips skim over the welts on her naked back.

She submitted to his attentions, marveling that big, rough hands could touch so gently. And soon to her own amazement, she felt the hunger of passion surge through her. She wanted him. She could not believe that it could happen this way and at such a time. But as the big man pressed her close to him again, she was ready to do whatever he might bid her.

He whispered in her ear, "There is so short a time, less than an hour until the dawn! Will you spend it with me? Give yourself to me until the moment comes when all must end?"

"Yes," she whispered. "Yes! What does it matter now? I will pleasure you as you ask!"

"More than that," he said. "All my life the memory of this night will let me live in the dirt and danger. A few blessed moments in a life of torment!"

He quickly stripped off his clothes, and she admired his strong, muscular body. Then they lay down on the blankets together. He kissed her hard and she wrapped her arms about his neck. His chest crushed against her breasts, and their thighs molded. His maleness thrust into her and she responded with spirit. A great flood of peace went through her and she gave herself wholly to this long, passionate union.

136

Surprisingly, the big man was a tender and considerate lover. Despite his size and strong passion, he paced her through the moments of love and left her replete and languid—indeed, almost happy. She had half expected to be violated, but his claiming of her body had been something close to an act of worship. She uttered a small moaning sigh as it ended.

The big man was on his elbow beside her. "Lass!" he said huskily.

She looked up at him. "How long until the dawn?"

"Soon."

She said, "I want you to know I'm not sorry. It was not a rape!"

The big man gave a distressed moan. "Stop!" he cried out.

"Why?"

"I cannot have you talk so when I'm soon to end your life," he said unhappily.

"You were not troubled before," she said quietly.

He stood up, still naked, and took a few steps away. He then turned to her and said, "I cannot do it!"

She sat up. "What?"

"It's useless," he said. "Some other will have to slit your throat! I cannot!"

She smiled. "I never believed you could! It is not in your nature!"

"God knows I have done enough wicked things," he said angrily. He made a fist and stove it against the brick wall. Wincing in agony as blood ran from his knuckles, he said, "I can't!"

Tessa rose and went to him, and taking his hurt hand in hers, she touched her lips to the bloody knuckles. She said, "You are a good man, whatever else there is about you. I knew it!"

They stood naked and facing each other. He said, "If I let you go, that will be no answer. Others would surely do what I turn my back on. And they will not be so gentle as I might have been."

"If I'm doomed, I have learned a lesson," she said. "I sat alone in my house wanting to die in my grief and

137

selfishness. I have learned what Charles Hart tried to tell me—life can be sweet until one has drained the very last drop of it!"

"What am I to do?"

"That is up to you."

"You are free to go," the big man said bleakly, "but it will be to your death. I know what Sir Edward has arranged."

Tessa said, "I do not care. Let me stay here until the morning. Then find me some clothes."

"I have a stock of stolen women's things here. It will be no problem."

"Then I will leave when morning comes and take my chances," Tessa said.

"And until then?"

Her smile was gentle. "Can we not bed together until then?"

"By heaven, we can and we will!" Dick Henry declared and took her in his arms once more.

Their second round of love was less frantic than the first. It was also more rewarding. And when they finished, they lay close together and slept until morning.

At dawn the big man let her search through his stock of clothes, and she found a dress and shawl. Then he set out a table of food and drink before she left. The large room was bare of furniture except for the blankets in the corner and a plank table with two rough chairs. There were doors leading to closets, and in these closets were piled all sorts of loot from various robberies.

One window with iron bars on it looked out on the muddy bank of the Thames. It was a somber morning with heavy fog, and Tessa did not relish going outside. Neither did she relish once again becoming a target for the thugs of the evil Sir Edward Montagu.

Dick Henry was strangely silent as they had their meal. Suddenly he gazed at her across the table with his single keen eye and said, "I do not see why it could not be!"

"What?" she asked.

"Why you could not assume another identity and stay safely with me."

138

She reminded him, "Sir Edward will be bound to keep a watch on you. If he is told you suddenly have a woman as a companion, he will certainly be suspicious."

Dick Henry scowled. "I could move out of London for a while. It might be a good plan in any case."

"I'd be recognized. I'm well known from the stage."

"We could dye your skin dark and keep a cap over your hair. In the sort of clothing you are wearing now no one would recognize you."

She studied the face of the big man. "And my life would not be in jeopardy."

"Not while you remain with me," Dick Henry assured her.

"It might be worth a trial," she said, considering it. She knew it would mean leaving all her other life behind her and throwing in her lot with a thief. But what life was there for her without Thomas? At least for now, the theater had lost its attraction for her. And now that she knew the extent of his evil, more than anything else she wanted to exact some sort of vengeance on Sir Edward Montagu.

Dick Henry eyed her suspiciously. "What is going on in that pretty head?"

"I do not want to be murdered by Sir Edward's hired killers."

"Your best hope is to hide out with me."

Her glance was stern. "And I do, one day, wish to make him pay for what he is trying to do to me."

The big man said, "If you survive, you ought to be able to even the score."

She thought for a moment. "What do you expect of me?" she demanded suddenly.

He looked flustered. "You would be my woman."

"That is fair enough," she said. "I like you. I suppose it also means I must involve myself in your thieving—become an associate."

"Only if you wish," the big man said sullenly.

Her smile was bitter. "Whatever you do, you're no worse than most of the robbers at court and in the government."

"You can be sure of that!" Dick Henry said, pleased.

"All right, Dick," she said. "Save my skin and I'll be your woman."

The big man jumped up delightedly, came around the table to take her in his arms, and gave her a hug and warm kiss. He laughed as he told her, "I couldn't bear to lose you now, lass."

"Then better be sure I'm not found by any of the others. Your friend, Mad Reevy, knows I was here. What about him?"

"He can be trusted," Dick Henry promised.

"What about the dye for my face? Will it wash off?" she wanted to know.

"Not without many scrubbings. I have used it when I want to pretend I'm a gypsy."

She scrutinized his good-looking face. "You're pretty brown as you are."

"Aye," he said with a smile. "I think it suits me."

As soon as they finished eating, she took the bottle of brown liquid he gave her and rubbed it into her skin. She was amazed at the difference it made in her. And with a cap to cover her hair, it seemed fairly certain no one would recognize her as Tess Shaw of the King's Theater.

She had just completed her disguise when Mad Reevy arrived. The foxy man gave a glance at her and whistled. "Your dead body was to be in the river before dawn!"

Dick Henry crossed to him. "There has been a change of plan. We're to pretend the lass is dead. She's disguised herself and is going to be my woman."

Mad Reevy looked shocked. "You've let the wench get around you!"

"I have not," Dick Henry said angrily. "I'm just not one to murder a fair woman in cold blood."

The foxy-faced little man groaned. "You're daft! You talked with Sir Edward and you know he means to have her dead. If you don't do it, you're likely to find yourself marked for murder as well."

"I'm willing to risk that," Dick Henry told him.

"Well, I am not," Mad Reevy said. "If you want to

keep this woman with you, I'll not stay for the trouble that follows. You'll keep her alone."

"Be that as you like," the big man said.

Tessa appealed to him. "Don't do anything rash, Dick. What about the things you took last night?"

Dick glowered at the little man with his one good eye. "He can keep all of it. We'll manage well enough without him."

Mad Reevy turned and slowly went to the door. He hesitated and said, "Mind, there's no hard feelings in this."

"Go on your way," the big man ordered.

"It's more risk than I want," the foxy-looking man said. "Good luck to you, lass. You'll need it when the rest of Montagu's hired thugs come after you."

"Be gone!" Dick Henry shouted at him. The little man hurried out the door and vanished.

Tessa gave Dick a worried glance. "Do you think he'll tell on us—let Montagu know I'm here?"

"I think not," the big man said. "But just in case, it would be better for us to pack and head for Windsor."

"I hope I won't cause you a lot of trouble."

He smiled. "Whatever trouble you bring me will be well worth it."

So they left London behind. To earn enough money to support the two of them, Dick Henry set himself up as a gambler in a tavern on the outskirts of Windsor. At the start he did well—in fact, exceptionally well. Unfortunately, as reports of his prowess with cards spread through the district, people became afraid to play with him, and there were fewer and fewer opponents to challenge. Finally he began to find himself sitting through the night alone at the gaming table. And with no games there was no profit!

Seated in their room at the inn one morning, he told Tessa darkly, "They are onto me. There will be no more winnings through the cards."

"Maybe we should risk going back to London," she suggested.

"No, I will hit on something!" He winked his eye at her. "Or someone!"

The elderly Lord David Gloster's house was robbed a few nights later. No one was hurt, but a large amount of money and a number of fine pieces of silverware were taken.

At the inn, Dick Henry hugged Tessa to him and chortled, "I have the cash we needed, and when it's gone I'll have the silver pieces disposed of through a fence in London!"

"I do not like your risking your neck," she worried. "You must be careful."

"And we must rise in the world," the big man declared. "I have a plan to own my estate with a big house on it one day. You shall take your rightful place as the mistress of the mansion!"

She smiled up at him. "Don't be too ambitious, Dick. I find myself happy enough with you just as we are!"

It was no lie. She had cut off all the ties of her old world, and now she was Tess, the companion of a robber. But there were compensations. Her sense of adventure had reawakened, Dick Henry was kind and considerate of her, and their lovemaking left nothing to be desired.

Nevertheless, as the days passed, she realized that rather than enjoying the pleasant country life, Dick was growing increasingly uneasy. He would pace up and down their small room and complain of inactivity.

Watching him one day, she smiled and said, "I swear you miss London!"

"Perhaps I do," he admitted. "There is a way of life there that I miss."

"Then let us return."

He frowned. "It is too soon. Word may have gone out that I did not murder you. Sir Edward's men may be waiting for just such an opportunity, expecting us to return!"

She sighed. "I cannot bear to see you restless and unhappy."

"Restless I may be, but as long as I have you at my side, I shall never again be unhappy!"

142

"You may count on me—if Sir Edward's men don't get me," she said.

Dick was staring out the window. Suddenly he turned to her and smacked his heavy fist in the palm of his hand. He said, "I know how we can liven up things here!"

"How?"

"We'll take to the road, become highwaymen—or a highwayman and his pretty partner! I think that would go down well—the mysterious highwaywoman! Should be good for a while!"

She laughed. "I'm a crack shot, and I used to ride a pony bareback in a circus!"

"I knew it!" he exclaimed. "It's a sign! We must do it!"

And so they embarked on a new adventure. Dick found two fine horses and equipped them with the best saddles money could buy. Tessa busied herself with the needle and made them identical black coats and breeches. They wore wide-brimmed black hats with dark plumes, and with their black masks, they would make a picturesque sight as they bore down on a stagecoach.

They would keep other outfits with them. These they would wear when they ventured into a village, where they would pose as traveling representatives of the king and his mistress. They had the best of firearms. Tessa discovered she had lost none of her cleverness with a pistol; Dick was also a crack shot. Together they made a unique pair of highway robbers.

The first time they held up a coach, one of their stout victims quavered aloud, "Bless me, one of them is a woman!"

Tessa leaned over the saddle, and placing the pistol under the portly gentleman's nose, she laughingly cried, "It is true, sirrah! And I'm the better bandit for it!"

The women standing by the stagecoach twittered at this. One of them, a delicate young thing, fainted dead away. By this time, Dick Henry had the cash chest of the coach company and they were riding away, leaving a bewildered and frightened crew behind them.

"It is too easy!" Dick said with delight. "And with it we get fresh air and exercise!"

"It is also risky," she warned him. "They'll have our descriptions out in no time. They'll arm the stages better and be ready for us!"

"Until then, it's our game!" Dick cried happily.

And so it turned out to be. Tessa was occasionally shocked when she thought how easily she had fallen into this rebel life. She was now a highway robber and the mistress of a highway robber, and yet she thought herself as good as most of them at Whitehall or in the Houses of Parliament! All of the upper classes were rogues, feeding on the weakness of the poor. So why not have her share by robbing a sampling of the rich?

It was easy to rationalize this way. Meanwhile, both she and Dick were careful to shoot no one. They had no desire to draw blood; besides, gunfire wasn't necessary— the sight of them swooping down in their black outfits with pistols in hand was enough. Most coachmen and passengers alike were delighted to part with their money and valuables as long as their lives were spared.

They made one strike after another. After a successful venture, they would often rest for days before hitting their next stage. Their favorite hiding places were sleepy little villages. In one of these one night, Dick, who had convinced the weak-minded landlord that he was a special messenger of the king, bought a cask of gin and ordered it taken out to the village square.

As soon as it was dusk, torches were set alight, and Dick invited all and sundry to partake of the gin. The villagers flocked to this free treat and there was such revelry under the stars as would be repeated for years by the oldsters of the tiny place. Dick and Tessa, feeling like royalty, stood on the sidelines and laughed until tears came into their eyes at the wild carousing.

It was a life of adventure and excitement such as Tessa had never dreamed existed. One wild prank led to another. They began to strike the busiest coach roads, where the stages had armed guards aplenty. It seemed that Dick continually thirsted for new challenges.

Still, once in a while, Tessa remembered Thomas. His body was long gone, she knew, but into her mind's eye came an image of his skeleton left somewhere under some strange sea. And often she thought of Sir Edward Montagu and of her desire to avenge herself on him. She began to think of returning to London for that very purpose. Vengeance cried out in her. But when she told Dick, he was loath to give up the excitement of the road.

Then one day they rode down on a stage bound for London. To Tessa's horror and Dick's surprise, there were no passengers aboard but only a lot of armed guards. The coach had been sent out to trap them. As they circled about the halted vehicle a tirade of shots rang out, and Dick was hit in the shoulder.

As he slumped over in his saddle, Tessa, covering her retreat with some shots, joined him and led him away on his horse. They rode for several miles before she felt they were safe. By that time the big man was pale from loss of blood and barely able to remain in the saddle.

She stopped by a spring deep in the woods and washed and bound his wound. Then she gave him a stiff drink of rum, and he came around a good bit. She changed into her other clothing and he did the same. She made him leave their bandit clothing behind in the woods.

"Too dangerous," she told him. "The game is up."

"What next?" he asked her as they prepared to mount their horses.

Her pretty face had a thoughtful look. "I think it is time to return to London."

He gave her a knowing glance. "I think I can tell you why. You're itching to settle with Sir Edward."

"Among other things," she said.

The big man shook his head. "It could lead us into grave trouble!"

BOOK TWO

Plague and Fire

Chapter Eight

The London they returned to was strange to Tessa, for she was dead, at least to all intents. There was no hope of her showing herself at the King's Theater or in St. James's Square, no looking forward to a warm embrace from Charles Hart or a friendly hour with Nell Gwyn. Nor could she turn to Sir David Farr for help. She was cut off from all the world she had known.

She and Dick took rooms in a lodging house in a mean part of the city. London seemed an overcrowded, stinking place after the freshness of the country. The sun shone day after day, and the rare showers brought no relief—it was said to be the warmest summer London had ever known. And the accumulated filth of the city brought a multitude of rats to roam the streets.

The rats grew bolder by the day. Once when Tessa went out to buy bread she heard a woman scream behind her in the street. She turned to see the woman snatch up a child from the edge of the overflowing gutter in the middle of the street. Tessa's stomach heaved at the sight of a great, gray rat with its fangs buried deeply in the flesh of the child's wrist.

As the child screamed with fear, the woman shouted, "Will no one do anything?"

A man passing by cried out in fury, and snatching up a heavy piece of wood from a wheelbarrow he was pushing, he ran to the aid of the child. He hit the rat a savage blow, and it let go the child's wrist and fell to the ground stunned. But as the man was about to strike it a second time, it bared its bloody teeth!

"Damned pest!" the man shouted in loathing and struck the snarling creature again and again. When it was little more than pulp, he picked it up by the tail and threw it into the gutter. There it floated for a moment before sinking into the murky scum of rotting food, excrement and other debris.

The stench and the sickening sight made Tessa's head

149

reel. She hurried away from the ugly scene and tried to put it out of her mind. But it was impossible. London was becoming a nightmare for her. Dick's arm was healing, but slowly, and he could do little. So he went in search of old Nestor, a fence who owed him what he called a tidy sum of money.

When Dick returned to their mean lodgings that afternoon she enquired how he had made out. "Did you see the fence and get what is owed you?"

Dick's manly face was grim. "You know what they're like!"

"I don't! Tell me."

"He complained of not having made the money he expected from the swag I left with him. And when I threatened him, he promised to get some money together."

"So he gave you nothing?"

"He's meeting me this afternoon at the Purple Owl. I think you had best come along to be a witness."

"A witness?"

"As to what I'm paid," Dick explained. "If he pays me short, I'll warn him I want the rest. He's a sickening sort, always whining about his poverty. And he's known as the largest fence in London!"

Tessa didn't like the sound of this any more than she liked the heat or anything else about this stinking London of the lower classes. She thought of her days in St. James's Square and of the cologne-sprinkled clothing she had wore. Now she was dressed in the clothing of the average Londoner, and the average woman of the lower classes had no such finery.

Her plan for revenge on Sir Edward Montagu had been put aside for the time being. Now she and Dick Henry were fighting for survival. She had no fear that as soon as the big man had his strength back he would be able to support them in style, but for now they were in a precarious position.

When the appointed time came, they went to the tavern and ordered a pint apiece. Dick, in an edgy mood, sat sullenly over his beer without drinking it, and everytime
150

someone new entered the tavern he glanced up to see if it might be the fence. And always he lowered his eyes again. It seemed the elusive gentleman was not to appear.

Then an incredibly dirty old man in a black hat with a wide brim came haltingly into the place. He had a stringy gray beard and heavy gray eyebrows; a hooked nose was the most prominent feature of his sallow, wasted face. There was a look of furtiveness about him. His shabby black coat reached so close to the floor that it sometimes dragged a little. Tessa thought him to be the picture of a miser.

Dick came to life and whispered to her, "That's him! That's old Nestor!" And he stood up and cried, "Nestor! Over here, my laddie!"

The dirty old man looked more uneasy and began shuffling across to them. In a whining tone, he said, "Forgive my lateness."

Dick was in false good humor to conceal his uneasiness. He clapped the old man on the shoulder and said boisterously, "Be as late as you like, as long as you're ready to pay me! Will you have a tankard of good beer?"

"No." The old man licked his lips nervously. "I never touch spirits of any sort!"

"Beer is not spirits, you old goat!" Dick said. And turning to Tessa, he said, "This is my girl! Don't you wish you had one like her, Nestor?"

Nestor offered a sickly smile. "I'm long past attracting the ladies."

"Or anyone else, I vow," Dick said with another laugh. "You are a smelly, creepy old walking bit of dung, Nestor, but as long as you bring me sovereigns, I'll not turn away from you!"

"Yes," the old man said in his strange, hissing manner.

"Let me have the money, old swindler!" Dick said.

Nestor gave a nervous nod and groped in his pocket. He reached deep in the oversize coat and brought out a few coins. He said, "I wasn't able to raise much, Dick, lad, but I'll do better another time."

Dick scowled and took the coins. "This is nothing, you

151

old reprobate!" And he made a move to strike the old man.

"Dick, please!" Tessa cautioned, taking him by the arm as old Nestor stumbled back in fear.

Then without warning four men appeared, moving on them from various parts of the rooms. Their leader, who had a greasy, fat face asked Nestor, "Is this the thief?"

"Yes, yes!" the old man shrieked. "They are the ones!"

"What foolery is this?" Dick Henry demanded angrily.

"No foolery!" the pig-faced one told him in a stern voice. "We're arresting you, in the king's name, for repeated robberies—and the young woman as well!"

"You'll do nothing of the sort!" Dick cried and began to fight the quartet.

It was an uneven match—hopeless with Dick's bad arm. One of the men seized Tessa and gave her a villainous grin while the other three fought with Dick until he collapsed to the tavern floor battered, bleeding, and unconscious.

The pig-faced man had a bloodied nose. He wiped it and told his helpers, "Take him away, men. It's Newgate for both of these worthies!"

Tessa cried plaintively, "Don't take him to that pesthole! He's ill. I can raise the money for his fine."

"No doubt," the pig-faced man sneered. "But you won't be able to, as *you're* going to the women's side of Newgate!"

"I have done nothing!" she told him.

The man holding her arm chuckled. "That's what they all tell us. Nestor put his finger on you both, and it's along to Newgate with your man, my dear!"

In a few minutes she was to learn the humiliation of sitting in an open cart and being dragged off to the jeers of the watching street crowds. In the background she saw the frightened face of old Nestor, the fence, peering over the shoulders of two tall men, to see that they were being taken away. Dick, sprawled on the floor of the wagon where he had been thrown, did not regain consciousness.

Guards were stationed both at the back of the wagon and up front with the driver, so that Tessa was caught between them with no chance of escaping from the rumbling wagon. It was a new mode of travel for her. She remembered her night of triumph when she had been taken through the fine streets of the city in the elegantly trimmed sedan-chair borne by two stalwart young men. What a great lady she had been then!

Now she was on the way to Newgate, the most evil and overcrowded of all the London prisons. Its very name sent fear through criminals, those who had been there and those trying to avoid it. For someone in Dick's condition it could mean death from fever, and for Tessa it might mean worse.

She had heard stories of women gang-raped by rough guards and horror tales of the diseased and mad women of the streets incarcerated there! Worn out and ill with the pox, these lost women seized on the young and innocent of their sex, and gloating over their pure bodies, tormented them without mercy. All agreed that Newgate was a dirty hell hole, a blot on the conscience of the nation.

And Tessa was bound there! She bent her head and saw Dick, his breathing labored, his face battered, and his eye patch gone, revealing the empty socket behind it. Perhaps he might die of his injuries before they reached the prison. Better for him if he did. She could not bear to picture this big, proud man tottering out of the pesthold a yellow-skinned, emaciated wreck.

One of the guards turned to her. With a smile that revealed crooked, rotting teeth, he told her, "I'm right fond of black-haired beauties!" At this his companion laughed loudly.

They continued on through the heat-ridden streets. She closed her eyes and tried to shut out the misery. When they finally reached the prison entrance, she and Dick were parted, and she was dragged roughly before a sour-looking old man at a high-topped desk. He laboriously recorded her name as Tess Henry, the name she'd decided to use. When he finished, he jerked his head for the guard to take her away.

The guard was young and had a cruel face, mean eyes and yellow hair. As he dragged her along a dark corridor

153

he said, "If you have money I can put you on the proper side of the prison. You pay for your comforts, but you gets them!"

"I have no money to pay," she said. "Where did they take my husband?"

"They took your man to one of the wards on the mean side," he said with relish. "By the look of him, he won't live until morning."

"He may surprise you," she told her captor.

The guard forced her down on a bench at the end of the grim corridor. He said, "Now it's time to shackle you!"

"Shackle me?"

"Those who can't pay have to wear the shackles," he said, and began selecting a set of chains and shackles from the wall.

"No!" she cried, drawing back.

"Crying out won't do you any good," he told her. "Nobody's going to hear you."

She moved her feet to avoid being shackled, but he was too expert for her. In a minute or two he had the chains locked securely to her ankles—a humiliation of which she'd never dreamed.

"Come along now, my love!" the cruel-faced guard gloated. And he dragged her up from the bench and along another long, black corridor. She could not keep up with him properly; the shackles held her back and ground into her ankles.

"Wait!" she protested. "They hurt!"

His reaction was harsh laughter. He strode on ahead of her while she shuffled painfully in an effort to keep up with him. The stench of this Newgate corridor was beyond anything in the foul streets. It closed in on her and made her feel like fainting again.

"What's wrong?" the guard leered at her as she faltered.

"That awful smell," she groaned.

"That's the fine Newgate air," he chuckled. "This is the day the hangman cuts the bodies down. They add a sweetness to the air, rotten bodies do!"

154

Knowing he was merely trying to make it more unbearable for her, she made no reply. Her anger had been aroused. Now she was determined to stand up to this ordeal, no matter what. She even managed to increase her shuffling pace a trifle. They went along a maze of underground corridors until finally they came to a halt before a forbidding iron door.

The guard fumbled with his keys. "This is where you're going to stay. If you could pay, you'd have better quarters."

"I have no money," she repeated bleakly.

"That's your misery, not mine," the slab-faced young man said. "The scum of London are behind this door— ladies who'll give you a proper welcome!" He turned the key in the door and pulled it open. "In with you!" He shoved her forward.

She literally fell inside the fetid ward. From all sides came a babble of voices. She tried to get up from the cold, slimy floor, but at the first attempt the pain of the shackles cutting into her ankles stopped her. She tried again and stood painfully facing the ghostly females crowding around her. It was like a weird nightmare!

The hag-like creatures crowded close to her, their hair wild, their faces thin and emaciated. They were dressed in the worst of rags. The faint light from a small window allowed her to see that some of the women were naked and had running sores on their faces and breasts. The greedy eyes of the women were fixed on her, and some of them stretched out claw-like hands to touch her.

She drew away. "Let me be!"

"Ha!" one of them shouted wildly. "Let her be, she says! What have you got to give us, lass? A few farthings, some nice lace from your petticoat, that blouse and skirt?"

"I have no money," she screamed, backing away as the acrid-smelling group crowded in on her. "I have nothing to give you!"

"Then we'll take what we want!" squealed the wild one who was acting as spokesman. There was a loud, gleeful shout from the other hags; then they were upon her.

Tessa sobbed in fear and revulsion as they tore at her blouse and ran their fingers through her hair, questing for loot between her breasts and in other intimate parts of her body, wise to the hiding places of street drabs.

They tore her clothing off down to her shift and then left her breathless on the floor as they moved away complaining that their search of her had yielded so little. Then they began to fight among themselves over the few poor things they'd stolen from her.

Moaning, she struggled to her feet again. As she did, one of the demented-looking women came to stare at her. The woman, who was completely naked, had long, greasy hair and her body was very thin—riddled, no doubt, with some dread disease—and there were running sores on her thin cheeks and body.

Tessa turned away from her, only to be confronted by another strange apparition. This woman wore a long, elegantly decorated gown which had seen better days, and on her head was a filthy cap which had once been white. Her face was bloated and her eyes wild, but she bore herself in a regal manner that was quite different from the animalistic behavior of the others in the charnel house.

In a booming, cultivated voice she declared, "I know you! You are Tessa Shaw!"

Tessa could not believe her ears. She stared at the old woman. Suddenly it came to her; this was Maude something or other, who had played older ladies' parts in the King's Theater company! Maude, who had been given to sipping gin too liberally and had descended to playing only walk-on roles.

"Maude!" Tessa exclaimed. "What are you doing here?"

"I might ask you the same question," the elderly woman retorted in her great-lady manner.

"I have fallen on evil times," Tessa said. "I have been unjustly accused of being a thief!"

"Newgate is a bad place to be," the older woman said with a grimace, "unless one has money. Then you can hire a private room of your own, have good food brought in so you don't have to eat the prison swill, and even re-

156

ceive guests when you wish. That is the way those on the rich side of the prison live . . . while we are treated like the rats that infest these filthy wards."

"My husband is here also," Tessa said. She felt Dick to be her husband though they had not had a legal marriage. "He is ill and I fear he may die."

"Many do," Maude intoned in her majestic way. "I was unfortunate enough to be caught picking the pocket of a gentleman who'd been drinking with me. He was not at all gallant. He condemned me bitterly and had me sent here."

"I'm sorry."

"Be sorry for yourself as well. You will be lucky to escape with your life, let alone your health. You see these ladies of the street, naked and clothed. More than half of them have the pox! You can be infected from their open sores."

Tessa glanced around her. "It is a horrible place. Are all the wards like this?"

"They throw the mad in with the sane until the worst off become so violent they have to be moved to Bedlam," Maude said. "I have established my position as a lady here by sheer force of personality. My training on the stage has not failed me. I was allowed to keep this dress, a costume from my stage days. You see how it is properly weighted with lead at the bottom hem so that it will hang right." She drew herself up. "Am I not still a fine figure of a woman?"

"You are!" Tessa agreed heartily, feeling it would be cruel not to, considering the woman's wretched state.

Maude preened the front of the filthy, ornamented gown and a smile creased her bloated, commanding face. "I shall return to the company when I'm released. Charles Hart says no one can play a queen like I do."

"You were always very good," Tessa replied, and this was true.

"Except when in my cups," the older woman confessed with a sigh. "But that is over. I have had nothing of spirits since I've been in here. I have conquered my thirst for gin."

"Thank Heaven you have gained some good in being here."

"I shall take you under my protection," Maude announced in her authoritative way. "We of the theater must support one another!"

"Thank you!"

"This scum will not harm you when I take you under my wing. Even in here they have respect for a true lady."

Tessa looked down at herself miserably. "My clothes! They took them!"

"I shall get them back—or something equal to what they stole," Maude promised. "Give me a little time."

"It doesn't matter," Tessa said in a tone of despair.

"But it does," Maude insisted. "It is cold and damp here. You must have some outer clothing."

Still suffering from the shackles, Tessa remarked, "You are fortunate they didn't shackle you!"

"The wretch didn't dare," Maude said imperiously. "I quoted some lines from my favorite role of Lady Macbeth, and they were humbled!"

Under other conditions Tessa might have been inclined to dismiss the old character actress's rantings as nonsense. But so desperate was her plight that she had nowhere else to turn; she must accept the older woman at face value. As it turned out, her decision was wise. Maude did have some authority over the mongrel lot in the ward, and warning them that Mrs. Henry was not to be further tormented, she soon had Tessa's clothing returned.

For this Tessa was grateful, but living on in the filthy place with the slop food was practically unendurable. Tessa and the older woman kept to themselves as much as possible, often whiling away the hours by reciting scenes from plays which they both knew. Eventually some of the less deplorable of the others noticed this scene-playing and began to listen, and soon the forlorn creatures were urging Maude and Tessa to do scenes for them, offering what poor payments of extra food and clothing they could.

After one such performance in the dank ward Tessa

turned to Maude and said, "What would Charles Hart say if he saw us now?"

"He would think us a credit to him and the profession," the older woman declared. "We have lost neither our dignity nor our hope."

"If only I knew something of Dick! I have no idea whether he is alive or dead."

"We must somehow try to find out," Maude said.

After many days, one afternoon they were allowed out into the upper courtyard of the prison for a little air. This was shut in by gray walls, but a few trees showed here and there as a reminder of the world outside. About a week before, Maude had used her influence with the guard to have him take the shackles off Tessa, and the relief went a long way to making her lot more bearable. Now, with the old woman by her, Tessa breathed the fresh air of the courtyard and felt a small ray of hope. Perhaps she might survive.

Maude nudged her and indicated a table on the other side of the courtyard with a group seated around it. "There are the ones what has the gilt! Enough to buy bread and comfort!"

Tessa stared at the chattering men and women, who seemed in a happy mood. She said, "You wouldn't guess they were prisoners."

"Money can buy anything here," the older woman scowled.

They and the other poor like them were held back from the privileged by the guards, but they were allowed to watch the gentry of the prison enjoying themselves.

One man held a quizzing glass to his eye and looked about him scornfully. Several of the women were naked, but many of them were dressed in fine gowns. These privileged feasted on hunks of meat, chickens roasted brown, meat pie and fine pastries! Not far from the table a man and woman openly made love on the ground, their laughter and screams of ecstasy unnoticed by most.

Beyond this group were the men who did not have the money to purchase the fine extras enjoyed by Newgate's elite. Tessa gave her attention to them. After a moment

159

she saw a tall, thin figure moving about in the rear of the scruffy group. He stood head and shoulders above all the others. Her heart leaped—it had to be Dick Henry! At least he was alive!

"Dick!" she called out happily and waved to him.

The guard came and shoved her back. "None of that! No mixin' among the prisoners."

"What about them?" She pointed to the ones gathered around the table feasting.

"They can pay for it," the guard said with an ugly sneer.

In the moment while she had been arguing with the guard, the tall figure had vanished. At least she had seen Dick; she knew now that he was alive. But he had become terribly thin, and she was sure he was not well.

Back in the ward she groaned to Maude, "He is ill! If only I could somehow help him!"

"You did see him," Maude commented.

"Yes, that was something. But I fear it has made me more impatient to get away from here."

"Better resign yourself," Maude advised her. "You may never get away from this place!"

"I refuse to believe that!"

Maude showed a smile on her bloated face. "I confess I like your spirit, my girl."

The days went on in grim fashion, a seemingly endless routine of wretchedness. Then, suddenly, there was a new and frightening development. In increasing numbers prisoners were taken ill, nearly all of them dying within a few days.

No more than a week after the first word of the disease, the haggard crew in Tessa's ward stood silently around a woman stretched out on the filthy floor. Her wide-open eyes stared up vacantly, her legs moved convulsively, and she was fouled with her own vomit. Her chest quivered and another gush of vomit issued from her mouth, spattering her face and hair and running in a streak on the ground beside her.

Maude and Tessa were in the background. The older woman said, "I know the signs. It's the plague!"

"The plague?"

"Aye, we've had it before. She should be got out of here and sent to the pesthouse to die; otherwise we're all liable to come down with it!"

"How does it take one?" Tessa wanted to know.

"Fever and chills and a great boil in the loin or the armpits," the big woman said worriedly. "When poultices are put on the boil to burst it, the pain is enough to drive a person to madness. If that doesn't kill you, the vomiting does!"

"Is there no cure?"

"None that I know," the old woman said dolefully. "Some are lucky enough to get over it, but it's pure luck and nothing more."

"Call the guards," Tessa said, on the edge of hysteria. "Get that poor sick creature out of here!"

"And more will be sick soon, mind!" Maude warned.

Again the old woman was proven right. No sooner was the dead body of the plague victim removed than someone else was stricken.

As the second woman was overcome, an ominous silence came over the usually noisy ward. Fear of the plague overcame everything else. It was as if they were all huddled together to wait for death. And the situation was equally bad all over the prison. Word leaked in to them that all London was succumbing to the plague. It was the worst visitation in years. The king was leaving to set up his court outside the city. All the wealthy gentry were leaving in the same way.

One morning Maude did not stir, and when Tessa tried to wake her, the old woman simply stared up at her in a dazed way. "I'm ill," she said. "I think it's my turn!"

Tessa knelt by her benefactor. "Nonsense! You will be all right."

But the old woman did not move, and when Tessa returned to her again she was dripping with perspiration. Tessa did what she could to help her, using some of the precious water allotment to wet a piece of cloth torn from her shift and placing the homemade bandage on the head of the former actress.

Later in the day Maude moaned and complained of a pain in her left arm. When Tessa investigated, she saw the red swelling in the old woman's armpit—the dreaded plague boil! Now Maude's body was shaken with trembling, and she moaned aloud.

"The pain is great," she said in a tense voice.

"I will remain by you," Tessa promised.

By the next morning it was evident that Maude was going to die. As she weakened, she drew Tessa close to her and whispered in her ear. "When I go, open the hem of my dress."

"Just rest yourself," Tessa soothed, supposing the old woman was in delirium.

"Don't forget!" Maude said in a shadow of her old regal fashion.

Tessa stayed with her as she sank further into a coma. About an hour later she shivered slightly and was gone. It was a shocking moment for Tessa. She felt dreadfully alone, for the elderly actress had been her protector since she'd arrived in the frightening ward. When she knew there was nothing more to be done, she went to the door to try to summon a guard, but without any success. She went back to the dead woman to wait until she could get someone to help.

It was then she thought of the old woman's mention of her dress hem. She reached down and held up a section of the dress bottom, feeling its lead weights that were designed to make it hang fully. Many such dresses were made in this fashion. Then a thought came into her mind—one which made her tremble with excitement. Suppose the weight were not lead?

Feverishly she went to work removing the thread from the broad hem. The thread was strong and resisted her efforts, but at last she managed to get a section open. She reached in and removed one of the weights. She stared at it and tears brimmed in her eyes. The weight was a golden coin! And without a doubt, the elderly Maude's dress hem was filled with them!

Now Tessa went to work even more frantically, but taking care not to attract the attention of the others. It was her good fortune that everyone shunned the bodies of those newly dead with the fever. She was herself taking a grim risk, but she could not help it!

In all, she rescued twenty golden coins and stuffed them in her own pockets. It was a small fortune the old woman had hidden in her dress, hoping to have something to take care of herself when she was finally freed. Maude had not lived to see that time. So now Tessa was the heir to the landfall!

Gratefully, she murmured a thank you to her dead friend. By using each golden coin frugally, she could have herself moved to the better part of the prison, could have her own room and decent food—and best of all, she would be able to search out Dick and look after him! She rushed to the iron door and pounded on it again until she caught the attention of one of the guards.

He came in and surveyed the old woman with annoyance. "Another one to take to the death cart," he said.

Tessa told him, "There is something else. Something good for you."

The bearded man eyed her suspiciously. "What?"

"I want to move to a room among the gentry," she said. "And I have money to pay you!"

His expression became crafty. "How much?"

She passed him a gold coin. "There'll be a second one for you when you take me out of here!"

"Where did you get this?"

"I've had it hidden away."

He eyed her greedily. "You're the one! Pretending to have nothing!"

"Well?" she asked.

"I'll look after you first," was his decision. "She can wait. The living take first place over the dead anytime!"

Tessa gave the old woman a sad farewell glance before she left with the guard. Maude had protected her in life and now was helping her after her death. The others in the ward shouted vile epithets after her as she left with the guard, suggesting she was selling him her body for a brief relief from the ward.

The room he found her was small and not too clean,

but it did have a bed of sorts, and it offered her privacy. He took the second gold coin and suggested that for a third he would provide her with good food for a fortnight. She accepted his offer.

Then she set about finding Dick in the men's section of the prison. She had to make her way along many dark corridors and pay out two more gold pieces to locate him and arrange his release. When she found him at last, she was saddened to learn he'd been stricken with the plague and was barely able to walk.

Tessa placed an arm around him and helped support him as she led him back to her room to nurse. She managed to get water and some herbs from one of the other guards, who guaranteed the herbs would help cure the plague.

Stretched out on the bed, Dick was a mere shadow of the man he had been. His big frame had hardly any flesh on it; his cheeks were hollow and the color of his skin was a horrid yellow. Tessa sat on the bed and kept fresh applications of cold bandages on his head.

He looked up at her with gratitude and affection. He had somehow found some dark cloth and made himself another eye patch to cover the empty socket of his lost eye.

He said, "I never hoped to see you again."

"I was beginning to think the same thing."

"How did you manage this?"

She gave him a small smile. "We had a good angel in the most remarkable form."

"I'm thankful to be able to die with you at my side," the once powerful man said.

"You must not talk of dying."

"How many get over the plague?"

"Some do. And I have some special herbs one of the guards sold me."

"Worthless, no doubt," the big man said as he began to shiver. "I have such chills and there is a lump under my right arm."

"The disease must run its course," she said. "But we shall fight it."

164

He studied her lovingly. "My poor Tessa. I brought a curse to you."

"No. We had a good life together!"

"Look how it has ended!" he said, his wasted face turning gloomy again.

"All London is being struck by the plague," she pointed out. "I would likely have been exposed to it in any case."

"You would not find yourself in this hellhole," he fumed.

"Don't upset yourself."

"I'm the one responsible. I started you in a life of crime."

"No, I just fell into it," she corrected him. "We shall get out of here and find ourselves that farm, with horses."

"The horses!" he exclaimed longingly. His thin yellow face showed a faint glow of happiness.

"Old Maude saved us," she said. "She had golden coins sewed in her dress hem."

"I was afraid you'd taken to selling yourself to the guards."

"Never."

"Don't, Tess," he implored her. "They are a bad lot—good deal worse than the so-called criminals on the street."

"I know," she said.

He closed his eyes and seemed to be sleeping. Leaving him to rest, when the guard came she enjoyed her first decent meal in months.

When she finished eating, she went out in the corridor, where she found a well-dressed old man who looked as if he might once have been an aristocrat. He bowed to her in the manner of the court gallants.

He said, "Your face seems familiar to me."

"Perhaps," she said. She knew that by now most of the dye had come off and she must be pale again.

"You look remarkably like a girl who used to be a member of the King's Theater Company," the old man said. He chuckled. "I understand she was the mistress of that straight-laced old fellow, Sir David Farr."

"You knew Sir David Farr?"

"I vow we were close companions at one time," the old man in the faded clothes said wistfully. "He and I used to stay at the same tavern when he was visiting in London. Then he rented a place."

"What about Sir Edward Montagu?" she asked.

A look of dislike crossed his face. "Ah, Sir Edward. He is a hard, cruel chap. He was one of those who had me put in here. I owed him and a few others a small amount of money. They took my bit of property and had me thrust into prison for bad debts."

"That is too bad."

He stared at her with rheumy eyes. "You are not the girl who lived with Sir David, are you?"

"No," Tessa said with irony, "I'm not that girl." And it was surely true, she thought, that she would never be that girl again. Life had changed her much.

"You're sure?" he asked suspiciously.

"Sure." And allowing her tongue to slip into the dialect of the streets, she went on, "Law, I wish I had been on the stage. Me and my man that I'm nursing with the fever would not have found ourselves in here! I'd have snatched onto some gent to pay me for my favors!"

The old man laughed. "I'm sure you would have. If your good husband is too ill to attend you, I'd be quite willing to have a try!"

She joined him in his laughter and nudged him in the ribs. "It's too bad he isn't that sick, for I'd swear you'd make a good job of it."

"I have been a rounder in my time," the old gent said with pride. "And should you need me, I shall rise to the occasion if possible."

"I'll remember," she said. "Just now I wish I could buy the services of a doctor."

The old gentleman shook his head. "You have no hope of finding one."

"You think not?"

"No."

"Not even for a sparkling gold coin?"

The old man said, "Not for a dozen, my dear. The

166

truth is that the doctors and the lawyers were the first to flee this plague-ridden city. The king and his crew led the way, but the gentry were not far behind him."

Tessa was angered by the idea of such irresponsibility. "Then how is the plague to be conquered? How are the sick to be saved?"

"No one cares," the old man shrugged. "You should know that, since you're in here."

"I know too well," she said bitterly.

"There is talk that if the plague gets worse, they're going to release us all. But to what purpose? We'll die out there the same way."

"No doubt," she said. Then, wishing him well, she excused herself, explaining, "I must go to my husband."

"Let me know how he is," the old man said. "You can always find me out here. I enjoy the air, what little there is of it."

"I'll remember," she said and hurried away.

So the doctors had gone and London was abandoned to the plague. This was grim news. She had heard it was bad outside but had not dreamed it could be anything like this. She wondered about Sir David, her mother, the theater company, and all the rest. Praying for the well-being of her old friends, she wished the evil Sir Edward Montagu would be stricken by the plague, but she doubted that its poison would have any effect on one so full of his own venom.

She returned to her room and found Dick still sleeping. But as she sat on the bed by him, a strange feeling surged through her—an eerie desolation. Bending to look closely at him, she felt her heart begin to pound. Dick was no longer sleeping. He was dead!

Chapter Nine

The guard arrived in short order, and Tessa's eyes filled with tears as she stood with him, staring at the body of the dead Dick Henry on the single, narrow bed. She turned to the guard and asked, "Is there any chance of a private burial?"

"None," the guard told her. "He'll go to the death cart like the rest and be burned. It's the means of controlling the plague—not that it is doing much to help."

"So I will bid him good-bye here," she said. And she turned away.

The wily guard followed her. "If you have a means of getting some more gold, there's no need for you to remain in here."

She turned to stare at him. "What are you saying?"

"Three gold coins will free you!"

"Is this some trick?" she asked suspiciously.

He shook his head. "There's talk of opening the prison and freeing everyone. I'm an ambitious man, miss. I can use those gold coins and get you out ahead of the rest."

"You are sure?"

"I swear it," he said.

"When?"

"Tonight after it is dark," the guard said. "Come to the main gate. I'll be there. My friend is on duty. I'll give him one of the coins as his share, and he'll let you out."

Tessa hesitated. "This is some sort of trick."

"No, I swear it! Upon the king's name!" He waited for her nod of assent, then said, "Be at the gate at nine."

"I'll be there."

At the door, he turned back. "And have the gold," he warned her.

"I'll have it," she said quietly.

She sat with Dick until the guard returned with a helper, and two men dragged the wasted body away to the death cart. It was the end of another period in her life.

It seemed to her that young as she was, she had already

lived many lives. First there had been the circus and her romance with Bob Wills. Where was the young acrobat now—perhaps pressed into service in the King's Navy? She had been taken from his arms fo Lady Pleasure, who intended to make a lady of her, until the deceitful Harry had seduced her and caused her quarrel with her mother. After Lady Pleasure had whipped her, Sir David Farr had taken her in his care. And she had lived a strange yet happy life with him in the house in St. James's Square. It was there she had met her true love, Thomas Montagu. But his father had come between them, and then Thomas had lost his life in battle.

At this point, Sir Edward had ordered her kidnapped and murdered. But Dick Henry, hired to take her life, had restored it to her on certain terms. And she'd liked the excitement and danger of life with Dick, even though it had finally ended in their disgrace and the ordeal of the dreadful Newgate Prison.

Now Dick was dead and she was the survivor, thanks to the old actress, Maude, whose last name Tessa had never found out. She was ready to pay for her freedom and escape Newgate. It was possible, of course, that Sir Edward Montagu might still be looking for her to have her murdered, but with London in its panic over the plague, it was likely she'd been forgotten. That was her hope and the reason she was willing to risk the outside on her own.

She had followed the elderly Maude's smart practice and sewed the remaining gold into the hem of her skirt. Now she bent and opened the skirt to remove exactly three of the shining yellow coins. Gold would buy almost anything, it seemed. She carefully sewed the hem closed again and began the wait until nine o'clock.

A few minutes before the hour she quietly left her room and made her way to the main gate of the prison. There she took a stand in the shadows. After only a few minutes the guard she knew came out of the shadows to her.

"You have the gold?" he asked.

Her reply was to give him the three coins. "They are

my last," she warned him, fearful that he might raise his price.

He gave her a sneering smile. "Of course, they would be," he said.

Then he walked away from her and was gone for a little. When he returned, he signaled her to follow him. He took her to the guard by the main door. The guard nodded to her, and she crossed to where he stood by the door. He unlocked it and opened it just a fraction and nodded again. She needed no second urging. Her heart hammering with excitement, she slipped through the narrow opening to freedom!

Once again she was on the streets of London, a free soul. She walked away from the prison district as fast as she could. When she reached a busy street some distance away from the prison gates, she was surprised at the amount of activity for so late at night. A number of families appeared to be moving. Sturdy wagons stood before several doors, and men and women were heaping them with household goods. Other wagons proceeded down the street in a somber parade.

Tessa questioned a toothless, old hag who was watching the procession from a street corner at which a torch glowed. She said, "Where are they all going?"

"Anywhere away from the city," the toothless one said.

"Is it that bad?"

The old woman grinned at her. "Where have you been, not to know?"

"I've been ill at home."

The old woman drew back from her. "With the plague?"

"No," Tessa said at once. "I had an injured leg. It is better now."

The brown-faced old woman still regarded her with some suspicion. "I'm not anxious to be near anyone who has had the plague."

"I promise you, I didn't have it," she said.

The old woman returned to watching the procession of carts. "Many of them will be struck down with the plague before they get away from the city."

170

"You think so?"

"I know it," the crone said. "I've seen most of my family go, but I don't seem to get it. I say the Good Lord knows his own."

"I trust you will continue to be blessed," Tessa murmured.

"Thank you, miss," the old woman said. "The king went to Hampton Court, then on to Salisbury, and now they say he is as far away as Oxford."

"He took the whole court with him?"

"Everyone including Nell Gwyn. We can't afford to lose our Nell."

Tessa said, "So the plays have ended."

"You may be sure of that. I hear King's Theater is abandoned and dirty as a dung heap. A sad business."

"It is," Tessa agreed. "Have you any idea where I can get respectable lodging? My husband is dead and now I am all alone."

"Die he die of the plague?" the woman drew back.

"I was not with him," Tessa said hastily.

"Oh." The old woman sounded relieved. "If it's a truly good room and bed you want, you can find it at the next corner. Place run by Isaac Cornwall, called the Hungry Pilgrim."

"Thank you," Tessa said. "I'll try there."

She left the old woman and made her way along the street, passing some carousing fellows who were far in their cups and arguing loudly. Torches burned in many doorways and in courtyards, since it was assumed that fire would help keep down the plague. She moved along as quickly as she could, hoping not to attract attention. She doubted that Sir Edward's thugs were still on the lookout for her. They would probably have decided that she had long since died. But she was very much alive, as was her determination for revenge. She looked forward to the opportunity of settling the score with the cruel nobleman.

The tavern room was crowded, but the room behind it was empty, and there she found the bald proprietor of the Hungry Pilgrim, Isaac Cornwall. He had a face the shape of an egg, and his bald pate made the resemblance stronger. His eyes were small but keen, and he wore a perpetually gloomy expression.

Tessa went up to where the dejected man sat on a high stool behind a desk. Putting on her best manner, she told him, "I'm a poor soul who has lost her husband and wish to find a decent lodging place. Are you the owner?"

"The sole owner," he said, "since my wife and two boys have been lost to the plague."

"My sympathies, sir," she said at once.

He frowned at her. "You look and speak like one of the gentry, not a common woman."

"If I were one of the gentry, I would be far from London in some village haven."

The bald man considered this. "That's logical."

"Can you offer me a room? I can pay."

"I'm not worried about the money," Cornwall sighed. "The way things are, I may be dead myself in a few days. Have you thought of that?"

"I think of it constantly."

He raised a pudgy hand as if in benediction over her. "You must make your peace with the Lord."

"I have," she said.

"It all comes from the looseness of Charles the Second and his court! He and his pestilent theater actors! They are the ones to blame!"

Tessa felt she should agree emphatically. "A pox on all of them!" she vowed.

The bald man blinked. "You are a smart girl."

"Thank you. And about the room?"

"You can have your pick of the second floor; it's almost empty. In return, I'll expect you to help with the beds of the other guests and work part of the time in the kitchen. You get your room and all you can eat."

"It is a fine bargain," she said.

He sighed. "I'm driven to it. My last maid left today and cook has no helper."

She said, "I can't believe that London has come to this. Everyone is fleeing!"

"We haven't had such a plague for sixteen years," the

tavern owner said. "It's been bad on the Continent, and I expect it came over on the ships."

"It began at the docks?"

"At the docks," he nodded. "Always a rat- and flea-infested spot. Now it's spread out everywhere in the city."

Tessa said, "It appears to strike young and old, rich and poor."

"Walk along the street and see the poor devils stagger and fall. At first it's just dizziness and blinding headaches. Then the swellings come."

"That's the bad sign."

"I swear some give up at the mere sight of the swelling," the bald man said. "They tried to lock and guard this place when my wife and boys got sick, but I fought them. They threatened to come back, but they didn't—too busy putting red cross marks on other doors."

Again explaining that she had been indoors for some time because of her injury she asked, "Is that the warning sign, a red cross on the door of houses where there have been deaths of the plague?"

"Aye," the man on the stool said. "The red cross and the words, 'Lord Have Mercy upon us!' "

"And the king has gone and all the theaters are closed?"

"All of them," the bald man said with disgust. "I wish they'd been closed long ago."

"You have a poor opinion of playactors," she said.

He scowled. "I'm a religious man. They are disgusting in the eyes of our Lord."

"I had not heard," she said with mock innocence. "No matter. I shall up to bed and be at work in the kitchen in the morning!"

And so she began her stay at the Hungry Pilgrim in plague-infested London. Business at the inn was poor, and the cook was deaf, so Tessa had only the proprietor to chat with. And Isaac Cornwall had spells of melancholy when he simply stared ahead of him and would not make a reply to anything.

From conversation with guests Tessa learned that in this hottest summer in years, on many streets there was

173

hardly a door without a red cross. This most fearful of diseases was striking England on a hideous scale. In the first week there were a hundred deaths, the next brought seven hundred, and now the corpses were rising in piles of a thousand a day!

London stank with death. Church bells tolled, and the mournful cry of the men with the death carts—'Bring out your dead!'—rang through the streets. At night gangs shoveled the corpses into open graves. The gravediggers were kept drunk out of their senses so they would risk this dangerous task. Tessa listened to frightened men downing their ale and indulging in all manner of wild rumors. Some poor fools, hearing that syphilis would make a man immune to the plague, raced to the brothels to try and get infected—and many did, catching syphilis and the plague as well. When it was suggested that the plague could be burned out of the air, for several sweltering days bonfires blazed in every street.

It was a time of fear and madness. Outside districts were refusing to accept fugitives from London whenever they could. The first to leave the stricken city had been the higher clergy and physicians; then anyone who could afford to had fled. Still life went on in the beleaguered city. People ate and slept, drank and worked; they went to brothels as well as to church. The beer gardens were busy and so were the cock fights. The streets were unlit save for torches, and footpads lurked frequently in the passageways. The ugly sewers ran along the middle of the streets and overflowed when it rained. Since there were no public lavatories, people relieved themselves in the street. The backyard industries of the brewers went on polluting the disease-ridden air, as did the horrid smoke of soap-boilers and dyers.

The work at the inn was light and Tessa found it difficult to fill in her spare time. It was this that led her to seek work with the good nuns who ran a hospital in an old warehouse down the street from the inn. The nuns welcomed her aid, and because she learned quickly, Tessa was soon one of their valued helpers.

It was here she took care of a young man who had

174

been a page for Sir Edward Montagu and who was miraculously recovering from the plague.

When the young man was well enough to talk, she asked him about the Montagu family. "Are they still in the city?" she wanted to know.

A wry smile trembled on his emaciated face. "Not likely," he said. "Sir Edward was one of the first to run off. He left us behind to look after his house and the fine things in it."

"Did he take none of his servants with him?"

"Only two or three," the youth said with some anger. "He cares for no one but himself."

"Where is he?"

"In his country place near Hampton Court. He and his wife and his son Claude. The other son, Thomas, was lost at sea."

"I know," Tessa said quietly. "What is his wife like?"

The youth shifted uncomfortably on the makeshift bed on the wooden floor of the warehouse. "She's a quiet woman, afraid of him. And the son Claude is like his father—or maybe worse."

"A cruel man."

"He is, even though he may be my master," the youth agreed.

"Are you going back to work for him?"

"Not if I can find anything else."

She smiled at the lad. "You'll be able to find something better when you are well. There's a shortage of strong young men."

"You've been most kind to me, miss," the youth said. "Like an angel."

She rose to leave him. "I fear I'm a far cry from an angel, but I try to do what I can."

Later, when she and the Mother Superior were sitting through a night watch in the ward of the dangerously sick, the bland-faced old woman turned to her and said with a smile, "You know you are a mystery to all of us, Tessa."

She raised her eyebrows. "A mystery?"

"You speak so well, you must be one of the gentry,"

the Mother Superior explained. "And yet you have not fled. You are still here."

"I feel I'm needed here."

"You are," the older woman agreed. "But we know so little about you. You are so lovely both in face and in spirit that you have been an inspiration to all of us."

Tessa smiled gently at the kindly woman in her nun's robes. She said, "You and your sisters are the ones who have done the great work."

"We are dedicated to God," the Mother Superior said. "It is our sole purpose in life to do good where we may. But you have made no vow of this sort. You are free. You could turn your back on the suffering."

"I have seen life from many points of view, Mother," Tessa said.

"I'm sure you have."

"I have seen humans at their best and at their worst. I have known degeneracy and filth which you wouldn't understand. I have seen wanton women stalking about in their nakedness and no one bothering to glance at them. I have seen eyes clawed out for valueless trinkets!"

The Mother Superior crossed herself. "God bless us! What evil there is in this world!"

"And at the same time so much good," Tessa said with deep sincerity. "I was attracted to working with you because of your good and the calm radiated by your peaceful souls. I feel as close to God here as ever I have been."

"Bless you!" the old woman said. "And may He spare you any more evil."

Tessa smiled wryly. "I would like to think that is possible, but I doubt it. I am only thankful for my health as this plague goes on!"

"Amen!" the Mother Superior said.

When Tessa reported to the warehouse the following day, she routinely visited all the new cases. Her mouth gaped open when one of those on the rough beds on the floor turned out to be an emaciated Sir Julian Dorley. The old fop had been struck down by the plague!

"Sir Julian!" she said, kneeling by him.

He opened his eyes and stared at her in dull fashion as he murmured, "Who does me homage?"

"Sir Julian, don't you know me?" she exclaimed. "It is Tessa, the little ponyback rider!"

The yellow, hollow-cheeked face took on a brighter look, and he showed recognition in his eyes. "Tessa! Tessa of the circus!"

"Yes."

"You look older," he said abruptly.

"I am older."

"But you are as lovely as ever, a better beauty now. It has bloomed more," the old gallant managed.

"You still have a magic with your tongue," she said.

"Fie on you," he said wearily. "I have about run my course."

"You must not talk like that," she said. "If your case can be helped, the nuns will cure you."

"Are you one of them? Have you joined the Church?"

"No," she said. "I'm only a helper."

He had a fit of nausea and she helped him through it. The beads of perspiration stood out on his yellowed forehead. He was truly far gone in his illness, and Tessa knew there could be very little hope for his recovery.

When he felt a little better, he gripped her by the wrist and in a feverish voice said, "Tessa!"

"Yes."

"Fever struck hard at Wilton. Your mother is dead. Lady Pleasure was the first to go."

"I shall pray for her," she said in a small voice, though she found it hard to summon any feeling of sadness for the wanton, cruel woman who had been her maternal parent.

The fop's jaundiced eyes fixed on her. "You hated her?"

"I did once. It doesn't matter now."

"She lives in you, remember that. Guide yourself well!"

Tessa's cheeks burned with this reminder of her passionate nature. Yes, she had inherited that from Lady Pleasure. She knew it too well. But she was trying to direct her passion into decent channels. She hoped that she would be able to manage this and would never end a wanton, as her mother surely had.

She asked, "What of the others?"

Sir Julian hesitated and then said sadly, "Sir David was the next to go."

Her lovely eyes filled with tears. "He was the kindest man I have ever known."

"He was your lover, girl!" Sir Julian said with a touch of his old self. "How Lady Pleasure hated that!"

"I'm sure," she said, willing to keep Sir David's secret. She was sure he would not have wanted Sir Julian to know the truth, not even on his deathbed.

"Well, that was a while ago," Sir Julian said, reverting to his weak manner.

"Yes, it was."

"Sir David was never the same after he left you. He was an old, sad man. And when death came, I think he welcomed it."

"It is sad news."

"Lady Eve and her children escaped the plague, and so did Lord Harry. He is here in London now. I came with him. I was stricken down while we were supping together, and he had me sent here."

"Why did he leave Wilton and his wife and children to be here now, of all times?" she asked.

Sir Julian winked. "Estate business, for one thing. More importantly, he has a mistress in Pall Mall, the wife of an old nobleman who refused to move from London. She is terrified and she begged her lover, Harry, to come here and be with her for a spell."

Tessa shook her head. "So he has not changed."

"He reaches out for any wench who shows interest," Sir Julian said. "You know!"

"I know very well," she said grimly. "My one experience with rape was his doing."

"You mustn't hold his nature against him," Sir Julian begged. "Harry can be a jolly companion. He should have come to inquire about my health, but I vow he's probably too busy bedding the wife of the Duke of Winchester."

178

"First things first with our Harry," Tessa said with sarcasm.

Sir Julian had another coughing spell and a fit of pain. He came through it gasping and with a look of fear in his eyes. He said, "I shall soon go."

"You must fight for your health!"

"No strength left," the old fop said. "I have done evilly by you, lass. I sided with Lady Pleasure against you, and with Harry! But damn him, he hasn't come to me! And so I will tell you something of value."

"What?"

"Go to Grimp & Wellwood, Solicitors, in Hampden Lane," he gasped. "Ask to talk with Mr. Grimp. He will have something to tell you."

"Are you jesting?" she asked, puzzled by it all.

"No, never was I more serious," Sir Julian said in a weak voice. "Do not forget the name or the address. I doubt that I will be here long to repeat it for you."

"You will get better," she consoled him. "And I shall come regularly to attend to you."

"Good girl!" Sir Julian said with a weak smile. "Sir David must have known much happiness with you."

She left him at this point, for she had to return to the tavern. The owner had taken a fancy to her and was much more friendly now. Besides she needed this refuge away from the hospital; the work there was heavy, and she inevitably returned home to bed in a weary state.

The egg-faced man was at his desk to greet her. "How did it go at the hospital today?"

She sighed. "There is no slackening of cases."

"And the nuns worked you as hard as ever?"

"No, I work of my own wish. All of them work until they are ready to drop, and then sit with the sick all night. I come here and take my rest."

"And so you should," Isaac Cornwall said. "You do not want to lose your bonny looks, not at your age."

"I don't think much about my appearance these days," she said.

"You should always do that, plague or no plague. A

179

woman's beauty is her gift from the Good Lord. One mustn't squander it."

She smiled in a weary fashion. "I'll try to remember that."

"The cool weather will come, and then the plague will end," the bald man predicted.

"What a blessing if that should happen."

"It always has in the past," he assured her. "I remember that was the way last time . . . though it wasn't nearly as bad as this in the first place."

She said, "I learned today that my mother and my stepfather have both died of the disease. I have no one left."

"I'm sorry, lass," the proprietor of the inn said with sympathy. "I know how it is. I had my own losses."

"So you did."

"When it's close to you, it truly hurts," he observed.

"My stepfather was one of the best men who ever lived," she grieved. "I shall always think of him that way."

"A good memorial, if I may say so," the bald man observed. "You might say his virtue is engraved on your heart."

"You have said it very nicely. Now I must say good night. I have to be at the hospital early."

"Mind you finish the beds first," he called after her.

She did not sleep for some time that night. Her thoughts were of Wilton and all that had happened there. She went over the various incidents in her mind. From what Sir Julian had said, Harry was the same rogue as when she'd been his innocent prey. Inheriting the title and the estate, being a husband and father—nothing had made any difference in him. It was he who had set her life on its strange course. She did not know whether she should curse him or thank him.

After a long while she slept and had dreams of the good days with Sir David in St. James's Square and her many happy experiences as a member of the King's Theater Company. She awoke in the morning wondering about Nell Gwyn and Charles Hart. What had happened

180

to them? She decided that at her first opportunity she would stop by the theater area and see if she could learn anything about them. She'd last heard they were at Oxford with the king.

When she returned to the hospital in the morning, she went directly to Sir Julian Dorley's bed, but it was now occupied by a younger man. She knew Sir Julian must have died, but she went to the Mother Superior for confirmation of this.

"What about the old man, Sir Julian?" she asked.

The Mother Superior smiled sadly. "The Lord took him last night. He died most peacefully, though he did ask for you before he died. He said, 'Where is Tessa?' "

"I wish I could have been here."

"I know," the Mother Superior said. "I told him you would be along soon. And then he murmured something about your not forgetting someone. I think the name was Grimp."

Tessa said, "He spoke that name to me yesterday. Strange that it should be on his lips at the end."

"It was the last thing he said," the Mother Superior told her. "After that he slipped into a coma and died."

"I knew him long ago," Tessa said. "Or at least it seems long ago."

The older woman nodded. "This year of the plague has been like ten!"

The next day Tessa took some time away from the hospital. The air was fresher, reminding her of the innkeeper's prediction about the cold weather cutting down on the plague cases. And coincidence or no, there were fewer new patients that morning. So she took the opportunity to search out Hampden Lane and the firm of Grimp and Wellwood. It was a commecial street near the middle of the city, and the doors on both sides of it had their share of red crosses.

She found the black and white sign of the solicitor's firm above a street-level door beside a many-paned bow window. As she opened the door and went in, a bell above the door rang and announced her. From a door in

181

the rear of the small office a bent old man with white hair appeared.

He glared at her and snapped, "What is your business?"

"Is this Grimp and Wellwood?" she asked needlessly. The sign had proclaimed the fact, but she was reaching for something to say.

"Wellwood died of the plague," the old clerk said, as if it were her fault.

"Then I'd like to see Mr. Grimp."

The sour clerk hesitated. "He is a busy man."

"My business is important," she said.

"What is your name?"

"Tell him Miss Tessa Shaw has called to see him. I was the daughter of Lady Pleasure Farr."

This seemed to impress the old fellow. He gave her a quick, interested look. Then saying, "One minute!" he darted back out of the doorway, leaving her alone.

It was not two minutes later that a giant of a man came out to extend a fat hand to her. This was Mr. Grimp, all friendship and warm heart. His many-chinned face and large stomach let the world know that this amiable fellow enjoyed his food and drink. He had a deep voice and wore an old-fashioned white wig.

"My dear Miss Shaw," he boomed. "I have been undertaking a search for you."

"For me?" she said in bewilderment.

"Did you not know?" he asked, raising his eyebrows. "What else could have brought you here?"

She said, "Your name and address was given to me by Sir Julian Dorley."

The fat man chuckled, his velvet jacket of brown and his ruffled shirt quivering with his mirth. "A charming old fop!"

"Yes," she said. "He died yesterday at the nun's hospital."

The fat man showed distress. "The plague?"

"Yes."

"Dreadful business!" Mr. Grimp said. "I lost Wellwood, you know—my friend and partner for twenty-five years. Dropped down with dizziness in this very room. They carried him off, and he was gone in a week."

"I know it is terrible," she agreed. "I understand my mother and Sir David Farr both lost their lives to it."

"Some time ago," the stout man said. "Have you only just heard?"

"It was Sir Julian told me before he died. And he seemed to think it important I see you."

The stout man touched a finger to the side of his nose in a significant gesture. "My dear young woman, you can be sure that it is. Do come and sit down." And he took her into his inner office, which was more richly furnished. They both sat in comfortable chairs. Mr. Grimp's had apparently been made for him especially. It was as wide as two chairs, and he filled it completely.

In a confidential tone he leaned forward, his hands crossed on his great stomach, and said, "My search for you has been a trifle complicated by Lord Harry Farr, who suggested that I give it up. He maintained it was a bad waste of time—insisted you were dead."

She was shocked and annoyed. "What could make him think that?"

The stout man raised his eyebrows. "He is a most strong-minded young man," he said in his deep voice. "He is stubborn and determined. He claimed that you must be dead since he had made an exhaustive search for you and you were not to be found."

"Fie on him," she exclaimed. "The most urgent search he will have made is for the bedchamber of the Duchess of Winchester. I'm given to understand he pleasures her more frequently than does the Duke, her husband."

Mr. Grimp's mouth gaped open but he showed surprise in no other way; rather, he said placidly, "That may surely be possible."

"I'm alive and here thanks to Sir Julian," she said. "Now, why were you searching for me?"

"It should be obvious. The usual reason."

"And what is the usual reason?"

The big man beamed with good news. "You have been left a legacy, my dear."

"A legacy?" she gasped.

"Correct," he said. "Only in the event of your being dead is the money to revert to Lord Harry and the estate. I assume that is why he was not anxious to find you and was quick to pronounce you dead."

Anger rose up in her. So Harry had wanted to do her out of her legacy! And he might very well have had his way, but for Sir Julian Dorley. The old fop had been her friend at the last. No one could question that.

She said, "Well, I'm sorry to disappoint Lord Harry, but I'm very much alive."

"And at once a wealthy young woman," Mr. Grimp said happily.

"Who was my benefactor."

"Your stepfather left you twenty-five thousand pounds free and clear. I have the money in safekeeping, and you may draw on it at will."

She sat there stunned. Without expecting it or even wanting it, good fortune had come her way. She was a wealthy woman. She could live in whatever fashion she liked and do as she pleased. Then a sadness crept over her. Was it so important? She had lost the man she truly loved, and the other men who had meant so much to her were also dead. How cruel fate could be!

The old lawyer must have noticed her change of mood. He asked, "Why should the news sadden you?"

"I'm sorry," she said. "I did not mean to seem ungrateful. It is a most wonderful gift. My stepfather was too kind."

"Money is a blessing, if used properly," the fat man said. "Sir David wanted to protect your future."

"That is difficult to do in these days of plague," she said. "When you see Lord Harry again, you will tell him I have come and claimed my fortune. I wish I could be here to enjoy his look of disappointment."

The fat man's eyes held a twinkle in them. "I shall be pleased to inform him."

She said, "I would like twenty pounds for myself. And would you send a hundred pounds to the Mother Superior at the hospital in the warehouse by the docks?"

The fat man said, "You're sure you're not being too generous?"

"No," she said. "They need it."

"Shall I inform them you are the donor of this generous gift?" Mr. Grimp wanted to know.

She shook her head. "No. Say it is from one interested in their work."

"Very well," the big man said. "It shall be done within the hour."

She rose, saying, "I would like to retain you as my solicitor, Mr. Grimp. No doubt we will see much of each other."

"My very great pleasure," the big man with the white wig said.

He saw her all the way to the street. She left him with her head literally floating. It had been so unexpected. She was financially well-off. She need not worry for the rest of her life—but what was she to do with the balance of her days? A hard expression crossed her face as she remembered Sir Edward. She surely had to settle her debt with him. Where had the lad said he'd gone? She thought it was Hampton Court. Never mind, it would not be too hard to discover. She walked on more quickly, thinking how strange it was that revenge should suddenly give her a purpose in living, but glad: It was better than no purpose.

When she arrived at the hospital the next day, the Mother Superior was in a state of rejoicing. The old woman said, "The Lord heard our prayers and moved someone to send us a most generous gift."

"I'm so happy," Tessa smiled.

The old woman beamed at her. "I declare, you have brought us good luck, my dear. It seems to me things have gone better for us ever since you came to help."

"That cannot be true," she demurred. "I actually do very little here."

"Your youth and beauty are an inspiration to our patients and the sisters alike," the Mother Superior countered. "I have said special prayers for you every morning."

"Then I feel repaid for anything I've done."

The Mother Superior sighed, then said, "Each day we get fewer patients. I do believe that the plague is abating."

"The signs seem to suggest it," Tessa agreed.

"There will still be some lingering cases," the older woman went on, "but I expect the worst is over."

Tessa smiled grimly. "Perhaps the king and his court will find the courage to return."

"Perhaps." The old nun paused before saying mildly, "Although the king is not a Catholic, I cannot condemn him, despite his excesses. He has a kind heart and has done much for the poor."

"There is still so much more to do." Tessa's tone was bitter. "I have lived among them. I know."

The Mother Superior gave her a kindly smile. "Still our lady of mystery. Never mind! Keep your secrets, my dear."

Tessa spent the day in the hospital. She was on her way home to the inn when she was confronted by a richly dressed young man standing in the street by the door of the warehouse. There was a sly smile on his florid face, and he had put on some weight, but there was no mistaking the handsome Lord Harry Farr.

"I have been waiting for you," he said.

Chapter Ten

Tessa could not help being amazed at the coarsening of the young man in the few years since she had last seen him. His complexion was more florid; he had an inclination to overweight, and there were subtle signs of aging in the handsome face.

She looked at him boldly and asked, "Did you come to make certain I was alive?"

Lord Harry laughed with some embarrassment. "Come now, Tessa, that is no way to greet a good friend."

"I fear I do not think of you as a friend," she replied.

In his fawn coat, dark brown breeches and matching brown plumed hat, he was dressed as elegantly as if there was no plague and London not in a panic of fear. He continued to study her good-naturedly.

He said, "It is true. Mr. Grimp told me where I might find you."

"So?"

"You were most generous with the good sisters. I commend your warm nature."

"Perhaps you would care to follow suit and give them a donation yourself," she said dryly.

He shook his head. "No, I do not wish to get the reputation of being friendly towards Papists. They are not in fashion these days."

"Goodness and charity are always in fashion," Tessa responded sharply. "And you will find nothing but that in there." She indicated the warehouse that had been converted into a hospital.

"I will not labor the point," Lord Harry said. "It is you I wished to see and talk with."

Tessa smiled bleakly. "I must be an unwelcome sight for you since, I am told, my being alive has cost you so many thousand pounds."

He shrugged. "There is plenty left."

"I'm glad to hear it. I'm also pleased to know your wife and children have been spared the plague."

"Yes, after the deaths of your mother and my father, we were hit only in the servants' quarters."

Tessa gave him a direct look. "Did you know Sir Julian Dorley is dead?"

The handsome, young man appeared upset for the first time. "I wondered where he was! So the plague reached him."

"You knew that full well," she objected. "And you knew he was brought here to the hospital. He fretted that you did not care enough to come and see him."

"The matter had passed entirely out of my mind until you spoke of him just now," Sir Harry alibied lamely.

Her smile was ironic. "Sir Julian mentioned that you might have been so busy warming the Duchess of Winchester's bed that you couldn't spare time for a dying friend."

The handsome man's face crimsoned. "Did he say that?"

"Something of the sort."

"Silly old fop! He should have minded his own business!"

Tessa looked away. Keeping her voice calm and cold, she said, "He died in the hospital. I was with him. So he will bother you no more."

Lord Harry said uncomfortably, "Let us get away from here. I know a decent place for eating and drinking in Westminster. It is one of the few such places remaining open. I have rooms above the dining room."

She expected to refuse him, but the prospect of a quick meal in the company of a gentleman exerted a strong attraction. It had been a terrible summer and it was ending. Before she could examine her emotions with regard to Harry, she had agreed to go.

They strolled along the smelly, plague-ridden streets arm-in-arm until he was able to get a hackney cab to take them to the Harp and Ball. It was only a short drive, and Sir Harry regaled her along the way with stories about his life in the country. She said little.

The Harp and Ball was like an oasis in the stricken city. Everything seemed to be much as usual there. A goodly number of the gentry were on view, dining and drinking. It was obviously a spot catering to the few of the wealthier classes who still remained in the city despite the danger.

Lord Harry was known, and they were taken to a good table with a candle flickering on it. They had barely sat down when a plump man jumped up from a table where he had been seated alone and came over to greet her. It took only a glance at the round face and the bulging eyes to know that it was none other than Mr. Samuel Pepys of the Admiralty.

"Heaven be praised," the little man exclaimed with a smile. "You have been spared, Tessa."

"And you as well," she said. "You know Lord Harry."

Pepys bowed to Lord Harry, who had risen. "We have met several times," he said. Then he went on in his gossipy way, "You know that the king is at Oxford and Nell there with him."

"I had heard rumors of this," she said.

"The last I heard, Nell was well and living discreetly in a tavern near the king's quarters. Charles Hart is also there; 'tis said he is doing some sketches with her to entertain the court. I had this news from John Dryden, who has visited there."

"I'm glad that Nell and Charles Hart are in good health," Tessa said. "So you remain in London?"

"I do," the stout man said. "I'm almost alone at the Admiralty, and the Duke of Albemarle is in sole charge."

"What about your wife?"

"I arranged for her to be evacuated to Woolrich when the navy office was moved there. She is well, though worried about me. Of course, since I'm the sole clerk left with the Admiralty here, I cannot desert my post."

"That is most commendable in you."

Samuel Pepys round face showed pleasure at this compliment. "Thank you," he said. "I am more than happy to see you alive and well. The last I heard was that you had vanished from your house in St. James's Square. It was said you were the victim of thugs who had robbed you and thrown your body in the river."

"I know some believed that," Tessa said evasively.

"Nell and the others were shocked by your disappearance," Samuel Pepys said. "They will be delighted to know you are alive."

Lord Harry smiled and said, "We are all pleased that she still lives."

"Most surely," Pepys said, missing the irony in Lord Harry's private joke.

"I made a hasty trip to the country for a time," Tessa said by way of explanation.

"You ought to have stayed there," Samuel Pepys advised her. "London is a cesspool of death these days."

"I know. For some weeks I have been helping nurse the sick with the good sisters at the hospital on the riverbank."

"What a splendid woman you are!" Samuel Pepys exclaimed. "And your beauty is more pleasing than ever. I trust good times will return, with the King's Theater open again and you again on its stage."

"It is too soon to predict that," she said.

"Well, we must hope," the stout man said firmly. "I shall not intrude on you longer—but I must put a note about our meeting in my diary tonight."

She smiled. "You are still faithfully keeping your journal?"

Samuel Pepys nodded. "You might say it has become one of my modest vices." He bowed again and returned to his table and the fine plate of mutton which awaited him.

Lord Harry sat down and gave her an interested look. "I did not know you were a friend of Pepys."

"I met many people of fashion while at the theater."

"My father claimed you were a good actress."

"I'm sure he was prejudiced," she said.

"No doubt," Lord Harry said flippantly. "You made poor Pepys uneasy when you inquired about his wife. The fact is, he is sleeping with one of the barmaids here. She has been his mistress for weeks."

"Pepys always appeared a pious man," she said, surprised.

"Not all that pious," Lord Harry responded. "I have

190

heard that he has given up many of his straitlaced views, and now that he has almost full power at the Admiralty, they say he has been filling his pockets with payments for arranging contracts."

She gasped. "And he used to lament such goings-on!"

"I fear complete power has corrupted him as it is wont to do with most," Lord Harry said with smiling satisfaction.

He ordered food and drink for them. Tessa noticed that Samuel Pepys soon left the dining room, no doubt for an assignation with his barmaid somewhere upstairs.

As the meal progressed, Lord Harry became more talkative. The wine was loosening his tongue. He smiled at Tessa across the table and said, "My father did well by you! You must have been a most satisfactory mistress!"

"You may think what you like."

"I found you eminently entertaining on our one occasion."

"I remember it as a painful experience," she returned.

"Your mother was a shrew," Lord Harry complained. "She had to punish you unduly to cover her own wanton behavior."

Tessa gave him a scornful glance. "You ran from the scene quickly enough and did little to help me."

Lord Harry showed no sign of remorse for his actions. He said, "That was a long while ago."

"It is like yesterday to me," she said.

"You are vindictive. That is not seemly after my father was so generous with you."

"The generosity was his, not yours," she pointed out.

The elegantly clad nobleman shrugged; then he leaned across the table and covered one of her hands with his own. "Surely we can become friends. It would be better for us both."

"I cannot see what I would gain," she said coolly, removing her hand. "Does your wife know of your present commitment to the Duchess of Winchester, or is she like the unhappy cuckolded duke, in ignorance of the affair?"

Lord Harry crimsoned. "I vow Sir Julian must have

191

talked out of turn. He was always too ready to gossip. No doubt at this very moment he is carrying tales in hell!"

"He is beyond the venom of your words," she said.

"For a good-looking wench, you were always cold and difficult," the young nobleman said with some anger. "I do not know why I sought out your company."

"Nor do I," she said. "And if you find yourself wearying of me, I suggest we leave here."

"An excellent idea," he said, still angry.

He paid his bill and they left the inn. Fortunately, they were able to find a hackney cab almost at once. Lord Harry sat beside her in sullen silence all during the journey back to the Hungry Pilgrim.

He descended from the carriage with Tessa and saw her to the door of the tavern where she made her home. He said, "I shall be leaving for Wilton tomorrow. It is not likely I shall see you again."

"Give my regards to your Lady Eve," she said. "And what of Mary?"

"She has returned to Wilton and is living with us. Her husband was a victim of the plague. She plans to remain at the castle and bring up her two children there."

"Give her my love," Tessa said. "I was always fond of Mary."

"Yes," Lord Harry said rather coldly. "I seem to remember that. Good luck in your ventures. At least my father has given you monetary independence." He bowed stiffly and walked back towards the cab to take it back to the Harp and Ball.

Tessa stood in the doorway watching after him for a moment. Then she drew in her breath sharply. He hesitated and swayed just a few feet from the carriage and all at once collapsed in the road. The driver, who had been standing with the cab door open, stared at the fallen man in consternation.

"God forbid!" the driver cried. "I declare, he's been taken by the plague!"

Tessa rushed forward to where the fallen Lord Harry still lay on the cobblestones. "No, I think it is only the spirits he had at dinner. He drank a good deal!"

192

"It is the plague," the hackney-cab driver vowed, still standing away.

Tessa examined Lord Harry closely and was stunned to discover that he was unconscious and perspiring profusely. From her wide experience in caring for plague victims, she knew at once that the driver was right. Harry's luck had run out. He was suffering from the dread disease.

She glanced up and asked, "Help me get him inside."

"No!" the driver said in panic. "No, I'll have nothing to do with him!" And he leaped up onto his carriage and drove off at a wild rate.

Tessa returned to looking after the fallen man. Without success she tried to rouse him out of the coma into which he'd sunk. In a few minutes, however, she saw two men come weaving out of the tavern, singing drunkenly.

She at once went to them and pleaded, "My friend is overcome with spirits. Will you help me get him up to my room?"

One drunken man winked at the other and swaying, told her, "For a lovely like you, no favor is too great!"

And much to her relief the two took Harry by the feet and by the shoulders and carried him inside and up the stairs. Tessa guided them to her room and had them put him on her bed.

The talkative drunk stood smiling and swaying before her, saying, "He ain't going to be much use to you for awhile, lass. Why not sell your favors to my friend and me?"

Desperate to be rid of them, she put her finger to her lips. "Fie on you both for such a suggestion! This man is my husband!"

"Her husband!" the first drunk guffawed, and the other joined in snorting and chuckling. But not really intending to make trouble, they both left her and stumbled down the stairs, coughing with noisy laughter. She was loosening Harry's collar when she heard a familiar heavy footstep on the stairs.

She turned and saw the angry face of the bald innkeeper. She said, "It's all right. This is an old friend of mine, a member of the aristocracy."

"I care not if it is the king himself," Cornwall cried. "This fellow has the plague, and you have brought him into my place."

"I'll look after him," Tessa said. "He'll be in this room all the while. It makes the inn no more dangerous."

"I'll lose the few I have here if they find out!"

"They needn't," she said. "No one has to know he is in here with me—unless you tell them."

"It's not right!" he continued to protest.

"It's his one hope of living," she said. "I can nurse him, and I have a supply of the healing herbs used by the sisters."

"What about the risk to you?" he demanded.

"If I'm willing to risk it, you should not worry."

The bald man stood there uncertainly, mumbling, "It's not fair!" After a little he turned and went back down the stairs.

Tessa gave a deep sigh of relief, knowing she had won the battle; then she went back to tending Harry, who was now breathing heavily. It took her a while to undress him and make him as comfortable as possible in her bed. Finally she placed a cold-water pad of cloth to his head and sat down to await the next development of the disease.

As she sat staring at him, she noted that his condition was growing continually worse. She realized she could have left him in the street. He would have died out there without treatment and no one need have known. But she had known, and so she'd done what she could for him.

Not that she might expect any thanks from the arrogant and selfish Harry. He had shown little such gratitude to anyone in the past, there was no reason to expect anything different from him now. Nonetheless, she meant to try and save him. After all, she had been doing that for strangers at the hospital.

For several days Harry threshed on the bed, his fever pitifully high. He raved aloud in his pain as a huge boil swelled up in his groin, pleading for his duchess, and rag-

194

ing at his poor wife before his mumblings became incoherent.

When he was at the worst point of his illness, Tessa sent a message to Mr. Grimp. A short while later that tremendously fat worthy appeared downstairs in the inn. He declined to go up to the room. He was determined to find out Harry's chances without being near him. Having been carried this message by the distraught innkeeper, Tessa washed thoroughly and came downstairs.

The solicitor met her in the lobby of the tavern, saying worriedly, "This is most distressing! What would you say his chances are?"

"No more than even," she replied grimly.

"Good Heavens!" the fat man exclaimed. "And he was well enough the last time he was in my office."

"That was a few days ago," she pointed out. "The plague hits one suddenly."

"All too true!" Mr. Grimp assented. "I know it is best to leave him in your care."

"Whatever my personal feelings towards him, I must do all I can to make him well."

"Most generous of you," the fat man said.

"Not at all. It is my duty as a fellow human."

Mr. Grimp frowned. "I expect his wife ought to be told."

"I expect so," Tessa agreed.

"I shall send a message this day."

"All right." Then she added, "If I have need of money, I will let you know."

"Send a messenger to my office," the solicitor said. "I shall also keep in close touch with you. I thought the plague was on the wane."

She made a helpless gesture. "Most people believe it to be, but there are bound to be some scattered cases in the wake of the disaster."

"And Lord Harry is one of them." With a knowing glance, the solicitor added, "I wonder how it goes with the Duchess of Winchester."

"Perhaps she may be lucky," Tessa said.

Now there began a period when Tessa had little rest

day or night. She made a bed on the floor of the room and was there whenever Harry needed her. As he grew more desperately ill, she despaired of his life. And meanwhile, day after day, the innkeeper strongly demanded that she remove her patient from the premises.

She was firm in her stand to keep him there. "He is not ready for the death cart yet," she told the bald man.

He said accusingly, "You brought him here without my permission and you have kept him here! It is not fair!"

"He is past the crisis," she said on impulse. "He is improving."

"I do not believe that," Cornwall said grumpily.

"You will see," she insisted.

Though she did not believe it herself, her prediction turned out to be true. After one dreadful night when it seemed Harry would go mad from pain, just before dawn the fever broke and impossibly he began to mend. Tessa had seen enough cases in the hospital to know that now he would be all right.

When he was able to talk, he said weakly, "You have been kinder to me than I deserve."

"I have done as much for strangers," she said, standing by his bedside.

"I am less than a stranger," he sighed, closing his eyes. "I have been your enemy."

"Let us talk no more about such things. Save your strength for your recovery."

A few days later, when he was stronger, he asked, "Would you return to Wilton with me, Tessa?"

She was surprised. "Return to Wilton with you? Whatever gave you such an idea?"

He looked up at her earnestly. "I love you, Tessa. I always have."

She smiled wryly. "Of course you have. That is why you ran from me and married Lady Eve."

"I was wrong and I admit it. I was a coward, but no one matched you in my heart."

"That is most complimentary," she said. "But it is too late for us."

196

"Why? You have no one. Your beloved, Thomas Montagu, was drowned at sea."

"You knew about that?"

"My father told me you were in love with Thomas Montagu," Lord Harry said. "I believed that is why Father stepped out of your life and came back home."

"What else did he tell you?"

"Nothing," Harry said. "He spoke little of you, though always with affection."

"He was the finest man I have ever known."

"I can try to be like him," the man in the bed insisted. "Give me the opportunity. Let me try to build my life over in his model."

"What about the Duchess of Winchester?"

"Fie on her," Lord Harry said. "She is a bawd with a title. I hope never to see her again."

Tessa stared at him thoughtfully. "So you would have me go to live at Wilton and be your mistress?"

"I would give my life for that to happen."

"And what would you say to satisfy your wife? What would be my excuse for being there?"

He frowned. "A governess to our children. They could not have a better one. And you could help Mary with her two."

"Yes, that would be a convenient arrangement," Tessa reflected.

"Then you will accept it? Admit you still care for me as I do for you?" he asked eagerly.

She sighed. "Perhaps I wish I could. But I do not want to lie to you, Harry, after having brought you back to life. I cannot honorably accept such an arrangement. And even if I could, I would like some example of your decision to be a better man. That will take a while."

Harry eyed her forlornly. "Why did you save me if you still hate me?"

"I do not hate you," she said. "Perhaps I'm fonder of you than I should be—but only because of your father. If you one day prove yourself as honorable as Sir David, then we might enter into a warmer relationship."

"Very well," he said. "I will go back to the wife I do

197

not love and who does not love me. I shall play the honorable gentleman and hope that in due time you will feel able to respond to me."

Tessa smiled thinly, certain in her own heart that this would never be, but not wanting to be too harsh with him. She said, "Just now you need further improvement before you can leave your bed."

As Harry gained in health, the days grew cooler and only a few cases of the plague were reported each day. Gradually Mr. Grimp began to call to have discussions about the estate with the young nobleman and to pay his respects to Tessa.

One afternoon when he was leaving, the fat man hesitated at the front door of the inn to say, "There has been a great change in Lord Harry's attitude towards you. I declare, his illness has been a cleansing thing. He has emerged from it a much better young man."

"I think so," Tessa smiled.

"Indeed, I believe he has inherited much of his father's sound character," the fat solicitor said. "I have high hopes that since his life has been saved so miraculously, he will try to justify his good fortune by being more like Sir David."

"That is also my hope," she said.

It was the following day that Lady Mary arrived from Wilton to escort Harry home. Tessa had expected Lady Eve would come for him, and she thought it significant that it was not the wife but the sister who elected to brave London and see him home. After Mary and Tessa embraced with a few tears of happiness, they sat and chatted briefly before seeking out Harry upstairs.

Mary looked older, and though she was still attractive, her manner was more sedate and she was dressed in mourning black for her deceased husband. "I live only for my children now," she admitted to Tessa, "and for Harry, of course. He is my brother."

Tessa asked, "Why did Lady Eve not come for him? Surely it is her duty."

"Theirs is a grim relationship," Lady Mary said. "She

198

is so soured by his cheating on her that she has nothing but hatred for him."

"I did not know his womanizing was so in the open."

"It was when I returned to Wilton," Lady Mary sighed. "Eve is a plain creature and a frump in dress. Happily, the children are attractive and seem to take after Harry. Eve will no longer bed with him. They have separate sleeping areas."

"Which makes him feel all the more free to do his wenching about," Tessa ventured.

"I have tried to make Eve see this, but she is blind to all but her hatred of him."

"No doubt she loved him deeply once."

"A plain girl like that, given affection by a handsome man like Harry . . . she was bound to lose her heart to him. I feel sorry for Eve, but I think she might have behaved more wisely."

Tessa said, "Perhaps things may be better when Harry returns."

Lady Mary raised her eyebrows. "Has the Duchess of Winchester tired of him?"

"I don't know," she said, "but I do know his illness has altered his views about many things. You shall soon see for yourself. I have the feeling he is returning to Wilton with the ambition to live a more useful life."

"If only you are right," Mary said fervently.

"He is still weak," Tessa warned. "Be sure he doesn't try to do too much until his strength is fully returned."

Lord Harry left with his sister the next morning. Tessa saw them into the stage that would take them directly to Wilton. Before Harry got up into the stage he took Tessa in his arms and kissed her. In a low voice, he said, "Remember our discussion. I shall not forget you!"

"Good luck!" she smiled.

The stage turned the corner of the street and was lost to her view. She felt a great sadness course through her. Once again Lord Harry had gone out of her life—this time, she suspected, for good. While he'd been ill, she'd felt a purpose in life; now that he was cured, she was alone and facing a pointless existence once more.

There would be no sense in going to the hospital. The worst of the plague was over and the sisters would not need her help. Besides, with the fortune she'd inherited from Sir David, she did not even need to work to live in luxury. She was rich beyond any hopes she'd ever had. Rich and alone.

One afternoon she visited Mr. Grimp in his office and told her doleful tale to him. The fat man listened with sympathy and said, "I confess yours is a sad case, my dear. Why not try to fall in love again?"

"My heart seems dead. Dead with Thomas."

"You are much too young for such thoughts," Mr. Grimp said.

"If the theater company would return, I might join them," she said. "Nell Gwyn and I were close friends, and I liked the stage mightily."

"That sounds like an excellent idea. With winter approaching, I'm sure the king will soon return the court to London."

It occurred to her: "Perhaps Mr. Pepys may have some word about all this."

The lawyer's broad face brightened. "You are right. I vouch that Samuel Pepys knows exactly what is happening and when."

"He often frequents the Harp and Ball tavern," Tessa said. "Perhaps I might find him there."

"Or at the Admiralty office," Mr. Grimp suggested. "Why not let me send word to him there and have him contact you."

She smiled. "That would be kind of you, sir. I do not wish him to think me overbold."

" 'Zounds," the fat man said. "You are anything but that!"

The next afternoon a messenger from the Admiralty office brought her a note. It was a message from Pepys, who wrote that he would call for Tessa at the Hungry Pilgrim and take her out to dinner on the following evening.

The little man, good as his word, arrived at six the next evening. For the occasion Tessa was dressed in a fine new gown she'd had made for her, a silk creation modeled after the latest French style—or so her dressmaker had said. In any event, the dress had a daring low bosom that almost revealed the scar on her breast, but it was cleverly cut so as not to show it. The back was higher, since she still had the welts that Lady Pleasure had inflicted on her.

They took a coach to a restaurant not far from London Bridge. Tessa was pleased to see that the streets were busier again, and many shops and eating places were reopening as people returned to London.

Still, throughout the city, a dreadful stench filled the air. It was strongest in the suburb slums, where the nameless poor had died in swarms. But now the cold air was ushering in a period of respite; the weekly deaths dropped from thousands to hundreds, and the death carts were seen less frequently on the streets. So, even with the stench as a grim reminder of the terrible times just past, hope was in the air.

Samuel Pepys had chosen a pleasant inn for their meal. And when they had ordered, he said, "I have brought my wife back to London. I think the danger is over."

"What about the king?"

"He will remain outside the city until after Christmas," Pepys said. "But if the deaths are still dwindling in January, he will return."

"I hope so. And Nell will be with him."

The man with the protruding eyes chuckled. "Well, it is not as open as that. But she will not be far away from him—of that you can be sure."

"What about the theaters? Will they open again?"

Pepys said, "I have visited the King's Theater. At present it is all dirt. They are altering the stage to make it wider."

Tessa was excited by this news. "Then someone must be ready to open it?"

"That is certain. But God knows when the players will begin to act again."

"The company must be in sad need of work," she pointed out. "Only a few followed the court to Oxford."

"True," Samuel Pepys said. "Some of the players must be near starvation."

Changing the subject, Tessa asked, "You knew that Lord Harry Farr was stricken with the plague and I nursed him back to health?"

"Mr. Grimp made mention of it," Pepys said, helping them to more wine, "but I would like to hear the account from your lips."

She told him about it, ending with, "He is now back at Wilton."

"A happy ending," Pepys approved, straightening out his napkin. "There are few enough of them these days. We are troubled at the Admiralty. The damned Dutch are far from finished."

"We can expect trouble from them again?"

"Not a doubt about it," the stout man said soberly.

Emotionally, she said, "I hate war! I lost my love because of this cursed war!"

Samuel Pepys eyed her with sympathy. "I know. It was I who had the sad task of sending you word of his death in battle."

"Yes," she said. "It is still a painful memory."

"It means his brother Claude will inherit the title," Pepys observed.

"I have never met him."

"No loss. He is a cold fish!"

"So I've been told," she said.

"And the father is the same. I take it that Thomas inherited his good qualities from his mother."

"He must have."

"The Montagus have returned to their London home," the little man said. "A great many of the gentry have returned."

Tessa did not let him see the interest this news aroused in her. She merely said, "In a short while London will have returned to normal again."

"I wonder," Samuel Pepys said pensively. "I wonder."

Tessa went back to the Hungry Pilgrim that night with a new weight on her mind. Sir Edward Montagu was back and she had not settled her account with him. And if he discovered she was still alive, it would be all too likely

202

that he would try to have her murdered, finishing the task Dick Henry had not completed.

It seemed to her that whoever struck first would be the winner in this deadly contest. But she would have to think about it, make some plan of action. And she wondered if it was possible for a lone woman to get into Sir Edward's fortress-like city house and confront him.

She was somewhat surprised at the turmoil this idea aroused in her. Clearly her desire for vengeance had not diminished. She was so upset by her thoughts that she slept only lightly. And this was fortunate, as it turned out, because she was awakened in the darkness to hear a stealthy footstep in her room.

She was prepared. Realizing the weakness of her position as a woman alone in the inn, she always slept with a loaded pistol under her pillow, and now she reached for the weapon and held it up ready to use. Her shadowy intruder moved a step closer and she could see the outline of his body clearly.

In a stern voice, she said, "I have a pistol pointed straight at you. Move once more and I shall ventilate your miserable carcass with a bullet!"

The apparition understood the message. He whined out a miserable, "Mercy, mistress!"

"One move and mercy will not be important to you," she warned him. And at the same time she got out of bed and slowly backed up to the glowing coals in the fireplace. She used her free hand to thrust a candle down to the coals. When it was lit, she held it up to inspect the intruder.

The would-be-robber sniveled, "Let me go, mistress!"

She held the candle closer to him . . . and let out a cry of astonishment. "Mad Reevy!"

It was his turn to gasp. "How do you know my name?"

"I know you too well, you scoundrel," she exclaimed. "I suppose you don't remember Dick Henry?"

"He was my pal!"

"And you deserted him!"

"He ran off with a fancy wench!"

"So he did," she said with triumph, "and I was that wench!"

Mad Reevy stared at her. "S'welp me God!" he said, awed. "You are the one!"

"I am," she said grimly, the pistol still directed at him. "This is not the first time you've tried to rob me."

"I didn't know it was you. They told me there was this woman had a swag of gold and kept it here in her room."

"You always were too quick to believe silly stories."

"Let me go, miss," the unhappy Reevy whined. "I never did squeal on you and Dick. I kept my mouth shut, and that old toff what paid us to do away with you—I told him Dick had done the job."

She gave him credit. "You did keep your mouth shut, I'll grant you that."

"And I'll do nothing against you now, I promise. Not to Dick's woman! I wouldn't," Mad Reevy said.

"You know what happened to Dick?" she asked.

"No."

"The plague got him in Newgate. He's dead!"

"In Newgate! They got him in there!"

She nodded. "Nestor did it! He put his finger on Dick and on me. We went to Newgate together."

"That was no place for a lady like you."

"I hadn't much choice. In any event, I stayed by Dick until he died."

"You're a good woman," Mad Reevy said earnestly. "And you have nothing to fear from me."

"I'll count on that." She placed the candle on the table. "But I'll keep this pistol pointed at you, just to be sure."

"You hurt my feelings," Mad Reevy whined. "I'm not one to steal from a pal."

She said, "So you found me by accident? You didn't come here deliberately?"

"I swear it. I didn't know your name or anything. I was told you had plenty of gold and kept it on you."

"Not likely," she frowned, "after all I know."

"I see that all right, but then I didn't know it was you."

"How did you survive the plague?" she asked.

"I held up an apothecary shop," Mad Reevy said with

a crooked smile. "Put my knife to his neck and told him I wanted powders to keep away the plague."

"And?"

"He gave me a lot of them," the robber said. "I ran out of them only a little while ago, and then the plague had begun to get over."

"I see. What about Nestor?"

Mad Reevy spat on the floor. "That snake! He's still in his shop and prospering."

"It seems all the villains escaped the plague," Tessa said wryly.

"Nestor is sure one. To think he put the finger on you and old Dick."

"You could say he caused Dick's death."

"Newgate—the filthiest jail in all London!" Mad Reevy exclaimed.

All the time she'd been engaging in this weird conversation with the robber in the semi-darkness, an idea had been forming in her mind. Now she said, "I'm going to let you go in a minute."

"Thank you, miss," Mad Reevy said gratefully. "I always liked you."

"You told Dick he should slit my throat and drop me in the Thames. And you deserted him because he didn't."

"I didn't know you very well then," the robber said. "And I was right afraid of what that Sir Edward might do to us. He's an evil man!"

She could not gainsay that judgment, but for the moment she let it pass, saying only, "If you are honest in saying you mean me well, I want you to return here in the morning."

He stared at her. "Return? What for?"

"You'll find that out in the morning. Now go!" And pointing the pistol at him, she herded him out of her room.

Chapter Eleven

If the summer of 1665 with its great plague had been hot, the winter which followed was more than usually cold. As the numbers of deaths due to the plague dropped, so did the temperature. No longer did bellmen run through the streets ringing their bells and calling, "Bring out your dead!" Gone were the death carts, into which corpses were thrown, some wrapped decently in linen winding sheets, others stark naked, with stiff, angular limbs. The accumulated dead of the summer nights had been dumped into huge pits which served as communal graves, and over the decaying flesh soil was spread so thinly that the mounds were often black with crows and ravens except when the gravediggers were at work nearby. All this excess had ended.

Tessa sat in her room at the Hungry Pilgrim the next morning, her mind made up about what she wanted to do. Mad Reevy had appeared in the room the previous night to rob her, not knowing who occupied the room; she had identified herself and had driven him off with a pistol, but she had asked him to return in the morning. Now she sat waiting, wondering if he would.

The thin, foxy-looking man had always been on the cautious side. He moved in only when he felt sure there was little risk. Perhaps she had scared him so badly the previous night he would not show up. This would be a pity, she thought, for he could be invaluable to her. The project she had in mind needed someone of his talents.

Dick Henry had been of a different stamp from the little man, but Dick had shown confidence in Mad Reevy. And when Dick had spared her life, Mad Reevy had kept his mouth shut. That proved he could be relied on to a degree.

Her reverie was interrupted by a knock on her door. When she opened it, the little man was standing there in his ragged clothes, looking wary.

She said, "So you decided to come."

"Yes." His animal eyes were watching her anxiously.

She smiled to put him at ease and said, "Come in. There is a chair for you."

He entered and sat down in the chair she had indicated as she closed the door and came back to stand facing him. She said, "I was beginning to think you'd decided not to accept my invitation."

"I did some thinking about it," he admitted.

"But in the end you decided to come see me?"

"I did. What is it you want?"

Tessa moved over by the window and looked out a moment; then she turned to him and said, "I have a plan that will require someone of your talents."

He showed a foxy smile. "You going to rob the royal jewels?"

"Nothing so ambitious."

"Must be something underhand or you wouldn't need me," the little man said, his crafty eyes on her.

"You are right," she said. "You will remember Sir Edward Montagu?"

"I'm not likely to forget him. He was the one sent Dick and me to rob and murder you."

"Sir Edward has returned to London with his wife and his son Claude. They are all living in his city house at Pall Mall."

"That's a toff's address," he sniffed.

"I wish to wreak my vengeance on him."

"You what?" Mad Reevy asked in awe.

"I wish to pay him for what he tried to have done to me," she explained levelly. "In short, I propose to enter his fine house and put a bullet from my pistol through his heart."

The thief gasped. "That's a big one!" he said, impressed.

"I know. It is why I require the services of someone like you."

The little man looked frightened. "I don't do no killing! Me neck is too tender for stringing up!"

She smiled at his reference to hanging. "I'll be the one to be strung up, if it should come to that."

"I don't like the sound of it. Montagu is powerful," he complained.

"I have money now, my man," she said. "A lot of money. So I'm not without power."

The foxy face showed interest. "Oh?"

"You'd like to even the score with old Nestor, wouldn't you?"

He looked angry. "That I would! Old swindler! Pays half of what the other fences do and then is liable to turn you over to the authorities for theft!"

"My plan is to settle with him first," she said.

Mad Reevy's small eyes were bright with interest. He said, "How would you go about it?"

"I have a plan," she said calmly. "But I do not propose to tell it to you until you have elected to throw your lot in with me."

"Law, you are a woman!" the little man said in wonder. "Dick Henry was right! You are no ordinary female! All right, let my neck take care of itself. Things haven't been that good lately. I'll join you in whatever you want to do!"

"Well spoken, Mad Reevy!" she commended. "And you shall be paid well in golden sovereigns."

"When do we begin?" he asked eagerly.

"Today, if you like. I want you to go to old Nestor and tell him that a lady has some treasure to offer him . . . that she is so innocent of values as to be offering them for almost nothing. Tell him you expect a commission for bringing her to him and arrange a meeting for this very night."

"That will be easy," Mad Reevy said. "Old Nestor will bite for that. What sort of surprise do you have for him?"

"I'll tell you later," she said.

"What time do you want to go there?"

"Say around eight," she said. "On these cold nights, there aren't many abroad at that hour."

"Precious few," Mad Reevy agreed. "When I get this arranged, what then?"

"Come for me about seven-thirty," she said. "I will

208

have a carriage take us to his place and wait for us there."

The little man nodded. "It's as good as done," he promised.

At precisely seven-thirty the two left the Hungry Pilgrim and took a carriage to the mean street in which old Nestor had his cellar shop. Tessa knew that Mad Reevy was jittery and worried about what she was going to do, but as they drove, she instructed him on his role in the matter. He had simply to guard the door and see that no one came in during the time she was with the old fence.

When they reached the entrance to the cellar shop, she saw the faint illumination of candles through a single low window on the street. She bade the driver wait while she and Mad Reevy left the vehicle and crossed the street, with its light covering of snow, to descend a few stone steps and knock at the door with its tiny window of glass.

In reply to their knocking, after a moment a ghostly face appeared in the window pane to peer out at them. It was the face of old Nestor with his hooked nose, flat black hat and droopy gray beard. When his eyes settled on Mad Reevy, his face vanished as he unlocked the door and let them in.

"Come in out of the cold, my lady," old Nestor said, bowing.

"Thank you," she said, entering the dingy place with its clutter of objects. Mad Reevy also came inside, but he stood back by the door as she went further into the shadowed room with the shuffling owner.

At a kind of counter, old Nestor stopped and turned to peer at her with a gloating smile on his ancient face. He had on wool gloves with the finger ends cut out so he could make better use of his hands.

He said, "You have some valuables you wish to dispose of, my lady?"

"I do," she said, pretending nervousness. "And I have been told to bring the things to you."

He smiled and nodded, rubbing his hands together. "I have a reputation for fairness. Everyone agrees old Nestor is fair. I make only a small profit. I am not greedy."

"And you always pay at once?"

Old Nestor looked wary. "That depends," he said. "What do you have, dear lady?"

"Something which should bring you a clear profit," she told him.

"Ah!" he said, his greed causing him almost to drool the word.

Mad Reevy was stationed at the door. There was no one else in the cellar shop but herself and old Nestor. From beneath her brown cloak Tess produced the pistol and held it on him.

The old man let out a soft, sorrowful cry. "What is this?"

"Surely you have seen a pistol before."

Old Nestor was shaking with fear. "You have come to rob me! I should have known Mad Reevy meant trouble."

Keeping the pistol fixed on him, she said, "You are wrong. I bring you amazing wealth." And with her free hand she brought out a small cloth bag with a drawstring on it. She said, "This bag is filled with precious stones."

Completely confused, he asked, "What do you want me to do?"

She kept the pistol on him. "Open the bag and take some of the stones in your hand."

Old Nestor gave her a strange look, but he opened the bag with trembling hands, took out a handful of the stones, and stared at them. There were rubies, pearls, opals, and even a few diamonds. All the stones were of various sizes."

"Excellent goods," the old man quavered. "I can pay you well for them!"

"Nay," Tessa said with a thin smile. "I'm going to make you a present of them. A present in the name of Dick Henry!"

"Dick Henry!" He raised his eyes from the gems and gazed at her in fear. "He died in Newgate months back."

"And you sent him there!"

"No!" old Nestor lied. "I had nothing to do with it!"

"It doesn't matter now," she said. "You have your present from him!"

210

Bewildered, the old man demanded, "Why should he give me a present?"

"It's a farewell present," she said mockingly.

"Farewell present! I don't understand!"

"You will," she said. "Take the stones in your palm and swallow them. Swallow them quickly!"

"What?" He scanned her face as if she were mad.

"Stuff those stones in your mouth and swallow them. This very moment. Or I'll shoot you!" Tessa ordered.

The old man was trembling more than ever. "I can't! I'll choke!"

"Eat them!" she commanded and waved the pistol menacingly.

Dismay on his withered face, he placed the gems in his mouth and tried to gulp them down. She held the pistol close to his chest and ordered him to put another handful of the stones in his mouth and swallow them also. The old man blindly did as he was told. As he tried to gulp down the second mouthful of the precious stones, he began to gasp and choke.

Tessa watched him calmly as he coughed and gagged. She kept the gun full on him as he began to stagger back, his hands clutched to his throat, his choking much worse. She watched and waited as his face turned blue and he dropped to his knees. Then he fell to the floor choking and writhing. She stood quietly until he stopped moving. There was a grimness enveloping her face as she stood over the fallen moneylender.

Mad Reevy came bursting up from the door, worry twisting his face. He stared at the crumpled heap on the floor. "What have you done with him?" he asked.

"Choked him with riches," she said sternly. "See if he still breathes."

The little man's face was a study. He bent down and listened to the old man's heart. Then he looked up at her in shock. "He's gone! Done with!"

"Good! We can be on our way."

Still on his knees, Mad Reevy asked, "What about the gems?"

"Leave them there," she said. "I want him to be found just as he fell!"

The little man stood up. "They're worth a fortune!"

She shook her head. "Most of them are imitations—glass! He didn't have time to make a close study of them."

Mad Reevy looked down at the dead man and whistled.

Tessa said sharply, "Let's us be on our way!"

On the way out the little man said, "I need a drink!"

"Where is the nearest tavern?" she asked.

"There's a grog shop by the docks, the Blue Parrot. It's not far off, and I'm known there."

She was wearing cheap clothing and a thin cloak. "Do women enter it?"

"Drabs," he said. "But you'll be all right as long as you are with me. I'm known!"

"Very well," she said. "Tell the carriage driver where to take us."

The little man called out an address to the driver; then they got into the carriage and were driven away. In the darkness of the moving vehicle's interior the little man hunched at her side. Suddenly he broke into hysterical laughter.

"It'll be the talk of London," he gloated. "Folk will think old Nestor went mad!"

She reminded him, "You and I know nothing about it."

"Right, my lady," Mad Reevy agreed. "We don't know a thing!"

They reached the grog shop, which was indeed on the docks. Fog wreathed the air around it, and there were drunken sailors entering and leaving it constantly. Mad Reevy escorted her in, and she found herself in a noisy, crowded place with a long bar, but Mad Reevy knew where there were some tables and took her to one that had just been vacated. They sat and he ordered from a burly waiter. Tessa was aware her presence had created a stir—she was not the sort of female who often came to such a place.

She said, "They're staring at me."

"Only for a moment," he answered. "They'll turn back to their own affairs when the novelty has worn off."

And he was proven right. Gradually the loud talk was resumed, and Tessa and Mad Reevy were left alone by the curious onlookers. When their drinks came, the little man gulped his down.

"A good night's work," he said, his little eyes bright with admiration.

"The big task is to come."

"Sir Edward."

"Yes."

"It won't be so easy," Mad Reevy warned.

"I know," she said. "Before we undertake it, I want you to go to his house in Pall Mall and become friendly with some of the servants. Find one you can bribe." When he nodded, she went on, "Then learn Sir Montagu's pattern of movement in the house, particularly the time he goes to his study and is alone. That is what we must discover."

"And if I find that out?" he asked.

"Next I want you to bribe this servant to let us into the house when Sir Edward is alone in his study. You will guard the door and I will deal with the gentleman."

"How?"

"You'll find that out later," she told the little man.

"It'll take a little while, maybe a week or two. I have to find someone I can bribe," Mad Reevy said.

"I can be patient."

"I'll see about it," he promised.

As he finished speaking, a tall, handsome man with long black hair and a black mustache approached their table. He was well-dressed in a green velvet jacket with white lace trim, fawn breeches and tall leather shoes in the same shade. He held a many-plumed hat in his hand as he made a sweeping bow and said, "Good friend, pray introduce me to the fascinating lady!"

The little man at once rose and said, "Mistress Shaw, this is Captain Nicholas Marle!"

"How do you do, Mistress Shaw?" Captain Marle said.

"Nicholas Marle, late of His Majesty's Navy, vows he has never seen a prettier face."

"You are too kind," she said, amused by his excessive courtliness in these rough surroundings.

"May I ask what you are doing in this coarse place?"

"I could ask you the same thing," she returned. "But I will be gracious. I'm here because Mad is giving me a tour of the city."

Captain Nicholas Marle said, "He might better have stared with St. Paul's or the Houses of Parliament."

She laughed. "I know all those places. I wanted to come and see where sailors drink."

"That's true, Captain!" Mad said, clearly in awe of the fancy-dressed man.

"In that case, you brought her to the right place," Captain Nicholas Marle said with a smile.

"You say you are late of the King's Navy," she said. "Perhaps you have heard of a Captain Thomas Montagu?"

The handsome man with the black curly hair and mustache said, "Of course! He went down with his ship in action against the Dutch!"

"That is true," she agreed. It seemed the Captain was not a bluff, but truly a former officer in the navy. "What are you doing now?" she wanted to know.

"I have my own vessel," he said. "I have become the owner of a merchant vessel, and I ply the seas in trade. With the war on with the Dutch, it is a somewhat risky but profitable line of work."

"I would imagine so."

"May I buy you a drink?" the captain wanted to know.

The encounter led to Captain Nicholas Marle's joining them and keeping them enthralled with his accounts of his many ocean voyages. He'd had many close scrapes and was now resting and taking on a new crew between voyages. Tessa found herself liking the big man for his courage and good humor.

"Come back again before my ship leaves," he said as he saw her to the carriage. "I have many more tales to tell you."

214

"Perhaps," she said. "Your company has been most pleasant and amusing, Captain."

His keen black eyes met hers. "I can be even more so."

As she drove away with Mad Reevy at her side, she went on thinking about the handsome Nicholas Marle. For the first time in a long while she had met a man who stirred her in a passionate way. She was certain the captain would be an experienced and satisfying lover. Still, for the present, her mind must be occupied with darker matters. She had one more score to settle, the most difficult and the most important to her.

It was nearly ten days later that an excited Mad Reevy turned up at Tessa's room at the Hungry Pilgrim to inform her, "I have it all fixed!"

"Tell me," she said tensely.

"I have me man ready inside," the thief went on eagerly. "I gave him the money as you said. He's going to let us in. Sir Montagu spends an hour alone in his study every night after his evening meal."

"How is it to be arranged?"

"The servant will let us in a side door," Mad Reevy explained. "There's a corridor goes straight to the library where Sir Edward will be."

"He's sure of this?"

"He swears it. We're to be there tonight at eight."

"Very well," she said. "You know how important this is to me. Nothing must go wrong!"

"I have it all fixed!" the foxy little man insisted.

The journey to Pall Mall that evening was unlike the one they'd made to the shop of old Nestor. They had both been more or less sure of themselves on the earlier occasion; this time each had his own fears. Tessa felt the arrangements had gone too easily and wondered if they might be stepping into a trap. But she couldn't turn down this chance to even the score with the cruel nobleman who probably still wanted her dead.

She dismissed the carriage a block from the great stone mansion of Sir Edward Montagu. She and her accomplice stood in the cold in a side street and gazed at the light glowing in the windows. The mansion was huge! She estimated there must be many servants in a place of this size and wondered how Mad Reevy had located the one who would be traitor to his master for the right purse. No matter, the man had been found.

"Watch by the gate," the little man whispered in her ear.

She studied the brick fence with the narrow gate in it, closed and locked to outsiders. She said, "It must be near the time."

"Aye," the little man assented. "Just about now!"

Just as he finished speaking the gate was swung inward, and a bent figure motioned for them to come through. They hurried across, their breaths trailing in the cold air to the gnome of an old man who was waiting for them. He led them across another short distance to enter the side entrance of the main house.

When they were finally inside the gray corridor, the gnome who had let them in vanished. Now they were strictly on their own. Mad Reevy led the way and she followed, her pistol under her cloak. At last they came to a closed door and he nodded.

"He's alone," he whispered.

"Best to burst in," she said. "You station yourself inside the door after you search him for possible weapons."

"I'll follow you," he whispered.

She drew a deep breath and flung the door open. Sir Edward Montagu was seated at the other side of the room with large windows behind him. He was poring over some volume on the desk when they burst in. He looked up with shock on his cruel face as Tessa marched towards him, the pistol pointed at him.

"What is the meaning of this?" he said, his face pale. "How did you get in here?"

"Never mind," Tessa said, motioning to her accomplice with the order, "Search him!"

The foxy little man rushed forward and roughly searched the nobleman for a weapon. Then he announced. "None!"

"Look in the upper drawers." she said.

Mad Reevy at once opened the desk drawers. In the

second one he found a gun, which he produced triumphantly to show her.

"Very well," she said. "Stand by the door so you are concealed if it should be opened."

"Aye, mistress," Mad Reevy said with relish and went back to stand guard.

Sir Edward was glaring at her. "May I ask what all this stage acting is about?"

"You surely remember me," she said. "I was a stage actress before you tried to have me murdered."

The hard blue eyes registered shock. He said in a strained voice, "You're the one who planned to marry Thomas. You lived with old David Farr!"

"The very same!"

"I paid to—" he halted himself at that point and ended lamely with, "you should not be here."

"But I am," she said, "and I plan to settle my account with you."

"Any move you make is bound to attract attention. The house is filled with people," he warned.

"Not close enough to this room," she said. "The walls are thick and soundproof."

Sir Edward shrugged. "Then get it over with. I do not bargain with my inferiors."

But first she wanted to know, "Why did you wish me murdered after Thomas was lost at sea?"

His expression was coldly condescending. "Because it suited my pleasure!"

"I shall kill you now for the same reason," she said.

"Get on with it," he said arrogantly. "I shall not beg for mercy. Besides, your neck will stretch for your crime."

"What about your crimes?" she asked him.

He did not reply because at that moment the door to the study was flung open and a young man who was a younger edition of the cruel Sir Thomas sprang inside, his pistol ready to fire.

The young man shouted. "I happened to see them in the hall, Father. It is all right!"

"Watch out! The door!" Sir Edward shouted as he edged around the desk towards his son.

The young man paid no attention to him. He was aiming at a frozen Tessa, who had dropped her weapon in her shock. As he pulled the trigger to fire at her, Mad Reevy jumped out from behind the door and brought the butt of his pistol down on the young man's head. The shot rang out. And Tessa, surprised to find herself unhurt, saw that a blob of red blood was spreading across Sir Edward's frilled shirt front. His eyes wide, the old nobleman bent forward and collapsed on the rich carpet where his son was already stretched out unconscious.

Tessa stood motionless, dazed by the unexpected drama, marveling: Sir Edward had been killed by a bullet from his own son's pistol!

Mad Reevy grabbed her by the arm. "We have to get out!" he cried.

She nodded, and swooping up her pistol from the carpet, she ran out with the little man. They heard voices from the other end of the corridor as they raced for the side entrance, but they reached the door before anyone caught up to them and in an instant were outside and through the doorway in the brick fence. And still they didn't stop but ran along several side streets, Mad Reevy scampering like a fox and Tessa, slowed by her skirts, stumbling behind, until at last she could run no more and lay back against a wooden wall, exhausted.

She gasped, "I can't run any further!"

He stopped up ahead and turned back to join her. "No need," he said breathlessly. "We are far enough away."

"Did anyone see us?"

"Only the son," her accomplice said. "And he had only a glimpse of us. I doubt if he really saw our faces at all."

"He didn't see you. You came up behind him."

"If I hadn't of, it would have been the end of you," the foxy little man retorted.

"I know. I owe you my life," she said, her breath beginning to come more easily.

"You fixed Sir Edward. I'll wager he was dead before we were out of the house—and his son will have some explaining to do to get out of the blame of doing it."

218

She said, "So our work is over!"

The little man said wistfully, "No more accounts to settle?"

"None." Satisfaction brought a brief smile to her lips; then she sobered and became businesslike again. "In the morning you go to Mr. Grimp and he will have fifty pounds for your final payment. I don't want to see you ever again."

The little man shrugged. "As you like. You can always come to the Blue Parrot if you need me."

"I don't think I shall have such a need," she said. "Now, if you will accompany me to a tavern, I must get a carriage to take me home."

"There's a stagecoach inn not far from here," Mad Reevy suggested. "If we go there, you're bound to get a carriage."

So the evening for which Tessa had waited so long came to an end. As to its outcome, she did not hear any word until two days later, when Samuel Pepys stopped by the Hungry Pilgrim, brimming with gossip.

The stout man joined her for a drink in the public room of the inn and said, "I am busy at the Admiralty, but I had to take an hour away from my duties to bring you this news in person."

"Pray tell me."

"Sir Edward Montagu is dead," he announced. "Shot by that booby of a son, Claude. I tell you, Claude has nothing of Thomas about him."

"Give me the facts."

Samuel Pepys sighed. "As I heard it, some thieves somehow got entrance to the house—a man and a woman, both armed. Sir Edward was held up in his study. But son Claude had glimpsed the two entering the library and he followed them, his pistol at the ready. He warned his father and aimed to kill the woman. But her accomplice struck him and sent his arm flying, with the sad result the bullet went through his own father's heart."

"And the intruders managed to escape?"

"Scot free," the little clerk said with annoyance. "This booby Claude can't even give a clear description of them.

219

He only thought of aiming his shot—and he is a miserably poor shot in any case. So we now have a new Lord Montagu, and you should have nothing to fear from him."

"We do not even know each other," she said. "It was his father who kept the feud alive."

"Then let it rest at that," Samuel Pepys said. "There is much consternation about what happened."

"I'm sure of it," she said.

"Old names and intrigues will come to mind once more," the little man said, his bulging eyes troubled.

She said, "I do appreciate your bringing the word."

"Law, my dear, I could not do less. You are a warm friend. Besides, there is other, more pleasant news. The King's Theater is transferring to Drury Lane when the king returns in a week or so."

"This is sure to happen?"

"I have it on the word of one high at court."

She smiled. "Perhaps I shall act again."

"Why not?" Pepys approved. "London will soon be its normal self again, and so will you!"

After the little man had left her, she thought about this declaration and wished it could be so. But she knew it was impossible. She would never be the Tessa of old. She had changed much and learned much. And London, too, was different. Its people would never again feel safe from the dread disease that had devastated it and could do so at any time in the future.

Some things could be better, however. For some time Tessa had been considering finding a new place to live, but she was waiting for the cold winter to end before making a serious search. Since she had money enough now to afford a pleasant establishment, she was thinking of taking a small house in Drury Lane. Once, in passing, she had asked Mr. Grimp to keep an eye open for a likely property there.

It would be the area of the theaters, and when King Charles returned to London, he would not be far from there. Tessa looked forward to seeing Nell Gwyn and Charles Hart, certain they could be persuaded to find her roles in a new season of plays. But she was thinking ahead, since she had only the word of Samuel Pepys that the king was planning an early return to London.

One evening the proprietor of the Hungry Pilgrim came up to her room to inform her, "A gentleman awaits your pleasure in the tavern."

She frowned. "Did he give his name?"

"No," the bald innkeeper said. "He simply gave me this message."

"Very well," she said. "I'll go down." And as she freshened herself to appear downstairs, she decided it must be Mad Reevy back to see her. The idea chilled her somewhat. She had warned him not to return to her again. She hoped he wasn't going to attempt blackmailing her; she had felt she could trust him not to do that.

In this troubled mood she went down to the tavern. But rather than the little thief, she found the colorfully dressed Captain Nicholas Marle waiting for her. She had forgotten all about the jovial merchant captain.

He bowed to her and said, "You remember me?"

"Captain Marle," she acknowledged.

"The same," he said, looking pleased.

"I thought you were bound for southern waters."

"So I had planned," he agreed, "but my sailing was delayed. It is hard to get a competent crew these days."

"I expect so," she said.

His manner became more sober. "I am here not only because I wished to see you again but because I am the bearer of some bad news."

Her eyes opened wide. "Bad news?"

"I judge it will be," he said. "It is about Mad Reevy."

"What about him?" she asked, suddenly afraid. Had her accomplice been picked up by the authorities? Perhaps he had told them of her part in the deaths of old Nestor and Sir Edward!

Captain Nicholas Marle said, "I regret to inform you that he died of the plague this morning."

"Died of the plague!" she echoed.

"One of the few cases lately," the captain said. "Odd that he lived through the worst of it and then was struck down when the cursed disease was essentially over."

"I am sorry," she said. "Thank you for telling me."

"I was at his bedside," the man said. "I had two of my men caring for him in the waterfront hovel where he lived. He made mention of you in his final ravings."

She felt her cheeks warm. "Indeed?"

"Yes," the captain said. "He spoke most highly of you and called you the finest looking woman in London. Which I agree you are!"

"Poor fellow," she said. "Has his burial been arranged?"

"Yes. He was taken away at once, as all plague cases are."

"Then there is nothing I can do."

The tall, swarthy man said, "I think there is. I would like to mark the occasion of this loss of our mutual friend by taking you to a favorite inn of mine for food and a drink."

This caught her by surprise. "I had not planned dining out this evening."

"There is still time."

"I would have to change to a more suitable gown," she said.

"Waiting will not bother me," he assured her. "I shall be here when you come down."

She selected her finest dress for the occasion, a silk with copious amounts of golden braid. Beneath it she wore three layers of petticoats against the chill of January and over her shoulders she placed a heavy woolen cloak with a hood attached. When she went down to join the captain he stood up and openly admired her.

"I shall be pleased to be seen in your company, milady," he said, bowing.

"You are most kind," she smiled.

They went a short distance to a small inn that Tessa liked because it was one of those places where one could dine in a tiny private room. She much preferred this privacy to the brawling that was so common in many of the public eating places. In this way they escaped curious eyes and the noisy conversations of the public room.

As she allowed the captain to remove her cloak and
222

pull out her chair for her, she smiled and said, "How thoughtful of you to seek out this place where we can dine peacefully!"

He said, "It is a sober occasion, marking the death of a friend. I felt that privacy should be part of it."

Tessa could not help giving the tall, dark man an admiring gaze. "You are sensitive, for a man who follows the sea."

"Some of us are actually bookish," he informed her. "During a long voyage there is little to do but read at times. I have a fine library of poetry, essays, and novels on board the *Flying Eagle*."

"That is the name of your ship?"

"Yes," he said. "I recently renamed it. And I trust that some time in future I may be able to invite you on board and have you see my collection of books."

"The collection is reflected in your good conversation," she said. "I'm most pleased to have you as a friend. At the moment I have few in London."

"I cannot understand why."

"Since I was on the stage at one time, most of my friends were theater people," she said. "These people left London when the plague broke out so fiercely and have been with the court at Oxford."

"Ah," Captain Nicholas Marle said. "I might have known that one with your beauty and easy speech had a knowledge of the boards."

"Do you like the theater?"

"I attend whenever I can, but I spend so much time at sea I often have to be content merely to read plays," he confessed.

The innkeeper, who seemed to know Captain Nicholas Marle well, seemed anxious to please him. The little man bobbed about bringing them excellent food and good wine. Tessa decided it was one of the most pleasant evenings she'd spent lately and told the handsome man with the black mustache so. "I'm only sorry it is to mark so sad an occasion," she finished.

The captain smiled. "Mad Reevy would be sure to wish us well. I drink to him!" And he raised his glass.

223

She joined him in the toast. And when she put down her glass she said, "It would appear I have a weakness for seafaring men. You know I was engaged to marry the late Thomas Montagu—you may remember I mentioned him when we met."

"Yes. I met Captain Montagu several times while I was in His Majesty's Service. But he did not tell me he had a fiancé such as you! No doubt he wished to keep your beauty and lovely nature a secret, so that he could enjoy it himself without intrusion."

She blushed. "How did you get out of the navy?" she asked.

"I was seriously wounded in a battle with the Dutch," he said. "And since it was not expected I would recover, I was given an honorable discharge."

"How fortunate for you," she said. "And how wonderful that you have regained your health."

"Some think that a miracle," he agreed. "But I know I still am not the man I was. On the other hand, I can function as a simple merchant captain."

"Which is risky enough these days," she replied.

"True," he said, smiling at her, but with rather an odd look, she thought.

She was embarrassed, for all at once she realized she must have drunk too much. The room was reeling about her in a most troublesome fashion. She strove to concentrate and drive this giddy feeling away before her escort noticed. Unhappily it grew worse—he spoke, but his words made no sense—and in the next instant she blacked out!

Chapter Twelve

Tessa opened her eyes and wearily decided it was shameful! The lantern in the ceiling was swaying gently, and the entire room seemed to be heaving from one side to the other in a rather sickening motion. She could not imagine how she had managed to get so drunk on such a small amount of spirits! What must the captain think of her?

She noted the small, low-ceilinged room in which she found herself stretched out on a bunk bed and decided she must be in one of the tavern's upstairs rooms. No doubt she had disgraced herself by collapsing at the table and the captain had carried her here to recover! How could she explain? What could she say to him?

She was still rather confusedly debating this when a door opened and a strange figure came into the room—a hunchback with a knitted cap on his head, wearing a striped sweater and loose trousers. The hunchback was old, with matted gray hair hanging down from under his cap. His mouth was sunken, since he was apparently toothless, and his small eyes were far back in his head, giving his face a strange, skull-like appearance.

She said, "Where is the captain?"

The toothless one offered her a grin and said, "*Si, signora!*"

She stared at him. "I want the captain," she repeated.

The hunchback did not seem to comprehend but stood there, a blurred, stolid figure before her glazed eyes. She struggled to a sitting position, and still there was no change in the motion. She groaned in disgust and held her opened palms to her temples in an effort recall clearly.

Her poor brain was still in a muddle. It seemed the room was creaking ominously, as if its very timbers were being torn at by some giant. What a dreadful fool she had made of herself! If only the floor would remain still, she would be able to stand. She could not keep the unfortunate captain down below in the tavern waiting for her indefinitely.

She clenched the edge of the bunk and getting to her feet, she stood there precariously. Through this the hunchback stood smiling and staring at her. The impudent fellow made her more self-conscious. And now that she was standing, she noticed that her head was aching painfully.

She decided to try once more, and raising her voice as one would to a deaf person, she shouted, "The captain! Captain!"

The hunchback responded at last, bowing his head and chuckling. He went to the door and motioned for her to follow him. It was extraordinary conduct, but she had no choice but to obey him.

She stepped through the door to find herself in a larger room, which appeared to be a kind of office. There was a large desk with a bookcase full of books built into the wall behind it. Captain Nicholas Marle sat at the desk studying some papers. He lifted his head and seeing her at once smiled and got up from behind the desk. "My dear Tessa!" he said in a friendly manner.

She stood in the swaying room with the hunchback grinning at her from a distance and the captain standing in front of her.

"What happened?" she asked. "I'm still in a terrible state. The whole room seems to be swaying."

Nicholas laughed, "You must not mind that!"

"I'm never ill this way," she protested. "How long have I been asleep?"

"About fifteen hours!"

She let her mouth drop open. "Fifteen hours! I did not hear you right!"

"Yes, you did."

"I don't understand," she said. As the room swayed again, even in her blurred state of mind she knew she was precariously close to blacking out once more.

"Let me take your arm," Nicholas said.

"Why?"

"You'll see," he assured her. And grasping her by the

226

arm he led her across the room to a tiny, circular window and said, "Look out!"

She did, and gasped. All she saw was the ocean—at close range, with angry waves of a giant size . . . the ocean extending all the way to infinity!

Turning to him, she said, "I'm on board a ship!"

"You are," he said genially.

"But how? Why did you bring me here? Why didn't you take me back to the inn when I collapsed?"

Nicholas smiled wisely. "I can explain."

"I wish you would. And then take me back to the Hungry Pilgrim. I wish to recover in my own room and in my own bed."

"I'm afraid that's impossible," the handsome captain told her.

"What are you saying?"

"We are many miles from London, I fear," he said. "Well out in the channel."

She stared at him and tried to balance herself against the sway of the ship. "This is monstrous!"

"Come sit with me at my desk, and I will have Manuel serve us some tea," he said. "Manuel is most efficient. He looks after my needs as steward. Unhappily he does not know much English." Nicholas now spoke some rapid words in a foreign tongue, and the hunchback bowed and went out.

Tessa touched a hand to her head. "I fear I may faint again. All this has confused me!"

"Do sit down," he said. "It will be best."

She allowed him to help her to the chair facing his desk. She sat heavily in it, filled with despair, not knowing what to make of the situation. "How can I have slept for all those hours?"

He smiled again. "I promise you that you did."

"And why bring me to your ship instead of to my hotel? I have never had this experience with spirits before! I do not understand it!"

The handsome Nicholas said gently, "Tessa, everyone has such an evening at some time. Manuel is bringing us some tea, and I'm sure you'll be able to think more clearly after you have had a warm drink."

"You said you would explain," she reminded him. "I'm waiting for your explanation."

"It will come best with the tea," he said.

At that moment the hunchback came lurching into the room, expertly balancing a tray on which there rested a teapot covered by a cosy, and cups. He placed the tray on the desk and left them.

"I shall pour," Nicholas said. "I think you had best have your tea black, without anything else in it."

"If only it will clear my head," she lamented, taking the cup and saucer from him. "I feel as if I were drugged."

He poured his own tea and sat down in the chair behind the desk. He said, "I'm certain the tea will help."

She drank some of the hot liquid and then waited for it to cool a little. As her head cleared slightly she gave him an accusing look. And she exclaimed, "Drugged! That must have been what happened—you drugged me!"

The captain smiled. "Don't upset yourself!"

She placed the teacup on the table and stood up. "Tell me the truth!"

He rose and came to her and placed his hands on her arms and forced her back in the chair. "Do remain seated and take the tea. Otherwise you run a severe risk of blacking out again."

Her reeling head told her this was true. It seemed the slightest exertion sent her back into a confused dizziness. She sat stiffly and took some more tea.

Then she looked at him sternly and said, "What have you done to me?"

"I'll confess," he said. "I did slip a powder in your wine."

"You scoundrel!" she cried.

He shrugged. "I do not mind what you call me."

"You drugged me and kidnapped me aboard your ship. Now we're far out at sea!"

"The tea must be working," he said. "You have it all most correctly."

228

"Why?"

"I could not bear to part from you."

She stared at the handsome man who stated this all so calmly. "Ridiculous!"

"You may think so, but I have taken a great risk in bringing you along with me. I had to make the venture. I have fallen in love with you!"

"You are making fun of me, sir!" she said angrily.

The captain looked solemn. "I wish I were, but what I am saying is true. I love you, my Tessa!"

"Then why not tell me in a normal way?" she replied in anger. "Why kidnap me and take me off against my will?"

"I had no choice."

"You had every choice!"

"Wrong!" he said. "I had to sail last night. I knew if I left without you, I might never see you again. So I made a rash decision, one which I hoped you might forgive—I decided to drug you and bring you along."

"I would not have expected such low-minded, treacherous—" She broke off, her dull mind refusing to supply an end to the sentence.

He looked pained. "Am I repulsive to you?"

"No," she said with spirit. "On the contrary, you were becoming most attractive to me. I might have found myself in love with you. By doing this you have ended it—spoiled it all!"

He stood up and came around to her. "Why?"

"You took a coward's advantage of me!"

"I have not touched you while you slept," he said. "I made no move against you!"

"Even so, you have taken me prisoner against my will!" she protested.

Gently, he asked, "Can you not understand my dilemma? I could not bear to think of losing you."

"You have done an evil, stupid thing."

"I'm sorry," he said. "I hoped you might show some tolerance and understanding. I felt certain you would see my side of it—how I could not bear to lose you."

She drank the rest of her tea. "You have behaved in a lawless fashion."

"Do not think I have arranged things simply for my convenience," he argued. "I have my crew to consider, and my first mate, Mr. Withers, is dead against your being on board."

"I should think so. Especially if he knows the way you managed it!"

Nicholas said, "It matters not how I managed to get you aboard. Sailor folk are a simple, superstitious lot. Mr. Withers, like the majority of the crew, believes firmly that a woman on board will bring bad luck."

"Surely it is bad luck for me," she said tartly.

"This is no small thing," he went on earnestly. "I risked losing my crew by bringing you on board. The danger is still not over. They are a sullen lot, and if Mr. Withers encourages it, they may decide to mutiny."

Indignantly, she said, "Yet you shanghaied me, knowing all this! You truly must be mad!"

"Mad about you, madam," he said gravely. "I fear it has been my undoing."

"Where are you bound?" she asked.

"Cadiz," he said. "I mean to bring back a shipload of perfumes, precious metals and jeweled articles which will make me rich."

She ignored this and said, "What is your first port of call?"

"We have none."

"Surely you can find a harbor on the French coast and let me off. I can get in touch with my solicitor in London and arrange my passage back."

He frowned. "I doubt that would work out."

"Why not?"

"The Frenchies are almighty slow. And you would have to live on something until the word came from London."

"Then you must arrange my passage on some returning vessel or give me money to pay for my being taken back. Failing that, as a former officer in the King's Navy and a
230

gentleman, you must turn about and sail me back to London yourself."

He laughed. "Turn about and go back to London? That is not likely. Especially with the Dutch out in their warships, looking for honest British merchantmen like this."

"You sailed out in the face of the Dutch!"

"I had no choice," he said. "But I do have a choice about turning back."

"And you will not do it for me?"

"It would not be convenient," he said.

"You think my plight is convenient for me?" she asked in a rage.

"Pray, be calm," he said. "We will reach Cadiz in a month or five weeks, do our trading and return to London. In all, it will not take more than three or four months. You will only miss the winter weather and the remaining threat of the plague. Why not settle down and enjoy the voyage? Consider it a kind of holiday."

She stared at him. "You are a cool villain," she finally said.

"Doesn't what I said seem reasonable?" he demanded.

"It might have . . . if you had made the same proposal to me fairly," she pointed out. "It is quite within the realm of possibility that the idea might have appealed to me. But you did not give me the opportunity of choice. Instead you took me in a criminal fashion."

"At some risk to myself and the welfare of this ship, as I have told you," he said.

"I see it as a selfish, cruel act!"

"So I have fallen in your esteem?"

"You have."

"Then I must try to win my way back into your good graces," he worried. "I shall be on my best behavior, I vow. You may have my cabin to yourself. And in your free time you may come in here and read from my goodly store of fine volumes. We can have our meals here in privacy, and when we reach warmer climes, you can enjoy the warm sun on deck."

231

"What a pretty picture you paint!" she said sarcastically.

"It could be so!"

"You do not think much about practical things, I fear," she said. "I have with me only the gown I'm wearing. What do you think my condition will be within three months?"

He smiled. "An excellent point. But I have a solution."

"Indeed!" she exclaimed. "Is there a seamstress among your crew? Are you about to have sails cut down into canvas dresses for me? Or perhaps you'll have some of your attractive frock coats converted into skirts for my use!"

"Not bad ideas," he said easily. "But they are not what I have in mind. I happen to have a trunk or two filled with female attire of the best quality. I will have them brought here and you may see what fits you and make your pick of them."

She was startled. "Why would you have trunks of women's clothing on board?"

"They were part of a shipment I undertook," he said. "The fee for their transport was not paid, so I confiscated the cargo. It is a common practice."

She stared at him. "You continually surprise me!"

"I care for you deeply, Tessa," he said. "It is my wish that you learn to love me on this voyage and that when we return to London I shall have the honor of making you my wife!"

She looked up at him and could not help offering him a small smile as she sighed and said, "I say it again—you are the most conceited villian I have ever met!"

The clothing in the trunks proved to be of the finest quality. And from the numerous items Tessa was able to select a wardrobe which was the equal of the finest in London or Paris. She considered it a fortunate quirk of fate that these things should have come her way. Moreover, Captain Nicholas Marle was lavish in his generosity. He insisted that she have everything in the trunks, whether the clothing was of immediate use to her or not.

So began his strange wooing of her. She slept untroubled in his cabin and joined him in the main area of his quarters for meals and socializing. She also took advantage of his many books and read a good deal, especially in the early days of the voyage, when she often had to remain inside because of the inclement weather.

Once there was a terrific gale and she did not see Nicholas for almost twenty-four hours. Through old Manuel she learned that the captain did not dare leave the bridge. The ship was in such danger that several times it seemed about to capsize. She stayed in the bunk and tried to read, but it was impossible. Once she was thrown out of the bed when the ship lurched wildly. Fortunately she was not injured, though the violence of the fall had ended her sleep for the night.

In the calm that followed the gale she spoke to Nicholas about his remaining on deck in the storm, asking, "Why did your subordinates not take your place for a while so you could rest?"

He smiled. "I feared no one was capable of steering a ship through such a gale but myself. So I lashed myself to the wheel and remained there."

"Are we apt to have other such storms?" she asked.

"No," he promised. "In a day or two we will be in warm, less surly waters."

Tessa greeted the calm sea and warm air of the South Atlantic with delight. She began to spend more time on deck, though Nicholas warned her to keep aloof from the ordinary seamen.

"They are a wild lot," he said. "A beauty like you is not safe among them."

She laughed. "You think not?"

"I do," he said sternly, "and you will do well to listen to me. I told you at the start that they consider a woman on board bad luck in any case."

"I shall have to try to convince them otherwise," she suggested.

He shook his head. "Useless. It's a legend as old as the sea itself. Just keep in the background so they don't notice you too much."

But this did not appeal to Tessa. She preferred to do

233

things her own way. And so she selected her best gown and worked for hours over her hair. When she finally appeared on the bridge one calm night when it was more like June than the January back home, she had her first glimpse of the crew. They were squatted aft to enjoy the same warmth that had brought her out.

Captain Nicholas Marle kept close by her in these few appearances, and she noted that even on shipboard his sword was on his hip and in its sheath. She did not think much about what this might mean, however, for she was beginning to enjoy the voyage.

She was charmed by the fine warm weather of these waters, and she was equally pleased by the patient friendliness of the captain. She began to forget that she should be discontent because she was a prisoner on the three-master. It almost seemed as if she were aboard by choice. After the stench and disease of London, the gentle motion of the ship and the endless, sparkling ocean seemed an enchanted world. The voyage became a fine holiday for her, and despite her early protestations, she and Nicholas became good friends.

He was a strange man, this handsome, dark-haired giant, light of spirit one moment and darkly moody in the next. He could be talking to her of history, art, and philosophy and in a twinkling be raging at the crew in the language of the gutter!

The crew were a conundrum. Old Manuel, who had become a sort of personal servant to her, was pleasant and harmless. A native of Portugal, Manuel was a most religious man, Nicholas assured her. The first mate, Mr. Withers, was hard-faced and silent. A man of middle age, he seemed annoyed at her presence on board, and when he talked with her he rarely looked her straight in the eye.

Not so ill at ease with her was a smiling, stalwart Spaniard, Miguel—young and dashing, with long black hair and gold rings in his ears, prone to sunning himself on deck in only his breeches. Miguel had paid particular attention to her from the start, smiling and trying to catch her attention, and Tessa, taken with his looks, would have spoken with him except that Nicholas warned her against it.

"Keep away from Miguel," he told her. "He considers himself a ladies' man, and the least encouragement will result in his making unpleasant overtures."

She thought that Nicholas was exaggerating the danger, but she obeyed him. Still, Miguel found ways to attract her attention, busying himself working on the deck near her cabin or sunning himself where she could not help noticing and admiring his brown, hairy chest.

The others of the crew were a motley lot. In tricornered hats, colorful handkerchiefs and knitted caps, you could almost sort out their nationalities by their headgear. Those in the hats were mostly English and Irish; the ones wearing the colorful bandanas were from Spain and Portugal; while those with the knitted caps were Scotsmen, Norsemen and Danes.

She laughed and told Nicholas, "I vow your crew is a veritable melting pot of nationalities."

Nicholas said, "You have no idea how difficult it is to get men for a merchant vessel in these times of war."

"Our voyage has been calm enough. I can't image the danger to be that great," she objected.

"Wait a bit," he warned. "You may see action enough, though I sincerely hope you won't."

One hot night Nicholas ordered dinner served on the deck outside their cabin. It was a fairy-tale setting, with a lantern swinging from the side of the cabin to light their table after night fell. The velvet blackness of the sky was soon alive with stars, and then a moon of startling yellow gold rose above the horizon.

Nicholas kept pouring wine for them, and Tessa found herself lost in a romantic haze. She listened as he recited from the playwright William Shakespeare, whose verse she knew almost as well as he did, and then she responded with lines from John Dryden.

As they stood close together by the ship's railing, he placed an arm around her and quoted from *Hamlet*, " 'Doubt thou the stars are fire, Doubt that the sun doth

move, Doubt truth to be a liar, But never doubt I love.' "
He finished by kissing her long and ardently.

When he released her, she smiled up at him gently and said, "John Dryden wrote, *All for Love*, or *A World Well Lost*. My world of London is well lost in my being here with you."

"Come," he said, taking her by the hand.

Alive with a new happiness and a new passion, she knew the moment had come for them, and so she meekly let him lead her into the cabin. With caressing hands he disrobed her, and when she stood before him in glowing nakedness, he kissed her body with a passion which banked the fires she already knew within her.

He placed her on the bunk and stood before her, naked, ready to make her body his. He was as manly and well-endowed as she had imagined, and she could scarcely wait until he slid down beside her. He was patient in his loving, but after a time his rigid thrusts melted her into ecstasy. They reached a perfect peak of frenzied passion and then lay exhausted side by side.

From that night on there was no question that she was his. Added to her enjoyment of his company, there was the new thrill of their sexual adventures together. He loved to watch her move about in the nude, never mentioning the scars on her back and breast, comparing her to a master's painting of female perfection. And she found herself anticipating his touch all day, impatient for the dark, when he could be free to caress her into ecstasy. Once again she felt a man's love had brought her to safe harbor.

Nicholas was forever telling her, "When we return to London the church bells will ring, and we will walk down the aisle man and wife."

And believing him, she was happy in what had thus far been an enchanted voyage. But a ship, she discovered, was like a great house—nothing of event occurred on it that did not get to be known by all. From the night she and Nicholas became lovers she was certain the crew knew about it. Was it just that they guessed, since they all were caught up together in this small vessel on a vast ocean, or had Manuel spied on the captain and his lady and recounted their erotic moments to the burly crew?

Surely Miguel's attentions became more noticeable. So brazenly did he try to thrust himself in Tessa's way that it became embarrassing. Still she did not take it seriously. Then one warm evening, when Nicholas was in his cabin conferring with Mr. Withers on matters of the cruise, she went by herself for some fresh air to a deserted portion of the upper deck.

But she was not alone. Out of the shadows there suddenly materialized the husky, handsome Miguel, naked to the waist. He uttered a cry and pounced on her. His lips crushed hers, and while he held her with one hand, the other madly sought out her body. She screamed and tried to fight him off without success. He ripped the bodice of her gown open so that her breasts were revealed and buried his face in them!

"Villain!" It was Nicholas who spat out the word as he mounted the steps to the upper deck.

Letting out an angry curse, Miguel stumbled back and away from Tessa. At the same time he drew a dagger from inside the top of his breeches and crouched in a position from which he could attack or meet attack.

Nicholas pushed Tessa roughly down onto the deck, where she lay sobbing, covering her bare bosom as best she could with the frayed cloth of her gown. Nicholas had drawn his sword and was now advancing on Miguel with deadly intent. At the same time the lower deck, which had been empty, filled with the crew.

Miguel moved about agilely, keeping out of the range of the sword. Nicholas lunged but missed, which gave the Spaniard a chance to get close to Nicholas and stab him with the dagger. It was only a wound in the arm, but it drew blood!

Miguel laughed harshly as Nicholas staggered back. Nicholas's move was partly strategy, however: He was putting some space between himself and the young Spaniard. Miguel crouched for a second attack, but he was never to manage it. For Nicholas, poising the thin blade of his sword, with deadly precision slid it straight through

237

Miguel's stomach until nearly a foot of its blade thrust out of his back!

As the crew howled their approval, Miguel looked dazed and then coughed blood, which spewed over his chest. Nicholas drew the sword out of him, its length crimson with blood. Miguel clenched his torn stomach, tumbled facedown on the deck, and lay still.

Tessa watched in horror. Shocked by the quick retribution which had overtaken the Spaniard and awed by the cruel swordsmanship of Nicholas, she was aware, by reason of the crew's enjoyment of it all, that a dangerous violence lay under the calm surface of life aboard the vessel.

Nicholas had cleaned his sword and returned it to its sheath as he came to her and lifted her to her feet. His face was dark with rage. "Did he harm you?"

"No, just tore my dress!"

"The scum!" Nicholas watched as members of the crew carried the dead young man away. "He has made his last sailing."

She gazed up into his angry face. "Was it necessary to kill him?"

"Yes," he said sharply. "You don't understand. These men are like wild wolves. Just undo the leash on them a fraction and they will attack you."

"I'm sorry," she said. "I oughtn't to have come out here alone."

His arm around her, Nicholas led her away, saying, "Something was due to happen. I knew Miguel had his eye on you."

She made no reply. But she noted that he was more lustful in his advances to her that night and his lovemaking was almost painful. When he'd finished with her, she felt almost as if she'd been raped. It was strange! In all their turbulence of lovemaking at other times he had never been savage with her. It was as if the violence of the earlier scene had brought about this change in him. He seemed a different person.

But this was only a start. A few days later she was in the cabin reading when Nicholas entered tensely to tell her, "I think we may be in for some trouble. I'm going to lock you in here!"

Putting down the book, she rose to face him. "Why?"

He was impatient. "An armed vessel is approaching on our port side," he said. "I'm sure it is a Dutchman. They arm their merchant vessels like fighting ships. If they get the first cannon shots at us, they'll sink us!"

"You're sure it's an armed vessel?"

"Yes, Mr. Withers saw it through his glass. We must get our cannon going first and be the victor!"

"Why can't you just sail by each other," she said, "if neither of you are ships of war?"

"You don't know much about war!" he said derisively. "We are enemies, regardless of the type of ships we sail. Even if we tried to pass them without notice they would engage us."

"You seem so sure!"

"I know," he said. "But don't be afraid! Our men are skilled with cannons, muskets and swords. We will engage this vessel, try to move in close and finish it!"

"What of those on board?"

"They will have their chance to take to the boats when the battle is settled. In these waters they will be soon picked up. But don't waste your breath worrying about them. Keep to this cabin and pray for our victory." With this he left her and she heard the door being locked.

Listening to his retreating footsteps, she realized she was frightened. She was to be part of a battle at sea. She had read of such events but had no idea what they might actually be like. She began to tremble. What if the Dutch shot first and their own ship was badly damaged? What if Nicholas and his men were killed? Quickly she envisioned herself left alone on a blazing hulk—or trapped as the ship filled with greedy ocean water and sank down into the murky depths!

She wished Nicholas hadn't locked her below, but she knew it must be for her own good. Above she heard the rumbling of the cannon carriage as the great guns were rolled into strategic places. She could also hear sounds of

239

running feet and angry, impatient cries and oaths. Everything had a sense of urgent haste.

Tessa went to the porthole and looked out. The other ship, a three-masted vessel like their own, seemed to be sailing by them about a half-mile distant. It did not look like an armed vessel, but then she knew little about such things. As she watched she heard the cannon above fire and felt the vibration of it. A few seconds later she saw the cannon ball strike the other vessel and watched as the foremost mast slowly collapsed amid smoke.

Now there was answering cannon fire from the other ship. She watched in fascinated horror. The cannon ball fell short into the sea near them. Again their own cannon sounded, and again its lethal charge found its place on the other ship. To her amazement all three masts had been splintered and were heaped on the deck of the Dutch vessel.

Nicholas then steered them close to the shattered ship, and Tessa could see men and a few women on the decks. There was another exchange of cannon fire at close range. Now she felt the shock of a great impact—this time the enemy cannon fire had found its mark. She prayed that Nicholas hadn't been in its path.

She tried to see what was happening as the melee grew, but now the vessels were actually scraping each other, and she could see little from below. Besides, great clouds of smoke hung over the scene, so that only occasionally did she get a brief glimpse of men fighting hand to hand. It was a terrifying experience.

The battle seemed to go on endlessly. After the din and fighting had lasted for hours, she felt the ships disengage.

At last they began to move away from the other vessel, and despite the clouds of smoke, she saw that it was low in the water. They had finished it. It was surely sinking. They changed course and swung around so that she could not see it any longer.

She sank into a nearby chair, wearied and sick with the violent experience. From above came the noise of the crew celebrating—hoarse shouting and laughter and cheering. Once she thought she heard a woman screaming

240

shrilly. This must have been her imagination, she decided; yet the sound haunted her and echoed in her mind.

An hour passed and she had still not been unlocked. In all, about five hours had gone by since the main battle with the ship. She had no water and she was thirsty and hungry. She pounded on the door to be let out and called to Nicholas, but there was no reply. Then she began to worry that he had been killed or badly wounded.

She was beset by these fears when she heard the cabin door being unlocked. When it opened, it was old Manuel with a tray of food and drink for her. She got up immediately.

"The captain!" she demanded, tugging at the old man's sleeve. "Is he safe?"

"*Si, signora,*" Manuel said in his stolid fashion. The hunchback put the tray on the desk for her and started for the door.

"Where is he?" she asked. "When will I see him?"

"Soon," the old man said. "Soon, signora." And he went out and locked the door after him.

It was night when Nicholas himself appeared. He was dirty and exhausted, and he appeared to be in a strange, tense mood. He said, "You managed all right?"

She ran to him and kissed him and pressed against him. "I died a thousand times for you!"

"I was safe enough," the handsome captain said, his arms about her.

"You sank the other vessel?"

"Yes," he said. "We had no choice. It could well have been us rather than them."

"Were many lives lost?"

He frowned. "We lost five men."

"What about them?" she asked.

He gave her a strange look. Then he said, "They fared little worse."

"Then they got in their boats safely?"

"I'd say so," he told her vaguely. "We moved away from them before they sank. They would not take to the boats until the last minute."

She sighed. "It is a dreadful business!"

241

His smile was bitter. "Only a while ago you were saying the ocean offered a peaceful existence."

"I'd had no taste of this."

"On shore or on ship, life is a struggle," he told her. "The spoils go to the victor."

"Spoils?"

He nodded. "Naturally. When you vanquish an enemy, you take what you like from him. That vessel was loaded with splendid silks and silverware from Spain. We made a fine haul and will be able to sell much of it when we touch port."

"This is the custom?"

"Always," he told her. "Wars are fought for trade."

"I see," she said, still a trifle puzzled. And then she asked, "What about the women? I saw there were some on board that other vessel, and I thought I heard a woman scream from our deck, above."

He shook his head. "Your imagination. We would not take a woman prisoner. In fact, we took no prisoners."

"The scream did not sound like a man's," she insisted.

"Men in pain often scream in a high-pitched way," he told her. "That must have been what you heard."

"I suppose so," she said uncertainly.

"There is still a lot of damage and gore above," he said. "I do not want you to go out there until the deck is cleaned and scrubbed."

"As you wish," she replied quietly.

He looked uneasy. "I must go back up there. I still have to direct the cleaning operation."

"Will you dine with me?"

"I will be back later. You dine by yourself. I won't be hungry. This sort of experience takes much out of me."

"I'm sure it does," she said sympathetically.

He left her and she dined alone. Manuel took her dirty dishes away, it became dark, and she still sat waiting for her captain. At last she heard stumbling footsteps, and the door opened and Nicholas lurched in.

She stood up. "You're drunk!" she exclaimed.

He swayed and nodded. "You are right, my dear. I am very drunk. I have had too much!"

Tessa said, "Come let me help you."

He smiled at her and placed an arm over her shoulders so she might guide his lagging steps into the bedroom off the cabin. She eased him down on the wide bunk on which they had so often made love. He looked up at her with drunken fondness on his handsome face. Then his eyes closed and he sank into a deep sleep at once.

She loosened his clothes and then left him. She put it down to the shock the battle had been to his sensitive nature. And she paced up and down thinking about it all; oddly, she could not forget that woman's scream.

Suddenly she realized she was no longer a prisoner in the cabin. In his drunken state Nicholas had left the door to the deck ajar. Cautiously she made her way outside. It was dark without any stars. Then she heard men's voices coming towards her and she darted to hide in a shadowed place where she would not be seen.

Two men came into view. As they came nearer, she recognized one of them as Mr. Withers. Then, to her horror, she saw they were carrying a body. Moving close to the railing, with a united effort they heaved the body into the ocean. She only had a momentary glimpse of the body, but she was certain it had been that of a woman!

Chapter Thirteen

The naked body of a woman!

The two men turned and muttered something and laughed, then walked off in the other direction. Tessa remained silent and unmoving in the shadows, sick with fear and stunned by what she had just seen. Her head reeled with the horror of it. These men had taken at least one of the more attractive women from the other vessel and had savagely raped her.

Probably all of them had raped her! Perhaps Nicholas had been a party to it. This would explain his strange drunken state—and the crew would surely not dare do such a thing without his approval. How could this man to whom she had given her heart be guilty of such a dreadful act? Was this what they called waging war?

Finally she crept out of the hiding place from which she had watched this horror. Standing there in a sort of trance, all at once she was aware of a fluttering sound above her head—the flag in the wind. She looked up, expecting to see the familiar Union Jack, but instead she saw the Skull and Crossbones! Now she had no more doubts!

Stricken by her discovery, she went back into the cabin. From the adjoining room came the drunken snores of the man who had so betrayed her. She felt soiled for having loved him. In her wildest imagination she had not suspected he was a pirate, but now she realized how naive she had been. He had been a friend of Mad Reevy's, and that crafty criminal had never associated with any kind but his own. Why hadn't she thought of this before it was too late?

Now she was far from England and the London where she had known both happiness and tragedy—trapped on a pirate ship, the mistress of a pirate captain! What hope could there be for her? One day the ship would be sunk and she would die with its pirate scum. If she were taken off alive, she would be raped as a pirate bawd or taken to some prison like Newgate. Better to drown!

She settled back in the chair by the big desk for what was to be a nearly sleepless night. She did not know what she would do. She knew only that somehow she had to survive and attempt to escape from this vile ship. With this uppermost in her mind, she finally slept a little.

Nicholas came in the morning and thinking she was asleep, lifted her from the chair and placed her on the bunk where he had been. Then he left her. She could not sleep for the smell of strong rum in the tiny room and the state of her troubled mind. After a while she washed and dressed. Manuel had set a breakfast out for her and she ate a little.

Then she went on deck. It was a lovely warm day with the sun shining and the sea placid. She almost automatically gazed up at the flag and saw that the dread Skull and Crossbones had been replaced with the respectable Union Jack. She was standing by the railing when Nicholas came up to her.

He said, "I'm sorry about last night. Battle affects me that way."

She glanced at him. "You always get drunk?"

"Often," he admitted. "Most of the men do. A celebration of being alive."

Soberly she said, "Some did not live to celebrate."

"True. But only a few."

She sighed. "I do not find the sea so pleasant today."

"It is an exceptional day. What is wrong, that you are so solemn?"

"I cannot get over yesterday as easily as you seem to have," she answered.

Nicholas was dressed elegantly again in velvet, but he wore no hat, and his black hair rustled slightly in the breeze. He said, "Perhaps you should have drunk like the rest of us."

"To drown my conscience?"

He frowned. "Rather, to lighten your mood."

She said, "I do not think whiskey would help me."

He sighed. "I'm sorry, Tessa. I know it was a bad
245

business. But England and Holland are at war, and as long as this situation exists, even honest merchants must be ready to do battle."

"So you told me," she said.

"I had hoped you would adjust to the reality of it," he said earnestly, "the necessity, in fact."

"Yes," she said, staring out at the ocean. "I'm sure you did."

"In a few days you will have forgotten," he said hopefully.

"Don't be so sure," she said, looking up into his handsome face. "I keep thinking about the men in the boats—and the women."

His face crimsoned. "I'm not sure there were any women aboard that ship."

Her eyes met his. "I told you I heard a woman scream on this very deck."

He looked uneasy. "And I seem to remember correcting you. You were wrong, as I told you yesterday evening."

"Yes, you did do that."

Nicholas hesitated a moment as the silence lengthened following her statement. Then, somewhat testily, he asked, "Are you hinting that I lied to you?"

She gave him an even look. "You are protective. And you do want me to adjust to this sort of warfare."

"What does that mean?"

"You might lie to me to protect my feelings," she said calmly.

Nicholas again crimsoned. "I see we are not in a pleasant mood. Very well, I can wait. We have plenty of time."

"Speaking of time," she said, "when do you expect to reach Cadiz?"

"Cadiz?"

"The port where your cargo is waiting."

"Oh, that!" he said. "In a week or two. We should be there in a week or two." He walked away from her, and meeting Mr. Withers, engaged the first mate in a serious conversation.

She remained at the railing, sick at what their conversation had made so clear. They were not sailing to Cadiz or any other port. This had been a fabrication on his part. They were casting about on the Spanish Main, ready to prey on innocent merchant vessels, and when the ship was gorged with loot, Nicholas would direct its course back to London.

She walked the length of the ship and soon discovered that it had not escaped injury. One of the cabin sections aft was splintered, and a mast had been damaged. Sailors were working on it now, trying to reinforce it with supports, but it seemed to Tessa that a bout of heavy winds and seas might bring this damaged mast hurtling down.

She passed a wounded sailor on the deck. He was stretched out in a drunken coma, his stump of a right arm bound with bloody bandages. And all the time she was haunted by the vision of that lithe female body with flowing golden hair being thrown over the side.

On the lee deck she came face to face with the dour Mr. Withers. She halted and said, "I see you have had some grievous damage, and at least one of your men was badly injured."

"Toby lost his arm—or a good part of it," Mr. Withers admitted, showing no emotion.

"But you expect these hazards?"

"Yes, ma'am," the first mate said.

"Were there many injured on the other ship?"

"More than us," he said.

"What about women? I'm sure I saw several women on the deck when the other vessel was close by."

Mr. Withers stared at her. After a hesitation he said, "You'll have to ask the captain about that, ma'am."

"Oh?" she said.

But Mr. Withers hurried away as quickly as he could. Staring after him, she found herself disgusted by him.

In spite of her upset state, she picked out a fine gown for dinner. Then, as she put it on, she realized it had been stolen and that the woman who'd owned it had likely died a violent death at the hands of her lover and his pirate crew. The logical conclusion was that yesterday's violence

247

was a drama that must have been repeated many times. This dress had come as loot on a long-ago voyage.

Nicholas had set out candles on their dinner table and was himself in a handsome outfit of yellow. They sat at the table and dined handsomely on venison preserved in wine. When they reached the end of the meal she glanced at him across the table.

"I like you better when you are sober, Nicholas," she said.

He smiled. "I like myself better."

"You were very drunk last night."

"I was disgusting, I know," he apologized. "You must forgive me."

"Yes, I suppose I must."

Nicholas looked troubled. "I do not like this distance you have suddenly put between us."

"Oh?"

"I think it unjust. Damn it, I do."

She took a deep breath before plunging into what she considered the business of the dinner. Then quietly she said, "I spoke with Mr. Withers this afternoon."

"Did you? He's not talkative."

"I'm aware of that. I asked him if there had been a woman prisoner taken . . . if she had been aboard. And he told me to ask you."

The handsome face of Nicholas clouded. "He said that?"

"Yes."

"I can't think why," Nicholas said irritably.

"I can," she said.

He glared at her. "What do you mean?"

"You are the captain of this ship."

"So?"

"You are responsible for what goes on. When Miguel stepped out of line, you dealt with him quickly enough."

He scowled. "The man tried to rape you! Would you have preferred that he was permitted to do as he pleased?"

"No, but your punishment was more cruel than was needed."

248

"I had no time to make choices," he replied impatiently. "It is over and done with. I would hear no more of it!"

"All right," she said. "Mr. Withers said what he did because he felt you should tell me about last night—that woman's scream."

He hesitated, frowning. "As I have told you, I know nothing about it."

"I think you do," she said quietly. "I *know* there was a woman."

He was taken aback. "You do?"

"Yes, I do," she said evenly. "Because I saw her naked body being thrown over the side by Mr. Withers and one of the sailors."

Nicholas looked crushed. He sank back in his chair and rubbed his chin moodily. Then he said, "I'm sorry, but you ought not to have been snooping about."

"Pray, which was worse?" she asked. "My snooping or the crew's murdering some poor girl?"

He looked at her grimly. "War is a nasty business. I have told you that."

"Is that an act of war—taking an innocent girl aboard and allowing the crew to rape and abuse her until she dies?"

This time his face went pale. He got up and began to pace back and forth in an agitated manner. At last he turned to her and said, "I couldn't help it! I wasn't able to stop it until it was too late."

"A fine excuse."

"It is true!"

"It occurred to me you might have been one of them," she said. "It seemed possible that in your drunkenness you too might have soiled her poor body, just as the others did!"

"Stop!" he cried. "You speak from a lack of understanding. This is war!"

She stood up facing him. "No! Not war! Piracy!" He opened his mouth to speak, but no words came. Instead, he picked up his wineglass and took a large gulp as she went on, "As you well know, what took place yesterday

249

was an act of piracy! That poor girl's murder was the degenerate work of a pack of criminals! Pirates!"

"Be careful!" he warned, looking as if he might strike her.

"Nicholas, the charade is over. I saw the flag last night—the Skull and Crossbones! How proudly it fluttered from your mast!"

He hit her full across her mouth with the back of his hand. "Slut!"

Blood trickled from her broken lip. She let it run down her chin without touching it, and it dripped onto the front of her lovely dress. She said, "I might have expected that from you!"

He sneered at her, "And what am I to expect from you? The leavings of the court! Whore to any of the gentry with the fee to pay!"

She said, "Captain Nicholas Marle! What a charade! You are no captain. You're a filthy pirate!"

"And what are you?" he demanded. "A pirate's mistress!"

"You tricked me!"

He smiled nastily. "You were happy enough in my arms. I heard no complaints!"

"You will never hold me in your arms again," she countered, "nor have me in your bed!"

He stood by the cabin door in an ugly mood. "We'll see about that. While you are on this ship, you will do as I say."

"You cannot force me to bed with you!"

Nicholas smiled nastily. "You think not?"

"I may be naive," she said, "but I have some character."

"I'm sure you do," he said mockingly. "No doubt a mite rubbed off His Majesty when he was pleasuring you at court!"

Having delivered this insult, he left her. Tessa sat watching after him, still in a rage. She knew she had acted rashly in revealing that she knew the *Flying Eagle* was a pirate vessel and Nicholas was its pirate captain, but she
250

had not felt equal to going on pretending. She had had to let him know and show him her contempt.

She had no idea what would happen next. She went to the room off the cabin and locked herself in. Then she undressed for bed and offered a prayer for forgiveness. Trembling, she thought of her days of working with the nuns during the plague, and she remembered that the Mother Superior had promised to pray for her protection. She surely needed such prayers now.

Before she could sleep, the door was tried, and then there was a banging on it. Nicholas, on the other side, called out in a fury, "Let me in!"

"No!" she shouted in reply.

"You cannot treat me in this fashion!" he raged.

"Go away," she told him.

"I'll break the door down."

"It will do you no good. I'll kill myself before I let you make love to me again."

He was silent a moment. Then in a different tone, he begged, "Tessa, you must forgive me!"

"I cannot!"

"You must!" he insisted. "It is your duty. You have told me you loved me. With love, forgiveness goes hand in hand, as does tolerance."

"I feel none of those things for you," she told him through the door. "What I feel most is disgust."

Again there was silence. After a long moment he said, "I will allow you to have your will this time. But in the end your will must give way to mine!"

"Never!" she said.

In the long days that followed an uneasy truce developed between them. Tessa continued to live in the small room off his cabin, but they barely spoke to each other. Her hope was that he would tire of the situation and find a way to put her off at a nearby port. Still he made no move to do this.

When she ventured on deck—at certain times and in certain areas—she noticed that Mr. Withers deliberately avoided her. The crew remained aloof; nevertheless, she was aware of hostile glances at her and lustful looks, which she preferred not to see. It was a battle of wills and she did not know how long it might go on.

She read and thought a lot about London. What would Mr. Grimp think, and Lord Harry Farr? Would her disappearance be put down to sudden death by the plague, and would her inheritance be lost to her because of her absence? She hoped not, but she could not help worrying.

The king surely must have returned to London with his court. If so, the theaters would soon be open. Nell Gwyn would be there and rehearsals would begin on a season of plays. Tessa felt sure that if she were there she would find work; but instead she was a prisoner in a pirate ship on an ocean a thousand miles away!

What a misfortune that she had met Captain Nicholas Marle; still greater was her mistake in falling in love with him. In her loneliness and despair, her heart had played her false. She could not now imagine what she had seen in the big, arrogant man. Finding out that he was a pirate captain had been one of the most shocking discoveries she'd ever made. Now all she could think of was escape.

They were in warm water now, and each day was hotter than the one before. Late in the afternoon on one of these sweltering days, Tessa met Nicholas on a deserted area of the deck. He halted and indicated a desire to speak with her.

He asked, "How long can this silly feud go on between us?"

"Forever," she said.

"Rot!" the pirate captain returned. "You cannot deny we made good lovers."

She gave him a scathing glance. "I can never love you again."

"Because of what I am?"

"Because of all you've done," she said scornfully, "your cowardly kidnapping of me and your murdering of that poor girl."

"The past is past," he shrugged. "Let us look to the future."

"There is no future for us," she said incredulously, turning her back to him.

252

There was a cutting edge to his voice. "You are pushing me too far, I warn you!"

"I have made up my mind."

"You will find I have a mind of my own," he warned
her.

"I am your prisoner," she said, "at your mercy."

His smile was unpleasant. "You may know that, but
you are scarcely behaving as if you do."

She told him, "I would prefer that you not address me
at all."

"You cannot hate me that much," he said lightly.

The next she heard of him was that evening. He came
drunkenly into the cabin where she was reading a volume
by Daniel Defoe. He stood before her, sneering belligerently at her. The sun had gone down, but darkness had
brought no respite from the heat. She pretended to be absorbed in the book and did not glance up at him.

At last he spoke, and she noted with alarm that his
words were drunkenly slurred: "I would take you to
bed!"

She did not move or lift her eyes from the book, paid
no attention at all, as if she had not heard him, though
she was quaking inwardly.

He moved nearer, so close she could smell the rum
from him. "Will you come willingly to bed with me, or
must I take you by force?"

She closed the book and glanced up at him with disgust. "I'm sure raping the weak is no new experience for
you!"

These words seemed to madden him. In the next instant he grasped her and dragged her out of the chair to
stand trembling before him.

"So it's rape you want?" he shouted in a drunken rage.

"Please!" she begged him, moving back a little.

He was beyond listening, past being reasoned with. He
came at her in his insane, drunken anger, saying harshly,
"Well, milady, you shall have what you want!"

She screamed and made a move to elude him, but he
was too quick for her. He grasped her cruelly and began
to tear the clothing off her. When he stumbled, off bal-

ance for a moment, she pulled away from him and in h[e]
terror ran out on the deck, her body bared to the waist!

But he came relentlessly after her. She crouche[d]
against the railing, threatening to jump over, sobbing o[u]
a plea for mercy. By now, however, there was no merc[y]
in the drunken captain's heart. He continued system[at]ically tearing her clothes to shreds.

When she stood naked before him, he lifted her, sti[ll]
struggling against him, and took her down to the lowe[r]
deck. She had no idea what he was going to do, but sh[e]
kicked and scratched at him, her fingernails bringin[g]
blood to both his cheeks in vain. Paying no attention t[o]
her, he went on his way with her squirming, screamin[g]
figure in his arms.

Laboriously he descended the steep steps to the com[m]on room of the crew's quarters. The rogues of man[y]
lands lay about the room in various states of undress. A[t]
their captain's dramatic entrance, they stood up to awa[it]
what would happen next.

With a vicious smile on his bleeding face, the drunke[n]
Nicholas held Tessa before them, cringing, sobbing, an[d]
totally nude. In a tone of satisfaction, he bellowed, "[I]
have a prize for you, lads. Use her as you like and use h[er]
well!" Then he pushed her towards them.

She screamed, aware of lustful eyes, bearded face[s]
greedy shouts, and hands clutching every part of he[r]
body. She cried out her fear as one of the naked ruffian[s]
set his naked body down on her and plunged his malenes[s]
into her savagely, causing her great pain. Now anothe[r]
was attacking her from the rear, and she was dimly awar[e]
of male genitals brushing against her face. She was sea[r]ing with pain and packed between sweating, besti[al]
bodies. It was a hell; it could not be endured . . . merc[i]fully she became unconscious.

When awareness returned, the first thing she knew w[as]
the pain which racked her. She felt as if the entire lowe[r]
part of her body had been torn apart by torture weapon[s]
She stirred a little and moaned, and the stinging of he[r]
breasts made her examine them with dull eyes. The[n]
254

vere bite marks on them, as if she had been ravaged by
an animal.

As her eyes wandered down her stinking, sweat-ridden
body, she saw that her genital area and her legs as far as
her knees were stained with blood, and blood still oozed
from her most intimate areas. She lay back and closed her
eyes and surrendered herself to her misery. Once again
she blacked out.

When next she became conscious of herself and her
surroundings, she was not alone. Old Manuel was
kneeling by her, bathing her with lukewarm water. His
wrinkled face was a study in shocked dismay. And when
he saw that her eyes were open and fixed on him, he
halted his work to speak to her.

"Signora," he said in a soft voice, "Manuel will make
you well."

She could not reply, but closed her eyes as the old man
went on with his efforts. After he bathed her completely,
he rubbed some soothing oils and salves into her skin. By
the time he'd finished, some of the worst pain had eased,
and she felt a great lassitude engulf her. He gave her a
sweet-tasting, warm drink and then covered her poor body
with a blanket. She went into a drugged sleep almost at
once.

The next morning the old man was at her side once
again with some broth and tea, and she had her first bit of
nourishment. Later he bathed and medicated her once
again. Each time she woke she felt a little less pain, and
gradually her strength returned. But the memory of the
horror into which Nicholas had thrust her remained. She
did not know how she had endured it, how her poor body
had survived. It was a wonder she had not died down
here from their abuse; if she had, she knew, she would
have been thrown over the side like the blond girl they'd
captured from the other ship!

All this time she had not left the tiny cabin, and only
occasionally did she get up from the bunk bed. But at last
the day came when she was able to dress herself and
emerge into the larger cabin. During the period of her
convalescence Nicholas had not come near her. The only

255

living soul who had any contact with her was the hunch-back, Manuel. It was to his tender care that she owed her life.

Now as she stood in the center of the large cabin, her legs still weak and unsteady beneath her, the door opened and Nicholas came in. In this hot weather he wore only his breeches, stockings, shoes, and a white blouse open at the neck. He looked devil-may-care and handsome as he stood facing her.

He said, "You're better. I'm glad."

She stared at him. "You might have been kinder to me. Why didn't you just slit my throat and throw me over the side?"

He shrugged. "I'm a proud man. I did not like your treatment of me. I had to have my revenge."

"And now?"

"It doesn't matter," he said. "I have humbled you. I no longer want you. Not since the crew had their pleasure of you. When the opportunity offers, I will return you to England."

"Thank you," she said with mock politeness, to cover the furious hatred she was feeling.

He gave her another look, as if to convince himself she had returned this well to her old self, then he went out and left her alone. She collapsed into the nearest chair and sobbed bitterly. She felt there was no longer any hope. She did not believe Nicholas would make any effort to see her safely home. More likely he would throw her to the crew again when he had another drunken tantrum. At this thought, she drew herself up. That must never be. She would go over the side before she let that happen a second time!

The day following this confrontation they sighted another ship. She heard Nicholas and Mr. Withers talking on the bridge, and from what she was able to catch, she knew the other ship was a British merchant vessel. As before, with the Dutch ship, Mr. Withers gave curt orders to the crew to prepare for battle while Nicholas remained on the bridge to direct operations.

But the sight of the distant British ship made Tessa

desperate. Instead of going back to the cabin, she found a hiding place in the aft part of the lower deck behind some large kegs and coils of rope. She knew that Nicholas would order the cabin locked, believing that she was down there. And she had decided she would rather take her chances on the deck, despite the cannon fire, than be trapped below.

In her mind was the hope that she might somehow transfer to the British vessel if the battle resulted in a close engagement like the one she'd witnessed before. In that case, she might make contact with some of the British crew, even if they lost the battle, and be able to take to the boats with them. It was a wild dream, but there was no other chance.

The pace on board the pirate ship quickened. The dark, ugly cannons were rolled from their hiding places and set up for action. Nicholas was busy shouting out orders and cursing when they were not at once understood. The villainous crew, all bared to the waist, had their various duties. Someone brought down the Union Jack, and the Skull and Crossbones took its place.

As the British merchant vessel drew nearer, from her hiding place Tessa saw that it was larger than it had seemed at first. This encouraged her in her fantasy of escape. When the stately vessel came within range, Nicholas gave an order and the cannons were fired. And once this was begun, the cannons were primed and fired over and over again.

The first cannon fire stove a mast of the British ship, and the second did damage to its hull. Tessa pressed back in her hiding place as cursing members of the crew rushed past her to shift one of the cannons slightly. Then there came a reply barrage from the British ship. The initial burst of fire struck the pirate ship and set it quivering. There was a huge amount of smoke, an explosion and then fire in the bow of the vessel.

Nicholas shouted, "Get that fire under control! Mind the powder! Get it out!"

Tessa listened to the orders with a pounding heart. She knew the powder for the cannons was kept in the fore of

257

the ship. And by a lucky strike the British cannon blast had hit this vital spot. Now there came another explosion of more fury. She saw several of the pirate crew blown into the ocean, and flames surged skyward!

As the smoke cleared for a little, she caught a glimpse of Nicholas on the bridge. He was in a frenzy, shouting all sorts of orders, which no one seemed to heed. At least one of the pirate ship's cannons was still in action. It sent a blast at the British vessel but seemingly did no damage. Nicholas shouted something to the crew.

Just then another burst of cannon fire hit the pirate ship, apparently close to where Tessa was hiding. Splinters flew around her and the ship trembled again. Mr. Withers, running by her hiding place, was struck by a heavy piece of flying metal and went down like a log.

Immediately she got up and hurried to him. His head had nearly been severed from his body, and the deck was crimson with his blood. She quickly retrieved the pistol that had fallen from his hand and began moving along the deck.

At the same time the British ship was beginning to close in on them, and since the last cannon of the pirate ship refused to work, probably because of overheating, there was nothing to stop the British ship from coming alongside. Many of its seamen, Tessa noticed, were perched high on the rope ladders leading to the masts— well armed British sailors, ready to drop down onto the deck of the pirate ship.

It now became clear to her that this vessel Nicholas had taken on probably was not a merchant ship at all but a navy warship disguised to seem a merchant vessel far from the trade lines—a decoy deliberately sent out to find pirate ships. Nicholas had taken the bait and had been trapped.

The pirate ship was ablaze to a point midway of her length. Tessa moved cautiously along the railing, hoping to be able to board the British ship and tell her story, yet wanting to avoid being noticed by Nicholas and his villainous crew. Her chances were good, she thought. There seemed little likelihood that the pirates were seeing any
258

thing besides raging fire and the need to meet the enemy in hand-to-hand combat.

The confusion was beyond belief. There was shouting and cursing, and men scurried here and there, some bleeding. Then Tessa saw Nicholas come down from the bridge and draw his sword as he prepared to lead his crew in battle with the victorious British vessel. The ragged band mounted the side of the ship and faced the Britishers grimly.

Tessa saw that the cannons on the British vessel were larger and looked more powerful than their own. The two ships drew close and there was a grinding of their wooden sides, accompanied by a great shout from the pirates who followed Nicholas, now going to meet their doom.

A British voice bellowed out through a horn from the bridge of the other ship, "Surrender! Good treatment is promised all who surrender!"

The motley crew of the pirate ship either laughed at this or pretended not to hear it. Yelling fiercely, they bounded onto the other deck.

Tessa dodged to one side and just missed being slashed by the blade of one of the British sailors. She screamed as she saw the blades glistening in the sun, heard the loud clicking of swords in contest over the harsh cries of the combatants. She crouched down and kept moving, hoping to come to a place where she might leap from the pirate ship to the safety of the other.

Men were fighting and dying all around her. There was another explosion from the front of the pirate ship, and great hunks of flaming debris filled the air. She dodged as one dropped directly in front of her. Then above all the wild chaotic sounds she heard her name, called out in astonishment.

She did not know whether someone had actually shouted her name or whether it was only in her mind. She turned to see and there was Nicholas, sword upraised, staring at her with disbelief. She did not hesitate but lifted the pistol and aimed at him. The shot made little impact on the whole chorus of noise, but she saw him flinch, saw

259

the spread of red blood on his chest. With a look of reproach on his handsome face, he fell to the deck.

Tessa was sobbing now. She did not linger where she was. Reaching the place where the railings of the two ships rubbed each other, with a great effort she leaped aboard the British ship. As she did so, something hit her, and she lost all knowledge of what was going on around her.

When she opened her eyes she was on the deck of the British ship and an officer in uniform was bending over her. "I vow you're not dead after all!" the man said. "And so you were one of them!"

"No!" she said feebly. "My name is Tessa Shaw. I was taken prisoner by Nicholas Marle!"

"A likely story," the hard-faced officer said with derision. "They dressed you well enough. That gown you're wearing must have come from some unfortunate Spanish noblewoman."

There was a lot of noise in the background, and her head was paining terribly. She fought to keep her mind clear and explain her position. "It is the truth," she insisted in a hoarse voice. "I was taken prisoner in London by that pirate crew!"

Another man came up and in a curt voice asked, "What is it goes on here?"

"A woman," said the officer who had been busy questioning her. "Claims to have been a prisoner aboard the pirate ship. I don't believe her. Says she hails from London and her name is Tessa Shaw."

"Tessa Shaw!" the man who had been identified as "Captain" said. " 'Zounds! That name is more than familiar to me. Let me look at her!"

In the next moment Tessa saw a face bending over her, a face older than when she'd last seen it, but one she could never forget. Not able to believe her good fortune, she cried out, "Bob Wills!"

"Tessa!" he cried, and kneeling down, took her in his arms to hug and kiss her.

Everything that followed was confused in her mind. But she was aware that she was carried below and the injury to her head was taken care of by the ship's doctor; sometime afterwards she found herself in a small cubicle in a narrow bunk. The noise of battle had faded into the distance and she no longer cared what was happening. She sank into a deep, exhausted sleep.

When she awoke, Bob Wills, in the dress of an officer in the King's Navy, sat by her. He said, "To think I would have to travel so far to find you, dear Tessa!"

She gazed at him. "You are older!"

"Who is not? Though I vow you do not show the passing of the years. You look as young and lovely as the lass whom I knew as the prize ponyback rider."

She smiled sadly. "I'm a much different person from that girl. Life has done much to me."

"To us all," Bob said.

"And how do you come to be an officer in the navy?" she asked.

Bob smiled wryly. "The death rate has been high among men and officers. The Dutch have given us a bad time, and so have pirate ships like the one you were on. I was promoted up the line until now I'm a junior officer."

"Lucky for me," she said. "Who else would have listened to my story?"

"Someone would have," he said. "Still, I'm glad I was on hand to help."

"You saved me!"

"I think you saved yourself," Bob Wills said. "And from what I've heard, you were the one put a bullet into that pirate captain. Several of our men witnessed your doing it and reported to us."

She closed her eyes. "He's dead, I suppose."

"Yes, he's dead! And his ship is at the bottom! There wasn't a survivor of the filthy lot except you!"

She opened her eyes and looked up at him frankly, soberly. "Would you think me cruel beyond understanding if I told you none of them deserved to live?"

Bob Wills shook his head. "No. I'd guess they treated you in such a way as to make you think like that."

"I'd given up all hope of seeing London again."

"You'll see it soon enough," he assured her. "We're on

our way back there now. They say the plague has faded out and it has been a quiet spring in the city."

"Is the king back?"

"I've been told so. What happened to you after that Lady Pleasure and her foppish friend took you away from the circus?"

Tessa smiled wanly. "A long story, Bob. You should have married me and ended it there."

The good-looking former acrobat said, "I wanted you to be a great lady. And you talk and look like one. But how did you come to wind up where we found you?"

She told him the whole story, skimming over parts of it, but telling him of the kindness of Sir David Farr, of her sad romance with Thomas Montagu, and finally of her being drugged and taken prisoner aboard the pirate ship. She ended with, "Thus far the fine life and a good home have not been mine."

"And I thought I had done what was best for you," Bob said sadly.

"You could not know," she said. "But at last we are together again. Fate sent you to me. You saved me from more disaster. Do you think we were ordained to meet this way?"

"Perhaps," Bob said with a frown. "You know I care for you deeply, Tessa."

"You were my first love," she said gently.

He took her hand in his and told her, "And you were mine . . . back in those carefree circus days." He paused. "But much has happened to me, just as it has to you. And I now am married to a lass I love well, and she has given me a son and a daughter."

Chapter Fourteen

It was a fine June day when Tessa stood by the railing of *H.M.S. Trevalyn* as it sailed majestically up the Thames. London had never looked better to her. Her eyes blurred with sentimental tears as she saw the great, gray huddle of buildings dominated by the Tower, London Bridge and St. Paul's Cathedral. She was back home!

Heroic-looking in his naval uniform, Bob Wills came to stand by her. He smiled at her and said, "In a short while you'll be setting foot on English soil."

She glanced at him. "Something I once thought might never be again."

"You are well and you are in London," he said cheerfully. "Dare you ask for more?"

"Not for the moment," she said.

"What are you going to do?"

She smiled wryly. "There will be no welcome committee to meet me on the docks. But I do have friends. First, I shall look up Mr. Grimp."

"Mr. Grimp?"

"My solicitor," she explained. "I have been away almost six months. He may have given me up for dead."

"I hope not," Bob said. "Would you like me to accompany you?"

She shook her head. "That won't be necessary. You are in a hurry to see your wife and children."

"It has been a long while," he admitted.

"Give them my love."

"You must meet them one day."

"I would enjoy that," she smiled.

"Where can I find you?"

"That is hard to say," she sighed. "Perhaps it would be best for you to contact Mr. Grimp; he will know where I'll be. I'll give you the address of his office."

The ship was soon docking, and the usual peddlers, small officials, and women of the streets were on hand to greet the new arrivals. Tessa bade a hasty good-bye to

Bob and engaged a hansom cab to take her to the office of Mr. Grimp. The clothes she wore had been given her by an officer on board who had bought some things in France for his wife. She intended to send him payment for his kindness as soon as she had called on her solicitor.

She had the driver of the carriage wait as she entered the street-level office of the fat solicitor. The wizened clerk recognized her at once.

"Miss Shaw! We feared you were dead!"

She smiled. "Not this time. Would you please pay the driver of the carriage, as I have no money with me. Mr. Grimp will repay you."

The old clerk nodded, "I'll announce you to Mr. Grimp first," he said.

When he called her name, Mr. Grimp immediately came out to meet her. "Dear Miss Shaw! Back from the dead!" the stout solicitor said, taking her by the hands.

"I was afraid you might give me up," she confessed as she took a chair in the office.

He sat down heavily at his roll-top desk. "I was nearly ready to. It was Lord Harry Farr who insisted you would return. He never lost faith."

"I have something to thank Harry for."

"You do, indeed," the solicitor agreed. "Now tell me, where have you been?"

She told him the whole story, ending with, "I still can't believe that I'm back in London after all I've been through."

"What incredible luck that you managed to get aboard the man-of-war and that one of the officers recognized you."

"I'm most grateful. My prayers were answered."

Mr. Grimp smiled benignly. "And your worries are over. Your affairs are exactly as they were when you left, except that your capital has accumulated some interest. You're still a rich young woman."

"Thank fortune for that . . . because I will need to start over again."

"What are your plans?" the solicitor asked.

"I would like a modest house; that taken care of, I

264

might enjoy going back to acting once again. I assume the king has returned and the theaters are open?"

"They are," the fat man said. "I think I have just the house for you. It is not far from the Hungry Pilgrim. The man who owned the house died of the plague, and his widow does not wish to live there. It is all furnished, and I can get it for you reasonably."

"When can I have occupancy?"

"At once if you like."

"I have nowhere else to go," she said.

"Very well," Mr. Grimp said. "I have the keys. I will escort you personally."

The house was a two-story wooden structure and was nicely furnished. It was pleasant and yet modest, exactly what she wanted. She took it at once. Mr. Grimp had her sign the required papers, after which she had him give her a cash advance for living expenses. It appeared that all was well with her again.

Getting settled in her new house took time, but it was pleasantly spent. She was out doing some shopping one warm afternoon when she passed a Punch and Judy show operating on the edge of the small patch of green known as Duncan Square. She was amused by the performance and watched for a moment, along with several other adults and a number of children. A youngster appeared among the spectators with a hat to collect for the show. She gave him a few farthings and then resumed her walk back to her house.

She'd only gone a short distance when she heard her name called out. She turned. A man was running after her, and as he came up breathless and red of face, she recognized him as her foster father, Tom Shaw.

"Tessa!" he gasped. "You were watching our show."

"I was," she said, delighted to see him. "But I had no idea you and your wife were the puppeteers."

The old man looked sad. "Not Ina," he said. "She was lost to the plague."

"I'd heard a rumor you had both died of it."

"Not Tom Shaw," he said proudly. "But I saw poor

Ina cut down by it and there was nothing I could do. It was a terrible shock for me."

"I'm sure it must have been," Tessa sympathized. "I liked Ina. She was like a mother to me."

"You look like a great lady now," old Tom said, admiring her. "Lady Pleasure kept her word. Where is she?"

Tessa sighed and told the shabbily-clad old man, "Also dead of the plague."

"So many," he said, shaking his head. "Of every station in life."

"Death has not shown the rich any special favors," she said.

"You, at least, are wealthy now," the old man ventured.

"I have done well enough. Did you know Bob Wills is an officer in the navy?"

Old Tom sighed. "He became restless after you left. Nothing would induce him to remain with us. And without you two, the circus didn't last long."

"And my pony, my lovely pony?"

The old man looked embarrassed. "Sold him to another circus," he said. "He'll be well looked after."

"I'm glad to hear that."

"I must be getting back," the old man said uneasily. "The lady working with me is my second wife. A woman of some talent, but possessed of a sour disposition."

"I'm sorry," she said. "It was good seeing you again."

"And you," he said. "Take care of thyself, lass."

"I will," she said, kissing him on the cheek. "And you do the same."

"Aye," he said morosely and started back to the Punch and Judy stand.

This meeting with the old showman brought pleasant thoughts of youthful days once again—and perhaps this was a good thing, for memories of her nightmarish adventures on the pirate ship still came to haunt Tessa. She often had vivid dreams in which the malevolent, handsome Nicholas was threatening her; later in the dreams she always found herself naked at the mercy of the villainous seamen.

266

The days were quiet, however; and she felt hopeful. She began to plan for the future. She had some clothes made, and she hired a little maid to live with her in the new house. The girl's name was Grace and she had a knack for cooking that made her valuable. Tessa enjoyed adding some personal touches to the place. Happily, the owner of the Hungry Pilgrim had carefully put aside the few belongings she'd left there and so she regained these clothes and other personal items.

One morning in early August Lord Harry Farr came to call on her in her new house. The young nobleman looked better than she had ever seen him before. He greeted her warmly with a kiss, and soon they were seated in the parlor of her new home with glasses of port.

In a gray frock coat and pale blue trousers, Lord Harry was a fashionable figure. He told her, "Lady Eve and myself have repaired our marriage. Plain as she is, I find she has an excellent head on her shoulders. In addition, she is a good mother."

"I'm happy for you," Tessa said, smiling. "So you have finished your sowing of wild oats?"

His eyes held a twinkle. "The right wench could start me again. What do you say?"

"I say I started you back on the path of your late father, and I'm pleased at the man you've become. I'm not likely to bring about your ruination by having an affair with you."

Harry sighed. "Ah, Tessa! I fear my father had all the best of you."

She laughed. "Perhaps that is true. My happiest days in London were with him."

"Have you so soon forgotten Thomas Montagu?" Lord Harry asked.

Tessa's lovely face clouded. "I shall never forget Thomas. That was a different sort of happiness. Call it the bittersweet variety."

"You know that Sir Edward is dead?"

She pretended ignorance of the fact. "Law, is he?"

"Yes," Harry said, giving her a searching look. "I thought you might have heard about it."

"But I was kidnapped months ago. I've lost all touch with what happened in London during my absence."

"Sir Edward was shot by his loutish son, Claude—now *Sir* Claude, if you don't mind!"

"Indeed!" She fought to maintain her calm. "I can't say that I'm sorry."

"I wouldn't expect that," Harry said. "Claude told some ridiculous sort of story about a woman and a man who came to hold his father up. Said he arrived on the scene to rescue Sir Edward and in the fracas shot the old man. The robber and his female accomplice escaped, of course."

"It is surely a strange story," she agreed.

His eyes met hers. "I was sure you'd relish it."

"I do," she said.

"I may add that Sir Claude Montagu is much like his father and hardly the most popular nobleman in London. It would have been different, had Thomas lived."

"Much different for all of us," she said. "What of Mary?"

Lord Harry sighed. "She has settled comfortably into her widowhood. She seems happy devoting her time to her children. She was delighted to hear of your return and she sends you her love."

"I must visit Wilton and see her," Tessa said. "I have always had a fondness for her."

"And she for you. Do come. Eve will welcome you, too, since she knows the role you played in my reformation."

Tessa smiled. "It was actually a selfish act on my part. Since I knew I could not have you as a husband, I decided I would like you as a brother—a brother molded in your father's pattern. So in the end I have won."

"Rather a brother than a lover?" he asked.

"Lovers are so much easier to come by," she said teasingly.

"I vow you've not lost your wit, lass," he said, enjoying this. "What do you propose to do, now that you are back in London?"

"I mean to go to the theater and look up Nell Gwyn

and the rest. I shall ask the opinion of Mr. Pepys, and if he advises me that it would be a good move, I shall try to rejoin them."

"You think much of this little clerk of the Admiralty?"

She smiled. "He is amusing and he knows most of the gossip in London."

"That he does," Lord Harry conceded as he rose to take his leave. "I must be going; I have much to do. See that you do visit us in Wilton."

"I promise," she said and saw him to the door.

About a week later she sought out Mr. Pepys, and by a fortunate coincidence, he was having a group of players at his house for a party that very evening. He gave Tessa a warm invitation and assured her that Nell Gwyn and Charles Hart would both be there. She was overjoyed at the news.

When she reached the Pepys house that evening, the revelry was already under way. Supper, games, cards, singing, and dancing were all going on at once. A servant let Tessa in, and her stout host came hurrying to greet her.

"I have announced you were coming," he said, his bulging eyes bright. "They are overjoyed—they thought you had died with the plague!"

"My absence made that story seem reasonable," she agreed. She had worn her most fetching blue gown and a blue hat that matched it. "Where is your good wife?"

Pepys looked embarrassed. "She is not present. She had to visit a sick cousin in Windsor. And to be truthful, I think this will be a better party without her. She has certain puritan leanings which make her suspect of theater folk . . . while they are my good friends."

"Has Nell arrived?" Tessa asked as Samuel Pepys filled a wine glass for her.

The little man poured himself a generous glass of the ruby liquid and beamed at her. "No, Nell will arrive a little later. She is at the top of her profession, a mature and experienced actress."

"She has much talent," Tessa agreed.

Pepys gulped his wine. "The people call her 'pretty,

witty Nell,' " he chuckled. "Few bother with her surname. And the playwrights capitalize on her impudence—writing parts, prologues, epilogues and the like to fit her personality."

"Then she has truly become a star," Tessa said.

"In every sense," Pepys agreed, sipping more wine. "When you have your breath, I shall introduce you to some of the others."

Listening to the ribald laughter in the adjoining room, Tessa was in no hurry to join the main company. She had come mostly to see Charles Hart and Nell. She asked Pepys, "What is the latest court gossip?"

His eyes twinkled. "Our good king is as fond of lechery as ever."

"And is Nell still a favorite?"

"One of several. I think the king is fond of her, but he is not the sort to be faithful to any woman—most especially not his wife."

"So the court is as licentious as ever."

"Perhaps more so," Pepys said. "Yet on Sundays the good and wicked attend church, sometimes both morning and afternoon services. If my experience may be trusted, not many Londoners are truly religious, but church attendance is looked on as a proper form of conduct. There are no laws to make it compulsory—except for those Roman Catholics who attempt to evade attending Church of England services. On the other hand, as you know, there is little else to do in the city on Sunday. Even Charles and all the court attend church."

"Is Lady Castlemaine still high in the king's regard?"

Pepys showed delight. "You might call her the king's senior consort!" And he laughed at his own joke.

"And who is the most powerful man at court?" Tessa wanted to know. "Have there been changes since I've been away?"

"Had you heard of Buckingham?"

"Only vaguely."

"He is the man of power at this time," Samuel Pepys said seriously. "He is a wit, light of temperament like Nell—in fact, he revised a play for Nell's use. He also has a talent for mimicry which the king enjoys. He grew up with Charles and has been almost a constant companion to him through the years. He is now thirty-nine, vain and ambitious and beginning to bloat a bit from the drink and his wild living."

Tessa smiled. "A too-common fate."

"So true!" Pepys agreed. "Withal, Buckingham prides himself on being a statesman. Actually, of course, he is too flighty to carry such projects to conclusion—and far too tactless for diplomacy. But no more of this talk! Let me introduce you to the others!"

She let him lead her within, to where some fifteen people were assembled, partaking of food and drink as they stood about laughing and talking. Some of them were small-part players from the King's Theater, and some recognized Tessa. Soon she was busy hearing about the latest plans for new play productions and enjoying herself thoroughly.

She was involved in a discussion of the merits of Shakespeare with a foppish young man, when she was interrupted by a female voice calling out heartily, "My dearest Tessa!"

She turned and saw Nell coming towards her. The lovely chestnut-haired girl was wearing a rose gown that set off her honey-colored beauty, and a single strand of pearls adorned her neck. Hurrying straight to Tessa, she threw her arms around her old friend.

"Word went out you were dead!" Nell exclaimed, kissing her.

"I was near it!"

Nell sized her up. "I vow, it agreed with you. You are more of a beauty than ever!"

"And you have become a star," Tessa returned, smiling.

"Fie on that," Nell grinned. "I was just as happy when I was an orange girl, and I did less work!"

"But you didn't have the king in your bed!" This sly taunt came from Charles Hart, who had joined them.

"A pox on you, Charles," Nell scolded with mock anger. "If you had not been the best Ophelia of your day, I would not tolerate you!"

Charles laughed heartily. "It's true I have never achieved the same fame since. Those female roles were my forte!" He embraced Tessa and kissed her. "I'm glad you're back again. We have a shortage of talented ladies!"

"And that is true!" Nell agreed as she helped herself to some bread and cheese.

Charles gave Tessa a questioning look. "You do plan to come back to us, don't you?"

She nodded. "It seems the theater is in my blood. I have dreamed of the day when I shall set foot on the stage once again."

"It need not be long," Charles Hart said, over a glass of brandy. "We are mounting several new plays."

Nell put in, "Rehearsals for the new pieces begin on Monday, September the third. That is when you should join us!"

Their attention was distracted by the abrupt entrance of little Mr. Pepys, chasing a stout, flaxen-haired girl who had managed to escape his pudgy hands. He turned to them, red-faced, to explain, "It was but a game of tag!"

Nell winked at him. "The game might have changed, had you captured her!"

Mr. Pepys, ruddy, perspiring, and more than a little drunk, said, "Nell, you are a queen among women. You understand me."

Droll Charles Hart could not let this pass. With a smile on his handsome face, he said, "Dear Pepys, you have it wrong. Nell is not so much a queen among women as she is a woman with a king!"

"Enough, Charles," Nell retorted with good-natured anger.

"I declare, a bit of singing would be in order," Mr. Pepys exclaimed. "Come, ladies and gentlemen, let us sing Flecknoe's warm tribute to Nell, 'On a Pretty Little Person'."

The group gathered around a smiling Nell and all began to sing the well-known ballad,

"She is pretty and she knows it,
    She is witty and she shows it,
    And besides that she's so witty,
    And so little and so pretty."

The song went on endlessly until they reached the last lines, "But for that, suffice to tell ye, 'Tis the little pretty Nelly!"

Someone then suggested they all sing a drinking song. This met with universal approval, and with Samuel Pepys in the lead, the song began. Nell gave Tessa a wink, and taking her hand, led her out of the room now filled with drunken harmonizing.

When they were alone in the adjoining room Nell wrinkled her pert nose in disgust and said, "I tell you, there comes a time when I tire of song!"

Tessa laughed. "Especially that sort of song."

Nell sat on a narrow bed and beckoned her, "Come sit with me, and tell me all that you have done since last we met."

Tessa smiled wanly. "It is a long story and, I'm afraid, not a pretty one."

"Never mind. I wish to hear it."

So Tessa told Nell everything. Nell listened intently, her sympathetic emotions—amusement, awe, horror—alternating in her face. She was clearly impressed. As Tessa finished, Nell said, "It is a wondrous tale. You must tell it to John Dryden someday. I know he could make a fine romantic drama of it."

Tessa shrugged. "John Dryden appears to keep busy enough with his own tales."

"His imagination is fertile," agreed Nell. "He is also an ambitious, rosy-cheeked young man, destined to go far . . . unless he annoys the king with too many barbed jests about him."

"That would be unwise," Tessa murmured.

Nell looked at her with concern. "But after all, you are alone. You still have no love."

"My one true love was Thomas Montagu. He lies dead beneath foreign waters."

"I had forgotten," Nell said, at once sorry. "I'm such a stupid, self-centered creature."

"You're much too hard on yourself."

"No, I'm like my mother in that respect, bless her poor gin-soaked body. She cared more for herself than anyone else."

"Really?"

"God's truth!" Nell said solemnly. "She put Rose out on the street when she was ten, then called her a harlot. I was not so easy for her. I kept my virtue and worked as an orange girl until I was of a better age. And then I picked my first gentleman for myself."

Tessa smiled. "You have done well. I hear you still have the king's friendship."

Nell eyed her and said frankly, "You mean he beds me when the whim strikes him."

"Is that all it amounts to?"

Nell relaxed and smiled thoughtfully. "No. If the truth were told—and surely it ought to be told to you—I have a warm affection for my Charlie. And I swear he feels the same for me."

"I'm glad," Tessa said. "I hoped you were content."

"You know he made Castlemaine a countess. She and all the other titled bitches he beds use him for their advancement. That is why they sleep with him and he knows it. He has no love for any of them."

"What about his queen?"

Nell's tone changed. Almost with awe, she said, "The Portuguese! The ugly one! There is a tenderness in his heart for her that must be close to love."

"Yet he continually cheats on her," Tessa said.

"Because she cannot give him an heir," Nell said soberly. "I think that made him doubt his manhood. To prove it he became a stud, of sorts, leaving a string of bastards by other women—and found the experience so pleasurable, he continued with it."

Tessa said, "You seem to have a great understanding of him."

Nell's eyes were gentle. "We talk for long periods. I think the talks we share are as important, or more so, than what happens when we are in bed. Yes, he is my dear Charlie, in spite of all the wagging tongues."

"There is bound to be jealousy of you."

"Indeed. A vice I abhor. I have never allowed myself to indulge in it. I think jealousy is close to stealing."

Tessa said, "I'd not thought of that, but you could be near the truth."

Nell placed an arm around her. "We must get you back on the stage, and I must find a good man for you."

"There is no hurry for that."

"Perhaps you should meet Sir Percy Hope. He is a member of the king's group of advisors and an important figure at court. He is a widower and is noted for his womanizing."

"I do not care for the sound of him," Tessa said.

"He is not bad," Nell assured her. "He is of good build and has a long face, but he dresses well and is a fine dancer."

Tessa rose with a laugh and said, "Let your matchmaking wait until I've found a place on the stage again."

They rejoined the others, and the party went on. At one o'clock in the morning the gathering broke up noisily, and windows were raised in the adjoining building. From one of the windows a man hurled epithets at the departing guests, and Samuel Pepys, thoroughly drunk, responded rudely.

Charles Hart and Nell accompanied Tessa home, and the three of them laughed and talked all the while the carriage rode over the cobblestones. In the morning darkness Tessa realized how much the stage and its people meant to her and how desperately she had missed this life.

Charles saw her safely inside and kissed her good night. He reminded her, "Monday, September third at the King's Theater."

"I shall be there," she promised.

And she intended to. In the time intervening she did some more work to make the house her own. She also wrote letters to Harry and his sister Mary. And she actually received a note from Sir Percy Hope, who wrote,

"Nell has spoken to me of you and I recall you from your earlier stage appearances. As I remember, you were the protegé of Sir David Farr, a fine gentleman. I hope when you return to the theater you will do me the honor of allowing me to pay you some attention. Your admirer, Percy Hope, Bart."

She grimaced and put the note aside. To some, she was still the girl who had run off with her stepfather. In the eyes of many Londoners, Tessa Shaw was that pretty young thing who had become the mistress of an older man—and Sir Percy Hope was clearly one of those who had enjoyed and believed the gossip about her. Would she ever be able to live it down?

It was early on Sunday, September second, that the maid, Grace, came running to her and said, "Mistress, there is a fire started near London Bridge. You can see it from the rear windows."

Tessa went to look. Flames and smoke were indeed visible from the area of the bridge. She sent the girl out to find out what she could about the origin of the blaze.

Grace returned after a little and with wide eyes told her, "The fire is spreading fast!"

Tessa returned to the window with the girl at her side and saw this was also true. The area of black smoke and flames rising in the air had increased greatly.

Grace was going on breathlessly, "The fire started in a baker's shop in Pudding Lane, Fish Street, near the bridge. It got out of hand at once. There's a gale blowing from the east."

"Lord help us!" Tessa exclaimed, staring out the window at the frightening sight. Was she to lose London so soon after she'd found it again?

All day she kept receiving new reports from the street. Over three hundred houses had been consumed, and the fire was spreading at a gallop, scorning the efforts of amateur firemen with their pickaxes, leather buckets and primitive engines.

Then it reached the region between Thames Street and the river, the area of warehouses where Tessa had once worked with the sisters tending the plague-stricken in the

276

emergency hospital. Many of the warehouses were filled with tar, oil, tallow and spirits. Here the fire grew madly.

When night came, the fire was almost all around them. The street was filled with people fleeing, clutching onto their few possessions. Many simply ran; others pushed big wheelbarrows filled with belongings; still others, more fortunate, had carriages of various sorts.

The girl, Grace, remained near Tessa and whimpered in a terrified fashion, pleading, "Shouldn't we leave, mistress? The fire may catch us and trap us here!"

Tessa knew she was right. Yet it pained her to think of leaving her house. It was fast becoming home to her, and she did not like the idea of abandoning it to the oncoming flames. As if she could save it by force of will, she tried to rationalize that the wind might change or abate, that the fire would end before it reached her.

She told the maid, "You can leave if you like. But I think the house will be spared. I intend to remain here."

Grace looked at her as if she were mad but said, "I will stay."

They watched the fire from the windows. Relentlessly it approached, a horrid, evil flame. There was one entire arch of fire on both sides of the approach of the London Bridge and a bow extended up the hill for almost a mile.

Tessa and the girl sat up all through the night. Once a neighbor came by to tell her, "John Evelyn, a scientist, though of amateur standing, swears that with the long set of fair and warm weather, the heat has ignited the air and prepared the materials to conceive the fire. Monstrous, it is! It is devouring everything—houses, furniture, bridges in an incredible manner!"

Another neighbor ran into the street screaming, "The Angel of God has come to scorch the earth with fire!"

But as dawn approached the wind changed, as Tessa had prayed it might. And although the fire continued, their area was spared, at least for the moment. Having watched until she was sure, Tessa sent the girl up to bed and settled herself for a nap in an easy chair.

She was wakened by a knock on her door. When she opened it, she was surprised to see the fat Mr. Grimp standing there. He was smudged with soot on his clothing and face, and he looked exhausted. At her invitation he came tottering in and sank down on the nearest chair.

"I came to see if the fire had reached you," he said, having difficulty breathing. He took out a handkerchief, mopped his perspiring brow, and set his wig straight.

"The wind changed and saved us."

He gave her a warning look. "Do not tell yourself that it will not change again," he said.

Fear returned. "Do you think it might?"

"Anything is possible in this inferno. My lovely office is in ashes."

"I'm so sorry," she sympathized.

He made a helpless gesture. "I saved all my records and important papers. But the premises are leveled to the ground."

"Mustn't it soon burn itself out?"

He gave her a grim look. "It's more likely to burn our poor London out. You should see the weary men vainly pulling down houses in the westward path of the flames. The streets are filled with the panicstricken. Outside your door, my girl, there is a procession of citizens with their goods loaded on dray carts and on their backs. In the river they're using lighters and boats! They run like terrified rats!"

"I thought we would have to leave last night," she admitted.

"You would do well to gather your valuables," he warned her. "Have them ready in case you are forced to leave in a hurry."

"How much of the city is already gone?"

He groaned. "By last account the fire had devoured Lombard Street, the Poultry, Cornhill and the Royal Exchange, plus some forty churches."

"I do not know what to do," she said uncertainly.

The fat man got to his feet. "Be ready, woman! That is the best advice I can give you. Be ready for the worst! I must be on my way." And he lumbered out without saying any formal good-bye, an oversight that was without precedent for the old gentleman.

278

Tessa went back into the house and gathered her best jewelry and most important personal documents and put them in a case. As she was thus occupied, Grace unexpectedly came down the stairs, red-eyed from weeping. "I'm sorry, mistress, I changed my mind. I'm frightened. Please, may I go to my mother?" she asked.

Tessa agreed at once. "Of course, if you like. Are you sure you can find her?"

"Yes, mistress!" Grace was eager to leave.

But Tessa was worried about the girl. "You're sure you can find the street? That it hasn't been destroyed in the fire?"

"No," the girl said. "It is back on the hill. I looked out. The fire hasn't reached there yet. I want to get there before it does."

"All right. Go along, and God bless you!"

Grace nodded. "When the fire is over I'll come back!" And she hurried out and joined the crowds of frantic refugees filling the street.

Now Tessa was alone. She knew the sky must be growing lighter with the morning sun, but the air was dense with smoke, and she could not tell the sunlight from the eerie glow of the fire. She went out to the door and saw there were still people in the streets. When she opened it, the crackling and the thunder of the hideous flames seemed almost upon her. Could she have been mistaken about the wind's change?

She wondered if little Grace had reached home and her mother before the flames. She was finding she could think of nothing else but the fire. The fear of it absorbed her completely. She paced from one room to another like a phantom creature.

When she opened the door again, a wild-eyed man dashed up to inform her, "The fires were set by the French and the Papists!" And with that he ran off to shout the news to someone else.

As Tessa remained on the steps, reluctant to be alone inside, the stout woman who lived in the adjoining house saw her and came over to her. She was a matronly woman who lived with her son.

Placing a comforting arm around Tessa, she soothed, "Do not be frightened! The fire is far from us yet! My son is in the midst of it, helping fight it!"

Tessa said, "I'm worried about my maid. She insisted on finding her way home. I'm terrified something may have happened to her."

"Not unless she went in the direction of the fire."

"She went up the hill," Tessa said.

"Then she should be safe."

"My solicitor came by and told me to have my valuables ready to leave in a hurry," Tessa said, her voice taut and her throat dry.

The older woman said, "I have my few things tied in a shawl. If it should come to that, I can leave without delay."

Tessa wondered, "Has the fire touched Whitehall and the court?"

"No, it is not gone that way," the older woman assured her. "But I hear that this morning the king and his brother James rode on horseback to see the fire. My son saw them. He said the king passed up and down the front line of the fire fighters, scattering silver, encouraging men like my son in their work of tearing down houses in the path of the flames."

"Charles is a good man, despite his failings," Tessa said.

"That is surely so," the older woman said. "My son said the king even dismounted and worked for a time with a bucket and shovel in his own hands!"

"And still the fire rages on!"

"There's never been anything like it before," the woman said. "Even the oldest say that. As fast as a gap is created, it is vaulted by the flames. Cheapside is destroyed; so is Cripplesgate!"

"I wonder if it has reached Mr. Pepys's home."

"I do not know him," the woman said. "But if his place is in the path of that fire, he will surely lose it."

"He is near Whitehall," said Tessa, "so I doubt that the fire will reach him."

"What will tomorrow bring?" the older woman lamented.

Tessa finally forced herself to go inside. After a time she fell asleep from sheer exhaustion. When she wakened, she hurriedly went to the window, hoping that by some miracle the storm of fire might have ended.

On the contrary, it seemed worse than ever. She forced herself to eat a little, but she could think of nothing but the fire. Again she went to the front door and hailed an elderly man carrying a pack on his back.

"What is the latest on the fire?" she asked.

The old man halted and stared up at her with bleary eyes. "Have you heard about St. Paul's?"

"No," she said. "Has it reached the cathedral?"

The old man nodded. "The fire has engulfed it. The lead roof melted and poured like lava into the streets. The heat exploded the stones of the walls and sent them flying out at us like cannon balls!"

"Then the fire is getting worse every hour!"

"Aye," the old man said. "And many are saying the wind is about to change. You'd best leave here!"

BOOK THREE

The King's Lady

Chapter Fifteen

The old man moved on, leaving Tessa standing in the doorway of her house. The acrid smell of smoke filled the air, cinders blew with the wind, and it was ominously warm. She went back inside, knowing full well that she could not wait for the fire to reach her street before leaving, but loath to go unless it seemed certain the holocaust was going to reach her.

The decision was made for her in an unexpected fashion. There was a knock on her door, and when she went to answer it she was confronted by little Mr. Pepys in a somewhat disheveled state. The stout man bowed to her.

"I feared you might have decided to remain here, Tessa," he said. "The wind is changing this very minute, and before the day is out the fire will reach here!"

"Mr. Pepys, it was so good of you to come," she said. "Are you certain about the fire?"

His evidence was hearsay, but he mustered authoritative names to back it in his earnest way.

"Then I shall surely leave," she said.

"I have a carriage and driver with me," the little man with the bulging eyes offered. "And my wife, Elizabeth, insists that you stay with us until the crisis is over."

"That is kind of you both," Tessa said. "Will you have a tankard of ale before we leave?"

"It would not be amiss," he said. "Thank you."

She went out and poured the ale. When she brought it to him, he sat down by the round table and took a large drink of it. She asked him, "Is the theater district intact?"

"Yes. All that section of the city has been spared."

"Thank goodness," she said. "The damage elsewhere must be the worst ever!"

The little man nodded. "Last night I crossed to the south bank of the river and found a vantage point in an alehouse to watch the fire from Southwark Bridge. I stayed there until it was almost dark, and while I watched, the fire grew. As night fell, more and more

285

flames appeared, in the corners and upon steeples, between churches and houses, as far as we could see up the hill of the city. A most horrid bloody flame, not like the fine flame of an ordinary fire!"

"I know," she said. "I've watched from the back windows."

"I stayed at the alehouse and watched the city burning and it made me weep—the horrid noise the flames made, everything being engulfed! I went home with a sorry heart."

She stood by his chair and glanced around her with a deep sigh. "I've only just purchased this house, my first true home. Now I have to leave it and lose it."

"Better than losing your life," Samuel Pepys said.

"I suppose anything is better than that," she agreed, "but I will feel pain at giving this up."

The little man stood up with a kindly expression on his plain, ordinary face. "I am sorry, my dear. I urge you to leave only for your own good. Now gather up whatever you wish to take and let us be on our way!"

This was how she left the house she had come to cherish so much in such a short time. In the carriage with Samuel Pepys at her side, she clutched her few belongings. She had only just begun a new life in London, and now she would be starting over again. She would have felt worse if it had not been for the pitiful cases all around them.

Old and young, many trudging on foot and dragging heavy carts of belongings, made their way grimly along the narrow cobblestone streets, with the smoke overhead and the flames approaching from a distance. It was an exodus such as London had never known before, and the story of it would be told for many a day.

Elizabeth Pepys was even more plain of countenance than her husband, but she made up for her ugly face with a warm heart. She gave Tessa a kindly welcome and installed her in a pleasant guest room. Tessa was to remain at the home of the good clerk and his wife until the fire was over and she could find herself a new home.

Tuesday was the worst day of the fire. It was on Tuesday that St. Paul's Cathedral was destroyed. The Duke of York and his soldiers labored all around the perimeter of the area, blowing up houses with gunpowder, a stratagem that succeeded in stopping the flames towards the east just short of the Tower, but which had small effect on the west. Gradually, however, the blowing up of houses confined the fire more and more, and on Wednesday, when the wind died down, at last the blaze came under control and burned itself out.

In four short days a third of the old city had been destroyed—from the Tower Hill on the east almost to Old Chancery on the west, short of the western suburbs, and in a semicircle north to Moorfields. Among the thousands of buildings consumed were the cathedral, the guild hall, and eighty-four churches. For weeks the waste of blackened rubble smoldered and smoked, and the ground was hot to the soles of wayfarers' shoes.

Mr. Grimp set up temporary offices in Jenner Lane, and soon as the fire was over, he found Tessa lodgings in the Drury Lane district, not far from the King's Theater. This time she rented an upper apartment from none other than Sir Percy Hope, who owned the brick building and lived as a bachelor on the ground floor.

This was the same Sir Percy Hope whom Nell had described as being an advisor to the king and a notorious womanizer. Tessa was not surprised when her new landlord called on her shortly after she had settled into the furnished apartment.

He came wearing elegant purple and fawn and carrying a silver-headed walking stick. His wig was a rusty brown, and he had hypnotic eyes in a long, rather pleasant face. It was difficult to judge his age, but some said he was much older than he admitted.

Sir Percy bowed low and in his most gallant manner said, "It is a pleasure to have someone of your youth and beauty renting these poor premises."

Tessa was garbed in a low-cut gown of pale green that she knew became her. She smiled. "I do not find the rooms poor. They are more richly furnished than the

287

house I lost in the fire. I'm sure I shall be most happy here."

Sir Percy smiled. "I understand you are thinking of going on the stage again?"

"I'm giving it thought," she admitted. "I have friends in the theater—Charles Hart and Nell Gwyn."

Sir Percy eyed her with his quizzing glass. "Nell Gwyn, you say! I have seen her. A lovely actress—and she has a good friend in the king."

"So I have been told," Tessa said.

"You have not met His Majesty?"

"I have only seen him at a distance."

"If you retain your friendship with Nell, you will surely make his acquaintance. They are often in each other's company." When Tessa made a noncommittal response the nobleman went on, "You know the theaters are still under an interdict."

"Oh?"

"Indeed. The bishops profess concern for the public health and are mainly responsible for their being closed."

She raised her eyebrows. "Surely they cannot continue this indefinitely!"

Sir Percy smiled. "The actors have sought the king's aid. The theaters should be offering plays in a few weeks. I shall look forward to seeing you on stage."

"Thank you."

His eyes held a twinkle, those strange pale gray eyes. "I spend a great deal of my time at court. The king depends on me."

"I admire King Charles," she said.

"It is an interesting court," the tall man said; and then with a hint of mystery, "and it is not the only court in the city. You should be introduced to them all."

He left her after this ambiguous comment. A few nights later, when she had Samuel Pepys and his wife to sup with her, she asked Pepys what Sir Percy could have meant.

Elizabeth Pepys drew a long face. "That awful man owns this building?"

"Yes," Tessa said. "He is my landlord."

"Take care," the older woman said across the table. "He is a libertine and worse, some say."

As usual Samuel Pepys was milder than his wife. He gave Tessa a knowing smile and said, "Sir Percy is an advisor of the king."

"He told me that."

"There are whisperings that he is not as loyal as he pretends but uses his friendship with Charles to work against our good monarch."

"A man of no principles," Elizabeth put in.

Tessa was at a loss. "I know so little of court affairs, I'm not sure I understand."

"Some say Sir Percy Hope is a Papist," Samuel Pepys explained. "It is rumored that he and some other prominent men at court secretly are working to put Charles off the throne and place his brother James there. James is a staunch Catholic."

"It is all news to me," Tessa said.

"And it may be only gossip," Pepys said cautiously. "There is much of that at court. Sir Percy may be quite innocent of these things."

Elizabeth looked grim. "I think he is involved in disloyal plotting."

"Admit you are prejudiced, my dear," her husband said placatingly.

"I say what I think. I trust that is not out of place," the plain Elizabeth snapped.

"Sir Percy has a rather mysterious air about him," Tessa observed after a moment. "I find his eyes strange. They seem to peer into your very soul. And he spoke to me of there being more courts in London than the king's court."

"Ah!" Elizabeth said with triumph. "Does that not hint of treason?"

"Quiet, madam," her husband rebuked her. "It may have only been a kind of double-talk to impress Tessa. You know that Sir Percy tries to conquer every lady he meets."

Tessa smiled. "Hope is an excellent surname for him, then." This caused laughter, and for the time they left their discussion of Sir Percy's loyalty to speak of less divisive subjects.

A few days later Tessa received a message from the King's Theater. Charles Hart wished her to report for rehearsal the following morning. She received the message with delight, for she was beginning to be uneasy. She was well settled in her new apartment and needed something to occupy her.

Her arrival at the King's Theater was like a reunion with old friends. She knew most of the company, and Charles Hart was directing with Nell as the star. The theater had been enlarged and made more pleasant. They were all anxious to work again, and the company gathered on the stage to work out the play in a mood of optimism.

The play was a revival, James Howards' *The English Monsieur*, which would open early in December. Nell had the female lead as Lady Wealthy, a rich young widow pursued and eventually won by Welbred, a fortune hunter, to be played by the director, Charles Hart. Tessa was to play Lady Wealthy's friend, a role she would do with some style. Most of the play was devoted to the antics of a group of bumpkins, fools and fops. Nell's part was not long, but she made it outstanding by her performance, in which she teased, insulted, and railed at her blunt wooer with gusto. Tessa felt the comedy was weak, but the cast made it sparkle and snap with their playing of it. Lines that were really ordinary were made to sound clever by the delivery of them.

When Pepys attended the opening of the play, he found it witty and pleasant. "All the ladies were excellent, particularly Nell and Tessa," he wrote in his diary that night.

Tessa was happy again, working in the theater. The king attended a number of the performances, and she thought he looked weary and older. But when she was presented to him, he had a smile for her that made her instantly understand the reports of his magic with women.

"Pepys tells me you played here several years ago," King Charles said, studying her. "But I cannot believe it. I would not think I could forget one of your unusual grace and beauty."

Kneeling before him, she said, "You are too kind, re."

"I pride myself on knowing beauty when I see it," he old her.

Later, when she and Nell, accompanied by Charles Hart nd another male member of the company, were enjoying ood and drink in a nearby tavern, Tessa related the in- ident to Nell.

The jolly Nell warned her, "I vow he has his eye on ou. And this time it may mean something."

Tessa blushed. "I'm sure it was just politeness on his art."

Nell said, "It sounds like more to me. Expect to be in- ited to the court soon."

"I wouldn't know what to say or do," she protested.

Nell showed a wise smile on her pert face. "Be pleasant o Charles. That will be enough."

Tessa gave her friend a serious look. "But you and Charles—I mean—" She halted, flustered.

Nell laughed. "You mean I'm the king's mistress. But Tessa, my dear, I'm only one of them. Surely you know hat! All England knows it!"

"But you are his favorite."

The other girl shook her head. "He is fond of me, and I believe that fondness will last. But there is Moll Davis, Barbara of Castlemaine and countless others. I hold no key to the king's favors."

"I know his love affairs are a scandal," Tessa agreed.

Nell laughed. "And a delight. What would the gossips do without them? In any case, my dear, if the king wishes to bed you, don't turn away from the honor out of loyalty to me. You are welcome to share him."

Tessa found herself blushing furiously. "I had not any- thing of the sort in mind."

"Perhaps not," Nell said, "but I have an idea he does!"

This was borne out when, a few days later, Sir Percy Hope paid another call on Tessa. Having seated himself at her invitation, he said with a smirk on his long face, "I think you are an entrancing actress."

"Thank you."

"I'm proud to have such a tenant in my house."

"I'm sure I do it no special honor," she said, "but I am enjoying living here."

"Good!" he exclaimed, and after a pause, "I come to you with a special and most important message."

"Oh?"

"The king is also charmed by you," Sir Percy Hope said smoothly. "And he requests the honor of your presence at an evening party at Whitehall tomorrow night."

So the moment had come! Tessa hesitated. "I don't know. I go out very little in the evenings. I find my performances in the afternoon so strenuous, I'm glad to retire after I have had my evening meal."

Sir Percy gave her a hard look. "My dear, this is not an invitation in the ordinary sense. I assumed you would realize that. It is a command. The king expects you."

This took her breath away. Faintly, she said, "I have no choice?"

"Unless you wish to offend your monarch." He added, "Most women would be thrilled by such an invitation."

"I know," she responded. "And I admire the king. I would not wish to hurt him."

"Then?"

She sighed. "Then I suppose I shall attend."

Sir Percy Hope smiled. "Sensible girl. I shall tell His Majesty that you were thrilled and delighted to accept his invitation."

"What sort of party is it to be?" she asked.

"Informal," he replied. "A girl with a sweet voice is to sing some of His Majesty's favorite French songs. He is lonely for his beloved sister these days, and she is far away in France."

"I have heard this."

"Only a small number will be invited."

"Will Nell be there?"

"No, I think not."

"What should I wear?" she wanted to know.

"Some charming dress," Sir Percy said. "The king likes the rustle of silk around him, and he enjoys lively colors."

He rose to leave. "I shall call for you here at seven. And I shall take the responsibility for seeing you home after the party."

She was also on her feet. "You are most kind," she said.

"I want us to be friends," the tall man told her. "I think it might be important to both of us."

She saw him out and was left with the identical feeling of puzzlement that she had remarked after his last visit. She had the impression that Sir Percy hoped to use her in some way, that he wished her to gain the king's favor so she would be more valuable to him. But this seemed senseless, since Sir Percy already had more power than most of Charles's other advisors. She could not sort it out.

During a break in rehearsals for *The Chances* she sought Charles Hart out and asked him about all this, explaining, "I'm to go to the king's party tonight, and Sir Percy is to escort me."

"Ah!" the dark-haired Charles said. "Something in the wind."

"Exactly how I feel," she said. "But I don't know what."

Charles thought for a moment. "Sir Percy has been the king's advisor long enough to know that Charles can be stubborn and devious but that where women are concerned, he is much warmer, more sincere. Sir Percy likely feels you might succeed in deals with the king where he could fail. That is your value to him."

Tessa said, "But I could not be of any real help in this way unless I were to become the king's mistress."

The director gave her a knowing glance. "That is surely what Sir Percy hopes."

"It is not my plan," she declared. "Let Nell deal with the king."

"Have you not heard the latest?"

"No."

"Nell has taken up with Lord Buckhurst."

"That profligate fellow who goes about with Buckingham?"

"The same," Charles Hart said. "He has looks and a
293

manner. He does not have money, I understand. Still, Nell has lost her heart to him, and there are rumors she'll leave the company, the king, and all, and go live with Buckhurst!"

"It would not last," Tessa predicted. "Nell loves the stage and she is truly fond of the king."

"I do not know what will happen in the end," Charles said dryly. "I can predict the future only in plays. But I do know that Nell is having trysts with Buckhurst and that she has warned me to be ready to transfer her leading parts to you."

Tessa gasped. "Then she must be in earnest."

"That is what I've been trying to tell you," the director said. "Sir Percy sees you as the next Nell, and so he is ready to be your protector."

"A most unlikely protector."

Charles smiled. "One who would prefer to protect you as your bed partner!"

"That is not likely to be," she said with a frown.

"You've asked me what is going on and I have told you," Charles said. "I wish you well at the party. Whitehall is a rather special place."

That evening she wore a gown of golden silk with white lace trim. When Sir Percy called for her he expressed approval. "My dear, you look like a queen!"

"Do you think it will fit in at court?"

"You'll be the best-dressed woman there, and that will truly delight the king!"

"Thank you," she said, relieved that her attire, at least, seemed adequate by court standards.

Sir Percy confided, "Charles needs cheering up tonight. Not only are he and Nell quarreling, but one of his other ladies has just given birth to another of his illegitimate children. That means he has six bastards in all now, while by the queen he still has none."

"How tragic that she is barren."

"And that he loves her," Sir Percy said. "He could discard her otherwise."

"I do not see him doing that," she said. "He is too kind."

294

"Exactly," Sir Percy agreed, taking her arm. "It is time we should leave."

When the carriage was on its way, Sir Percy again droned on with idle gossip of the court, but Tessa was not listening. Her nerves were on edge and her heart was pounding wildly. Eventually the carriage slowed and she heard the sound of curt voices outside. Looking out, she saw a dark-liveried servant wearing a powdered wig and holding a flaming flambeaux above his head. When the carriage stopped, the servant opened the door and helped Tessa down.

Sir Percy Hope was at her side. "This way," he said, leading her into the courtyard.

They were met by a tall footman in a powdered wig and elaborate crimson livery who escorted them into the palace. He strode ahead of them down a corridor softly lighted with candles in sconces on the walls. There were flowers set out at various intervals to give the air a pleasant scent.

Then Tessa heard the sweet sound of a girl singing. This would be the lass offering the French folk songs. The footman halted by a door and then led them up richly carpeted stairs to a great ballroom where the entertainment was going on.

The girl finished her song and there was polite applause, then the murmuring of many voices. Tessa leaned on Sir Percy's arm. She was finding this entrance more trying than any stage appearance, but breathing deeply, she stepped into the big room. People were standing all around it in colorful dress. The floor was of glass-like black marble, which reflected everything. At the end of the ballroom, on a dais of crimson and gold, was the huge chair in which the king was seated.

Sir Percy smiled at Tessa. "Do not be awed by the splendor," he said. "You are the most beautiful thing here."

"I have the most awful stage fright!" she whispered.

"You, an actress of experience? I don't believe it!"

A tall retainer in gold and red livery was standing by the king. This servant bowed to them as they approached

295

and struck the marble floor with the staff he held. In a clear, high voice, he announced, "Miss Tessa Shaw and Sir Percy Hope."

The room reeled, and Tessa thought she might faint, but Sir Percy, having bowed to King Charles, was leading her forth to kneel. The king gave her a friendly look and offered her his hand to kiss. She touched her lips to the hand with its many ringed fingers and felt a thrill surge through her.

In a warm voice Charles said, "Enough of kneeling! I would see your pretty face more clearly."

She rose and looked into his intelligent face. His dark eyes were fixed on her with admiration. "It was kind of you to invite me, Sire," she said.

"I have long wanted to talk with you in a leisurely way," the king said. "Thank you for bringing her to us, Sir Percy."

"My pleasure, Sire," the nobleman said, and recognizing this to be a signal for him to leave, he drew back and joined one of the circles of people chatting.

Tessa stood at the king's left. Now that the first excitement was over, she was quickly regaining her poise. She had often played court scenes on the stage, and except that the scenery was real, this was not much different. The people she saw were no more special than the dignified actors playing such roles on stage.

A group of musicians on a balcony at the other end of the room played pleasant music. Charles suddenly stood up, looking much the king in his court dress. His coat and breeches were a warm brown velvet; the decoration was in gold thread and white frills. His hands were so covered with jeweled rings than when he moved them they created a rainbow of light.

He turned to Tessa and bowed, "Shall we begin the dance?"

She smiled in return, curtsied, and offered her hand to His Majesty, and he led her out to do the minuet. She was conscious that all eyes in the room were upon them, but she called on the experience of her stage training and played her role with zest. They were joined by other cou-

296

ples as the dance continued. Charles smiled at her as they danced and held her hand tightly on occasion. The dance went well, and after it he led her back to Sir Percy.

"Our dance was much enjoyed by me," Charles told her.

"It was a unique experience for me to dance with a true monarch," she said, "after having been partner to so many make-believe ones on the stage!"

"You have wit as well as beauty," the king said. "Enjoy the evening, and I trust that on another occasion soon we may have an opportunity to enjoy a conversation at our leisure." He bowed and left them.

Tessa watched the king cross the room to join an angry-faced Barbara, Countess of Castlemaine. Turning to Sir Percy Tessa remarked, "The Countess of Castlemaine seems upset."

Sir Percy showed amusement. In a low voice he said, "She is! The king invariably gives her the first dance. And tonight you were his choice."

"So that is why she looks so pale," Tessa said, watching as the Countess and the king stood together.

"He left you not because he wanted to but because he feared Castlemaine might create a scene. She has done so before."

"I had no idea I was involved in such a game. I was only honored because he invited me to dance."

"You did well," Sir Percy commended her.

"It is a frightening experience to be here for a first time," she said. "But I expect one eventually gets used to it."

"I feel quite at home here," Sir Percy assured her. And as the music began again, he added, "Shall we dance? I'm sure the king will be occupied with Castlemaine as his partner."

And he was. From the corner of her eye Tessa watched Charles and Barbara as they danced; there could be no mistaking the angry looks on both their faces. It was evident they had been having a private quarrel, but at least the king had prevented the countess from causing a scene.

The evening wore on. Tessa met the Duke of Buckingham, the Duke of Clarence and many more titled folk. It was like a magnificent stage play and had as much reality for her. At last it was over. The king retired and his guests left. Tessa did not have a chance to speak with him again, but as they drove home, Sir Percy was emphatic in saying she had made a fine impression on all.

He saw her to her door and gallantly kissed her good night. Following this, he lived up to his reputation as a womanizer by trying to force his way into her apartment. But when she told him she was not in the market for a lover, he at once changed his manner and became quietly respectful again. It was a strange interlude.

She went to sleep that night dreaming of the magnificence of the court and the king's handsome face. She could not deny that he had a winning way about him. For the first time since her ordeal on the pirate ship she dreamed of love again. But she knew this love could only be a frustration. No matter how much they might be attracted to each other, she was a commoner and Charles was the king of England!

Next morning, when she appeared for rehearsals of Ben Jonson's *Cataline,* she was notified by Charles Hart that Nell would not be in the play. She was taking a rest.

"A rest?" Tessa asked the director.

He nodded. "A rest with Lord Buckhurst. They've taken living quarters together."

"Fie!" she exclaimed. "The king will not like that."

"I should imagine not," Charles Hart agreed, "but he will not be slow to find a new diversion. By the way, how did you make out at court last night?"

She blushed. "Very well. I saw the king only briefly, but he was most pleasant, and we led off the dance together."

Hart lifted his eyebrows. "Sounds promising. What about Sir Percy?"

"He escorted me," she said, "and afterward attempted to rape me on my own doorstep. I needed all my experience to fend him off."

Hart laughed. "He thinks a lady should consider it an honor when he attacks her."

298

"I have explained to him I see matters differently," she said. "And I assume I shall not be bothered in a like manner in the future."

"Not if the king has his sights set on you," Hart assured her.

This comment did not make her happier, but her misgivings were soon lost as she applied herself to the play. The company was to offer the play in sixteen splendid scarlet robes donated by the king. The drama itself had all the usual banter and indelicate speech that were designed to put the audience in a good humor.

When Tessa returned home after the rehearsal, she found she had a visitor waiting for her. The portly Mr. Grimp was seated in her parlor in the finest easy chair. He rose to greet her with a certain ponderousness.

"How good of you to call," she said.

"May I sit down?"

"Of course."

"I have come on behalf of Lord Harry Farr," the solicitor said as he made himself easy in the chair.

"How is dear Harry?" she asked.

"He is very well," Mr. Grimp said, "but I regret to say that his wife, Lady Eve, is grievously ill."

She was at once concerned. "How unfortunate! I know how he must be troubled."

"He has been almost constantly at her bedside for some days," the fat Mr. Grimp said with a sigh. "She seems to have a weakness of the lungs."

"That she should come to this after escaping the plague!" Tessa murmured. "What are the chances for her recovery?"

"Scant," the fat man said, "but it is possible she may linger as an invalid for a long while."

"Is there anything I can do?"

"Lord Harry would have you visit them," Mr. Grimp said. "He thinks your presence might be beneficial to his sick wife."

"Oh!" she said unhappily.

Mr. Grimp stared at her. "Is it not convenient?"

She made a gesture of helplessness. "I'm afraid it is not

299

even possible. Mistress Nell Gwyn has left the King's Company, and I have taken her place as leading lady. We are about to open in a new play."

"I see."

"I'm sure Lord Harry will understand. Let me write him a personal note for you to send to him."

"I shall be happy to act as messenger," the fat Mr. Grimp said.

Composing the note was an unpleasant task. Tessa felt that saying no to Harry's request was like turning her back on an old friend. And this she didn't want to do. So she thought hard for a few minutes, and then carefully selected the proper words to offer Harry sympathy and to wish a swift recovery for Eve. After explaining why she could not leave London, she promised that she would leave the minute her play ended. In the meanwhile she wrote, she would pray for Eve's recovery, and she urged Harry's wife to take cheer and live for her husband and children. Tessa sighed. It would have to do. She signed it and sealed it in an envelope and handed it to Mr. Grimp.

Mr. Grimp rose to leave and took the letter in his pudgy hand. "I will send this on. If there should be any change in Lady Farr's condition, I will advise you."

"I wish you would," she said.

The fat man glanced around him. "You seem to have made this apartment your own."

She smiled. "I have it much as I like it now."

"Good!" her solicitor said. "And your landlord? Do you get along with Sir Percy?"

"Yes, I'd say so."

"I'm glad," the solicitor said. "I was a trifle worried. He has the reputation of being a difficult man."

"So I have heard."

"Even a dangerous man," Mr. Grimp went on. "He is said to have the king's ear on most things. Well, I shall be on my way." And the big man picked up his hat and started for the door.

It was not more than an hour later that Tessa had her second caller. This time it was Sir Percy Hope. She was a little shocked to see him back so soon.

300

After he came in he took off his gloves and hat and placed his walking stick with them. Clasping his hands behind his back and planting his legs apart, he told her, "You did better with the king last night than I suspected."

"Really?"

"Yes. He called me to him this morning. And what do you think?"

"What?" she asked nervously.

His smile was knowing. "He wants you to go to the palace again tonight."

"I couldn't!"

"Why not?"

"It would cause a great scandal!"

"No," Sir Percy disagreed. "No one will know about tonight. You will use the famous back stairs."

"The back stairs?" Tessa did not like the sound of that.

"Nell could explain. When the king gives anyone a private audience, he always has them use the back stairs."

Tessa's cheeks crimsoned. "Are you suggesting I keep an assignation with His Majesty?"

"Of course not," Sir Percy said blandly. "You are merely going up there for a conversation. He is lonely and he considers you a diverting wit."

"I do not like the sound of it!" she maintained.

"I would have no part in the scheme if I saw harm in it."

"Come!" she said. "I'm not an innocent child!"

"You made me aware of that last night."

"Does the king want to make me his mistress?"

"It is a possibility."

"I do not see myself in the role."

"You are committed?" Sir Percy Hope asked with some sarcasm.

"Must that be my only reason for refusal?"

"The only one I can think of," Sir Percy said. "You would refuse him?"

"I would refuse his bed, yes!" she said with spirit.

Sir Percy shrugged. "Then I say you should tell it to him yourself."

"Why not you?"

"He has not put the question to me," her landlord retorted with ironic lucidity.

She frowned. "You make my position most difficult."

"I do not wish to," the nobleman said. "I am on your side. I want you to do as you wish. But the king will think more of you if you speak frankly to him yourself."

"I see," she said, considering. "Are you to escort me again?"

"No. This time you will go alone." She felt a brief flash of fear. Having noticed it, he went on to explain, "The king has to be discreet in his private audiences. He has entrusted me with his message. And he wishes you to know that a carriage and personal attendant will call for you at seven."

"So it has all been arranged?"

"It is the king's way of doing things."

She said, "I think it all wrong, but I shall go."

"Thank you," Sir Percy Hope said. "I am greatly relieved. The king is not a bad-tempered man, but I would not care to take back a message saying you would not attend him."

Tessa gave him a wry look. "It appears I'm not at all versed in the ways of court."

"It takes time."

"I gather that."

"You are being greatly honored, and the king will listen to you," the nobleman assured her. "I have an idea you two will get along handsomely."

"I wonder."

"But you did last night."

"Last night was somewhat different."

"It was, but you are a young woman of considerable resources. You will be able to meet the situation. That is why I shall soon propose that you meet my court."

She frowned. "You spoke of that before."

"Did I? I'd forgotten," he said lightly. But she was sure that he remembered.

"What sort of court are you referring to?" she pressed him.

"A personal court, unlike His Majesty's, but perhaps even more entertaining. I will discuss it with you again after you have seen the king."

"You mystify me," she said.

"Only for a little," he assured her. "I will come by tomorrow and perhaps we will discuss it then. By that time you and the king will have come to an understanding."

"I would be his friend rather than his mistress," she said firmly.

"No one can better explain that than yourself," Sir Percy said. "And so you must do it."

"I fully intend to," she said.

Sir Percy Hope smiled thinly. "I shall be most anxious to know His Majesty's reaction to this unusual declaration."

Chapter Sixteen

Tessa spent much of the afternoon in meditating about the position in which she found herself. From a poor girl earning her living by riding a pony in a circus she had risen to be the leading actress at the King's Theater. The road she'd traveled had not been an easy one, but she had survived much that might have finished others and now was back in London a star of the stage.

She had been loved by many men but had lost the only man who truly meant anything to her—the only one with whom she might have built a secure life. Now she was being offered the ultimate—the king himself was making a bid for her to become his mistress! It was so fantastic as to be unbelievable, and yet she knew it was true.

To complicate matters, Charles was a monarch whom she admired. She respected him for his liberal attitude towards his people, if not for his licentious view of love. And knowing he had done much for those in need, she could forgive him for his scandalous personal life.

In a sense, even that was not so terrible. In all his sexual conquests the king had not, to her knowledge, hurt anyone as she had been so deeply harmed by selfish men on several occasions. She could not bring her heart to hate this man whom Nell described as Charlie. And surely Charles's treatment of Nell had merited something better than her running off with the profligate Duke of Buckhurst.

No, Tessa could not hate this king. On the other hand, she did not feel bound to give herself to him merely because he found her comely of face and figure. She had always tried to include the value of love whenever she'd given her body. In an instance or two, as with Captain Nicholas Marle, she had been cruelly deceived. But always the deceit had been on the part of others. She had never entered an affair with the thought of betraying the trust of her lover.

Nor would she do so now. So, given her present frame

of mind, she could only meet the king as he had requested and tell how she felt. If, as she believed, he was a fair man as well as a monarch, he would be grateful for her honesty.

As the hour of seven drew near, she sat waiting. For the evening she had chosen a rose silk dress of simple design, and over it she wore a black cloak and hood. Promptly a few minutes before seven there was a soft knock on her door. She opened it to find an elderly man in somber black garb.

He bowed and said, "I have come to escort you. The king is waiting."

They were driven to Whitehall in a plain carriage. This time they rode past the regal front entrance of the palace and halted at a flight of outside stone steps leading to a rear entrance. The elderly man helped her from the carriage and saw her up the stairs.

Inside, she was received by another stolid-faced male servant of more than middle age. He showed her into a large living room elegantly furnished and dominated by an almost life-size portrait of the king on one wall.

"Make yourself comfortable," the servant said. "The king has been kept late signing documents. He will soon be with you."

Having helped her remove her cloak, the servant carried it away, and she was left alone to examine the large room. It was like the best room of any luxurious home, but it had little of the palace about it. This was clearly a place for the king to retire and enjoy himself. Tessa moved about, examining the fine paintings, particularly the one of the king.

She was studying it when she heard a step behind her and turned quickly to see that Charles, a faint smile on his face, was standing behind her.

"Well, Tessa, do you approve?"

She made a curtsy to him. "It is a good likeness, Sire, though I must admit the real man interests me considerably more."

Charles, in a tolerant mood, laughed. "Gad, you know how to say the right things, my dear." He kissed her on the cheek, then, taking her by the arm he said, "The table awaits us within."

He marched her into a large dining room, sat down at one end of the candlelit table, and gestured that she should be seated on his right. Tessa was a bit overwhelmed when she saw that the two of them were to dine alone at this huge table, which could easily accommodate forty or fifty people.

Servants waited upon them silently and poured out wine into the great goblets when there was any sign of a shortage. The great roast of beef was the best Tessa had ever tasted. And when the feast ended they lingered at the table over brandy.

The king was handsome in a great lounge-coat worn over his ruffled white shirt. He said, "I would have danced more with you the other night, but the countess was in an ugly, jealous mood."

Tessa said, "I was honored by that single dance, Sire."

"The court is a breeding place for scandal," he sighed. "I try to be discreet, but I fear I do not always succeed."

"The people love you, Sire."

The king looked pleased. "I think they do understand me—better than my advisors think. And I know I understand them better than a hundred advisors. Thus I make many decisions of state on my own."

"You are king, Sire," she said. "That should be your right."

"Tessa, you are not only lovely to look at, but I vow I would rather listen to you than all the ministers and ladies of my court!"

She laughed. "I cannot but speak frankly. I'm still in a state of shock at finding myself in such a high place."

The king shook his head. "Forget I am the king. It wearies me to be constantly referred to as 'Sire.' Call me Charles and I shall call you Tessa, and we shall get along much better."

"If that is your wish, Charles."

His eyes met hers. "Sir Percy Hope is your friend?"

"He is my landlord," she corrected him. "I know him

306

only casually. He infers that he is an important advisor here at court."

The king smiled thinly. "Not quite as important as he thinks. There are a few mysteries about that gentleman still to be solved. And beware of him if he pays you court. He is known widely as a fornicator."

Tessa could not resist saying, "But that is not unique among gentleman of your court."

The king gave her a startled look and then he laughed. "What I have liked about you on the stage," he said finally, "is the manner in which you speak the words of the various plays. You do not recite or declaim them; you give them meaning. You make me believe I am listening to a real person with real thoughts, not merely an actress."

"That is a great compliment, Charles," she said, meaning it.

"And you carry this same frankness into your real-life conversations. That too is in your favor."

"Honesty is of great import to me," she said. "And my friend Samuel Pepys is also most emphatic on that point."

His Majesty said good-humoredly, "You know our Clerk of the Admiralty. He joined us briefly during the days of the plague and he much amused me. He is filled with self-importance; still, he is intelligent and honest—at least, to a degree. Rather a prodigious combination. He returned to London and ran the Admiralty almost alone. I understand he has come out of it a rich man."

"I would say he deserved it," Tessa said. "Many gain wealth in less desirable ways. Pepys is your loyal servant."

"I do regard him so," Charles said. "And I think of you in the same fashion; otherwise why would you sup with me here tonight?"

She said, "I am your strong supporter, Charles. I came tonight to let you understand that."

"Are you not also my good friend?"

"I would most willingly be," she said.

"My court spies tell me you are not wed, nor even betrothed."

She blushed. "That is so."

"Why?"

She hesitated a moment. "Let us say my life has been rather complicated. There have been romances, but some of them ended grimly. And the great tragedy of my life is that my betrothed died in naval battle defending England."

There was sympathy on the king's Stuart face. "I am truly sorry."

"So, except for my stage career I have nothing. I am alone."

"What about Lord David Farr?"

The king's question came as a shock. She grimaced. "Your spies have done well. I knew Lord David before I met Thomas Montagu, the man I would have married. Lord David was my stepfather."

"And you were his mistress."

"London gossip would have it so. I can say only that Lord David was a man of honor. Now that he is dead, I must uphold that honor with my silence."

"Your mother was Lady Pleasure," the king said with meaning.

"That fact has never filled me with pride," Tessa said. "I would prefer not to be known as Pleasure's daughter."

"Why?"

"My mother was a beauty and a wanton! I have never chosen to trade on whatever looks I may have. I want to be a person, not a mere object for the bedchamber."

The king gazed at her admiringly. "By Gad, you have managed it, Tessa. You are a person—one of the few women I have been able to admire for their intelligence alone."

"That pleases me, Charles," she said lightly.

"You know that Nell has left me?"

"Yes."

"She has gone off with that booby Buckhurst. He is not half good enough for her."

"I'm glad you feel that way."

The king showed surprise. "You would not think I'd turn against my Nell? No. She has chosen to make me a subject for court jesting, but I care for her still."

308

"As she does for you, Charles."

"Nell's position at court was not secure enough. I should have done better for her. She generously shared me with others without complaint. I shall not hold Buckhurst against her."

"I do not think they will long be happy together," Tessa ventured.

"She will return," Charles said emphatically. "And I shall take her back and cherish her more than ever. Buckhurst, however, is a different matter. Buckhurst is finished, banished from England. He was on the verge of my displeasure in any case. This had decided his case."

"I'm pleased to know your feelings," Tessa said. "I have a great fondness for Nell."

The king sat back. "You have seen the queen at the theatre, I'm sure."

"Many times."

Charles stared at his brandy glass thoughtfully. "Although she is not pretty nor greatly intelligent, she is a good woman and devoted to me beyond what I deserve. Our marriage was a mistake. She is barren. I shall never have an heir. But I shall never dismiss her. It would break her heart, and I will not do it to her."

"What of England?" Tessa said. "If you are the end of your line, who will rule our poor country?"

"My brother James, more than likely," Charles said with some derision. "We must insure the succession. But if I may speak in confidence"—Tessa nodded—"I would rather it be my son by Lucy, the Duke of Monmouth. He is dear to me. On the other hand, he is a hothead whom I fear will cause trouble for the monarchy."

"Is there no way to arrange that he take the throne?"

"The line must be kept—that above all," Charles said. "If all my bastards were to make a claim for the throne, there would be enough left over to fill the rest of the thrones of Europe!" He laughed without mirth.

She joined him in the laughter, saying lightly, "At least you are human in your faults, Charles."

"I trust so," he said. "And I am also human in my needs." His eyes met hers. "Never have I encountered a

309

female with your combination of intelligence and beauty. I need a love such as you can offer. But I have nothing to give you in exchange. As a king I have been profligate and have bestowed both my person and favors too lightly. I can only come to you in private as the man and beg you to be generous with me."

She was silent for a moment. "You ask a great deal, Charles."

"Yes, I do," he agreed with a kingly nod. "I ask your all."

"With nothing in return."

"Because I have nothing of value to you," the king said.

"That is true," she murmured.

He rose and took her hand. She gave him a look that told him his answer. Together they left the great dining room and went to the more modest sleeping area. And in the scented and satined luxury, Tessa surrendered herself to Charles the king.

He was an experienced lover but not one of great passion. Indeed, the actual mating of their bodies was tame in contrast to the frenzy she'd known with previous lovers. But this joining had a poignant quality, and when it was over they were both at peace.

She knew he would never be more truly hers than at this time and that she could never truly own him. But there was a quality of goodness to this bedding which she had never known before and which she vaguely realized she would never know again. She had become part of a group, was one of the king's mistresses. But she fully believed what he'd said—that her role in his life was a special one. She was important to him in more than a physical way.

So the romance between them began. Each week she paid at least two visits to the palace, always under the same discreet conditions. Often there was nothing more than talk between them, and she gradually became one of the king's closest advisors.

It was the wish of both Tessa and the king that their love affair be kept as secret as possible. Only a few people knew about it, one of them being Sir Percy Hope, but he rarely made any mention of it to her. She carried on with her stage career, and though the king sometimes came to see her performances, he showed no special interest in her at these times.

During this period John Dryden produced a new work called *The Royal Martyr*. The ingenious playwright had hit on a way to employ Tessa's talents to their fullest in a tragedy. As Valeria, daughter of the cruel Emperor Maxim, persecutor of St. Catherine, Tessa had a strongly dramatic role that climaxed in a histrionic suicide scene— Valeria stabs herself when it seems that her stubborn beloved must die—though, ironically he survives to marry another.

Samuel Pepys, delighted with the new play, held a party the evening following the first performance. It was the first such party he'd held in many months, and Tessa accepted his invitation to attend. John Dryden was there to share the honors with her, and there was plenty of food and wine along with music and games.

Soon after her arrival the jovial Pepys took her aside and said sotto voce, "I hear you are occasionally in the company of Sir Percy Hope."

"Yes. You will remember I live in the upstairs apartment of his house."

"Ah, indeed, I'd forgotten," the little man said. "I have been hearing some strange stories about him."

"Really?"

Pepys nodded. "I have heard that he heads a kind of secret society, which holds meetings at his place."

"I do not know," she said, "though several times he has made mention of secret courts."

"That may be what he is talking about," Samuel Pepys said in a low voice. And looking around to be sure that no one overheard them, he added, "I have been told on the strongest authority that he is a satanist!"

She was shocked. "Sir Percy?"

"No other," Samuel Pepys said in the same confidential fashion. "It is said they hold meetings and indulge in the most contemptible practices."

311

"He is not reputed to be a man of good morals," she agreed, "but I have never heard anything like this."

"It is being whispered about," Pepys said. "And one of the members of his group is said to be the Duke of Buckhurst."

Nell's lover! Tessa's eyes widened.

The little man nodded again. "I do not like the sound of it at all!"

Tessa said, "I should think not. I have never liked Sir Percy, but I have had to tolerate him since he is my landlord and also an advisor at court."

"A man of influence," Pepys agreed. "But I felt I ought to warn you about the rumors."

"I will try to get to the bottom of them," she said.

In a normal tone of voice, Pepys said, "Enough of that. I have a surprise for you!"

"Oh?"

"A most unexpected guest, who has stolen away from her lover to be here with us tonight!"

"Who?"

"Can you not guess?" Pepys said. "Who would want most to celebrate the new success achieved by yourself and John Dryden?"

It took Tessa only a moment to decide, "Nell!"

"You are right! Come and meet her. She is in the room adjoining the kitchen!" And he led Tessa in the direction of the room.

In the soft candlelight of the square room Nell stood laughing and talking with a group of actors and admirers from other fields. She carried a small fan, which she used to make points as she told her stories. The rosy-cheeked Dryden was standing beside her sharing the spotlight.

But when Nell spied Tessa coming into the room, she called out, "Come here and join me! We would honor you!"

Tessa ran forward and the group moved back to allow Nell to embrace her friend. Tessa sobbed happily, "I began to fear I would never see you again."

Nell winked and said, "Buckhurst has kept me busy, but I slipped away from him tonight!"

312

"How wonderful that you are here!" Tessa said.

"She makes it all worthwhile," John Dryden agreed.

Toasts were proposed to Dryden and Tessa and all drank heartily. Then there were more toasts to Charles Hart, His Royal Majesty, and to their host, Samuel Pepys.

Pepys then stood on a plank table—to the great alarm of his wife—and excitedly offered the most popular toast of all, "To our Nell! May she soon be back with us again!"

There were cheers and shouts of encouragement to Nell, who nimbly jumped up on the table beside the stout host. With her arm around the little man, she called out, "Ducks, I've missed you more than you could possibly miss me! Nellie the slattern will soon be at the King's Theater again!"

This was greeted warmly. Music and games began, and Samuel Pepys and Nell were helped from the table by friends. Nell at once came over to Tessa and said, "Let us find a corner where we can talk."

"This way," Tessa said and led her to a small room that was used mostly for storage. Here they were able to shut the door on the other guests and talk freely.

Nell's eyes were twinkling as she said, "My friends at court relay the latest news to me. It seems the king has a new mistress."

Tessa replied warily, "Is that news?"

"Not really, but it becomes so when the new mistress is also a friend and advisor." Nell paused. "I told you that you and Charles would do well together."

"You know!" Tessa said.

"Yes. Even though the secret has been guarded well. I can say I have known of it for weeks."

The two women stood in the near darkness of the small room, Tessa holding the single candle to give them light. Her intelligent, lovely face was solemn in the glow of the candle's flame as she said, "You will forgive me if I do not discuss it."

"I understand," Nell said.

"He still loves you."

"And I him."

"Are you returning to him?" Tessa asked.

"If he will have me."

"He will. He has told me so."

Nell's face was sober as she said, "There is a strong link between us that I doubt anything will break."

Tessa warned, "He will not be so lenient with Buckhurst."

"Buckhurst is a scoundrel," Nell said flatly. "I have wasted my time with him. And I felt it was to be a great romance. We hated each other after a few days."

Tessa was sorry for Nell's disappointment, but she was relieved that her friend had come to her senses. Deciding it was better to say nothing, she waited until Nell went on:

"Now he drinks too much and attends his meetings. And I fret and wish it were over."

"Why not end it at once?"

"I intend to leave him shortly," Nell said. "Somehow, these things are never simple. But it is helpful to know the king's feelings about me."

"He has never spoken ill of you."

"Surely I deserved it," Nell said. "But then I'm a ninny—my mind never matched my heart. All my life I've made stupid mistakes."

"We all are prone to such failings," Tessa said sympathetically.

"How is Sir Percy Hope?"

"He seems careful to avoid me most of the time these days. I'm not sorry he does. But he makes me wonder. And Mr. Pepys had some strange tales to offer about him."

Nell looked knowing. "About a satanist cult?"

"Yes."

"I've heard the same story."

"Pepys said your Lord Buckhurst is one of them."

"He's always hurrying off for secret meetings," Nell said with a frown. "He is gone somewhere tonight— maybe to be with Sir Percy and the drabs he has caught up in his satanist rituals."

314

"It sounds frightening," Tessa worried. "And I live in the same house."

"Be watchful," Nell warned. "The thing I fear most is that behind it all there may be plots against the king."

"Have you any evidence of this?"

Nell shrugged. "Not truly—but the Papists have never given up. They want to control England. And I wonder if this satanist business isn't a cover to hide Papist activity."

"A strange sort of cloak!"

"It's very nature would prevent suspicion," Nell said. "I think Sir Percy and his group bear watching. If you find out anything of import, you would do well to pass it along to the king."

"I shall," Tessa promised.

They returned to the group in the big room, fearing their absence might cause some talk. Fiddles were playing gaily and Samuel Pepys was exerting himself in a merry dance, partnered with a giggling red-headed wench a third of his age!

Nell slipped away soon after this, but Tessa remained to the end of the party, and John Dryden escorted her home. The youthful playwright was full of plans for new plays, and she enjoyed listening to him.

He saw her to her door and kissed her good night. Then he said, "It was good to see Nell again. Will she return to the company?"

"Yes, I'm certain of it. And soon."

"Then I'll write splendid parts for both of you," Dryden said. "We'll put on the finest plays London has seen!"

The next week passed in normal fashion. On one of her visits to the king, Tessa told him of her meeting with Nell. He was at once interested.

He said, "Did you let her understand I will not punish her?"

Tessa smiled. "Yes. And I think she almost wishes you would. She is aware of the wrong she did you."

"Buckhurst has been punishment enough," Charles said with disgust. "I don't know how she can abide the fellow!"

"They are at odds," Tessa told him. "They have been since a few days after their running away."

"I knew it would be like that," Charles said. Then he gave her a questioning glance. "Did you tell her about us?"

"She already knew."

"I might have guessed that. What did she say?"

Tessa smiled. "We agreed it was something that we did not care to discuss."

"Good girl," the king said approvingly.

On the late afternoon of a cold day she was on her way up the stairs when Sir Percy Hope came out of the door to his lower apartment and spoke to her. He asked, "May I come up and have a brandy with you?"

Tessa considered this for a moment. She did not want Sir Percy's company; still, she did not wish to appear inhospitable, and she also was curious to discover if there were any truth in the satanist story. She said, "Come along. I'm chilled. I would enjoy a drink."

Sir Percy lost no time joining her, and shortly they sat before the blazing log fire in the comfort of her living room. He cradled his brandy glass in his hands and said, "You are popular in the new play."

"There'll soon be another new one. Dryden is working at it."

"Good," he said. "I enjoy the theater. And there was none of it until Charles came back to England."

"It is hard to believe."

"But the truth," Sir Percy said sipping his brandy. "You and the king are happy, I venture?"

Of course he must see the carriage when it came for her and know that she was regularly seeing the king, but Tessa decided she would reply to him in a way which would show her attitude. She said, "I see him fairly often—when he attends the theater."

Sir Percy raised his eyebrows ever so slightly. "Of course," he said in a quiet voice, "at the theater."

She said, "We hope that Nell will soon return."

His smile was knowing. "To the theater?"

316

Her cheeks crimsoned. "Yes. Dryden is going to write a play with parts for us both."

The tall man took a sip of his brandy before observing, "Nell may return to the theater, but I doubt if she will be taken back again at court."

"I would rather not comment on that," Tessa said. "Nell is my dear friend."

Sir Percy nodded benignly as he purred, "Naturally. You two share such a lot."

She hated this sarcastic-tongued man with his odious arrogance, yet it seemed unwise to make an enemy of him. She said, "You have not been to the theater much of late."

"I have had other things to occupy me. That is why I have come up to speak with you."

"Oh?" She waited to hear what he might have to reveal.

"I have several times mentioned a secret court of which I happen to be a leader," he said.

"You told me there were courts other than the king's," she said. "But you did not say you lead one."

"I do," he said. "I have for some time. It is a kind of secret society."

"What sort of secret society?"

He leaned forward. "Are you truly interested?"

She carefully assumed an air of casual disinterest. "Who can say? I would have to know more about it."

"It is rather complicated to explain," he said. "We operate on more than one level."

"In what fashion?"

Sir Percy permitted himself a sly smile. "Well, on one level we cater to the improvement of enjoyments of the flesh. On the other we seek an improvement of our society."

She said, "The latter would seem to be a worthwhile aim."

"I can assure you that it is." Her landlord paused before continuing, "We have a full membership except that we lack one female. And I thought of you as a prospect."

"Why me?"

"We want someone of intelligence and spirit, not to mention beauty."

Tessa smiled, "Your entry requirements are substantial."

"We must pick our members carefully."

Tessa was sure she was onto something. If, as it seemed, Sir Percy's society were dedicated to satanism—and perhaps to dethroning the king—it would be helpful if she found out about it. She could then give Charles warning. So she decided to gamble on this assumption.

She said carefully, "Your tale of secret meetings intrigues me."

"We have such a meeting downstairs this very evening," Sir Percy said. "Would you care to attend?"

"I can," she said. "What does one wear?"

"Any pleasing dress you may have," he told her. "We will provide you with suitable robes for our rituals."

"What are the rituals?"

"They are most impressive—all in Latin, like the Catholic mass."

"Is it a Catholic group?" she inquired innocently.

"No. We are of no denomination, but we do take the mass as a pattern for our ritual. I think it proper to borrow from anything that is good."

Tessa said cautiously, "Without doubt. But what does taking part in this mass entail? Does one make certain obligations, a bond of friendship which cannot be violated?"

"There is a promise to secrecy," he said. "And since this too is in Latin, I cannot offer it to you word for word. Primarily it is a dedication to the purposes I have mentioned."

"I see," she said. "What time is your meeting?"

"We gather in the big room of my house at eight," he said. "And by the way, it is our practice that all wear masks of the same sort. I will send you up a silver mask."

She smiled. "It truly is a secret society!"

"Some of my group are well known and do not wish to be recognized as members of a secret society."

"It sounds more exciting each moment."

He rose with a smile. "So I can count on you to attend?"

"Yes. Must I remain a member?"

"That will depend entirely on you. I can only say that few have left us. I think we offer too much."

"It would seem so."

"I will not forget the mask," he said. "And I trust you will come downstairs. Just be on time!"

The hours between her talk with Sir Percy and her attending the secret society meeting were tense. Tessa wished that she might think of someone to discuss the project with. She did not have time to seek out Samuel Pepys; as for the fat Mr. Grimp, her solicitor, he would be too shocked by the idea to listen. Only Nell would be truly helpful, and Tessa did not know the address of the tavern where Nell and her lover were living.

She found herself trembling a little, fearful of what the experience might be. She did not wish to place herself in a position where she might be thought to be plotting against the king, and yet she had no choice but to risk this if she were to obtain the information about the secret group.

Sir Percy had not said anything about satanism; he'd merely told her the rituals were in Latin. Still, this suggested some sort of secret black mass, and that could only mean Sir Percy and his associates were devil-worshipers. He had mentioned that part of their aim was to encourage pleasures of the flesh. It sounded ominous.

She dressed carefully in a gown of plain blue and put on the silver mask that Sir Percy had sent up to her. It covered three-quarters of her face, and she was grateful for that. It would make it very difficult for anyone to recognize her. She made her way down the dark stairs to the heavy wooden entrance door of Sir Percy's apartment.

The door was opened by a stalwart young man wearing a silver mask to match her own. He bowed to her and held open the door for her to enter. At once she smelled a pungent smoke in the air—incense must be burning. The hall was in darkness, and the young man led her down to the big room Sir Percy had mentioned.

As she stepped into the room, Tessa was startled to see

319

that it had been transformed. Along its walls were whit
drapes, on which were painted life-size figures of nake
men and women in all manner of erotic positions. Thes
went all about the room and depicted every form of se
ual encounter one could imagine.

Tessa drew a deep breath and felt her cheeks bur
Once again she was grateful for the mask. The room wa
filled with perhaps twenty men and women, an equa
number of each sex. They were gathered in small group
of three and four, and all were engaged in low conversa
tion. None of them paid attention to her. It was as if sh
had not entered the room.

After the shock of the erotic drapes, her attention wa
drawn to a small platform at the end of the room mos
distant from her. On it there was a brass vase and some
thing was burning in the vase—obviously the source c
the pungent odor. Tessa did not know whether she fan
cied it or not, but the acrid smell seemed to have mad
her head light.

As she gazed around one of the silver-masked me
came over to greet her. She could tell it was Sir Percy. H
smiled at her behind the mask and said, "You did not dis
appoint me."

She said tensely, "No. But you did not prepare me fo
anything like the drapes."

"Unusual."

"Very."

"They were done on commission by one of London'
finest painters," Sir Percy Hope said urbanely. "He con
siders them his masterpieces. What do you say?"

"I would say he has an imagination and experience t
match it."

"Very good," Sir Percy said. "Now that you are here,
think we are almost ready to begin."

"What shall I do? I don't know any of your rituals."

"You will manage," he assured her. "Just take you
place with the others and follow their example."

He left her and went to confer with a ramrod-straigh
man who was unusually thin. This man slowly made hi
way down to the altar and stepped up behind it. Like Si

Percy he wore a suit of black velvet. Tessa noted that the masks and the identical clothing made the men seem much alike.

Now the thin man began to intone in Latin. At the same time one of the women began passing out lighted candles for all to hold in their hands. When Tessa's turn came, she took the tall white candle, which flamed nicely. The group now made a kind of semicircle in front of the man at the altar holding the lighted candles. Tessa's tension increased and she felt more lightheaded than before.

Now the man at the altar intoning Latin reached under it to produce a love dove. The beautiful white bird tried to escape, but the thin man gripped it firmly in his left hand. His voice became higher in pitch, and he spat out the words of Latin ever more rapidly, his frenzy growing. The group in the semicircle began to moan.

Tessa was appalled. She drew in her breath and for an instant thought of turning and running out of the room, but before she could do this, the man leading the ritual took a knife up in his right hand and with a deft movement slit the neck of the dove. Then, while the bird was still in its death convulsions, he stepped down from the altar, and dipping his hand in the bird's blood, touched the lower cheeks of each of the cult members.

When Tessa's turn came, and the weird leader approached her still muttering words of Latin in a low voice, she thought she might faint. She was sickened at the touch of his sticky wet finger. As he moved on to the man at her side, she felt she must cry out her misery and attempt to get away.

But again she was frustrated. Silver wine goblets were being passed, and the woman who had handed out the candles was retrieving them and blowing them out, after which she filled each of the goblets with a rich, ruby wine. Tessa saw that the others were all drinking the wine, and so followed suit. She found the drink refreshing, it renewed her hope of seeking out Sir Percy and telling him she wished to leave.

Staring at the masked men and women around her, she tried to single him out, but she had no success. To make it worse, her dizziness had returned and it was even worse now. She fought to clear her brain and steady herself, but everything seemed suddenly to rush at her. She saw the silver masks turned to her and then she blacked out!

Chapter Seventeen

When Tessa opened her eyes, she was in a small room on a narrow bed. Standing by the bed was a figure wearing a silver mask and a long, enveloping silver robe with a high collar. She recognized the man as Sir Percy Hope.

"What happened?" she asked.

"It seemed the potion was too strong for you," he said.

She touched a hand to her head. "I liked none of it," she moaned. "The business of the dove nauseated me."

"The most gentle sacrifice we could make," Sir Percy said. "The actual ritual calls for a child, but we modified it."

Tessa gazed up at him in horror. "This is not something I wish to go further with!"

He smiled cruelly. "You have gone far as it is."

Only then did she realize that she was wearing a silver robe exactly like the one worn by Sir Percy. And under the robe there was nothing. Her clothes had been removed and she was naked except for the robe!

Raising herself up in anger, she demanded, "What liberties have you taken with me?"

He stood there with his robe completely covering him. "We only took the liberty of changing your dress to conform with ours."

Still slightly dizzy, she struggled to her feet and said, "I want my clothes. I intend to leave."

"And miss the best part of it all?" Sir Percy said mockingly. And opening his silver robe, he displayed his nudeness to her.

"You disgust me!" she cried.

"No doubt!" he sneered. "I cannot hope to compete with so famous a lover as the king!" And he advanced on her with what seemed the intention of rape.

"Don't!" she cried. And she dodged away from him and rushed out the door.

She had not known that it led into the large room. Now a lunatic orgy was taking place within. Men and women were sprawled over the floor, squirming in every manner of sexual union. Many had discarded their silver cloaks and were completely nude; the cloaks of others hung back over their shoulders so as not to interfere with their coupling. There were shrieks of delight, mixed with moaning.

For Tessa the sight of the orgy brought back memories of the night aboard the pirate ship when she had been tossed to the common seamen and gang-raped. Terrified, she turned her back on this new scene of passion unleashed, but as she did so she was confronted by a large young man whose stiffened member told of his state of arousal. He seized her in his arms, and ignoring her screams, forced her under him on the floor.

She felt him entering her and kept up her protesting, but it did no good! He ravished her and ignored her struggles and protests. When he had spent himself, he sprang up with a curse and left her sobbing on the floor.

"Let me help you." It was Sir Percy who spoke. He assisted her to her feet. As he led her back to the small room away from the orgy, he added, "You ran from me to worse!"

"Scoundrel!" she sobbed. "You are responsible!"

"I brought you here for myself," he said. "I have long wanted you. But you spoiled it by rushing out and allowing Buckhurst to rape you. I dared not interfere. He is like a mad bull when in passion!"

The name cut through her hysteria. In a hoarse whisper, she exclaimed, "Buckhurst! Nell's lover!"

"The same," Sir Percy said. "You seem to be attracted to the same sort of men as Nell."

"There was no attraction!" Tessa said angrily. "As you know full well, I was cruelly attacked."

"I regret it," Sir Percy said. "You are in no mood for further loving, though I promise I would be tender."

"Give me my clothes!" she demanded and tore off the silver mask.

"I will bring them for you," Sir Percy said.

She stood there weakly, the silver cloak drawn about her, still hearing the shrieks and laughter from the other
324

oom. She felt ill and wondered why humans must debase hemselves in this way.

Sir Percy returned with her clothing in a bundle. He aid, "I will return after you dress to escort you safely ut."

Tessa said nothing but hurriedly dressed herself. She vas ready to leave when Sir Percy reentered, still wearing is mask and cloak.

He said, "You are missing a lot by not joining us."

Angrily, she said, "If what happened is an example of what it would mean to be one of you, I would prefer to be on the outside."

The tall man said menacingly, "But you have been on the inside."

"You tricked me!"

"Folk might find that hard to believe in a woman of your sophistication."

She stared at him. "You have harmed me enough! What are you trying to say?"

"Keep silent about tonight!"

She gave him a derisive look. "Do you think I will suffer such abuse without trying to revenge myself?"

Sir Percy said, "You had better consider—especially before speaking to the king."

"What are you saying?"

He went on firmly, "There is no one the king more despises than His Grace, the Duke of Buckhurst! I can produce half a dozen witnesses who will swear that you willingly coupled with Buckhurst before all the company. This would surely please Charles."

"You wouldn't!" she said in a tense whisper.

"I promise you, I shall if I need to," Sir Percy said. "It is well known my taste runs to debauched evenings. No one will criticize me more than they ordinarily do. But the story about you will make a juicy tidbit at court. Even Nell might hear of it and wonder what you were doing with her lover."

Tessa said, "You propose to blackmail me into silence about all this and what happened to me!"

"A most mild sort of blackmail!" he protested.

"Blackmail is always the same," she said.

He shrugged. "As you like. But speak out of turn, and I will make you the despised jest of all London. You will come into your own wanton fame, Lady Pleasure's daughter!"

"Villain!" she said in a low voice.

"Yes, I suppose so," he said casually. "Now I shall take you out by a side door so you will not be again subjected to the pleasant goings-on of the company."

She made no reply. She was seething with rage as he escorted her along another passage and out a door she had never used before. She then made her way around the house, entered the front door, and went up to her room. When she was safely in her own quarters, she threw herself on her bed and sobbed.

After her rage and sorrow, she tried to sort it all out in her mind so that she might decide what she was going to do. She had no doubt that Sir Percy would not hesitate to libel her if she complained about what had happened. It was doubly unfortunate that the man who had raped her had been Buckhurst. She doubted that even Charles, tolerant as he could be, would understand.

Ironically, she had subjected herself to this in the hope of finding out something for the king's protection, but as it had turned out, she had mired herself in filth for nothing. She was unable to make use of anything she had learned; worse, actually she had learned very little. Going over it all in her mind, she was left with the feeling that it probably *would* be best to say nothing at this point in time. With luck, other information about Sir Percy and his crew of satanists would come her way. If so, she might eventually be able to make so strong a case against him that he would not dare to remain in London to attack her.

She debated leaving the city but decided against this. Her best opportunity to spy on the debauched Sir Percy was to remain in the upper apartment of his house. She felt fairly sure he would not bother her again. He had attempted to have his way with her and had failed. So she would dare to remain and watch those who paid visits to the evil man.

326

Though she continued her visits to the king, she made no mention of the horrible ordeal Sir Percy had put her through. Whenever his name came up in their conversation, she tried to change the subject.

One evening the king was in an unusually good humor, and as they sat at the dining table, he told her, "One of my predictions came true today."

Tessa smiled. "I did not know you were a seer, Charles."

He laughed. "I rarely am. But this was a safe prediction. I said Nell would return and she has. She is installed in her house in Pall Mall once more."

"I'm glad." Tessa could not help asking, "And what of Buckhurst?"

"Gone!" the king said. "Banished—and his estates taken by the Crown. A rotten fellow! England is better without him!"

"Unquestionably," she agreed. Then she added carefully, "Are you sure he has left the country? Sometimes these fellows go underground and then try to strike back."

"Are you worried for me, Tessa? I'm pleased."

"I am worried. If there were enough of Buckhurst's type and they joined together, you could be in great danger."

The king looked interested. "You are thinking of the Papists and their wish to be rid of me in order to restore a Catholic to the throne."

"Yes."

"I don't see this as a serious threat," he said. "I have a Catholic background, and I have shown tolerance to them. The intelligent ones know that and are grateful for my stand."

"But there are always agitators, Charles," Tessa insisted anxiously. "Men who scheme for power and use religion or anything else as a pretext. These are the ones whom you must think seriously about."

He stared at her. "Have you heard whispers of such a traitorous group?"

"I cannot tell you anything definite," she said. "But

327

there is a strangeness in the air, something building that I don't like. I worry much for your safety."

He reached out and touched his bejeweled hand to hers. "Dear Tessa, you are too protective of me."

She later blamed herself for not having the courage to name Sir Percy Hope as one she suspected. But she still had no specific evidence against him, and until she did, she would keep silent on him and what he had done to her. Meanwhile, she was pleased that Nell was back. The theater seemed more lively with her, and together Tessa and Nell would work hard at offering a new season of plays.

Nell was promptly assigned the leading role in the new two-part play that Dryden had written for the King's Company. Dryden wrote a prologue and epilogue to suit Nell's talents and there was a good part in the play for Tessa. The play was called *The Conquest of Granada*.

Since the current styles in men's clothing in France were the butts of many jokes, in the play Nell appeared as a boy wearing a short coat with a very wide belt and a hat the circumference of a cartwheel. The audience roared with laughter and applause.

One afternoon after the play was over Nell and Tessa went to a nearby inn for a quiet tea. At once seeing that the usually jolly Nell was not in the best of spirits, Tessa asked her, "Is something wrong?"

Nell sighed. "It is Charles."

"Oh?"

"Does he ever mention me to you these days?" Nell asked.

"Not since your return," Tessa said.

"That is diplomatic of him," Nell said wryly. "I'm worried. He does not want me to remain on the stage."

"Why not?"

"I have a child by him," Nell confessed. "It is not very well known."

Tessa's eyes widened. She had known Nell for years without suspecting this.

"I had not heard," she said.

328

"The story is gradually getting around," Nell said. "I wanted you to hear it from me."

Tessa said, "So it is because of your child."

"Yes. Charles has promised that he shall be named a duke."

"How wonderful that you have given the king a son."

"He has many, all bastards," Nell shrugged. "Monmouth is his favorite but tugging at the bit, I fear. Too ambitious a youth. In any case, the king does not want the mother of his child on the stage."

"I can understand," Tessa said.

"So can I," Nell sighed. "I have seen the knowing glances, the raised eyebrows; I've heard the sly allusions. The stage is my love, but even so it is second to the king. When I finish with this play, I shall have to retire."

"The king will look after you well. You'll be a great lady."

"I shall be an acknowledged mistress," Nell corrected her friend. "I expect that is how I will go down in history—not as a great actress but as the king's whore!"

Tessa blushed. "Nell!"

"Sorry. You mustn't take that as applying to yourself. It is different with you. I believe he truly loves you and wishes you were of royal lineage so you could be his proper queen. He'd rid himself of poor Catherine for you. He wouldn't for me or any of the others."

"I don't think so," Tessa said. "I see Charles as a man who needs more than one love . . . and he surely has had his full share!"

"Amen to that!" Nell said. And they both laughed.

A few evenings later, when Tessa was leaving to go to Samuel Pepys's house to have a quiet dinner with the clerk and his wife, she had an unusual experience. She came down the stairs to get into the carriage Pepys had sent for her, and reaching the vestibule, she came face to face with Sir Percy Hope with a young girl on his arm.

This would not have been particularly remarkable, except that the girl could have been Tessa's twin. She was her double in every way—hair color, features, build, eyes. It was shocking, and Tessa could not hide her surprise.

Sir Percy seemed to thoroughly enjoy her upset. He said, "Let me introduce my protegée, Miss Elmore."

"How do you do," Tessa said, trying to seem casual.

The girl replied, "My pleasure to meet you. I have seen you in the theater."

Sir Percy said, "Miss Elmore is something of an actress herself, though she has only played in very minor companies."

"That is interesting," Tessa said.

"Folks say I resemble you," the girl said boldly. "Indeed, that is how I came to get my London job. They hired me in the hope that some of the dull-witted might think they had a star from the King's Company."

"Yes," Tessa said. "I see the resemblance."

Sir Percy said jovially, "I was going to mention it. I have recruited Miss Elmore for my group. Since I couldn't have you, I decided to have your lookalike."

Tessa thought this decidedly impertinent of him, and said, "I do not like your insinuation, sir." And to the girl, she said, "I wish you good luck—and I advise you to mind the company you keep."

She heard Sir Percy's mocking laugh as she entered the carriage and felt her anger rise again. She had never forgiven him the humiliation he had caused her. No, Sir Percy Hope was her enemy and the enemy of the king, and she still hoped to find a way to expose him.

For the girl who resembled her she felt nothing but pity. She had no doubt that Sir Percy would use and abuse her and then cast her into the gutter. Whatever chance Miss Elmore might have of making something of herself on the stage would be shattered. The debauched noblemen of Sir Percy's company would set her well on the road to ruin.

At Samuel Pepys's house Tessa brought up the strange experience over dinner. She said, "The girl was hanging on Sir Percy's arm as if he were all the world to her, and she was my twin. It was like watching myself!"

Pepys nodded. "I have heard of this girl. One of the small Drury Lane theaters is using her and billing her as the second Tessa Shaw."

330

"What a strange business!" the plain Elizabeth exclaimed.

"It would be odd enough," Tessa said, "but then to have Sir Percy latch onto her . . ."

"He and his friends will be no good influence on her," Pepys said with a frown. "You surely heard about Lady Blake?"

"I haven't," Tessa said, at once interested.

Pepys touched his napkin to his mouth. "I fear it is not a fit subject for dinner conversation."

"Fie on you Samuel," Elizabeth snapped. "You brought the matter up. Get on with it."

Tessa said, "Yes, I would like to know. I'm not so delicate."

"Very well," Pepys said. "Lady Blake was found dead in a ditch by her house. She had been throttled and she was stark naked!"

"Thugs!" Elizabeth Pepys lamented. "They will murder you, rob you and then strip you of clothes. London needs more law and order."

Pepys told his wife, "Do not blame the thieves in this instance, good wife. The rumor is that Lady Blake was a crony of Sir Percy. And at one of his wild parties, which her husband did not attend, she was coupling with a man who strangled her in his frenzy!"

"Shocking!" Elizabeth gasped.

Tessa remained silent, thinking of the orgy she had been an unwilling party to. After a moment, she said, "It is not impossible!"

"I quite agree," Samuel Pepys said. "They say the group has been strangely quiet since this happened. Members have not been seen together as they were in the past. Of course, when the scandal dies down, it will begin all over again. I hope this child you mention doesn't become one of Sir Percy's victims."

"How can you live under the same roof with such a man?" Elizabeth wanted to know.

"I do not enjoy it," Tessa said. "But I am doing it for a reason."

"May I ask what reason?" Elizabeth said sharply. "You surely don't hope to reform the creature!"

"No. That would truly be folly."

Samuel Pepys chuckled. "Agreed. Sir Percy relishes his debauched state."

Tessa said, "There are some things I wish to learn about him. When I find them out I shall leave."

The older woman gave her a warning look. "You are much like a daughter to Samuel and myself. My advice is to leave that place before something happens to you."

"Elizabeth may have a point," Samuel Pepys said.

Tessa promised, "I'll think about it."

And of course she did. But she could not see herself backing away from the situation just as it might become interesting. She would never feel truly safe in the apartment again, but she had to remain if she were to keep a close watch on Sir Percy. To bolster her courage, she purchased a pistol again and kept it loaded in her bedroom.

She did not dare confide fully in anyone. Sir Percy still held his dark threat over her head, and she did not doubt that he would go forward with his campaign to disgrace her if she crossed him. It seemed there was nothing to do but wait—if not too patiently—and hope things would soon come to a stage where she could speak frankly.

She paid a visit to her solicitor, Mr. Grimp, who had now become accustomed to his new office. She had to wait to see him. The ancient clerk had vanished and had been replaced with a new one, and the sign outside the office now read "Grimp & Seddon." Seddon, a younger lawyer who had become a partner, occupied an office next to Mr. Grimp's. Several of those waiting had announced that they wished to see Mr. Seddon.

The young clerk called Tessa's name and then ushered her in to see the ample-stomached Mr. Grimp. He seemed to have put on more weight. His mouth was like a petulant baby's in his broad face, and he now had three chins, yet his gaze was still sharp and he studied Tessa as she sat opposite him.

"You look a bit peaked, my dear," the old solicitor said.

"Do I?"

"Yes. Has something been worrying you lately?" His three chins wobbled as he spoke.

She smiled wanly. "No, not exactly."

"I do not consider that a proper answer," he said, taking a huge handkerchief from his pocket and loudly blowing his nose.

She said, "I do not get along well with Sir Percy Hope. He makes me very nervous."

"You have lived in his house for some time. Am I to understand you've always been afraid there?"

"No," she said. "It has only been of late. I have found he is an evil man."

"There has been much gossip about him"—Mr. Grimp hesitated and then leaned forward to say in a hushed voice—"since they found the body of Lady Blake."

"I worry that they might find me next!"

"Pray not!" he exclaimed in a distressed tone. "You are not the sort."

"Is there a sort more easily murdered than others?" she asked with some bitterness.

The fat man waved a pudgy hand. "There are those who seek danger as a moth seeks out a flame. Lady Blake was one of those lovely creatures, bent on her own destruction. More than once I saw her in her cups, risking attack by thugs as she walked alone on a dark street after midnight."

"I do not doubt this to be true."

"But this does not condone Sir Percy Hope for creating a situation in which the murder could happen," the old lawyer said. "I do not like this satanist cult he is said to have founded."

"They are blamed in Lady Blake's death."

"Yes," Mr. Grimp sighed. "Her husband, Lord Alfred Blake, is one of my valued clients. He speaks of murder. Yet he dares not pursue the matter because he is aware he would only succeed in further blackening his wife's character after death. So he has been forced to be content with dropping a word now and then about the vileness of Sir Percy."

"I have heard much the same story," she said. "I think I would like soon to purchase another house of my own. Would you look for a suitable one?"

"It shall be done," Mr. Grimp assured her. "My new junior partner, Mr. Seddon, is younger and more active than myself. I shall have him undertake to find the right property."

"I noted his name on your sign," she said. "And the old clerk you had has been replaced by a younger one."

"Attrition!" Mr. Grimp sighed. "The old clerk was worn out. I sent him on an errand one day, and he collapsed on the street and died. This is a fine youth we have now—energetic and wants to get ahead. Indeed, I shall soon be retiring myself. And if Mr. Seddon should decide to article him, the lad may one day be the replacement for Grimp!" The fat man chuckled at this.

Tessa joined his laugh. "No one will replace you pound for pound, I'll vouch."

"True," Mr. Grimp said happily. "If you were to count the cost of me by the pound, I'd be a great bargain!" And he laughed once more.

Tessa rose regretfully, "I must go. I have a rehearsal."

"I understand Nell Gwyn is leaving the stage," Mr. Grimp said. "What a loss!"

"I agree." Then she remembered to ask, "What about Lord Harry Farr? I have not had my usual letter from him."

"That would be because he is coming to London for several days. He has some property to sell, and I'm attending to the legal side of it. No doubt he will be calling on you." He added with a smile, "You two get along well these days."

"We are true friends," she said.

"The world has too few of them," Mr. Grimp declared with a touch of philosophy.

So Tessa was not surprised when Lord Harry arrived at her door a few days later. She greeted him happily and at once prepared food and drink for him. He was continuing to put on weight, but his good-looking face was ruddy and healthy looking.

She said, "I was worried that I'd had no letter."

"I saved my news so that I could tell you all personally," he said. "I have a chance to sell a section of the estate, and I shall do it. We have too many acres."

"But things are going well?" she asked anxiously.

"Couldn't be better," he assured her. "My family are all healthy; even my dear wife has enjoyed better than usual health since she recovered from her severe illness. I swear it rid her of all the evil in her system."

"Some people believe in that," Tessa allowed. "How long will you be in London?"

"Until tomorrow. I had an intent to ask you to have dinner with me at some fine inn tonight."

She was at once embarrassed. It was one of the king's nights, and of course she could not tell Harry this. But since she usually returned early from the palace, she decided she might meet Harry later.

She said, "I have an appointment in the early evening. But I shall return in good time. Why don't you come here and wait for me?"

"If you cannot cancel the appointment."

"I cannot," she said, "but I will give you a key to the rear door that gives access to this apartment. I would prefer you come in the back way when I'm not here."

He laughed. "You do not wish any undue scandal."

"Actresses are continually under the scrutiny of the curious, and we are always gossiped about."

"True," he said. "I'll willingly enter by the back way to guard your reputation."

She kissed him on the temple. "I knew I could count on you, dear brother."

Lord Harry remained for a while, and she had to hurry to be at the theater in time for the important afternoon show. Charles Hart was pacing on the stage, worried by her lateness. He came to greet her when she arrived.

"Where were you?" he wanted to know.

"A friend came and kept me," she apologized. "I'll be in costume in a minute."

"Thirty seconds would suit me better," the actor said. "I must raise the curtain now!"

She had never dressed so quickly, but she entered on cue. And the play went well. Though she was tense because of her lateness, Tessa somehow managed to give one of her best portrayals.

After the final curtain Charles Hart embraced her and smilingly said, "Whenever I decide to give you a lecture, wind up having to congratulate you!"

She smiled her thanks, but when he was gone her expression became worried. And the feeling of tension remained with her after she left the playhouse; in fact, it seemed to grow. She could not quite understand it but decided it was because she was planning to see both the king and Lord Harry that evening. Probably she would be on edge until she finally returned to meet Harry. At least he could take his ease in her apartment.

Her maid was away visiting her family in the country for a week, so Tessa was making do on her own. She prepared only a light supper for herself, since she knew she'd be dining with the king and later having a drink and perhaps some food as well, when she and Lord Harry went out.

She put on the brown velvet dress that was a favorite of the king's and got out her black cloak. Then she sat to wait for the arrival of the footman who always accompanied her on these visits.

After a moment or two there was a knock on the door and she went to answer it, expecting to see the footman. But when she opened the door, Sir Percy Hope, an ugly look on his long face, burst into the room and seized her roughly as his companion, a big, puffy-faced man, quickly bound her wrists and ankles.

Fighting wildly for her freedom, Tessa managed to bite Sir Percy's hand. He drew it back with a yelp and then slapped her across the mouth.

"Vixen! Let that teach you a lesson!" he snarled.

"What do you want of me?" she cried.

"All in good time," Sir Percy said, smiling mockingly at her as he tightened the ropes.

When she lay trussed up on the floor, she warned him, "I am expecting someone at any moment."

"I know," Sir Percy gloated. "The king's footman and his carriage. This is one of your palace nights."

"When the king finds out about this, it will go badly with you," she cried.

"Ha!" Sir Percy said and addressing himself to the puffy-faced man, he said, "You hear that, Buckhurst?" To Tessa he said, "This is the gentleman you were so friendly with that night down below."

Buckhurst looked at her with his thick lips wet with desire, and a sickening smile widened on his broad face. "Our first meeting was a pleasure I would like to indulge in again."

"Later, maybe," Sir Percy said. "Leave her alone now."

"I could finish the business without delay," the duke bantered.

"No doubt," Sir Percy said dryly, "but we have other work to do. Where's the wench?"

"Below," Buckhurst said. "I'll go fetch her."

"And don't tarry for any nonsense," Sir Percy said sternly. "The carriage will soon be here."

"I'll have her here right away," the big man promised and hurried out.

Sir Percy sneered at Tessa. "You are going to be most useful to our cause—truly one of us!"

"What do you mean?"

"You are to strike the blow that will free us!"

"You're mad!" she said, straining at the bonds which held her and having no success in loosening them.

"I hit upon the idea when I saw your lookalike on the stage," Sir Percy said. "As you know, I recruited her for our little band. And I must say she has been popular. Not too bright, but a passionate little thing! We have all enjoyed her!"

"Beast!"

"Maybe," Sir Percy said. "At any rate, we have made her see things our way. And now she is about to do the deed for which you will be blamed."

"What?"

"She will take your place and go to keep a rendezvous

337

with the king. In her dress she will have a dagger. And as he embraces her she will bury the dagger in him a sufficient number of times to free England of a libertine!"

"No!" Tessa exclaimed, seeing it all and knowing that it might well work. Fear chilled her. No one would question this girl who so resembled her. And before the king could find out, he would be dead.

"As soon as she has done her task, she will hasten out those same back stairs you use, and Buckhurst will be waiting for her. And together they'll leave England."

"You'll never manage it!" she cried, though she knew all too well that he might.

"I shall remain here with you," he gloated. "Perhaps while you're securely bound I'll pleasure myself with your lovely body—a privilege you've denied me. Afterwards I shall free your bonds and leave you, and you can meet the king's men with protests of your innocence. I doubt that they will listen to you. In any event, I'll be on my way across the Channel to blessed France."

Before she could make a reply, Buckhurst appeared with her lookalike. The girl was pale and looked scared, but it was clear they had talked her into being their instrument for murder.

Sir Percy smiled at the girl and embraced her. "All England will worship your name one day. You will be known as the liberator."

"I am afraid," the girl whispered and seeing Tessa on the floor looked aghast. "What are you going to do with her?"

"Nothing," Sir Percy said. "She will be freed shortly after you leave."

"I do not like the idea of killing," the girl said.

"It will be over in a moment," Sir Percy told her. "Just remember to do it as we rehearsed. You have the knife?"

"Yes," the girl said in a small voice.

Buckhurst moved to the door. "I'd better leave," he said. "I want to be at that rear stairway and have the guard out of the way before she comes down."

"Don't fail me!" the girl pleaded.

Buckhurst scowled. "I'll be there!" And he vanished out the door and went down the stairs.

Sir Percy picked up Tessa's black cloak and placed it on the girl. Then he pulled up the hood and paused to kiss her. "You are so lovely," he said. "You are brave. For tonight's work you'll live well all your days."

"And become a great lady?" the girl asked plaintively.

"I promise it," the villainous Sir Percy said.

The girl shivered and gave a deep sigh. "I wish it was all over."

"It soon will be," Sir Percy promised. Then he moved back to Tessa. "You'll forgive my treating you like a potato sack, but you are too clearly in view here. I should have moved you while Buckhurst was on hand to help." And seizing her roughly by the shoulders, he dragged her over to the rear of the room so that anyone entering would not be able to see her.

"You!" Tessa shouted to the girl who was standing nervously by the door. "It won't work! They'll know you are not me! You'll be thrown into prison or killed!"

"Law!" the girl said in horror and gazed at Sir Percy with terrified eyes.

"She's trying to frighten you," he rasped. "Nothing will happen!"

"They'll know and pounce on you!" Tessa cried.

"You slut!" Sir Percy said, kicking Tessa so that she cried out in pain. Then he took a handkerchief from his frock coat and roughly bound her mouth so she could no longer speak out.

The girl was at the door watching it all. "Do you think she was right? That they'll know me?"

Sir Percy said, "The footman comes for her on these nights. He will come up here to take you down. Say nothing to him here or on the journey to the palace. The only moment of danger will be right here. If he seems to think you're an impostor he'll show it in his manner or say something. If he doesn't, go with him!"

The girl nodded miserably. "You'll meet me and Buckhurst at the boat?"

"I will never be parted from you, my dearest," Sir

Percy said. Going to her again, he fondled her face with his hands and kissed her.

She stared up at him. "I never thought the king so wicked until you told me. I'm only doing this because you say it has to be done."

"For England, my dearest," Sir Percy Hope said. "You will live in history."

"I want to live in France with you," she said. "And damn Buckhurst! I don't want him pawing over me any-more. I hate him!"

"What a temper you have!" Sir Percy said in his best purring manner. "Never worry about Buckhurst. I have plans for ridding us of him. There'll be just the two of us."

"Law!" the girl said in a frightened voice. "I hear the carriage outside."

"Excellent," Sir Percy told her. "Open the door when he knocks. Then go with him."

"Where will you be?" the girl worried.

"Hiding in yon room," he said. "After I know you are on your way, I'll untie this wench and leave to meet you at the boat."

"Can she make any sound of warning?"

"No," Sir Percy said with disdain. "She's trussed like fine fowl! She can neither move nor speak!"

And it was true! Tessa rolled her eyes at him in despair as she strained at the bonds holding her. And the gag he'd tied across her mouth was burning into her flesh! She was helpless, and the moment had come. She heard the foot-man knock at her door.

Chapter Eighteen

Tessa felt she would go out of her mind. The sickening frustration of her plight was more than she could bear. She heard the footman knock again. Then the girl cleared her throat nervously and opened the door.

The footman's familiar voice came, "Are you ready, miss?"

The impostor spoke in a near whisper, "Yes."

There was the sound of her going out and the door closing after the two. Tessa again made a fearful struggle to escape her bonds but she succeeded only in hurting her wrists. When she tried to moan, only a muffled gasp issued from the gag.

Sir Percy Hope came into the room and went over to the window that overlooked the street. "Perfect!" he said with delight. "Perfect! They're getting into the carriage. He has closed the carriage door, and now they are on their way!"

He stood for a moment longer at the window and then came back to gloat over Tessa's prone figure. She thought she had never seen a face so evil—not in Newgate, not anywhere. His face was the face of all corruption.

His smile was arrogant. "So you see it worked just as I predicted. Within the hour the king will be dead and I shall be on my way to France. After James is on the throne I will be able to return safely. The Duke of York knows more than he'll ever admit, and his gratitude to me will be boundless."

She tried to show her hatred of him with her eyes. But she did not think he was even seeing her. His ecstasy in his crime had swept him away to a world of his own.

"You could call me a true genius," he said with awe. "I planned this out with every incident fitting perfectly. No flaw! Of course it was sheer luck I found the lookalike, but after that it was easy."

Tessa managed to wrench her body to the right a little

341

so that she hit a chair leg and it made a sound. The sound attracted his attention.

He said, "You could have done it! I hoped that first night to enlist you in our band and have you do it! You were privy to the king. You alone could catch him at a moment when no one was guarding him. That was our first plan. But when I saw you would never help us, I began to try to work out some other way. And when I was almost ready to admit failure, I heard about this girl who not only resembled you but was an actress. Then it was easy!"

Tessa closed her eyes, finding it all too painful. She was thinking of the king innocently waiting for her, looking forward to their evening together. And with the passing of each minute, death was coming closer to him. Soon that girl would reach the palace back stairs. A footman would show her into the private apartment and take her cloak, after which he would discreetly retire.

Then it would be only a matter of the girl's waiting until the king appeared. When there were no affairs of state to keep him, he was always on time. And even if he had visitors or was asked to sign papers, he was never very late.

"Well, what do you think of yourself now? They'll take you to prison for the king's murder or perhaps place you in an asylum. I think Bedlam would suit you well!"

She tried to glare at him again, but he turned his back on her to look out the window again. Sickened, she waited for his return. Was there any hope of having him halt the plot and spare the king's life, even at this late hour? If she willingly gave herself to him and swore to be his mistress as long as he wished, would he spare the king?

She had no time to think of this further, for at that instant she was aware of a faint sound. Someone was downstairs! Sir Percy gave no indication of having heard it, and Tessa realized that her position on the floor at the back of the room gave her an advantage; Sir Percy at the window had noticed nothing as yet.

Her heart gave a great leap. It had to be Lord Harry she heard. She had given him the key and not named a

pecific time when he should come. It appeared he had
ecided to arrive at the apartment early. She listened.
'es, she heard his footsteps coming up the stairs!

Then the possibilities of a meeting between Sir Percy
Iope and Lord Harry loomed in her mind. There was al-
nost sure to be violence. Once Harry saw her bound and
agged, he would turn on Sir Percy. And if Sir Percy be-
ame aware of him first, he would be liable to place a bul-
t in Harry!

Her immediate fear now was transferred to Harry. She
new he was just outside the door of the room and prayed
nat he would not be killed. Sir Percy, deep in his own
houghts, still stared out the window. The door opened.
As Harry gasped aloud, seeing Tessa, Sir Percy wheeled
round and uttered a sharp curse. She could not see what
appened next, but she heard an exchange of shots and
melled the powder from the pistols. She prayed as she
ad never prayed before!

She heard a body collapse to the floor, and there was
o moan. One of them was dead. As she struggled to turn
erself to see, suddenly she felt hands working at her gag,
nd tears of relief sprang into her eyes. Harry was alive!

"What is going on here?" Lord Harry asked as he tore
way the gag.

"Plot against the king," she cried. "Untie me!"

"Give me a moment," he said, kneeling and worked at
er ankles.

She glanced across the room. "Is he dead?"

"I don't know," Harry said. "He shot at me and I had
o return fire!"

"I hope he is dead!" she said angrily.

"He hasn't moved," Harry said breathlessly as he finished with her ankles and began working at her wrists.
'What is this about a plot?"

"Now," she said, "at this very minute a girl who looks
like me is on her way to the king. He'll receive her and
she will stab him to death before he finds out she's an impostor!"

"Good God!" Harry exclaimed. "The country will be
thrown into turmoil!"

"Hurry!" she begged him.

"There!" he said. "But you'll have little feeling in yo
hands and feet for a time."

"Help me up!" she said.

"Easy," he told her as he assisted her to her feet. H
ankles were swollen and throbbed with pain, but the
would support her.

"Downstairs!" she said.

"Do you want a cloak?"

"Never mind. Must get a carriage!"

"It won't be easy," he warned.

"No time!" she cried and ran ahead of him on he
shaky legs. She held tightly onto the banister as she race
down the steep stairs. All she could think of was gettin
to the palace.

At her heels Lord Harry said, "Is there any hope? Ho
much start has she had?"

"Ten minutes," she said. "But the carriage goes at
leisurely pace."

"Still, that doesn't give us much time," Harry said, hi
breath coming with difficulty.

They both rushed into the street, but there was no hin
of a carriage or even a passerby. Tessa ran frantically
down the cobblestone street in the cool night. Ahead wa
the tavern. As she reached the glow of its windows, sh
saw a rider dismount from his horse and pay a lad
penny to watch it while he went in for a drink.

She did not hesitate to consider. Before the man ha
even entered the tavern, she ran up to the lad, tore th
reins from his hand, and falling back on her old ridin
skill from the circus days, swung into the saddle an
started the frightened horse off at full gallop.

"Stop her! Thief! She's taken my horse!" the indignan
owner of the horse screamed into the night after the van
ishing Tessa.

Bent forward in the saddle, she called out tense encour
agements to the horse, urging it on. The cold wind sen
her hair streaming back and billowed her skirts. The fev
people on the street turned to gaze after her in curiosity

...is girl riding her horse so recklessly through the narrow ...reets at night.

Once a wagon rolled across her path and she had a ...oment of terror. She was certain she and the unfortu...ate horse would crash into the heavy vehicle. But some...ow the driver of the wagon egged his horses on, clearing ... small passage for her just in time, and she rode through expertly.

Finally she was on the straight, broad highway to the ...alace. Still at a gallop she rode around the huge building ... the back stairway entrance. As she rounded the corner, ...e saw the carriage that had brought the other girl being ...riven away. She tore up to the stairs and quickly dis...ounted. But the guard on duty blocked her way.

"You have no business here, miss," he said roughly.

She said, "Don't you recognize me?"

The man who had often seen her come and go by this ...rivate entrance stared at her. "But I saw you go up the ...airs a while ago."

"No matter," she said. "Let me by. The king is wait...g."

He hesitated, "Well, if the king expects you!"

She was already on the stairs. "Look after my horse!" ...e called back.

Breathlessly she raced up the narrow stone stairway, ...raying that as on other occasions the king might be ...elayed for a few moments. If he had arrived on time, she ...as almost certain to find his lifeless body awaiting her. ...he thought increased her panic. She fairly leaped up the ...nal few stairs.

She threw the door open and then the inner door. The ...ootman standing on duty gave her a blank look but did ...ot make any move to hold her back. He evidently recog...ized her from her many previous visits. Now she ran ...long the corridor which led to the king's private living ...oom.

Flinging open the door of the living room, she saw the ...irl posing as herself standing in the middle of the room. ...he king was approaching her from the doorway at the ...ther side.

Tessa ran forward with her hand raised. "Sire!" she cried, "Stand back! Don't go near her!"

Charles halted and looked at the two young women who could be twins. He seemed stunned. At the same time the impostor, startled and needing to improvise, brought out her dagger and held it up defensively. This was Tessa's cue to leap. In a flash she was on the girl struggling with her for the possession of the dagger.

"Call the guards!" Tessa had the presence of mind to shout, even as she battled with the other girl.

Charles lost no time doing so. Within a few seconds elegantly uniformed members of the guards rushed in to seize the battling two and to restrain them from inflicting further harm on each other.

Charles, in his dressing gown, came to Tessa. "What does all this mean?"

Still breathing hard, she managed to curtsy. "A plot, Sire. They found this girl who resembles me. She was sent here to stab you to death with that dagger!"

Charles frowned. "Take her away. I'll deal with her later!"

As the guards dragged off the screaming girl, Tessa went on, "She was only a pawn in this game, Sire. Sir Percy and the Duke of Buckhurst are the true villains. Buckhurst is even now waiting at the private door for her to join him!"

The monarch's face was dark with anger. He turned to the captain of the guards, "You heard her! Arrest Buckhurst!"

"Yes, Sire." The captain of the guards at once hurried off.

Now the King and Tessa were alone. He came and took her in his arms, "My dear Tessa, you are so disheveled! Did those villains harm you?"

"In no lasting way, Charles," she said. And then she quickly told him of how it had all come about. She added, "Sir Percy Hope was to meet the other two at the dock. They were planning to sail for France tonight. But Lord Harry Farr shot him, and he may be dead."

Charles said, "We'll find out. If he has by some miracle

vived and gone to meet the other two, we'll have a
arty of guards go after him and return him to prison."

She said, "Thank heaven you were saved."

"I owe it to you," he said, "and to Lord Harry Farr."

"An insidious plot," she said. "And it almost worked."

"You must tell me everything—how long this has been
ing on, why you suspected Sir Percy . . . but it can
ait until tomorrow. You are exhausted from your or-
al."

"Yes, I had better go," she agreed. "You will have
ore than enough to do this night."

Charles nodded. "So it seems. When you are ready,
en, I'll have the carriage take you. Meantime the horse
ust be returned to its owner and the fellow recom-
nsed."

She smiled. "I hadn't any time to make a polite request
r the use of his animal."

"A bit of silver will put him in a more understanding
ame of mind," the king said. "And when you go back to
ord Harry Farr, give him my warmest thanks."

"I will," she promised.

The king kissed her tenderly, then called for the car-
age and saw her safely on her way. She reached the
ouse in time to see Sir Percy's body being carried out by
embers of the palace guard. Lord Harry was standing
watching.

She went to him as soon as she got out of the carriage.
You killed him?"

"Yes," he said. "The king's men came to get him, and
ey're taking his body. They want something to show for
eir effort. I understand you reached the king in time."

"Yes," she said. "He is safe."

"I would have sworn all was lost when you left," Lord
arry said in a tone of wonder. "You must have ridden
ke the wind to have reached the palace soon enough."

"My days as a circus performer stood me in good
ead."

"There is blood on the floor of your living room," the
oung nobleman worried. "Sir Percy bled a good deal in
ying."

347

"It can be cleaned up later."

He stood facing her in the cool darkness. "What you wish to do? We can stay here or go out somewhe for food and drink."

"I'm surprised at myself," she said. "It's incredible. I actually hungry after all this!"

"It's normal that you should be. Is your cape war enough?"

When she left the palace the servant who had taken t cape from the other girl had returned it to Tessa, and no she held it closely around her. "It will do," she said.

Lord Harry took her to the tavern where she'd stol the horse. The man who'd had his mount taken was a ready a center of attention as he related the incident to number gathered along the bar.

The young nobleman found them a quiet table, and t owner came to serve them. Tessa smiled as she listened the owner of the horse making as much as a hero of hi self as he could.

"I tell you, gentlemen, the king's own personal guan brought my mount back," the man said. "I believe it w used on an important mission. I have been invited to a tend the palace tomorrow morning."

Someone yelled jokingly, "Chances are they'll thro you in prison!" The man looked embarrassed and ever one else guffawed.

Lord Harry smiled at Tessa across the candlelit woode table and said, "They don't realize the heroine of the ev ning is seated here only a short distance from them."

"I don't want them to guess," she said.

They had an ample dinner and remained to drink brandy. She was finally relaxing after all the strains of t evening.

Harry gave her a knowing look. "I had no idea yo were so close a friend of our king."

She blushed. "It has not been a long friendship, but is a meaningful one."

"I'm sure of that," the young nobleman said smilin wryly. "That girl was able to gain the king's compan simply by resembling you."

"It came near being his death."

"At least all has turned out well," he said. "But do you think it will influence your friendship in the future?"

She frowned slightly. "Why should it?"

"No sound reason," he said. "Yet I think you may find it will make a difference."

"Perhaps," she agreed. "We shall see."

Lord Harry sighed. "I should be the last to reprove you, Tessa, but why have you not married? You are lovely enough to win a fine husband, and a sound marriage would be a protection for you in this age of scandal."

She gave him a wistful smile. "I'm married to the theater. Isn't that enough?"

"I think not," Lord Harry said. "The theater can be fickle. Audiences turn their backs tomorrow on the talent they worship today."

"I'm financially independent," she said. "Your good father saw to that."

"But you need more!" he insisted. "Is it not dangerous for you to live alone in London? To be exposed to the wiles of villains like Buckhurst and Sir Percy?"

"I managed well until this present crisis," she said.

"But other problems will present themselves, I promise you," he said. "I do not think you should return to that apartment alone tonight. Yet the king can offer you no shelter."

She sighed. "I might seek out one of my theater friends."

"You need someone of your own," he insisted. "I shall not be happy until I see you married."

Tessa gave him a meaningful look. "You had the chance to marry me once, and you chose Eve."

"I was a young fool!"

"No," she said. "Eve is of your own class and she loves you truly. She has made you the best of wives."

He glanced down at the tabletop in a shamed fashion. "You are right. I had no reason to speak of her in that manner."

"I'm glad you're aware of that, Harry."

349

"That doesn't alter my deep feeling for you," he said. "I shall always look upon you as a lost love."

"And I have come to regard you as my brother," she said.

He waved a hand of protest. "Nay! Let me be a favorite cousin, many times distant, but one for whom you have a special fondness."

She smiled. "I'm willing, if that is what you would prefer."

"It is," Lord Harry said. "Tomorrow I shall have to return to Wilton."

"I shall miss you," she told him. "You probably saved my life tonight. And the king asked that I offer you his thanks for your role in saving his life."

A strange light showed in the good-looking Harry's eyes. He said, "There is a time when every man wishes he were king. I have that feeling tonight."

She stared at him. "Oh?"

He reached out and took her hands in his. "The innkeeper has rooms above. I think it might be fitting if we hired one."

"I see," she said quietly.

"Well?"

She said, "Perhaps it would do no harm for you to be king for just once—just for tonight!"

So the turmoil of that eventful night ended with Tessa and Lord Harry bedded together in a large room over the inn. Tessa was glad not to be alone, and she was satisfied that she had made it clear to Harry that the tryst was not to be repeated—that this night of passionate loving between them would not become a pattern for the future. It was a civilized acceptance that they cared for each other and that a sharing of their bodies would help each of them get through a difficult night.

The next morning they breakfasted together. Then Harry kissed her with great warmth and began his return journey to Wilton and his wife and family. Tessa went back to her apartment and was relieved when her maid appeared, having returned from her short vacation. She at once set the girl to work cleaning up the apartment.

350

She did not go to the theater but sent a note complaining of illness. And she truly was upset. Early in the afternoon she had been called upon by the mysterious Mr. Seddon, junior partner to Mr. Grimp. Mr. Seddon, whom she had not seen before, was a pleasant young man with reddish hair, dressed quietly in dark blue velvet with little fancy trimming.

She received him and asked, "Pray, what has brought you here, Mr. Seddon?"

The young lawyer said, "You spoke to Mr. Grimp about wishing to find new quarters."

"Yes."

His eyes met hers. "I hear that Sir Percy Hope, the owner of this building, was killed last night. Supposedly, he was involved in a plot against His Most Gracious Majesty and was shot while attempting an escape."

"It was much like that," she said.

"Many wild rumors are going about the city," Mr. Seddon told her. "And I trust you will not be offended if I tell you that one version has it that *you* shot and killed Sir Percy."

"That is not so," she said.

Mr. Seddon's pleasant face crimsoned. "I did not mean imply the rumor was true."

"Oh?"

"I simply wished you to know the sort of gossip that is going on. I have heard that a girl, an actress in one of the small theater companies, was involved in the plot, as was the Duke of Buckhurst."

"That piggish lout might be capable of any evil," Tessa said bitterly. "Nell Gywn is well rid of him."

"She is not likely to see him again," Mr. Seddon observed. "He faces a long prison sentence, as does the girl."

"The king should show her lenience."

"Gossip has it that she tried to stab him with a dagger," the young lawyer said awkwardly.

Tessa smiled at him thinly. "May I also suggest that gossip has it that I arrived on the scene and saved the king from this plot."

The young man cleared his throat. "That is the situ
tion exactly, miss. I'm pleased that you seem to ha
taken all this . . . ah . . . in stride, as they say."

"I'm satisfied England is at last rid of that scoundrel
Percy!" she declared. The rug was still drying from t
cleaning she'd had given it because of the bloodstains.

Mr. Seddon continued, "If the usual practice is f
lowed, the government will confiscate his estate. Th
means this house goes."

"So it would," she agreed. "I have had no time as y
to give thought to such matters."

"Of course you wouldn't," the young lawyer said wi
understanding. "But Mr. Grimp and I have conferre
and we wondered if you might wish to make a bid for t
house. It is well located and near the theaters. And y
are comfortably established here."

She considered the various aspects of this for a lo
moment. Then she said, "You have a good idea there.
might be an intelligent move to make an offer for t
property. In the event that I should win it, I would pref
to move down to the apartment below."

"That would be the least problem of such a change
the lawyer said, rising. "I shall inform Mr. Grimp of yo
feelings, and he and I shall discuss how to proceed in o
der to gain hold of this house."

"You are most thoughtful," she returned.

The young man bowed and flushed with pleasure at h
comment. She saw him on his way and speculated
what other changes might be brought about by the even
of the previous night.

Her next visitor was an excited Samuel Pepys, his h
in hand. He stood with her in the living room and glanc
around him in a conspiratorial way. "So this is where o
of the thrilling moments took place. Is it true that S
Percy was stretched out dead on this very floor?"

She said, "Is that what is being said all about the city?"

Little Mr. Pepys nodded. "That is what is going t
rounds. And you are lauded as the one who saved t
king's life."

"It sounds like one of Mr. Dryden's plays," she smiled.

"Better," Pepys chuckled. "In the end Buckhurst made a run for it with the king's men after him. The story goes they found him in a pigsty, smelling most foul!"

"A pigsty would be suitable for him."

Samuel Pepys went on, "The girl who tried to plunge a dagger into the king is in Newgate."

"God forgive her and pity her," Tessa murmured.

The little man's bulging eyes showed amazement at his. He said, "You are of a forgiving heart!"

"I know something of Newgate," she said soberly. "I would not wish it on the most foul sinner. And that girl was more sinned against than sinning."

Pepys continued to be astounded. "You would know, of course," he said. "Now I must back to the Admiralty before someone asks for me. But I had to spend a moment with you."

"You are most kind," she said.

"I am your humble servant, my dear Tessa," he said. "I shall be in touch with you shortly. Elizabeth is talking of having another fairly large party."

"I shall look forward to it," Tessa said politely, though she felt little enthusiasm for the idea. She saw Pepys to the door.

Her third visitor did not arrive until the afternoon theater performance was over. Tessa had not expected him, but she did greet him with warmth. It was her oft-time director and leading man, Charles Hart.

The handsome actor said, "The show has left me thirsty, my love! The audience was composed mostly of dull dogs, more interested in their own exchanges than in what was going on before them on the stage!"

She smiled. "Then you would not refuse a drink?"

"I beg you for one!" he said with strong theatricalism. He paced up and down. "Why did I choose to be a player of parts in a world where none of the important parts are those of players?"

She brought him a brandy and had one herself. "You do very well. One stupid audience will not ruin your life. We have known many. Another day will bring a more pleasing group of patrons."

Hart downed half the drink and smacked his lips. "Law, I declare you're right! I feel much better already!"

"You see!"

He gave her a fond glance and cupped his drink in his hands. "To be truthful, dear Tessa, my afternoon was spoiled by your absence. And by worrying about you."

"You are too kind."

"How could I not be aware of you and what went on last night," he said with mock sarcasm, "when all the audience did nothing but talk about the plot against the king, despite our princely plotting upon the stage?"

"So Pepys and my lawyer told the truth. The story has been spread by the gossips."

"You were wise not to show up today," Charles Hart went on. "I'm sure we could not have kept control of those dogs in the pit!"

"They will soon recover from it," she said. "Another bit of scandal will supplant it. Last night will be forgotten."

Charles Hart downed the rest of his drink and handed her the glass. "Another, my love!"

She poured it for him. And asked, "You do not think it truly serious?"

The actor sighed. "You want the truth?"

"You have always been truthful with me."

He sat on the arm of a chair and gazed at her sincerely. "Very well, I'll be truthful now. I think this event is going to have a marked effect on your career."

"I see," she said worriedly.

"You have become notorious overnight—the latest known consort of the king. That will stay with you."

"Nell is known to be his longtime mistress, and it has not hurt her popularity."

Charles Hart said, "They have a different feeling for Nell. In the long run it will not hurt you, but . . . well, for a few months your appearance in any play would be too distracting. The audiences would see you and not the character you'd be playing. They would gossip about you openly as you tried to speak your lines. You must spare yourself that humiliation."

354

"You are saying you cannot use me for a time, until the scandal dies out," she said.

"I am," the actor admitted. "And I deeply regret it. We need you."

"I also regret it," she said. "I need to be occupied. To be kept busy."

Charles Hart took part of his drink. He gave her a knowing look. "You have the king."

"I wonder," she said.

"Of course you have," he said. "The bond between you will be stronger than ever. He cannot help being grateful to you."

She said quietly, "There is more to it than that."

"And you know how it is with Nell," Charles Hart said. "He has refused to let her do any more plays."

"I know."

"He might decide the same about you."

Alarm showed in her eyes. "That would be horrible!"

He nodded. "I'm sure Nell finds it a grim sentence."

"Poor Nell!" she exclaimed. "I had not thought much about it before, but it is truly tragic."

"I agree," Hart said. "If this keeps up, we'll have to turn to men playing the female parts again in the King's Company. I don't relish the idea. Now I'm used to having ladies in the cast."

"It will not come to that," she said.

The actor finished his drink. "Well, I must be on my way. I wanted you to know we are all thinking of you. And I thought I should explain to you why you must remain away from the stage for a little. I'm certain the king would say the same thing."

She smiled bitterly. "I thought we had ended Sir Percy's evil last night. But I see it goes on, and we all continue to suffer because of him."

So she found herself living in forced seclusion. She made one sally to the shops on a fashionable street not far from where she lived and was shocked to find herself being pointed out by both men and women. The whispers, winks, and sly faces sickened her. From that day on she had her maid take care of the shopping.

She began to read a good deal. As an exercise she read all of Shakespeare's plays over again and memorized a share of the leading female parts. It gave her a sense of being on stage and the feeling she was not completely wasting her time. Still, she was greviously lonely.

Then one morning she received a message. It was from the palace. The carriage would be calling for her tonight as it had so often in the past. She felt both thrilled and saddened. Thrilled because she felt a true need to see Charles again and saddened because she knew deep in her heart the romance could never be the same as before the attempt on his life.

Still, she wore her best pink gown and spent much time with her hair. And when the footman came to the door she felt her heart begin to pound wildly. This excitement remained with her as she reached the palace and mounted the stairway to the private apartment where she and Charles had always met.

She stood waiting as he was somewhat late. At last he entered and came to her. And she was shocked to see that in a short time he had aged perceptibly. There were new lines of weariness on his aristocratic face.

"You are a picture of beauty tonight, Tessa," he said.

She made a curtsy. "Thank you, Sire."

"Charles," he said. "I would always be Charles to you." And he took her in his arms.

At dinner she sensed that he was not fully at ease. And she suggested, "Is something troubling you, Charles?"

He eyed her soberly. "Yes."

"Pray, share it with me," she said, a tremor in her voice because she felt she already knew what he would say to her.

The king frowned. "I fear I have no choice."

"Please," she begged him to continue.

He said, "Children are taught by fairy tales to dream of being kings or queens. It is a stupid, evil practice! Grown men and women go on believing this fallacy. In fact, to be a royal figure means most to bear burdens from which ordinary men would hastily turn aside."

"I know," she said softly.

"I have flaunted the conformists," the king went on. "My name is often the butt of obscene jokes. But still I have the loyalty of the majority of my people. That is why schemes like that of Buckhurst and Sir Percy are bound to fail."

"That is so true, Charles. The people love you."

"It is too late to win their respect," the king said. "But I do not want to tarnish the crown more. Ours has been the one love which depended less on physical mating than any of the others, with the exception of Nell, who amuses me. You have made me feel like a man of worth—like a king!"

"You are! You are a true king, Charles," she whispered as their hands met in a fierce clenching.

"To preserve what is good of what we have had, it must end," the king said sadly. "You must not be snickered at as another of the king's whores!"

"I have never been concerned about that!"

"I have," the king said. "And so this will be our last meeting of this kind. You will be invited to court whenever it is possible. I shall always be your friend, and I beg that you shall remain mine, dear Tessa."

She spoke gently, "Always, Sire."

"To practical matters," he said. "The house in which you are living has become royal property, and I am turning it over to you."

"I need nothing," she said. "I have money enough."

"No matter," he said. "It is a fine house and it suits you."

"One favor, Sire," she said, using the term of extra respect which she felt their new relationship demanded.

"Anything you ask," Charles said.

"That girl!"

He frowned. "The one who would have stabbed me?"

"Yes. Where is she?"

"In Newgate. She will rot there or perhaps be eaten by the rats! I have ordered that she be detained there for the rest of her natural life."

"I beg you to have mercy!"

"Mercy for that wanton hussy?"

"She was molded into madness by Sir Percy and others like him," Tessa said. "She was not as guilty as they! I beg you to free her!"

"Free her?" The king seemed stunned.

"Yes," she told him. "You said any favor, Sire."

He considered for a long moment. Then he said, "Very well. There is a ship leaving for the New World. A group of female criminals are being sent to the Virginia Colonies to be wives to the men exiled in that distant land. She shall be among them."

Tears brimmed in Tessa's eyes. "You are a good man, Sire!"

Charles took her in his arms, and before he touched his lips to hers, he said, "I vow you will always remain close to me, in my heart forever!"

That relationship severed, life became a pattern of dull gray tasks for Tessa. She became a recluse. Cut off both from the theater and from the king, she had little to do and few friends. It was a blessing that Samuel Pepys and his wife invited her to dine with them occasionally. But it seemed that whenever she joined them, half the gossips in London were among the guests. And she was often spoken to sarcastically about her affair with the king.

One foppish fellow had the gall to mince up to her and say, "I never did like you on the stage as well as Nell. And it appears the king liked you less in bed than her. She is still seen with him!"

To which Tessa exclaimed in anger, "I suggest you bed with the Duke of York—he has a taste for your sort!" And she slapped him hard across the face.

Justified as it was, her reaction distressed her host and hostess. It seemed that the fop was a cousin of the Duke of Bancroft, prominent in the Admiralty. And so, because of the unhappy scene, Tessa felt she had to decline the further invitations which Pepys and his wife extended.

So she remained at home.

One day Mr. Seddon came to call on her. The pleasant lawyer was one of the few people she saw regularly. He often came about money matters and the like. This afternoon he seemed to be in an excited mood.

358

He said, "You have done nothing about the large apartment below."

"True, I have not," she said. "It is just as when Sir Percy left it."

"A fine, large space and well furnished," Mr. Seddon said in his practical way.

"Sir Percy often entertained upwards of a hundred down there," she told the solicitor.

"What do you propose to do with it?"

"Nothing," she said. "I have made no plans."

"You once spoke of taking it for your own use," he recalled.

"I have since changed my mind."

He smiled. "A lady's privilege."

"These simpler quarters are more suited for my use," she said. "Even more so since I have been less active. There are just myself and my maid here."

The young solicitor said, "It would be better if the downstairs apartment was occupied. Not only would it bring you a good rent to help defray the expenses of the property, but it would also mean you would not be isolated here alone and so prone to robbery or other crimes."

She offered him a melancholy smile. "It would seem you have something in mind."

"I do," he said. "I have a possible tenant for your apartment. And I think you might find the offer most exciting."

Chapter Nineteen

"Pray explain this offer to me," Tessa said.

"Very well," the young solicitor said. "I have a client, a man with a sound reputation for paying his debts—and in all ways a most moral person—who wishes to open a gaming house for private members."

"A gaming house?"

"Yes," the young man continued. "Not at all the rough sort of place you might be imagining. As it happens, he is at present in partnership with another gentleman in a somewhat similar venture in another part of London. But his partner insists that there be a cellar with cock-fighting and a rat pit. My client objects to these cruel and vulgar attractions and wants to establish a house in which dice, cards, and other similar games can be indulged in by gentlemen of worth and reputation. I suggest the premises below as being ideal for such a purpose."

Tessa said, "Your proposition comes as a surprise. I have always considered gaming establishments to be evil places."

"They need not be if properly operated and restricted to members and their guests. Some spirits would be sold, but there would be no ladies to offer their services on the premises, if you understand me. My client does not wish to be involved in prostitution."

Tessa raised her eyes. "Your client would seen to be a man of strangely mixed principles—certainly of very fixed ideas."

"He believes the one way to make such a venture a paying and respectable business is to run it along stern lines," the young lawyer told her.

"He is probably right in that respect," she agreed.

Mr. Seddon went on seriously, "I would not have presented this project to you without previously giving it severe scrutiny. Mr. Grimp has heard all the facts, and he has given his approval to my discussing the possibility with you."

"I have been living a quiet life," she remarked.

"I know," he said.

"Would this not bring a great deal of people to the house, many of dubious reputation?"

"My client proposes to restrict his members to a high type of gentleman. And the membership will be limited. I do not think you need fear a mass of people coming each evening. My client assures me there will be no noise, no unpleasantness."

Tessa smiled wanly. "I must say, you make it sound attractive. Of course the money from the rental would be welcome. At present I am draining my capital to pay the running expenses of the house."

"Exactly. This would reverse that. You could how a profit as well as having a free living here."

"What does your client propose to call his club?"

"The Green Room," Mr. Seddon said. "Many of the gaming tables would have green covered tops."

"You see no possible ill results for me?"

"None. You would no longer be alone in the house, and your income would be greatly increased. And if you wish to protect yourself, you could easily insist that the lease be only on a yearly basis. In this way, you need not renew it unless you are satisfied."

"That would give me a degree of safety," she said. "Let me think about it."

"Very well," Mr. Seddon said, rising. "If you wish to go through with the project, send me a message. On your approval, I will arrange to bring my client here to view the premises and sign a lease with you for the first twelve months."

"I will let you know," she promised.

She had a hard time making up her mind. Finally she sent a message to Samuel Pepys and asked that he come and see her on a matter most urgent. The little man did not keep her waiting long. He came to visit her that very night.

Tessa outlined the offer and invited his opinion. "Do you think I might be criticized for entering into such an agreement?" she worried.

"Law, no!" Pepys said. "There are gaming clubs all over the city, places for every class to gamble. And while I have some strong opinions about gambling, I cannot see any harm in this. It is a private club and apparently to be run under strict rules in a most genteel manner."

"My solicitor has promised me that."

"Then I say, go on with it," Pepys said. "And good luck!"

She smiled. "It will mean there will be much coming and going downstairs."

"All the better for you," he said. "You have become too much of a recluse."

"I know that is true."

"You need to see more people. We sorely miss you at our small gatherings."

She gave him a grateful look. "You and Elizabeth have been stalwart friends," she said.

"And always shall be," he told her. He paused a moment, "Have you heard from the king?"

"No," she said. "I have not heard from him."

Pepys sighed. "Well, perhaps that is best."

"I'm sure it is," she said quietly.

The conversation with Mr. Pepys weighed her decision in favor of seeing the mysterious client who wished to open the gaming club. She made up her mind to let the matter hinge on whether she felt she could trust him personally. If so, she would give her permission for a year. She sent a message to the solicitor and arranged a meeting for the following afternoon.

When Mr. Seddon arrived with his client, no one was more shocked than Tessa. For the sturdy, assured gentleman at the young solicitor's side was none other than an older Bob Wills! He was elegantly dressed in red frock coat, yellow breeches and expensive buckled shoes. He had become a dandy. He had aged a good deal, and his face wore a stern expression which was intensified by a bristling black mustache.

She gasped, "Bob! It is you!"

Bob Wills bowed, "Yes, Tessa. I only discovered you were the owner of this property on my way here today."

362

Mr. Seddon was delighted that they knew each other. He said, "How fortunate that you have had previous acquaintance."

"Previous acquaintance, indeed!" she said with a small laugh.

The solicitor said, "There is no need of my introducing Captain Robert Wills."

"None," she said. And turning to Bob, she went on, "Did I hear right? You are Captain Wills?"

"Yes," he said, his hat in hand. "I was retired from His Majesty's Navy after suffering serious injuries in a battle off the French coast, where the Dutch fleet was under the command of De Ruyter. Because of my conduct in battle, I was promoted to the rank of captain."

"I'm proud of you, Bob," she said sincerely.

The new sternness in him relaxed a trifle. "Thank you, Tessa. We circus people always remain true to each other. I wish I could say the same about all people."

She said, "Pray be seated, both of you." And she sent the maid out to bring them some liquid refreshment. As she sat facing Bob, she sensed there had been a remarkable change in him and wondered if it had been in his injuries which brought this about. She asked, "Were you badly injured?"

"My back," he said. "A musket shot entered me near the middle of the spine. At first it was thought I would die; later they said I would never walk again. Happily, I came out of it. But my back is painful and weak. I was no more use to the navy."

"You are in constant pain?" she sympathized.

"Almost constantly," he said. "My small naval pension would not support me, and of course my days of somersaults and the like are far behind me. So I could not return to the circus."

She said, "And so you entered the gaming business?"

"Myself and another former naval officer," Bob Wills said. "We have done well. But I do not see things as he does. I wish to operate a more genteel sort of place."

"Yes," she said. "My solicitor explained that to me."

363

They were interrupted for a moment as the maid brought in their drinks.

Mr. Seddon resumed the conversation by saying, "The fact you two are old friends should simplify matters."

Bob gave her a questioning look. "That depends on Tessa. I would not force this on her."

She smiled. "I think we can come to an agreement. What about your wife and children? Are they in London?"

His face clouded suddenly, and she feared she had made an error in mentioning them. He said in a grim voice, "I have no wife nor family!"

"Bob!" she exclaimed. "What happened?"

"The slut ran off with a rich wine merchant," he said bitterly. "They are living in Oxford. She took the children with her."

"I'm sorry," she murmured. "I truly am."

Bob went on darkly, "I offered to take her back, forgive her. The life of a sailor's wife can be a lonely one. But she turned her back on me. Worse, the children no longer want me as their father. They prefer this new man!"

Tessa hardly knew what to say in the face of this personal tragedy. But she now understood why Bob had become so stern and aloof. He was living with more than physical pain; like herself he had an aching soul.

Mr. Seddon cleared his throat. "I would take it, then, that you are willing to rent your premises to the captain?"

She said, "I think we should inspect them first. The apartment may not be as suitable as he thinks."

They went downstairs, and she gave the lawyer and Bob a tour of the place. When they came to the large room where Sir Percy had held his satanist gatherings, Bob stared at the erotic paintings on the curtains that lined the walls.

She remarked, "These can be removed and whatever decor you like substituted."

But Bob surprised her by saying, "No, I would leave them. Let this room be known as 'The Venus Room.' It could very well become a topic of gossip and increase interest in the club."

Tessa smiled ruefully. "If you like. I guarantee no one will fine their equal anywhere in this city."

Young Mr. Seddon's face was boiling red. "So lifelike and so unusual!" he breathed.

An hour later the arrangement was concluded, and Captain Bob told her he would like to begin moving in some of the gambling equipment and other furnishings within a few days.

"Whenever you like," she said.

"I shall hope to see you from time to time," he told her.

"Come up and visit whenever you like," she said. She felt truly sorry for him. Yet there was a hint of passion in her feelings for the good-looking man who had been her first companion in bed. She hoped that he had no thought of renewing a relationship with her on an intimate level.

As the weeks passed it was inevitable that they would grow more friendly. Captain Bob opened his club, and so discreetly did he operate it that Tessa was almost unaware of the traffic and noise below. At the same time she felt less open to attack by robbers because of having company in the big house.

It became a ritual for him to join her for his evening meal several times a week. He would regale her with talk of his club and its customers and discuss the general events of the day. They had a warm, comfortable relationship, and she began to take pleasure in planning the food and drink for him.

One evening as they sat together in her dining room, he said, "I have a regular member whom you may have met. You knew his brother."

"Really?" she said. "What is his name?"

"Lord Claude Montagu," Captain Bob said with a knowing look. "I understand it was his brother, Thomas, to whom you were betrothed."

"Yes," she said. "Much against the wishes of Lord Edward and the family. Then Thomas was lost in battle."

"And this Claude took over the title at his father's

death," Bob said. "You know he shot him in trying to prevent a robbery. He is a stupid, sour clod! Instead of killing the thief he killed his own father! People still whisper about it."

"I can imagine," she said. "And you say he is not a pleasant fellow?"

"Neither in looks nor personality," Bob said with disgust. "I would like to exclude him from my club, but unhappily he is a founding member and it is difficult."

"I see." Tessa was thoughtful. She was recalling her single meeting with the ugly Claude . . . on that fateful night when she and Mad Reevy had invaded the great mansion of Sir Edward in pursuit of vengeance. She had intended to put a bullet through the man who had wanted her murdered; but, by a quirk of fate, in the melee it had been Claude's shot which had killed his father.

"He comes to play dice often," Bob added. "I wish he would tire of it. He has been losing recently and grumbling."

"He would be a bad loser," Tessa agreed. And she wondered: Had the loutish fellow had a good look at her that night before she fled? Would he remember her if they should meet again? She thought not. It had happened years ago.

Bob smiled at her, one of his rare smiles, and it a sad one. He said, "Where are your thoughts? Still with Thomas?"

"In a way," she said.

"You have had many lovers since then."

"A few."

"I have been thinking," he told her, "about us."

"Have you?" She guessed this might be the moment she had been fearing—the moment when he might try to renew their affair of long ago.

"What is to happen to us?" he asked earnestly. "We shall grow older and our circle will narrow. London is a cruel city, a bad place to be alone when one is old."

She forced a small smile. "We have a long way to go before that. I pride myself on still having some remnants of youthful beauty."

"And you have," he said quickly. "Indeed, your beauty has veritably blossomed with the maturing years. You are more interesting now than when you were that little girl riding a pony."

She said, "I fear that little girl was lost long ago."

"Never," Bob said, taking one of her hands in his. "I see her in you more than you would believe."

"I think you imagine it."

"No," he said. "I was your first love. And now we meet again after many storms. It seems to me we might do worse than form an alliance, you and I."

She could not meet his earnest gaze. "I've been expecting you to say something like that," she said.

He showed surprise. "You have?"

"Yes. And I've feared it."

"Feared it?"

"Because I have nothing to give you but my friendship," she said. "Oh, we could bed together . . . perhaps we could even find enjoyment in the act. But it would be a hollow thing, and it might spoil our friendship. I would not wish to live with you pretending love."

He looked down and sighed deeply. "Is it still the king?"

"No," she said.

"Who, then?"

She sighed. "My memory of Thomas," she admitted. "He alone won my heart completely. I would not sully the memory of that love with any more casual affairs."

"Ours would not be casual."

"I know that," she said. "But I fear in the end it would not work out for either of us."

Bob kept his eyes on the carpet. "Would you prefer that I not visit you again?"

"Certainly not!" she exclaimed. "I want your friendship. I need it badly. Do not desert me."

He raised his sad eyes and told her, "Never, Tessa! I'll never desert that little girl I taught to ride a pony."

"How I loved the applause!" she smiled. "And how I miss it now!"

"Why not go back to acting?"

"They don't want me just yet," she sighed. "Maybe they'll never want me again."

"Return anyway!" Captain Bob said stoutly. "It is not fair of them to keep you off the stage."

"It is a matter of the king's interest in supporting the theater," she said. "I can blame myself for placing myself in the sorry situation."

"I would say the king is equally to blame," Bob suggested.

She shook her head. "Don't condemn him too quickly. No, I must remain away from the King's Theater or run the risk of embarrassing the king and myself."

"Is that why Nell Gwyn is seen no more on stage?"

"Yes," she said. "Though the circumstances are rather different. She has a son by the king."

Captain Bob suddenly thumped a fist in the palm of his other hand. "I have a thought!" he said.

"What?"

His expression was more animated than she had seen it since their getting together again. He said, "There are times during the evening when it seems the club becomes too quiet—lulls in the activity now and then."

"So?"

"What I need is a kind of hostess, a lady who occasionally would come and conduct gracious conversation with my members. Someone like the hostess of a fine mansion, but who could join with the harpsichordist and sing a sweet song or two when the moment called for it."

Tessa said, "I think it an excellent idea."

"I'm pleased that you do," Bob said. "For I see in you the ideal person to fill this role."

"Me!" she exclaimed in surprise.

"You can sing, I'm sure," he said. "And you can be a charming hostess. It would get you out of this lonely apartment."

"I couldn't," she protested.

"Why not?"

"I'd be afraid!"

"I'd always be on hand to protect you," he told her.

And you'd be exposed to only a small company—not like being on the stage in a noisy theater."

She hesitated. "It is appealing. I won't deny it!"

"You would hear applause again! And that means much to you," Bob said. "I know it from myself."

"Could I be criticized for appearing in a gaming house?"

"A private gaming club," Bob corrected her, "one of a most dignified nature, if I do say so myself."

She smiled. "I don't know."

"Try it," he urged. "If it doesn't work out, you needn't continue."

"You tempt me," she confessed.

"Because I know you'll be a great success!"

And she was. Each night she spent several hours of the mid-evening at the club. She came to know the members and made it a point to learn all their names. She congratulated them when they won and sympathized when they lost. Many of them knew her from the King's Theater and were glad to meet her again. She became one of the club's attractions.

Not the least of her appeal was her singing of ballads. She varied from sweet love songs to rollicking numbers satirizing London society. The proof of her popularity was that many ceased their play at the gambling tables to enjoy her entertaining.

Bob was delighted that he had been responsible for her success. He said, "I wish some of the circus people were around to see you now!"

She smiled at him. "And you! What a success you have become!"

He shrugged. "To what purpose?"

"Someday you may think differently," she said lightly, but aware that he was still saddened by the loss of his errant wife and his two children.

The club became more successful with each week, and Bob had to close down membership. But those on the outside managed to enjoy the club's atmosphere occasionally by coming as guests of members. It was in this capacity that Samuel Pepys arrived one night with a convivial group of men from the government.

He sought out Tessa and confided to her, "Elizabeth would punish me if she knew I had been to a gambling place."

Tessa smiled. "You could be in worse places than this."

"It is elegant and genteel," Pepys agreed. "And you adorn it well."

"Captain Bob is my friend," she said. "I sing chiefly for him."

"I have heard about your being here from mutual friends," Pepys said. "They all agree you are the best thing about the club."

"Have you seen Charles Hart?" she wanted to know.

"Yes," Pepys told her. "He was ill with the gout for some weeks, but he is back on stage once again."

"I did not know. I miss him—and all the others."

"There is talk of a new company."

"To rival the king's?"

"Yes. The story is the king was persuaded to back another group."

"I hope not," she said. "I don't think there is enough talent to form a second company with the high standards of the King's Company. Charles Hart is a genius."

"True," Mr. Pepys agreed, "but it may be that the people wish a change."

Tessa was to hear more about this a few nights later when Nell Gwyn arrived with a merry company that included the Earl of Shrewsbury and Lord Cleveland. She left her party when she saw Tessa and came and threw her arms around her old friend.

"Love!" the former orange girl said in her impulsive way. "I've missed you so!"

"And I've missed you, Nell," Tessa laughed as they exchanged kisses. "I'm glad you've come here."

"I came to see you," Nell said. "You are getting to be a London favorite. Everyone likes your songs!"

Tessa told her, "I can't compare with you. Indeed, you can do me a great favor by appearing for me tonight!"

Nell's eyes shone. "I've not entertained for what seems donkeys' ears. I can't remember the words of my songs!"

"They're bound to come back to you," Tessa urged. "And the man who plays the harpsichord has an excellent ear and will be able to accompany you with ease."

"You must sing for me first," Nell said. "Then we shall see."

So Tessa did what she considered her best numbers while Nell and the others watched and listened. When she finished, the applause was loud and sincere.

Tessa bowed and said, "A little later my friend Nell Gwyn will sing for you."

At this there was another burst of applause and cries of "Bravo!" Nell was still a big London favorite. She and Tessa went out to Tessa's small dressing room so that Nell could freshen up.

Tessa stood beside the pretty chestnut-haired girl and helped her repair her makeup. Nell gazed into the mirror studying the effect of her fashionable rose gown and the golden pendant on her bosom that was studded with diamonds.

In her jolly way, she said, " 'Tis not the makeup which needs renewing, but the face!"

"Nonsense!" Tessa said. "You're not much over twenty. I'm older than you."

Nell looked up at her. "You are wearing better! I vow it!"

Tessa took a brush and fixed some straying wisps of the seated girl's hair. "It is so good to see you," she said.

"I miss the stage," Nell said.

"I know how you feel. That is why you find me here."

"You are lucky," Nell said. "The king will not allow me to take any regular acting work. So I shop and play the lady and stay at home with my son."

"How is Charles?" she asked.

Nell looked up at her. "I never mention your name, but he looks sad," she said.

"I think of him often," Tessa said.

"You have heard about the new theater company?"

"Samuel Pepys mentioned it. Is it likely to come about?"

"It is a certainty," Nell said. "I predict that before long Charles Hart will retire. He is displeased at the idea of a competing group sponsored by the king."

"I think he has a right to be angry," Tessa said. "He has produced such fine plays."

"Everything changes," Nell said with a sigh. Then she smiled and announced, "I'm ready to appear! Sound the cymbals!" And she laughed at her own exaggeration.

Yet she was received with warm appreciation as she took her place by the harpsichordist and entertained the company. Tessa stood at the back of the room with Bob and admired the lively talent of the former orange girl.

Nell ended with a lively song:

"I come, kind gentlemen, strange news to tell ye,
I am the ghost of poor departed Nelly,
I beg you, be not distressed. I'll be civil,
I'm what I was, a little harmless devil!
Gallants, look to it if you say there are no spirits,
For I'll come dance about your beds at nights!
As for my epitaph now I'm gone,
I'll trust no poet, but will write my own,
Here Nelly lies, who, though she lived a slattern,
Yet died a Princess in Saint Catten!"

It was a version of the song Nell had sung at the end of *Tyrannic Love.* Her audience went wild over it and coaxed her to sing some songs that were more earthy in type. Bob later complained that though he'd been honored by Nell's visit, he'd lost a great deal at the tables because there had been little gaming that night.

Nell left promising Tessa she would return another evening. All in all, her visit had proved most pleasant. But there were other not-so-pleasant things about to happen at the club.

One winter night when Tessa came down to appear at the club, Captain Bob came up to her and growled, "It is
372

a good thing you are here. There is trouble in the air tonight."

She gave him an anxious look. "What has happened?"

"It is Montagu," he said, nodding to one of the side rooms.

"Sir Claude Montagu?"

"Yes. He has been away from London, and I wish he still were absent! Now that he is back, he is in his usual foul mood!"

"That is too bad."

"For the first time we've had an argument," Bob said. "He and the Duke of Beesley came to words about a card game."

"What did you do?"

"I managed to placate the duke and calm him by telling him Lord Montagu was overcome by drink and not responsible."

Nodding, Tessa said, "Which was probably close to the truth."

"It was," Captain Bob said bitterly. "Now he is playing with a rich merchant, and I fear what may happen."

"Can I help in any way?"

"Sing as soon as you can," he told her. "Montagu may get bored and leave. He is not one to enjoy a sweet voice."

She smiled. "I shall feel complimented if he goes."

Shortly afterward she took her usual position in the corner of the big room with the harpsichordist and began her program of songs. She was partway through it when she became aware of a drunken figure standing almost directly in front of her. It took her only a moment to recognize the ugly face of Lord Claude Montagu. He watched her with owlish disinterest until she finished.

The applause was friendly and she thanked the members for their appreciation. She was about to cross the room and return to Bob when she was waylaid by the drunken Lord Montagu.

"You!" he said. "Mistress Tessa Shaw! Have I not met you before?"

Nervously, she said, "I think not!"

"Your face is damn' familiar," he insisted. "While I watched you singing, I tried to place where we'd met."

She said, "I have an ordinary face. You may have met someone who resembled me."

Claude Montagu stood swaying slightly and still blocking her way. "Your face is lovely," he slurred. He waved to the erotic nudes on the wall and added with a leer, "I understand you have a lovely body also. They tell me Sir Percy had these wantons painted with you modeling!"

"You have been misinformed!" she said sharply.

"You caused Sir Percy's death," he accused her. "He was my friend."

"Please," she said. "I would rather not discuss the matter."

"Ah!" he said. "Guilty conscience! I'll wager you had yourself a fine time at his orgies here! I attended a few, but I'm sorry to say I missed you."

"I must go," she said. "Captain Wills wishes to see me."

Lord Montagu laughed and lurched to the left a little. "Captain Wills! My what airs we give ourselves! He's nothing but a discharged navy man who rose from the ranks!"

"In my opinion that is to his credit!" Tessa returned, angered.

"A commoner who once was an acrobat in a country circus," Claude Montagu sneered. "Of course he is your lover now! What a rise in the world for him—to bed one of the king's discards!"

"Scum!" she cried, unable to restrain herself. And she slapped him hard across the face.

He staggered, and wiping his mouth with the back of his hand, he saw the blood from his broken lip. His eyes were filled with mad rage as he hissed, "Slattern!"

Someone came up behind Tessa and asked, "Has this fellow shown you impertinence?"

She looked and saw it was John Sheffield, Earl of Cumberland. He was a stalwart young man with a handsome face that was now white with anger as he glared at his fellow nobleman.

Tessa said, "It is all right!"

"Keep out of this!" Claude Montagu told the younger man.

"I'll leave only when I'm certain the lady has not been unduly provoked by you, Montagu!" John Sheffield said with cold contempt.

Montagu smiled nastily. "I see no lady here!"

"Enough!" John Sheffield cried. And seizing Claude Montagu by the arm, he dragged him staggering and arguing out to the hallway.

Tessa felt numbed by the unpleasant experience. She was still standing alone when Bob came striding across the room. His face was flushed as he asked, "What did that lout say to you?"

"It doesn't matter," she said wearily.

"I say that it does," Bob insisted. "Sheffield has taken him out and made him leave."

"Then that settles it."

"No!"

"Let it end there!" she begged him.

Bob studied her with a grim expression on his face. "You struck him. I know you wouldn't do that unless he had insulted you in some way."

"I acted without thinking!" she protested.

"What did he say?"

She knew she would have to tell Bob at least part of it. He was standing there trembling with anger, and he would not let her be until she had in some way satisfied his curiosity.

She said, "He spoke of you in demeaning words. And he suggested that I was one of Sir Percy's whores. I denied it and slapped him!" She felt this was more than enough detail.

She had never seen Bob so enraged. He said, "That ends it. I shall arrange for a meeting and have Montagu asked to resign from our membership!"

"That will only cause unwanted gossip," she objected.

"We can survive the gossip," he said. "On the other hand, I doubt the club can survive many nights of that fellow."

"He is a poor example of the nobility," she said. "Shef-field despises him!"

"So do most of the members," Bob said. And then with a deep sigh, he told her, "Don't let this bother you. I suggtst you go upstairs for the rest of the evening."

"I'm all right. I can sing again if you like."

"I think not," Bob said. "The atmosphere has beer poisoned by that fellow. Better to wait until another night."

"If you wish," she said. And then she gave him a pleading look, "You are not going to involve yourself in a quarrel with Claude Montagu—I mean on a personal level?"

"I would be pleased to make him apologize," Bob said with fury.

"Let the club membership committee handle it," Tessa urged.

"The sooner we are rid of him the better," Bob said, his hands still clenched with rage.

Tessa left him reluctantly and went back to her own apartment. At this hour her maid was always in bed and asleep, so she looked after herself, taking off her fancy gown and preparing for bed. Sitting before her dresser mirror and combing her long hair, she thought of Bob. She always worried that some night he might become involved in some sort of quarrel and be shot or stabbed.

Fortunately, at least until tonight, he'd been able to operate the gaming club with very little trouble. But handling Lord Claude Montagu was another affair. She had seen a mad gleam in the loutish man's eyes. How little like Thomas he was!

He was also a poor imitation of his father. Thinking of the late Sir Edward, Tessa remembered what a thorough villain he had been. It was fitting that he had come to the end that he had. Her thoughts wandered. Claude Montagu had given her a bad moment when he insisted that he had seen her before. Of course he had, the night his father had been killed, but thus far he hadn't been able to straighten it out in his rather stupid head, and Tessa

:ould only pray that he would never be able to recall it
:learly.

She was in her nightgown and ready to retire when she
:eard someone in the living room. This startled her, but
3ob had a key; she decided it probably was he. He might
:ave come to update her on what had happened to the
:runken Lord Claude.

She donned a dressing gown and went out to the
:hadowed living room. A figure stirred in the darkness
:cross the room from her.

"Is that you, Bob?" she asked nervously.

There was no reply and she asked again, "Bob, are you
:ere? Answer me!"

The answer came by way of a low, unpleasant laugh.
And then the figure advanced towards her and in a
:lurred fashion demanded, "Waiting for your lover?"

"You!" she cried, recognizing the drunken Lord
:laude.

"Will I do instead?" he asked mockingly.

"Go!" she ordered him.

"You're not so fussy, we know that!" he went on in the
:ame sneering fashion.

"How did you get in here?" she asked.

"I found a way," he said slyly. "You forget I was here
vith Sir Percy. I know about the back stairway."

He was right! There was a little used back stairway,
vhich led up to a storage room. The storage room had a
:ght lock, but any heavy man throwing his weight against
: could easily break it and so enter the apartment. This
vas what Claude had done.

She said, "You would be wise to leave!"

"Not likely!" he said, reaching out to grasp her.

"I have a pistol!" she warned him. And she ran into
:er bedroom to get it from the drawer of her bedside
:able.

He uttered an oath, and before she could get the pistol
:ut, he was upon her. She fought to get free, or just to
:ree her hand so she could get the pistol. But he swung
:er around and then hurled her to the floor.

"Please!" she begged. "Bob will kill you!"

"You think I worry about him?"

"You would do well to," she said, creeping back along the floor and stalling for time until she could get to the doorway.

He moved quickly to her. "Think you're getting away?" he jeered. "Not tonight!"

"You're mad!" she cried and jumped up again to try to run out.

He raced after her. Catching her by the arm, he ripped both her gown and nightdress so that she was completely naked but for the shreds of clothing hanging from her shoulders. Then he drew her close to him, mumbling crazily and pressing his lips to hers.

But as she moaned and gave up all hope, suddenly the drunken Claude was seized and torn from her and hurled across the room. He hit the wall with a loud thump and slumped onto the floor, stunned.

Meanwhile Bob stood over him and said, "You've fixed it nicely, Lord Montagu. I demand satisfaction from you on the field of honor."

Chapter Twenty

The duel was held in a field not far distant from the King's Theater. It took place at dawn and Tessa was here, trembling with fear. Pistols had been named, and Bob had chosen John Sheffield to be his second. She did not know whom Lord Claude Montagu had chosen, but she could see that the man was as ill-featured as Montagu himself.

She stood on the sidelines with a doctor and several of the founding members of the Green Room Club. She watched through the thick mist as the seconds of the two men met and went over the final matters pertaining to the contest. Bob stood by himself, looking cold and determined. Lord Montagu seemed less at ease, talking agitatedly to another friend who had remained at his side when his second left him.

The doctor, a middle-aged man asked Tessa, "Have you been to one of these affairs before?"

"No," she said, her teeth chattering from a combination of fear and chill. "Never."

The doctor said, "They can be bloody affairs. Perhaps you should wait in the carriage." He indicated the carriage in which she had arrived.

"No," she said. "I must be here to see it through."

"You are a friend of Captain Wills?"

"Yes."

"He is a good shot, but so is Lord Montagu," the doctor told her. "It will be a fairly even match."

This was not cheering news as she stood there in the heavy mist of the cold dawn. The great elms that rose above them in the field were shrouded in the mist. The seconds finished conferring and returned to the principals in the duel.

The moment had come!

Lord Montagu and Bob Wills advanced to meet each other, turned back to back, then took the required measured paces forward. Tessa, watching with mounting apprehension, cried out as the two men whirled about face each other with their pistols ready.

It was Claude Montagu who fired first, and it was once apparent that he'd missed. A white-faced Bob restrained his fire as a shaken Claude Montagu gazed him in horror and dropped his pistol. Then Bob carefully aimed and fired. Lord Montagu flinched, and his second and the doctor rushed to his side.

Tessa saw that Bob's bullet had grazed the ear of the villainous Montagu. The ear was bleeding profusely, and he had applied a white handkerchief to it to stanch the blood as the doctor opened his bag and prepared to attend to the slight injury.

Giving his pistol to his second, Bob came straight across to Tessa. He said, "I could have killed him, but was content to teach him a lesson. I don't think he bother us again."

Tessa, Bob, and his second, John Sheffield, the Earl Cumberland, all stepped into the carriage that had brought them to the field. As they were driven back, Sheffield said, "The membership board had voted Montagu out of the club, and you have bested him on the field honor. That should liberate us from his unpleasant company."

"I dallied with the idea of finishing him right there Bob said bitterly. "I could have, but I decided against it."

"You were right!" Tessa told him. "I do not approve duels."

The handsome John Sheffield gave her a warning look "Your mercy does you honor, Miss Shaw. But you and Bob might have been better off if Bob had taken the more violent course of killing Montagu. That way there would be no possibility of his bothering you again."

"I approve of Bob's choice," she said. "I can live with the risk."

"A noble stand," John Sheffield said with a cynical smile. "I hope the future justifies it."

"I'm not afraid of him," Bob said. "And what can he do to us now?"

Tessa would have been the first to agree they had re
380

red the unpleasant Claude Montagu impotent. She
ped never to see or hear of him again. She could not
ve imagined at that time that a development shortly to
e place would send her pleading to the obnoxious no-
man.

A few days after the duel she and her maid were out
a morning shopping tour. It was a crisp but sunny day.
ey had accumulated some items for dinner and were
out to return home when they came by two men carry-
g a barrow. The load seemed to be heavy, and the thin,
gged man at the front faltered, then stumbled and fell
wn on one knee on the cobblestones.

At this, the other man—a big, burly fellow—let go the
afts at the rear and ran forward. Dragging the thin man
his feet and holding him, he began to abuse him with a
ade of foul language. The thin man seemed dazed and
ade no attempt to defend himself as the burly man fin-
ed by shaking him.

Tessa and her maid watched this little drama from the
pposite side of the street, and Tessa was so touched by
e fate of the thin man that she felt impelled to rush
ross the narrow street and address herself to the large,
gressive fellow.

She said, "You should be ashamed of yourself. Your
rtner is clearly ill!"

The big man turned and glared at her. "Mind your
siness, madam! He is lazy and doesn't have all his
its!"

"That gives you no right to abuse him," she
aintained. Then she gave her attention to the thin man
d found herself stunned. The emaciated face of the man
re an amazing likeness to that of her dead fiancé,
homas Montagu, except, of course, that this man was
der and thinner. He also had a dreadful livid scar down
s right temple and onward on the cheek to the
eekbone. She was so startled she could not speak for a
oment.

In a tense voice she asked the emaciated man, "What is
ur name?"

He turned to her with fear in his eyes and mumbled

381

words she couldn't understand. The burly man releas
him, and the moment he was no longer restrained, t
thin man ran off to vanish at the turn in the street.

The burly man glared after him and then accused he
"See what you've done with your interfering!"

"I meant no harm," she said. "I could not stand to s
you abuse him."

"That's the only kind of treatment he understands," t
burly man said. "I've given him food and a corner
sleep in at my warehouse. But this is the end. I'll not u
that loony anymore. Let him starve in the streets!"

"If he is really mad, he should be receiving care
Tessa said.

The big man laughed harshly. "Care! He'll wind up
Bedlam! Maybe they'll put him on display in one of the
cages. He's mad enough!"

"Don't speak so cruelly!" she retorted.

"It's plain fact," the big man said. "Without me to pr
tect him, he's bound to be picked up and placed in Be
lam."

"Where did you find him?"

"In the streets," the big man said. "You asked h
name. He can't tell it to you. He doesn't know it. He tal
wildly!"

"You've never found out anything else about him?"

The burly man spat contemptuously. "Why should
stay here answering your questions after the troub
you've caused me? How am I to get this barrow moved?"

She took a few coins from her purse and gave them
him. "These will hire you someone else."

He took them and grunted, "Least you could do!"

Tessa said urgently, "I'd like to know anything mo
you can tell me about the man. He looked much li
someone I once knew."

The big man shrugged. "He's mad! Doesn't know an
thing about himself or his past. I'd say he was in the arm
once and that is how he got that sabre cut down the si
of his face."

"What about the navy? Did he ever mention ships
sailing?"

382

"Never talks at all. Mumbles to himself, snatches any
od you give him, sleeps a lot," the big man said with
ntempt.

"You say he sleeps in your warehouse?"

"He did," the burly man said. "I doubt if he'll return
w after your interfering. When I first met him, he was
eping in the stables of the Bull and Horse Stagehouse."

"That's the big stage exchange in his part of Lon-
n," she recalled.

"All the main stages and their passengers stop at the
ll and Horse," the big man said. "It is likely he'll wind
there again."

"Thank you," Tessa said and left him to return to her
aid and then walk home.

She went downstairs to see Captain Bob Wills at the
een Room Club shortly after her encounter with the
o men carrying the barrow. Still haunted by the face of
e emaciated man who so resembled the lost Thomas,
e sought out Bob in his small office to get his advice.

Having told him of the incident, she ended with, "I
obably am being silly, but the vision of that sick, terri-
d face haunts me."

Bob frowned. "How could he possibly be Thomas
ontagu? He was listed as being lost at sea."

"Suppose he somehow survived and because of his in-
ies lost his mind?" she worried.

"There seems small likelihood of that," Bob said.
here are many people in the world who look alike—
at actress who resembled you and wound up being
ipped to the Virginia Colonies for example."

"I know that," Tessa sighed.

"I'd say you are worrying yourself over nothing."

"Perhaps."

"My best advice is that you forget this fellow. You only
d a slight glimpse of him, in any case. If you'd had a
od look at his face before he ran off, you might have
alized there and then it was not Thomas returned from
e dead."

"You are probably right," she agreed. "The man was
ill and emaciated that there was only a shadow of com-

parison with Thomas. Still, I'm worried by what ha
pened."

"What can you do?" Bob said. "He ran off, and no or
can be sure where he went."

"I suppose you are right," she said. And she went bac
up to her own apartment and tried to forget about t
troubling encounter.

The club was having a period of prosperity. Fort
nately, there were no ugly incidents following the expu
sion of the loathsome Lord Claude Montagu. In fac
since Montagu had few friends and cronies, his absenc
was considered a blessing by the majority of the members.

The Duke of Cumberland, John Sheffield, came to th
club almost every night. He was one of those who alwa
paused in his gambling to listen to Tessa's singing, ar
over a period of time they became good friends.

The night after the barrow incident, when she finishe
her performance of songs, the handsome John Sheffiel
came up to her and said, "What is wrong? There was
sadness in you tonight that showed through your songs."

"Was it that obvious?"

"It was. Do you care to confide in me?"

"Why not?" Tessa replied with a wan smile. And the
moved away to chairs in a corner of one of the smalle
rooms. There she told him her story.

He listened and said, "Strange!"

"Yes. I'm sure that Bob is right. Unquestionably th
man is someone I never met before. Yet the face, becaus
it reminded me of Thomas, keeps haunting me."

John Sheffield gave her a keen look. "It is my belie
that you will continue to be bothered by the inciden
That is unfortunate."

She sighed, "If only I had not crossed that street!"

"Perhaps fate intended that you should."

She stared at him. "What are you saying?"

"The chances are truly small," he said, "but suppose
should be Thomas, ill and maddened by his suffering fro
his war injuries?"

"You think it might truly be he?" she asked breath
lessly.

Sheffield spread his hands. "Who can say?"

"What will I do?" she worried.

"I think you have only one choice—to try to find this ick, ragged fellow and see if you can discover anything nore about him."

"At least then I would know."

"Exactly," John Sheffield said.

"It will not be an easy task," she said. "He might be nywhere. In fact, he was so ill, he could be dead by ow."

"If he has survived so long, I'm sure he's still alive," he young nobleman assured her. "Will you allow me to help you in your search?"

Her eyes widened. "Would you? Bob seems not at all nterested."

"I met Thomas several times years ago," John Sheffield said. "I was younger than he, but I admired him and have always had a sort of hero-worship for him. If by any chance he is alive, I would like to help."

Tessa's eyes were alight with eagerness. "When can we begin?"

"As soon as you like," he said. "I'll come by for you tomorrow morning in my carriage."

"I'll be ready," she promised.

She had difficulty settling down to sleep that night. Her mind was filled with excited thoughts about the morning. She had visions of that gaunt face and knew that John Sheffield was right. Unless she pursued this mystery, she would never have any peace. She had loved Thomas Montagu deeply, and the sight of a face so like his had given her a bad shock.

When John Sheffield called for her the next morning, she told him about the Bull and Horse Stagehouse. She said, "The man with the barrow told me that is where he once stayed. He slept in the stables."

"Then let us try there," John said. And he told his driver where to take them.

As they rode through the narrow streets with the horses' hooves clopping over the cobblestones, Tessa gave the young man at her side a troubled glance.

"What if we find him and he turns out to be Thomas, and yet is too mad to recognize me or remember anything?"

"That would surely be tragic."

"He seemed incoherent and vague in the few minutes I saw him."

He said, "I think you should postpone worrying about such things until we locate the man."

"True. We may not be able to find him at all."

"We'll certainly make a yeoman's effort," John Sheffield smiled.

The Bull and Horse Stagehouse was a jumble of buildings all joined together and built around a large courtyard with only one broad gate for entry and exit. As they drove into the busy courtyard, Tessa decided this place must be the scene of the most activity in all of London. Stagecoaches were arriving; others were leaving; some were being unloaded while others were being weighed down with baggage. And everywhere people stood about waiting to be assigned to their particular coaches.

She and John Sheffield stepped down from the carriage and found themselves surrounded by ragged, begging children and scrawny, yapping dogs. The young nobleman flung out a handful of pennies, and the youngsters deserted the couple to give their attention to picking up the pennies.

John drawled, "One has to handle these things the most appropriate way!"

They passed by a smithy shop where the horses from the various stages could be shod without leaving the area. A woman with a tray supported by straps around her shoulders shouted out her offerings of pork pies and kidney pudding. It was a scene of noise and confusion.

John Sheffield led Tessa to the stable area and asked for the man in charge. After waiting a little, a lean, hard-faced man approached them with a suspicious look on his face. "Why are you mucking around here?" he asked harshly. "Can't you see we're busy?"

John Sheffield smiled and handed him a golden sovereign. "For your trouble."

The man's sour expression vanished and he showed a smile. "Thank you, master," he said pocketing the sovereign with a grimy hand. "Always time for a gentleman! And you, my lady!" He bowed to Tessa.

John said, "We're looking for someone—a vagabond. We wish to help him."

The man said, "Plenty of vagabonds around here. You can take your pick!"

"We want a special man," John said.

"Yes," Tessa chimed in. "He has a bad scar all down one side of his face, and he has no memory of his name or his past!"

"Mad Mark!" the stableman exclaimed. "He's the only one fits that description!"

"Do you know where he is?" John asked.

"I do," the stableman said. "He's in a horse stall in the last building. He came here last night barely able to walk. He's that sick, I don't know whether he's still alive or not!"

John gave Tessa a meaningful glance. "Come along!" he said.

They hurried to the building the stableman had indicated. When they reached it, they went inside and moved along the horse stalls until they found the one in which the emaciated man lay very still in a corner, with straw heaped around to keep him as warm as possible.

She knelt by the man and looked closely at the face which had haunted her. "It's he!" she said. "What will we do now?"

"They rent rooms here," John said. "We'd best get him out of here and into a warm bed. Then we can call a doctor."

John lifted the emaciated man, who showed no sign of consciousness, and carried him slung over his shoulder out of the stable. The innkeeper was reluctant to accept such a guest, but when John paid him double his rate in advance, his manner changed.

The innkeeper and John carried the unconscious man to a good room one flight up. Then they all helped get him into bed. After that the innkeeper sent for a nearby doctor while they kept a vigil at the bedside. Obviously the man was very seriously ill.

Tessa stood at the foot of the narrow bed and asked John, who was standing at one side, "What do you think? Could it be Thomas?"

He stared at the man in the bed. "There's surely a remarkable resemblance."

"As I told you."

"It's hard to say more until he recovers and we can talk with him."

"I trust the doctor will be here soon," she worried.

John nodded gravely. "Yes. I think his condition at a low ebb. He needs some help soon if he is to recover."

"Then perhaps we can learn some things," she ventured. "We are so much in the dark."

"I'll make some more inquiries at the stable while we are awaiting the doctor," John offered. When she nodded her agreement, he left her with the unconscious man.

She did not have to wait long before the doctor came fussing into the room, old, nearsighted and spindly of shanks. Tessa's heart sank when she saw him. The tall old physician squinted at her and demanded, "Are you the sick man's wife?"

She said, "No, I may be a friend. I'm not sure."

The old doctor fumbled about, finding a place on the dresser for his bag. He opened it and glanced over his shoulder. "You do not know him?"

"Not really," Tessa said unhappily. "Please hurry and examine him and let me know what you think is wrong with him."

The thin old doctor held out a skinny hand. "Not until I'm paid. I can't afford to make charitable calls to those who have no friends!"

She gazed at his wily old face in dismay and wished that John Sheffield had not left her. But she had some money with her. Offering several coins, she asked, "Will that do?"

"For a start," he said grudgingly. Then he gave his attention to the patient. He fussed over him for a little and then straightened up and informed her, "This fellow has a
388

fever. There has been a great deal of fever lately, especially among those who have not had sufficient food."

"Will he recover?"

"With medicine and nursing. I have the proper medicines. I used to be an apothecary."

"I'll pay you for everything," she said. "Give him the best treatment available."

The elderly doctor rubbed his knob of a chin. "He will need someone to nurse him until he comes out of his coma."

"Surely there is a nurse we can hire," she said.

"You can, madam," the elderly doctor said. "My good wife is an excellent nurse, and her services are available. Shall I send for her?"

"Please!" Tessa begged.

"I shall require a sovereign in advance," the elderly physician informed her, back to his favorite subject of money again.

"Whatever you like!" she said, out of patience with him. "Can't you understand that money is of no importance? We are only interested in his recovery!"

The doctor's thin visage showed interest. "Is the fellow some noted highwayman?"

To Tessa's relief, John Sheffield returned at this moment and took over. He said, "We would have fewer of your useless questions and more evidence of your healing talents!"

The old doctor scowled at him, fussed in his bag, moved about on his spindly legs, and seemed in an extremely ill humor. Still, calling for a messenger, he sent for his wife; then, still grumbling, he did manage to get some medicine into the sick man.

After an endless time a jolly old woman in a bonnet and long gray dress arrived. She had twinkling eyes and was as pleasant as her husband was grim. "I'll nurse him to health," she promised as she gazed at the man on the bed.

With this Tessa felt a sudden, refreshing relief. The man was safe in a clean bed with someone to nurse him. She went to the bedside again and gazed down at the emaciated, scarred face and tears blurred her eyes. So much like Thomas—and yet she could not be sure! She struggled to remember if he'd had any birthmarks or other blemishes by which she might identify him. But she could think of none.

John Sheffield touched her by the arm. "You'd best leave now," he said. "There is nothing to be done until he comes around."

She was reluctant to leave, yet she knew he was right. She said, "I want to know as soon as he recovers from the coma."

"I'll arrange with the nurse to have a message sent to you," John promised.

It was two days later that a lad arrived at her door with the word that the mysterious man had recovered consciousness. Tessa at once arranged for a carriage to take her to the Bull and Horse.

The old nurse met her in the doorway. "He is still weak," she whispered, "but he is on the mend. He has had some broth this morning, and you may talk to him for a little."

Tessa went in, nerves on edge, almost afraid to face him. He looked up at her with gratitude on his thin face. She said, "You are feeling better."

"They have been kind to me," he said in a voice so low she could barely hear him.

"We want you to get well," she said. "Do you recall me?"

"Yes," he said.

Her heart bounded. "From where?"

"When I stumbled—when the barrow was too heavy for me," he said, casting her hopes down again.

She sighed. "Yes, that was when I first noticed you. You remind me of a dear friend. What is your name?"

"Mark," he said. "Mad Mark, they call me."

"But that can't be your real name?"

"I don't know," he said.

"You can't remember?"

"I try, but my head pains me," he said. "There was a

crash and something fell on top of me. It is all a confusion!"

She listened intently to this longest bit of conversation, and she could tell his speech was that of an educated man. And though he spoke weakly, his voice sounded much like Thomas's, as she remembered it.

She asked him, "Does the name Thomas mean anything to you?"

He shook his head. "No."

"Montagu," she tried again.

"I think I have heard it before."

"What about Tessa?"

"It is a pleasant name. I like it."

"Do you remember someone called Tessa Shaw?"

He closed his eyes. "I'm very tired."

The nurse came to her and touched her arm. "You'd best not trouble him anymore just now. Later, when he is stronger."

"Yes," she agreed. And she left the room. But as she returned to her carriage, she felt almost positive the man she had rescued was her long-lost lover, Thomas Montagu.

Bob Wills frowned as she told him this when they were dining in her apartment that night. He said, "I'm afraid you're bound to convince yourself this is Thomas."

"I feel it deep inside me," she insisted as they faced each other across the candlelit table.

"He may never recover his memory," Bob warned her. "What then?"

"I hope that he will."

"Suppose he doesn't?"

She sighed. "I don't care to think of that."

"You'd better," he told her. "You've rescued this fellow from the gutter. You're having him nursed back to health. When he is fully recovered, what are you going to do with him? Bring him here?"

Unhappily, she said, "I've always counted on his memory returning as he recovers."

"The time you might have expected his memory to

come back was when he came out of the coma. That didn't happen."

"Not so far."

"Nor is it likely to," Bob said. "In which case you will be saddled with a man known only to you as Mad Mark, who may be a complete stranger."

"Let us hope he improves and recalls who he is."

"Would you bring him here and live with him if he doesn't? Risk your life with a madman under your roof?"

"He seems in no way violent," she said meekly.

"That does not mean he will never take a turn to violence," Bob countered. "He is not in his proper senses."

"He is," she protested, "except for his memory."

Shaking his head at her stubbornness, Bob Wills rose to go. "I think you are in serious trouble, Tessa," he said. "I'm glad I did not encourage you in this. And I feel John Sheffield did you no kindness in helping you find this fellow."

"I'm sure it will work out," she insisted. "He is Thomas. I was positive from the first. You will see." But she was not as positive as she tried to pretend. And she knew Bob was right. If the man was not Thomas, he could become a burden to her.

John Sheffield accompanied her on her next visit to the sick man. He told her, "I agree he speaks as an educated man, but that does not prove him to be Thomas."

"Surely that added to the resemblance?" she asked hopefully.

The young nobleman smiled at her tolerantly. "I know you want this to be. But you must remain objective and not try to convince yourself, whether you are right or not."

The old nurse was all smiles. "He's so much better today. In a short while he'll be on his feet and able to get about."

The man was sitting up in bed when they went into the room; when he offered them a smile of greeting, Tessa was almost tempted to rush to him and take him in her arms and cry, "Thomas!"

392

He said, "It is good of you to take such an interest in my welfare."

John Sheffield approached him in a friendly fashion. "We wish to see you fully recovered."

"The nurse says it won't be long," the man said.

"You seem stronger," Tessa encouraged him, "and your color is much better."

"I was strong enough before the fever hit me," he said. "I did hard labor."

Tessa said, "But you cannot always have been a common laborer?"

He held up his calloused, scarred hands. "My hands look it."

"I still wonder," she said. "Has your memory improved at all?"

"Just the same," the man said.

John Sheffield tried him on a few questions, but the replies were all negative. Tessa began to worry that Bob might be right. Probably they had rescued some stranger whose identity they would never truly know.

When she and John Sheffield left the sickroom, at his suggestion they stopped by at a pub on the way back to her place. It was called the Cheshire Cat and was a favorite of the players of the King's Company.

When they arrived, the place was empty except for two venerable old gentlemen. John Sheffield ordered for Tessa and himself and then gazed at her across the small table.

He said, "What do you think?"

"I hope he is Thomas," she said. "He seems much better physically."

"Yet his mind remains a blank."

"We must pray his mind will improve eventually." She realized this was becoming her constant refrain, but she could not help herself; she half-believed that repeating the words would bring about the reality she so desperately wanted.

"I agree," the young nobleman said dryly.

She sighed. "What do you think?"

"To speak frankly, I'm discouraged. It's hard to believe

393

that such a vacant shell could be the Thomas Montagu I knew. Thomas was a wonderful, exciting person."

"I know," she said.

"Perhaps, after he has had time to recover," John suggested, "you could give him some money to start fresh in life. But I think you should not let him know you suspect he may be Thomas, your lost love come back."

"That would be the safe thing to do," she said.

"You don't like the idea?"

"I wonder if I'm not admitting failure in agreeing to consider it," she said. "Surely if I talked to him about the love we once knew, it would help him to remember."

"Indeed . . . but what if he should be sly enough to pretend he remembered some of it, even though in fact he recalled nothing. Then you might be trapped into marrying a good-for-nothing stranger."

"He must prove himself and be able to take his title," she said.

John smiled grimly. "Lord Claude would not be happy with that."

"He would have no choice," she said. "Thomas, by birth, inherits the title."

John Sheffield said, "What do you propose to do?"

"I guess we can only wait," she said.

The innkeeper brought their food and drink and John Sheffield said, "May I speak for myself?"

Her eyes widened. "For yourself?"

The handsome nobleman said, "Yes. In this time of helping you with this mystery man I've suddenly discovered that I don't want him to recover his memory. I don't want him to be Thomas."

She was startled. "Why do you say that?"

"Because I suddenly find that I am in love with you," he said, "and I do not want to lose you."

Tessa crimsoned. "You are a dear, good man, John!"

"But I'm not Thomas Montagu?"

She sighed. "I was betrothed to Thomas. We meant to marry. If this man is he, I cannot turn from him."

"It grieves me to think that I helped you find the fellow," John said wryly. "I worked for my own defeat."

394

She smiled at him and said gently, "John Sheffield, you are a fine man and I'm truly honored."

"But Thomas is first in your heart. I suppose I cannot blame you."

"Thank you for showing understanding," she said.

"And I will go on helping you with him in any way I can," John said. "I only beg you, do not marry him if there is any doubt as to who he really is."

"I promise that," she said quietly.

They finished their drinks. As they stood up to leave, a company of several men entered the pub, and Tessa recognized them as actors she'd worked with. Charles Hart was among the four.

The famous director came and embraced her. "My dear Tessa," he said, "I have been thinking of you recently. What a pleasant trick of fate that we should meet like this."

She smiled and said, "You know the Duke of Cumberland!"

John laughed. "Plain John Sheffield will do."

Charles Hart shook his hand. "You have often be[...] the theater. I've seen you in the king's box occasio[...]

John nodded. "Charles and I have a warm f[...]

Charles Hart turned to her again, "You kno[...] rival company now."

"I'm sure you do not play to empty seat[...] smiled.

"We seem to be the people's preference still[...] said, "and the king's, of course. Meanwhile, I he[...] are making a remarkable name for yourself at the [...] Room Club."

"Who told you that?"

"Many people—Nell Gwyn for one."

"Nell sang for us one night."

"She told me," Charles Hart said. "I've been thinking that enough time has passed. It is a shame for you not to be acting. I can offer you roles again."

She said, "This is a moment I have longed for and dreamed about. I've even prayed it might happen. But now that you are making the offer, I find I cannot accept

395

it. I am busy singing at the club and I have become in
volved with a friend who is ill and whom I'm trying to se
brought back to health. Between these two activities, .
have no time for theater work."

"I'm sorry," the actor said. "Perhaps later."

"Should the situation change, I will let you know a
once," she promised.

"I cannot ask for more." Charles Hart bowed an
kissed her hand. "Good luck, Tessa."

When she and John were back in the carriage, he said
"So Hart wants you on the stage again."

"Yes," she said. "I should be deliriously happy, but un
der the circumstances, it doesn't mean very much to me."

"I'm glad you feel that way," the young nobleman ap
proved. "If you returned to the stage now, you migh
never break away from it, and as you grew older yo
could well regret the move. You should choose a husban
and make a home for yourself."

She smiled. "I'll probably continue singing at Bob'
until I'm such a withered drab no one will want to
me."

effield said, "That is a long way off."

door of her apartment and stood
a moment before saying, "
today. Please do not forget

win you if he is alive, so I mus
ve found is not Thomas."

er told him gently.

er is settled, I shall consider myself in
handsome nobleman said. And drawing
planted a loving kiss on her lips.

t him in a confused state of mind. It seemed
her friends, each for his own reasons, were ben
rsuading her that the man she'd brought to health
not Thomas. And she was beginning to be afraid they
uld succeed. Certainly, if he did not recover his
memory, it would be hard to argue against them. As she
considered this, it became clear to her that if Mad Mark

was Thomas, the one person who might help restore his memory was Lord Claude Montagu!

Loathsome as he was, Claude was the brother of Thomas Montagu. He might be able to arouse some faint bit of memory in the ailing man. As the idea took shape in her mind, she knew she must try it. Yes, it seemed she would have to humble herself and beg the evil Lord Claude for his help!

Chapter Twenty-One

Tessa did not dare to tell anyone else of her plan to call on Lord Claude Montagu. She knew that Bob Wills would be especially resentful at the thought of it. But all she could think of at the moment was trying to prove that the man called Mad Mark was Thomas. This meant more to her than her pride or her fear of the evil nobleman.

She made the visit early in the evening before she was due at the club so she would not be missed. She told the driver of the carriage to wait for her; if she didn't come out of Lord Claude's mansion within a half-hour, she told him, he was to drive back to the club and inform Bob Wills where she had gone. She hoped this would serve as protection for her.

The servant who took her name gave her a cold look, and she feared, as she waited in the hall, that she would not be allowed in to see Lord Claude. But after a few minutes the servant came back and led her down a long [corridor] to a room that appeared to be the nobleman's [study].

[...] she was shown in, and despite the gravity of [...] he could not help noticing that his hair was [com]bed down to hide his ear, a good part of [it mi]ssing because of Bob's calculated marksman[ship. The br]utish Sir Claude was plainly puzzled by her [presence.]

[Gaz]ing at her, he asked, "May I ask why you have come [he]re?"

"I ask your pardon for the intrusion," she began.

She paused, but he did not invite her to sit down; nor did he move from the place before his desk where he'd received her. With an impatient wave of his hand, he said, "Let us have no pretty speeches. We both know where we stand. We are enemies!"

"Your frankness is refreshing, my lord," Tessa said mildly. "I am in your debt for receiving me. But I think the reason for my visit is important to you."

398

"Say what you have to say!"

"Some years ago I was in love with your brother, Thomas. We were to be married."

His eyebrows lifted. It was evident that this came as a surprise to him. He said, "So you were the one! My father——" He caught himself and stopped.

"You might have finished it," she said. "Your father tried to have me killed."

Sir Claude pointed a finger at her. "Now I remember. You were here that night! The night I accidentally shot him! You and some male ruffian!"

"I fear you are mistaking me for someone else," she said. "But no matter. I have come here on a friendly mission to ask your help. I believe I have found your brother, Thomas. It appears that he was not lost at sea, only badly injured, and that he returned to England without memory of the past and has been wandering about London as a laborer."

"Thomas, alive?" the evil nobleman gasped.

"I believe so," she said. "Unhappily, I have not been able to do more than restore his physical health. He was suffering from a severe fever, which threatened his life. He is recovering now, but his memory is still a blank. He does not know who he is or anything of his past."

"Why do you say it is Thomas?"

"He looks and speaks remarkably like him."

"That proves nothing," Lord Claude said angrily.

"I know," she said. "I have tried to help his memory to no avail. But I am convinced that if you, his brother, go to him and speak of your boyhood days and other matters, these memories might strike a note in his mind. With your help his past might come back to him."

"Why should I do this?"

She said, "For decency's sake. He could well be your brother."

"He is more likely some impostor whom you and Wills have brought forth in an attempt to steal my title from me," the loutish nobleman said accusingly.

"You must believe I have no ulterior motive," she said.

399

"I can only say you have been a threat to my family over the years!"

"Your brother and I were in love."

"Thomas was a fool, and he is better dead!" Claude cried.

She stared at him in disgust. "Why did I think you might help? I ought to have known better!"

"I'm not interested in your nonsense," he snapped. "And you can so inform Captain Bob Wills of the Green Room Club!"

"He knows nothing of my coming to you," she said stoutly.

The evil nobleman gave her a strange look. "You came here on your own?"

"Yes."

"And quite alone?"

"Yes."

A sneering smile crossed his face. He moved towards the door to the hall to block it. "Suppose I decide to keep you here to complete the unfinished business of that other night?"

She said, "I thought you might have some such idea. My carriage waits outside. If I don't return to it within a few minutes, the driver will go to Bob Wills and tell him where I am."

Lord Claude Montagu looked discomfitted. "I do not believe you."

"Have one of your servants check. He will be able to see the carriage."

"You would still hope to marry my brother?"

"Yes," she said.

"You would then be my sister-in-law," he said, but there was less belligerence in his tone now. "Does the idea not offend you?"

"I could live with it if I had Thomas," she said. His manner had shifted perceptibly. Perhaps, after the initial shock, the idea was taking root in his mind. Hoping to take advantage of his wavering, she repeated, "As his brother you have a duty to find out whether this man is Thomas or not."

Lord Claude was silent for some time. "Where is he?"

"At the Stagecoach House, the Bull and Horse."

"And you seriously think he could be Thomas?"

"I have strong hopes that he is."

"What do you offer me in return for helping you in this?" he wanted to know.

"My forgiveness and my friendship," she said.

"Indeed!" he replied sarcastically. "I suppose that is a good deal."

"I think so."

"What about Wills? Would the bargain include his forgiveness and friendship also?"

"I would ask him," she said. "I cannot promise. But he very often does as I request."

"How about my membership in the club? Would he restore that? I find it awkward not to belong. My friends taunt me on being expelled."

She said, "If Bob Wills forgives you, he can extend membership to you again."

"Very well," Lord Claude said. "If I go ahead with this, you will not turn your back on your bargain?"

His pettiness disgusted her, but she kept her face expressionless. "You have my word."

"Very well," he agreed, "I'll see the fellow. Though I'm sure you will find he is not Thomas."

"I only ask that you make an effort to help him."

"I shall," he said.

"I'm very grateful. I hope some good may come of this, specially for Thomas."

"We shall see," Lord Claude said.

Tessa returned to her carriage with a feeling of encouragement. Lord Claude had reacted better to her visit than she had expected. While she trusted him no more than she had before, it seemed likely he would make at least a token effort to identify the man named Mark—if only because Claude hoped to get back in the good graces of Bob and return to the club. She was certain that was why he had agreed to cooperate with her.

She arrived back at the club in time to make her first appearance of the evening. And though she had promised

herself to tell no one what she had done, when the hand
some John Sheffield arrived, she felt the need to confide
her accomplishment and thought he could be depended
on to keep silent.

Taking him aside, she told him, "I called on the devil
tonight."

He looked at her in surprise. "What are you saying?"

"I paid a visit to the devil in the interest of finding out
about our mystery man."

"Explain, please."

She smiled. "You mustn't breathe a word to Bob!"

"How could I? I haven't a clue as to what you're talking about," he said. "Pray, be clear."

"I felt there was one person who might rouse the
memory of Mark, and that man was Claude Montagu. I
went to his mansion tonight and pleaded with him to see
our man and try to revive his memory."

John's mouth opened in dismay. "That was stupid,
Tessa."

"Why?"

"It was too dangerous for you to go there, and it was
pointless. Nothing will be accomplished."

"I did better than you'd expect," she insisted. "I made
a bargain with him."

"What sort of bargain?"

"He wants to get back in the club and have my friendship. I promised him both if he would only see that man
and prove him to be Thomas!"

John said, "There is not a chance in the world he will
do it. He has been leading you on, making a fool of you!"

"Why do you say that?"

"The last thing he'd want would be to have Thomas
proved alive. It would mean turning over his title and
most of his income to Thomas. Second sons get very
little!"

She began to feel uneasy. "You think he'll refuse to
come, after all?"

"Regardless of what he may have told you, he'll never
help," John Sheffield predicted. "Why didn't you speak to
me or Bob?"

402

"I knew you'd try to stop me from going and pleading with him."

"Better if we had."

"I think not," she said. "I believe he'll go see Thomas and realize that he is his brother."

"Did you tell him where Thomas is?"

"Yes."

"Another mistake," John groaned. "He might well do something to harm our man."

"Why?"

"To eliminate him," John said. "As I explained, Claude can't afford to have Thomas alive."

"What can I do?" she worried.

"Not much now," he said. "We'll have to pray that Claude is too afraid of Bob, or too stupid to get any foolish ideas."

"Ideas?"

"I don't want to frighten you, but I think our Mad Mark should be moved from the Bull and Horse tomorrow. He is well enough."

"Perhaps I'd better bring him here."

"Let Bob find a room for him down in the club," was the young nobleman's suggestion. "He can employ him as a worker and keep an eye on him."

This seemed a reasonable idea. But before she could reply, Bob himself joined them. With a smile on his broad face, he said, "You two are having a very confidential talk."

John Sheffield said, "I'm suggesting some songs I'd like to hear."

"She can do them now," Bob replied. Putting a hand on Tessa's shoulder, he said, "It's time you did your second show."

She rose automatically, but the conversation with John had shaken her. She now saw that she might have made a bad mistake, which could cost them all dearly. She went about her song program and did the best she could under the circumstances. But her mind was with the man she believed to be Thomas, wondering what all this would mean to him.

Her program concluded, she accepted the applause of the gentlemen of the club, who shortly after returned to their games. Then she saw Bob coming to her. His face was clouded and she at first worried that John Sheffield might have broken his word to her and told Bob what she had done. If so, she realized, it had probably been done for her good.

But Bob had other things on his mind. He said, "Your maid is waiting in the hallway. She has a message for you."

"A message?" Tessa repeated.

"Better see her," Bob said. "She seemed upset to me."

"I will go to at her at once," Tessa said, and hurried out. The girl was waiting white-faced and alone in the hall, and her eyes were large with alarm. "A message just came from the Bull and Horse, mistress. There has been a bad battle there. The sick man was injured and is in great danger of dying. They want you to come at once!"

Tessa drew in her breath, and a single word escaped her, "Claude!" Now she saw it all. Claude had encouraged her only to trick her into giving him all the facts about the man with the memory loss. Then he had hired thugs to go to the inn and murder the unfortunate man. Tessa was sickened that she had not realized how he would react.

To the girl she said, "All right. I'll take care of it. Go back to the apartment." Then she went inside in search of Bob. She first met John Sheffield and told him.

The young nobleman looked grim. "I'm not surprised. As I told you, I was sure Claude would attempt something of the sort—that's why I suggested moving our patient. But I didn't expect Claude to strike so soon."

Tessa lamented, "If Thomas dies, I shall have signed his death warrant!"

He placed a comforting arm around her. "He's not dead, and he may not even be Thomas."

"What shall we do?" she said, panic-stricken.

"Tell Bob, for one thing," he said. "After that, make haste to the Bull and Horse."

Tessa sought out Bob. And when, in faltering fashion,

he had explained the situation to him, he was not angry with her; he simply said, "I thought you had more wit!"

"I know," she said, near tears. "I was a fool."

"I'll go with you to the Bull and Horse," he said.

"Are you sure you dare leave here?" she asked. "It could be some sort of ruse."

"I think not," Bob said. "What happened is about what would have expected from Claude Montagu."

They left the club at once and used John Sheffield's carriage to go to the Stagecoach House. When they got here they found the place in more of an uproar than usual. The owner of the place greeted them.

"We have had a most damaging night," he said. "Villains came and attacked the man you left here and chased his nurse from the building. By the time she reached me, they had started a fire, and I had to ask all my help to leave their other tasks in order to extinguish the fire and bring that poor fellow down here."

"Is he still alive?" Tessa asked anxiously.

"Barely," the innkeeper said.

"What about the men who made the attack on him?" Bob asked.

"There were three of the villains," the innkeeper said angrily. "Two escaped, but one of my faithful coachmen drew his gun on the third. That fellow is here and is also at the point of death. I have him in a room adjoining that of your man. It was a sad day I received that fellow in my house!"

"No lamenting," John Sheffield said sharply. "Take us to them."

They first went to the room of the man who so resembled Thomas. Bob remained only long enough to see the man was alive; then he went on to the adjoining room to see the thug who had been shot.

But Tessa had no interest in the thug. Trembling, she watched the face of the man who might be her long-lost love. The old nurse was standing tearfully by her patient's bed as her spindly-legged physician husband tended to him. Mad Mark looked deathly pale and was barely

405

breathing. The doctor turned to John and Tessa and eyed them sternly.

"You placed my good wife in needless danger. You shall pay for your deed," he warned them.

"How is your patient?" Tessa said urgently.

"Alive—though I can't expect that to be his state for long. He has stab wounds all across his chest. There is much internal bleeding!"

"Can he speak?" John Sheffield demanded.

"He spoke a few minutes ago, asked for the lady," the physician said.

"Try to reach him!" John urged Tessa.

She at once knelt by the bed and tearfully said, "Thomas! Don't die—not after all this! I beg you, hear me!"

The man stirred slightly and then his eyelids fluttered open. He gazed up at her and something like relief came over his wan face. He gasped, "You!"

"Yes," she said, "Tessa! You must live! Live for me, Thomas!"

He stared at her and then with great effort said, "No!"

"What?" she asked.

"Not Thomas," he said. "I remember!"

"What do you remember?" she said, leaning closer to him so she might hear his strained whisper.

"Gault," he said, "John Gault, served under Leslie at Dunbar! Wounded at Dunbar!" He gasped and closed his eyes.

Tessa listened to the dying man's words with relief and distress in about equal portions. She was relieved that it was not Thomas of beloved memory who was dying there on the bed, and horrified that she had brought about this poor man's death because of her insistence that he must be Thomas.

The old physician roughly shoved her aside and proceeded to examine the man on the bed. After a minute he turned to them and said, "It is over! He is finished!"

John Sheffield placed an arm around Tessa, who was sobbing. He said, "You must be comforted by the fact that he lived long enough to tell you his identity."

406

"I betrayed him to Claude Montagu," she lamented.

"You were trying to do good for him; it was not your fault this happened," the young nobleman said.

The doctor's wife was crying. "He had come along so well. He would have been able to leave his bed by tomorrow. They came into the room like devils, put me to rout, and attacked that poor man! Savages!"

The physician eyed them gloomily. "I shall expect payment for the danger in which you placed my dear wife!"

John Sheffield gave him an angry look. "Present your bill to the Duke of Cumberland. You shall be paid whatever you ask!"

"Who, pray, is the Duke of Cumberland, and what has he to do with this?" the spindly-legged doctor wanted to know.

"I am the Duke of Cumberland," John exclaimed. "And I wish no more conversation with you at the moment!"

He and Tessa left the room and met Bob in the hallway. Bob asked grimly, "Is he dead?"

"Yes," she said.

"Did he manage to tell you anything?"

"Nothing about his attackers," John Sheffield said. "But he did say the most important thing of all before he died. He gave us his true name. He was not Thomas Montagu."

Bob looked at her. "Thank God, that ghost is at last laid to rest!"

"I have been wrong in living in the past," Tessa admitted with tears in her eyes. "I shouldn't have looked back and wished him alive."

Turning to Bob, John Sheffield asked, "What about the villain they shot?"

"He'll live," Bob said. "The shot went through his upper leg and shattered the bone. He is bleeding and in great pain, but he should not die from it."

"Has he talked?" John wanted to know.

"Yes," Bob Wills said scowling. "It was indeed Claude Montagu who hired them. This fellow's willing to testify against him. I'll have the physician make sure he lives, and as soon as we return to the club I'll send a messeng[er] to a magistrate. We ought to have Claude under arrest b[e] fore morning!"

"Good!" John Sheffield said. "Newgate is too good f[or] the likes of him!"

Tessa, near collapse, paid small attention to what w[as] going on. She hardly knew that they were driven back [to] the club and that John Sheffield was taking her upstair[s] but worried about her, John stayed with her while Bo[b] went about contacting the magistrate.

It was a night of tension and terror. Once home, Tes[sa] insisted on waiting for word from Bob, despite John She[f] field's pleas that she should go to bed.

"You must rest," he insisted. "I'll wait up to see Bo[b] Then, if you wish, as soon as I know what has gone o[n] I'll come in and wake you."

"I cannot sleep," she declared. "We will stay here un[til] Bob returns."

John poured them brandies, and drinking the war[m] pungent liquid, Tessa felt better. In retrospect she no[w] was aware that there had been many things about t[he] dead John Gault that should have proved to her he w[as] not Thomas Montagu. Gault had been of smaller buil[d] and his face, even allowing for its emaciation, had bee[n] sharper in its structure than Thomas's. On the other han[d] he had much resembled her lost love.

"It was a little like having Thomas die again," she said.

The young nobleman said, "Surely he is dead for y[ou] now. You will no longer hold hopes."

"None," she said. "Our romance was in the past. W[e] loved truly. But it ended long ago and I was wrong to [be] harking back to it always."

"You were devoted in memory," he said kindly. "N[o] one can condemn you for that."

"I was also stubborn. Foolishly stubborn."

He smiled. "You are a rare woman in that you will a[d] mit it. I vow that makes you a paragon!"

"Hardly," she said.

"So now you face life again," he said. "You ha[ve] Charles Hart's offer to return to the stage."

408

"Yes, I can consider that now."

His eyes met hers. "And you have my offer of marriage."

She looked at him with gentle eyes. "Pleasure's daughter, the Duchess of Cumberland? I do not think so. In my heart I am still a circus performer, I think. And Bob Wills, my old partner in the circus, has made me an offer to be his common-law wife. We have gone through much together."

John Sheffield said, "Bob and I have discussed you."

"Discussed me?"

"Do you know two gentlemen more concerned about your welfare?"

"I do not," she admitted.

"Bob agrees that being his mistress would not be good enough for you. Moreover, his wife still lives and has lately sent him a note of repentance. The wine merchant has deserted her and she has begged him to take her back, and the children."

Tessa's eyes filled with tears. "Bob will take her back. He is at heart a generous soul. And he loves his children dearly and has been sorely unhappy without them."

"So?" John said.

"So I'm left with Charles Hart's offer to return to the stage and your offer of marriage."

"Yes," he said. "I do not expect an answer tonight. I only ask that you think it over."

"I will, John," she said softly. "I will not decide lightly. It will have my best judgment."

They sat for a little longer and were very weary before they heard Bob's footsteps on the stairs. Since the door to the apartment was open, he came straight in. But he did not speak at first. He stood before them, his face a study in grimness.

"Get me a brandy," he told John Sheffield at last.

John rose and poured him the brandy. "What happened?" he asked as he gave it to him.

Bob gulped the amber liquid down. Turning to Tessa, he said, "I saw the magistrate myself."

409

"Good!" she said, but she could tell by his set feat[...] that there was more to hear.

"I accompanied the arresting party," he went on. "[...] by the time we reached Montagu House Lord Claude [...] received a warning and was on his way to Dover in a [...] riage. He planned to sail to France and escape the law!"

"The wretch!" John Sheffield said with disgust. [...] might have known he'd do something like that."

"Let me finish," Bob told him with a knowing look. [...] returned to the magistrate to see what we might do [...] stop him. While we were conferring, word arrived t[...] three miles outside the city a wheel came off Monta[...] speeding carriage and Claude was thrown out. His n[...] was broken!"

"Dead!" Tessa exclaimed, shocked.

"As if the hangman's rope had been placed around [...] neck," Bob said. "And since he'd probably have esca[...] the hangman, I'd say it was a fitting end for him."

"Amen!" John Sheffield said.

And so the most terrifying night Tessa had ever expe[...] enced came to a close—or so it seemed at that mome[...] though perhaps she had been through many nights t[...] had exceeded tonight in horror. Bob excused her from [...] club for a week and she spent most of the time recover[...] from her ordeal.

A few days later, when Samuel Pepys and his wife s[...] her another invitation to dine with them, she decided [...] accept. When she arrived at the little clerk's fine hou[...] she was surprised to find another guest there, John Sh[...] field.

Pepys went about happily, as if delighted with the si[...] ation. At the table he became overwhelmed by his w[...] and made some insinuating toasts concerning those w[...] might soon be wed, heedless of the plain Elizabeth, w[...] continued to signal him fiercely to stop. Finally M[...] Pepys was forced to say firmly, "Samuel, we have h[...] enough of your poor nonsense!"

"Merely a bit of good humor, my dear," he placa[...] her.

Pepys and Elizabeth discreetly left John and Te[...]

ne for a little after dinner. The clerk went off on pre-
se of completing his diary for the day, and Elizabeth
it incumbent upon herself to supervise the cleaning up
he kitchen.

n the library John stood with Tessa, studying a re-
tly produced print showing a scene of the great fire.
smiled at her and said, "It is most lifelike."

"Indeed it is," she said. "I well remember the smoke
l flames."

"Poor old London," John said with good humor. "She
s survived Cromwell, the plague, and the fire—not to
ntion the lechery of the court."

"Do not speak against Charles," Tessa begged him.

"I shall not," John said. "He is not a bad fellow. I wish
n happiness—him and poor Nell!"

"So much has happened in so short a time," Tessa
eathed, "I can scarce believe it all. It seems only yester-
y I was an innocent proud of my ability to ride a pony
a circus."

John said, "I have never managed to do anything half
clever!"

"You jest with me!" She looked up at him fondly.

His eyes became serious. "Our hosts have left us for a
rpose," he said. "Let us come to it! Are you to be
ne, or is it the London stage for you?"

She looked up at his handsome face with loving eyes.
he decision is too easy. I would be with you, my good
hn."

He took her in his arms, and she knew this was safe
rbor at last. All the buffeting of fate, the romances bad
d good, the dangers and the ordeals, had in due time
l to this moment. This had been her destiny, even in
ose darkest days in the plague-infested dungeons of
ewgate. She would be loved by this good man whom she
ved so dearly, and she would take her place in London
ciety as the Duchess of Cumberland.

The marriage was set for a day in July. Weeks went
o the preparations. Gifts came from all sides. The
embers of the Green Room Club and her old friends
om the stage all remembered her. Tessa spent days hav-

ing dresses fitted and getting ready for the honeymoo
France that John had proposed.

Among the gifts Tessa received was a string of pe
from Nell; then, by special messenger, was a small
with no name of the sender on it. When she opened t
she found it contained a dainty ring, gold with a
crown of diamonds. Immediately she knew from whe
it had come, and it became the most treasured of all
gifts.

The wedding took place at St. Dunstan's on a wa
sunny afternoon, and a great reception was held af
wards at the mansion where Tessa and John would re
on their return from France. The house and grounds w
filled with relatives, friends and well-wishers.

When Tessa and John were riding happily through
streets on their way from the church to the recepti
they passed many people waving to them and wish
them good luck. As they paused at a corner, Tessa sa
little old man raising a pudgy hand to offer them g
luck. She gasped. Surely that was old Tom Shaw, her
ter father, who had given her his name. But they mo
on so quickly she had only a brief glimpse of him.

At the reception Bob Wills proposed the toast to
bride. And Tessa thought about what a fine man Bob
become and what an impressive presence he made in
brown frock coat and trousers. Lord Harry Farr
there, too, with his wife Lady Eve. And he was one of
first to kiss the bride.

The celebration continued and became riotous. As d
fell, torches were lit in the gardens and at the front of
mansion, and dancing and drinking continued. Cha
Hart rose on one of the tables and declaimed a po
written especially for the occasion by John Dryden.

When he finished, the applause was loud and appre
tive. Amid shouts of "Bravo!" the handsome ac
jumped down and came and kissed Tessa. "A great
to our stage, my dear," he said.

"You'll find someone else," she said. "I only wish
had chosen to be here today."

412

Charles Hart said, "Perhaps this was one of those days en she should be near the king."

"Perhaps," Tessa said quietly.

Then John came to her smiling and more handsome n ever in his wedding suit of golden silk. He placed an n around her and said, " 'Zounds! We had better make r departure, or the party will go on all through the ht!"

Tessa nodded, and arm in arm they moved on past the npany in the torch-lit garden on their way to the use. In the morning they would take a carriage to Do- and thence to France.

The guests parted to let them through. Suddenly they re passing Samuel Pepys and his wife Elizabeth. Tessa iled at them and said, "Good night, dear friends!"

Samuel Pepys stepped forward as she and John moved him. The little man's bulging eyes were glazed with ne, but his face was a study in bliss. He kissed her hand ickly and with a wink, whispered, "And so to bed!"

Reading Fit For A Queen

QUEEN-SIZE GOTHICS offer the very best in novels of romantic suspense, by the top writers, greater in length and drama, richer in reading pleasure.

ALL TIME BESTSELLERS
FROM POPULAR LIBRARY

☐ ALWAYS IS NOT FOREVER—Van Slyke	04271-0	2.25
☐ DIANA ROSS—SUPREME LADY—Berman	04283-4	1.75
☐ YOUR SINS AND MINE—Caldwell	00331-6	1.75
☐ THE HESS CROSS—Thayer	04286-9	2.25
☐ THE UNORIGINAL SINNER AND THE ICE-CREAM GOD—Powers	04287-7	1.95
☐ HOW TO MEET MEN NOW THAT YOU'RE LIBERATED—Gellis	04288-5	1.95
☐ AFTERNOON MEN—Powell	04268-0	1.95
☐ MARINA TOWER—Beardsley	04198-6	1.95
☐ SKIN DEEP—Hufford	04258-3	1.95
☐ MY HEART TURNS BACK—Patton	04241-9	2.25
☐ EARTHLY POSSESSIONS—Tyler	04214-1	1.95
☐ THE BERLIN CONNECTION—Simmel	08607-6	1.95
☐ THE BEST PEOPLE—Van Slyke	08456-1	1.95
☐ A BRIDGE TOO FAR—Ryan	08373-5	2.50
☐ THE CAESAR CODE—Simmel	08413-8	1.95
☐ DO BLACK PATENT LEATHER SHOES REALLY REFLECT UP?—Powers	08490-1	1.75
☐ THE FURY—Farris	08620-3	2.25
☐ THE HEART LISTENS—Van Slyke	08520-7	1.95

Buy them at your local bookstore or use this handy coupon for ordering: